Blind Temptation

(Bitten by Love #3)

Stacy McKitrick

MYTHICAL PRESS * DAYTON, OHIO

MYTHICAL PRESS * DAYTON, OHIO

www.mythicalpress.com

Cover designed by Maria Zannini of Book Cover Diva
http://bookcoverdiva.blogspot.com/

Edited by Michele Stegman and Stephanie McKitrick

Formatted by Enterprise Book Services
http://www.EnterpriseBookServices.com/

This story is a work of fiction. Names, characters, places, and incidents are either products of the authors imagination or are used factiously. Any resemblance to actual events, locales, business establishments, media title, or persons living or dead, is entirely coincidental.

Print ISBN: 978-0-9839097-8-1

:

Books by Stacy McKitrick

Bitten by Love Series

My Sunny Vampire (Book #1)

Bite Me, I'm Yours (Book #2)

Ghostly Encounters Series

Ghostly Liaison (Book #1)

Short Stories in the Following Anthologies

Home for the Holidays

Love's a Beach

ACKNOWLEDGMENTS

The publication of this book wouldn't be possible without my husband's enthusiasm in wanting to help me succeed. He took it upon himself to learn to format (thanks Jennette Marie Powell for teaching him!) so I would have one less thing to worry about. He's also my website guru and takes hints really well. I only have to hit him, like, one or two times!

Thanks to the talented Maria Zannini (of Book Cover Diva) for such a wonderful cover. It's like you read my mind—or my story—and I know you haven't done either. Yet.

Thanks to Michele Stegman and Stephanie McKitrick for your fine editing. Everything you found or suggested only made my story better. Ignore all the moans you heard after sending me your comments. It wasn't me at all. Honest!

Thanks to Jennette Marie Powell (again!) and Mythical Press for welcoming me into your publishing family. I hope I do you proud.

And finally, thank you to the creator of Auggie Anderson (a character on "Covert Affairs"). Auggie was my inspiration for Ben.

DEDICATION

iii

Dedicated to my dear friend, Mary

.

CHAPTER 1

When life became rough, nothing worked better at soothing her spirit than the silky texture of her handkerchief. Now if she could only get her life upgraded to rough.

Victoria sat with her head down, the smooth material failing miserably to calm her. She couldn't have heard the Head of the Committee correctly. Never in all her years had she been called into his office for disciplinary action.

"Do you understand me?" he asked.

"You had a meeting without me?" she asked. "What have I done wrong?"

Barnet came from behind his desk looking more fatherly than her own father had. The smattering of grey in his hair only enhanced that image. He sat in the chair beside her. "Victoria, we're concerned. Staying holed up is not healthy and it's not been fair to the other members."

"I am not holed up. I go out." Just because she lived at Headquarters, which was her right, didn't mean she stayed in her room. The Underground Atlanta shopping mall was but a doorway away.

"The Underground is not going out. Seeing the stars, walking in Centennial Park, driving to an assignment, now that's going out."

She didn't even know where that park was located. Had it even existed before 1967? And what was so great about seeing the stars? They couldn't have changed. But what he was asking her to do… "You don't play fair, Barnet."

"Don't go there, Victoria. We've been more than fair. Forty-plus years of exile is long enough. Actually, it's been too long. If you wish to remain on the Committee, you will attend class tonight."

"Why can't you just give me the manual? I'll read it. I promise."

Barnet smiled. "That would kind of defeat the purpose. We want you out of Headquarters, mingling with the population. You can't get that with reading."

"And a driving class is supposed to accomplish this? I don't even own a car."

"Are you afraid to drive? Is that it?"

Not so much driving, only what driving stood for, but she wouldn't admit that. "Can't very well be afraid of something I've never done before."

He rose. "Then there is nothing to discuss."

"But Barnet…"

"What?"

"Is this at least an adult class?"

He let out an exaggerated sigh. "I won't lie to you. It's possible the class will be filled with teenagers. Most adults already know how to drive. As Henrik should have taught you."

She moaned. It was worse than she'd thought. "You can't do this to me! They're going to treat me like…like one of them."

"Only if you act like one."

Oh, what did Barnet know? He hadn't been turned at seventeen. No, his turning had happened after his forty-second birthday.

"The school thinks you're twenty-two. You act like twenty-two, they'll treat you accordingly."

How about if she acted three hundred and eighty-one? How might they treat her then?

* * * *

The front door slammed and Ben all but jumped off the couch. That's what he got for reading *'Salem's Lot*. Vampires. He shuddered. Thank God they didn't exist.

The scent of lilacs preceded Susannah's entrance. "Ben! I'm so glad you're here."

"Where else would I be?" he muttered. Sometimes he really

wondered about her mind. Had turning forty done that to her? Is that what he had to look forward to next year? Papers to his right rustled and the scent intensified. Ben marked his spot in the book and turned toward his sister. "What's wrong?"

"My instructor for tonight's class quit on me. Last minute. I can't afford to cancel this class. I need you to teach it."

Ben laughed. Sometimes Susannah had a rich sense of humor. She sure knew how to play it, acting all serious. "That's a good one."

"I'm not kidding."

Shit. "Why can't you do it?"

"Because I'm already teaching another class."

"Then put them together."

"I can't. It's the driving portion. Do you want to take that one over instead?"

"Very funny."

She placed her hand on his knee. "I'm sorry, but I need the money. *We* need the money. You have to help me, here."

"No one's going to believe I can teach them the rules of driving."

"You've taught it before. You know the class."

His pulse raced. Yeah, but that wasn't the point and she knew it. "Can't you just cancel tonight's class? I'm sure you'll find someone."

"Not last minute. And not at the rate I can afford to pay. Please, Ben. I haven't asked for much, have I? I let you live here."

He rose. "So you're saying if I don't do it, you'll kick me out? Nice, Suze."

She grabbed his arm. "No, of course not. But if I cancel this class, we may both be out. I'll be short on rent. Your tutoring income can't cover it."

He sat back on the couch. "You said it was enough."

"Normally, it is. But..."

The emergency room. *Shit.* He covered his face. "I told you I shouldn't have gone."

"Like I was going to stitch you up. Sure. Next time maybe I will." She was getting angry. Her voice raised an octave, usually a good indication.

He puffed out a breath. "Suze, I want to help, but if I'm the teacher on record—"

"You won't be. I will."

"That's fraud."

"No one's going to know. After I'm finished with my driving class, I'll take over yours. Please, Ben."

Who in their right mind would believe he could teach driver's education? Maybe agreeing would make her see what a terrible mistake it was. "Fine. I'll do it."

"Thank you, thank you, thank you." She hugged him tight and nearly knocked him over. "Now hurry up and get changed. Class starts in an hour."

Crap. What the hell had he gotten himself into?

CHAPTER 2

Victoria smoothed the front of her blazer as she observed herself in the full-length mirror. She only owned the one mirror and normally kept it hidden. No reason to depress herself by seeing the same reflection year after year, but there were times she needed to make sure she looked professional. Or less like a teenager.

How could she look older? Maybe if she wore spectacles. They would make her look studious, if not unflattering. That would certainly deter any pimply-faced kid from hitting on her. Sure, she could use her powers so mortals would see an older adult, but that would take too much energy and then she might need to feed before the mall opened.

"Knock-knock!" Perry stuck his head around the corner. "Your driver has—whoa, what the hell are you wearing?"

She turned toward one of the crudest men she'd ever met and nearly choked on her breath. "Maybe I should ask you the same thing. What happened to your old Hawaiian shirt? Or those ripped pants?"

He tugged on the button placket of his green polo shirt while staring at his navy Dockers. "I thought they needed replacing."

"I've told you that for years, but you never made an effort." She turned toward the mirror and pulled her hair back.

"Times have changed."

More like he'd met someone. About damn time. Maybe now he would act like a gentleman. She secured her hair in a bun and double-checked it. Perfect.

"Why are you dressing for a Committee meeting? I thought you're going to a driver's ed class."

"I am. What does that have to do with anything?"

He shook his head. "This outfit will only bring attention to yourself. You need to wear something casual. You know, like jeans. Or a pretty sun dress. And your hair…" He walked over and pulled out the pins, spilling her blonde hair around her shoulders. "Much better. Now hurry up and change. Don't want to be late."

Scheisse. She fisted her hands. "Just because you're older than me doesn't give you the right to come in here and tell me what to do."

"Maybe not, but Barnet could. You need to blend in, so change."

"You want to keep your head, you'll leave me alone. Barnet didn't say anything about how I should dress for class. He only said I had to attend." She yanked the brush through her hair and secured it back into a bun. Damn, impossible man.

"Fine, but don't say I didn't warn you."

She grabbed her purse and followed Perry down the hallway. Not a sound leaked from any of the closed doors they passed, because no one lived in any of the rooms. Any Committee member could reside at Headquarters, but only Victoria and Barnet took advantage—the other members had mates and preferred to live elsewhere. Any other vampire could live here temporarily whenever Barnet required their assistance, and apparently Perry's assistance was requested in chauffeuring her to and from class. Otherwise, the rooms were provided for vampires who needed them during the Committee Meetings.

She followed Perry up the stairs to the garage, a structure with over a thousand parking spaces. During a Committee Meeting the place would be full of cars, but today it only housed one. A minivan she would eventually learn to drive. A van with many windows. Sure, they were tinted and made of UV glass, but that didn't mean she could trust them. "How am I supposed to get from the van to my class? The sun won't set for over an hour."

"Barnet's not out to get you hurt and neither am I. There should be plenty of shade this time of day. Just make sure you don't sit next to a window in class. They probably aren't treated."

She gasped. "There are windows?"

"It's an office building. Of course it has windows. But don't worry that pretty little head of yours. There won't be enough light to do any damage. And if there is, you can always feed after."

Feed outside? Where it was stinky and filthy and…noisy? She much preferred the convenience of the Underground. She only needed to lure her donors over to Headquarters and into an empty room. It had been decades since she'd been out. Before Henrik's death. Why did he have to die? She wouldn't have to go out by herself at all if he were still around.

She pulled the sunglasses out of her purse. At least Barnet had the sense to give her these, even if she didn't have a pair of spectacles for class. She would hide behind the dark lenses instead. She slipped them on and climbed onto the backseat of the van, ready to face…whatever.

"What are you doing? Sit up front."

"I don't want to."

"Just because I'm chauffeuring you around doesn't mean I'm your chauffeur. It's safe up here."

"Says you. I'm staying back here."

"Damn it, woman. How did Henrik put up with you for 300 years?"

Make that 322 years, thank you very much. And what was there to put up with? Henrik had turned her. If he hadn't known what he was getting, it was his own damn fault. "You could always tell Barnet you can't do this. I don't mind."

Perry laughed. "Yeah, I bet you wouldn't. Just for that, you can walk back, *Vicky*."

"Ooh, you did not just call me—Wait. What do you mean walk back? You can't mean that."

"Sure I do. It'll be dark."

But alone? In the city? She'd never done that. Damn Perry. Damn Barnet. Damn Henrik!

By the time Perry pulled into an underground garage, she was still steaming.

"There's the elevator." Perry turned in his seat and smiled. "When you leave you can just get off on the first floor. No need to come all the way down here."

"And you'll be outside waiting." She made it sound like an order, because damn it, it was an order.

"Uhh, no. I told you. You can walk back. It'll be good for you. You could stand to get some fresh air."

Like she needed fresh air. The man was seriously deranged.

"Perry, you're…you're…you're a *Backpfeifengesicht*." And she'd like to be the fist to hit that face.

He furrowed his brow. "What's that mean?"

"Wouldn't you like to know." She opened the door.

"Well, then, you're a…a…blunderspooner."

"That's not even a word. You just made that up."

"Wouldn't you like to know. Now you better get going. Hate to see you late on your first day."

"I will see you out front after class. Do you hear? If not, I'll make your life difficult."

"Not as difficult as Barnet can. I bet he rewards me for this. Have fun. And don't forget to learn something. Barnet expects you to pass, legitimately. He'll be testing you."

"Oooh. I hate you!" She slammed the door and he drove off. This was no fair. She was a member of the Committee. Shouldn't that garner her some respect? Especially from the likes of Perry?

She spun around and collided into one hunk of a man who was waiting by the elevator. Her anger was no reason to be rude. "I'm so sorry. I should have watched where I was going."

He laughed. "No problem. I run into people all the time. Fight with the boyfriend?"

"He is not my boyfriend. The woman who goes out with that Neanderthal would need to have her head examined. I have better taste than that." Say, for a man like him. Someone who was definitely not a sniffly-nosed teenager like her classmates would be.

Tall and broad shouldered, he was closer to Barnet's age—even had a bit of grey at the temples. And while his size and age were more than desirable, his lovely sea breeze scent reminded her of home. A scent she hadn't come across since last December, when Katarina had brought Justin to Headquarters. He had smelled the same.

Victoria inhaled deeply. Simply wonderful.

Which only proved her theory. Justin had been wearing cologne. That's what she reacted to. Not his natural scent. No two humans ever smelled the same without help. Katarina owed her an apology.

Victoria took another whiff. She would definitely have to find out the name of that cologne and then buy some.

The elevator doors opened. The man put his hand up against the side, keeping the way open. "Ladies first."

"*Danke.*" A gentleman, too. Ah, but he probably saw her as a child, not a woman. She smoothed her hair back and brushed against her sunglasses. Oh gosh, she was still wearing them. He never said a word, but then, he also had on a pair, the kind with mirrored lenses. Maybe his eyes were sensitive, too.

"Floor?"

Her floor was already lit on the display. She smiled. "Same as yours." Maybe going to school wouldn't be so bad. Not if she ran into him every time. Maybe he was in her class. He would certainly make attending bearable. Of course, the odds of that happening were pretty slim; he probably already knew how to drive. Well, she could dream.

The elevator arrived on their floor and he let her exit first. She thanked him and wished him a good evening when she really wished she was spending the evening with him. But she appeared young and he clearly wasn't, so she ventured out. The last thing he probably wanted was someone who looked like a teenager hitting on him.

His tantalizing cologne hit her again and she nearly glanced over her shoulder.

Oh, why had Henrik turned her so young? Stupid man couldn't have waited a few more years? Maybe she should just be thankful he hadn't turned her on their wedding night. Then she'd be stuck at the age of fifteen.

She stepped inside the classroom and stopped. Windows lined the wall straight ahead, but they faced east, thank goodness. A woman in her twenties sat in the back of the class, but the rest of the students were teenagers. Figured.

As she maneuvered her way toward the woman, staying away from the windows—she could never be too careful—several students snickered, causing several more to follow suit. Maybe Perry was right about her wardrobe. Oh, who cared, anyway?

"Hello, class. I'm your instructor, Ben Martin."

Victoria halted. His voice. It belonged to the man in the elevator. He was her teacher? Well, she did want him in her class.

"Is this some kind of joke?" a boy to the right asked. "How are you supposed to teach us to drive?"

"I'm not. I'm here to teach you the rules of the road."

What was that child's problem? She found her seat and smiled at the woman next to her, but the woman's mouth hung open as she stared ahead. And what was her problem? The man was good looking, but it didn't warrant a shocked expression. Unless he'd grown a horn since leaving the elevator.

Victoria looked ahead. Nope, no horn. Ben, or maybe she should call him Mr. Martin, was one gorgeous man. However, he still wore his glasses. Then again, so did she.

Sitting behind the desk, he looked out over the room. Did he see her? Should she wave? Maybe not. That would be weird. She must resist looking stalker-ish.

"I will be calling role at precisely seven o'clock. If you are not in attendance then, you will not get credit for the class. I am also giving you a seat assignment, so be prepared to move."

Several students groaned at this announcement, probably because they sat with a friend. Victoria didn't care one way or another. As long as she wasn't near the window.

"When I call your name, please acknowledge and start filling in the seats in the front on your right. Peter Abernathy."

The students in the front row vacated their seats. Peter yelled out "Here" and moved to the first seat.

"Zachary Abernathy."

"Here." He sat next to his brother.

"Twins, huh?" Ben said.

"You could tell by our voices?"

"Yeah…sure."

What kind of classmates did she end up with? Zachary was an idiot. He was a mirror image of his brother, so why wouldn't Ben know they were twins.

"Victoria Braeden."

Great. Front row. Now everyone would see her. At least her seat wasn't near the window. She stood and smiled. "Here."

He frowned briefly. What was that about? Had she insulted him in the elevator? Maybe she had stared at him too long and he thought she was a stalker. Great. Nothing she could do about that now.

She settled into her seat where she had a nice, uninterrupted view of him. Okay, so maybe the front row wasn't all that bad. Maybe the class wouldn't be all that bad. If only she didn't look like another teenager in a sea of teenagers. He'd never believe she was older, not without spilling her secret. As if she would be stupid enough to do that.

Ben continued with his roll call until everyone was seated. "In an effort to ensure you've attended all thirty hours of this class, you are not to leave this room without permission. And trust me when I say, I'll be able to hear you leave if you try to sneak out."

Sneak out? Why would anyone need to sneak out? Besides, wouldn't he see them leave? The man was making no sense whatsoever.

"Are we supposed to raise our hand?" a boy behind her asked.

Several students snickered.

"That's a good one," Ben said. "How about you tap your desk with your pencil?"

Tap the desk? What the—

"Will you be teaching the driving portion, too?"

A roar of laughter filled the classroom. What was wrong with these kids?

Ben stood and placed his hands on the desk. His biceps strained against his blazer. Henrik never had biceps like that. Damn. Victoria swallowed the lump in her throat.

"Bring it on, I'm okay with it. I understand this is an unusual situation. But if we all work together, you'll forget you even have a blind teacher and you'll be on your way to earning that driver's license you so badly want."

"You're blind?" Victoria slapped her hand over her mouth. *Scheisse.* Had she said that out loud? She must have as Ben turned his head toward her.

"Yes, and if anyone has a problem with it, I'm sure we can reschedule you for a later class. I think there's an opening in a couple of months. Guess it depends on how soon you want your license."

He *was* blind. How had she not seen that? He hadn't used a cane that she could remember and he didn't have a dog. And then it was all about avoiding the windows and she hadn't seen him enter.

But wait. He was *blind*. That meant he couldn't *see* her. That meant maybe he wouldn't treat her like a child. He would only go by what he heard. She straightened in her seat. This certainly changed things. She would make sure he heard a woman.

She smiled. This was turning out so much better than she expected.

* * * *

After Ben had at last dismissed the class, he leaned back in his chair. He'd forgotten what a rush teaching gave him and so far, he hadn't had a problem, especially after he'd thrown out that threat of postponing their class. Yeah, no teenager he'd ever encountered wanted to wait any longer than necessary to obtain their driver's license. Of course, it was only the first day. How many students would actually return for the second? Or how many parents would demand their money back? Susannah better know what she was doing.

The room became silent, yet Victoria's scent lingered in the air. When she had collided into him in the garage, he pictured someone older, closer to his age, and had nearly asked her out. He hadn't dated since his accident and he was now ten years older. Did he still have what it took or would women be turned off by his blindness? Still, the thought had lingered and he had promised himself if he ran into her again, he would be bold and ask.

Then she had answered his roll call. The disappointment at her being a teenager had stung. Good thing he hadn't asked for her number in the elevator. He could just picture her eyes rolling at that.

Damn, she smelled good, though. These next two weeks could wreak havoc on his unused libido.

"Excuse me."

He jumped at the sound of Victoria's voice. Damn, she was quiet. Normally, he would have heard the door open. Or her footsteps. He'd heard neither. Then again, her scent had lingered, so maybe she'd never left.

"Sorry, didn't mean to startle you. I wanted to say I'm sorry about that blurt in class. It's just I didn't realize...I mean, you didn't have a cane so I assumed... Oh *Hölle*."

The last part came out quiet and he laughed. She certainly didn't sound like a teenager. "Don't worry about it, Miss Braeden."

"Wow, you are good. But technically it's Mrs. Braeden, but seeing as he's dead now... *Scheisse*. You can call me Victoria."

"You're a widow?"

"Yes. You don't think I'm one of those crazy teenagers, do you?"

"No, not at all." He'd only assumed and assumed wrong, thank goodness.

"Oh, good. Because I'm not. One of those teenagers, that is."

Her scent intensified and the faint clicking of heels indicated she had walked toward him. Too bad he couldn't see her, see if she was interested, because one signal from her and he might go ahead and do something wild and stupid like grab her and kiss her. How crazy was that? Better to ignore her scent before he embarrassed himself. "You're not from around here, are you?"

"What do you mean? I live in Atlanta."

"Your accent. And the fact you've spoken German."

"You can hear an accent?"

"It's faint."

"You really are good. I, uh…grew up in Germany, but I haven't lived there in ages." The door squeaked open. "Oh. I guess your ride is here. I'll see you tomorrow night."

Ben stood. "Goodnight, Victoria."

Was she smiling at him? She'd sounded disappointed at the door opening. He certainly was disappointed. But he'd see her tomorrow. And since she was a widow, no harm in asking her out once he determined her interest.

The scent of lilacs overpowered Victoria's light summery fragrance. "She's too young."

"What are you talking about?"

Susannah placed her hand on his shoulder. "The girl who left. I'm assuming she's a student. You seem awfully interested. Just warning you. Jail bait."

"She's not jail bait. She's a widow."

"Yeah, right. If she was married, she'd had to have had parental consent."

"Maybe she has one of those faces." He ran his hands over the desktop searching for his papers.

Susannah beat him to it and gathered them up. "Maybe, but she's still young enough to be your daughter. Which means you'll have nothing in common."

Disappointment burned in his chest. He'd been crazy to think Victoria would be interested in him anyway. Now he not only had blindness against him, he had his age, too. Getting old was the pits.

* * * *

Victoria stepped off the elevator. Goodness, but that man smelled good enough to eat. In a sexual way, of course. All during class his scent had distracted her. Once, she had stopped herself from climbing out of her seat. How embarrassing would that have been? Well, only temporarily. She'd have wiped everyone's memory. But *Hölle*, she'd still remember.

She had hoped to leave the classroom with Ben. Or at least have more time to talk, but not with his ride hanging around. The woman held a certain resemblance to him, so she was most likely a sister or cousin, but not a wife. No, he had frowned when she appeared, almost as if he'd heard or maybe smelled her. And how could he miss that perfume? Victoria had nearly choked on the fumes.

The glass exit to the great outdoors greeted her, but no van stood by the curb. She pulled out her phone and brought up the GPS tracker. She'd installed the tracker on the van herself when Perry started driving it regularly and it was a good thing, too. That man mixed up business and personal usage all the time.

No tracker signal? She shook her phone as if it would do any good. The van could be in the garage here or... No, he couldn't have been serious. She punched in Perry's number. He didn't even get a chance to say hello when she lambasted into him. "Where are you?"

"Hey, Vicky. I'm in my room watching *Castle*. I really love this show."

She gritted her teeth. "Get your *Arsch* over here and pick me up."

Perry laughed. "Enjoy that fresh air."

The line went dead. No...he didn't. She glared at the phone. Damn him. If she had known he had such a cruel streak, she would have brought money for a cab. Sure, she could manipulate the driver into thinking she'd paid him, but that was an abuse of her powers and she refused to stoop that low. When she returned to Headquarters, she'd give Perry a piece of her mind. Better yet, she'd let Barnet know. He'd be able to control the miscreant better than she.

She opened the door and stopped. Even at ten o'clock, traffic was heavy. How big had Atlanta gotten anyway? Used to be she could walk outside at night and barely see anyone.

Better to get this over with. She stepped out, but stayed close to the building. Her heart hammered. And where was the fresh air? The exhaust nearly choked her. Maybe she wouldn't have to walk far. Holding her breath—something she could do for about twenty minutes at a time—she brought the GPS map up on her phone. Ten miles? Too many people to zip down the roads. Too many people, period. What the heck was she going to do?

Jack. Why didn't she think of him earlier? Of all the Committee Members, he probably lived the closest. She quickly located his number.

"Hey, Victoria. What's up?"

"I need a ride home. Can you come get me?"

"Sure, where are you?"

"At the place I'm taking the class. Didn't you know about that?"

Jack laughed. "I know about the class. What's the address?"

She looked around. "I don't know. There aren't any numbers on the buildings."

"What intersection are you near?"

She took a few hesitant steps away from the building. Once she found the signs she returned to the wall and read them to him.

"Give me about thirty minutes."

"Thirty minutes!" She could zip back in less time than that, if she could zip, that was. Or leave the comfort of the building.

"What's the matter, Victoria?"

"Oh, nothing. I thought you were closer. I'll be here waiting. *Danke.*" She disconnected the call and put the cell in her bag just as a car stopped at the intersection. Ben. His mere presence calmed her and she waved. But of course he couldn't see her. His sister/cousin could, though. She glared at Victoria.

What the heck was her problem? Seemed Victoria would need to win this woman over if she wanted Ben in her life. He was certainly on her radar. She couldn't wait until the next class.

* * * *

Graham was prowling the streets looking for his next meal when his cellphone vibrated against his hip. Fantastic contraptions. One of the few marvels he actually enjoyed. If he didn't wish to talk to the person calling, he could send them to his voicemail. And if the caller was lucky, he'd actually listen to the message.

He pulled his phone out. Maybe he should answer this one.

"What's up, Ian." God, he hoped the man wasn't calling about another job. The last one had been horrendous. But favors cost more than money at times.

"She left the compound, today."

If he slept, he would assume the call was a dream, because he couldn't have heard Ian correctly. "What are you talking about?"

"Victoria, who else?"

He froze. "Is this a joke?"

"No joke. I saw her come back with Jack. Found out she's taking a driver's education class."

Well what do you know? About damn time. He'd waited much too long as it was. Now that Henrik was out of the picture, no one could stop him now.

Victoria would finally be his.

CHAPTER 3

Victoria held the brush in her hand and gazed into the mirror. Hair up or hair down? Did it really matter? Ben couldn't see her. Better to wear it up and keep those adolescents at bay. She certainly didn't want to waste all her energy sending them away.

But if by some chance Ben had the opportunity to free her hair, would he have trouble with the pins or find it a turn on? Listen to her. When would he ever get the opportunity? Class was definitely off limits and that sister of his—Victoria had done her research—seemed awfully protective. But who was the woman protecting? Ben or her own self interests?

Victoria pulled her hair back. Except she didn't feel very sexy with it up and if she didn't feel sexy, then she wouldn't sound sexy and if she didn't sound sexy how would she ever get Ben's attention? Down it was. She'd risk the flak it might cause.

She glanced at the clock. Six-thirty? *Scheisse.* Where was that idiot anyway? She grabbed her purse and stormed out of her room.

"Perry!" Her voice echoed through the hallway. Damn man was going to make her late. She continued screaming his name on her way to the garage.

"Will you stop?" Perry emerged around the corner holding his hands to his ears. "Jesus, woman. They can hear you down the street."

"Where have you been?"

"None of your business. What's your hurry?"

"I don't want to be late."

Perry blinked several times. "Yesterday you didn't want to go at all. Why the sudden change?"

A certain someone she would not divulge to him, or anyone for that matter. "Yesterday I wasn't aware that if I miss any part of the classes, I would have to take the whole class again."

"Uh huh, sure. That's why your hair is down and you're wearing younger duds."

"Duds?"

"Your clothes. What's with the jeans and frilly blouse? Some kid catch your eye?"

Technically, Ben was younger than most vampires, so he could be considered a kid. "Maybe."

Perry smiled. "Go you."

"Yeah, rah-rah. Now, let's go."

"All right, all right. Don't get your panties in a bind." He stared at her jeans. "That is, if you're wearing any."

What lady dressed without underwear? She smacked him in the arm. "Didn't your mother teach you any manners?"

"Sure she did. I know exactly what to do in the presence of *ladies*." He grinned and batted his eyes.

How dare he? Victoria nearly struck him again. But if she kept this up, he might take his time driving to class and then all her efforts to arrive early would be for naught. "Very funny. Can we go now?"

When they reached the van, she climbed into the back.

"I told you the front is safe. Do you really think I'd go out into the sun if it weren't?"

No, she didn't. And he hadn't seemed in pain during that drive, either. Still… "Maybe tomorrow."

Perry sighed. "Then until you do, you're on your own coming back. And Jack has been told not to pick you up."

It seemed as if everyone was against her. When she had complained to Barnet about Perry, the man had the gall to side with the fiend. So she secretly stashed money down her bra in case Barnet saw fit to disallow a cab ride.

Victoria crossed her arms. "What difference does it make where I sit as long as I'm going to class? I think you've become power hungry."

"Maybe, but right now I do have the power. And it has six

cylinders." Perry started the vehicle and waited for the garage door to open. "It might be easier on you if you watched me drive from up here. You know, since you'll be doing it in a couple of weeks anyway."

She would worry about that when the time came. "Why do you care anyway?"

"Girl, why are you being so difficult? If you don't cheer up any, you'll never get that kid's attention. Of course, at that age, you'd probably kill him if you smiled. So maybe the sourpuss look would work."

"Did you ever think my attitude has to do with you?"

"Me?" He laughed. "Nah. I'm a charmer."

Slowly, he drove down the street, weaving around car after car after car. How did anyone drive in this traffic? It hadn't been this congested when Jack took her back. Would she have to drive in this? She shivered at the thought.

Perry pulled up to the front of the building. "Here you go."

"This is outside. Why aren't you in the garage?"

He turned around in his seat. "Maybe when you ride up front, I'll drive into the garage. Besides, it's not sunny here, you're safe."

But Ben would be coming in from the garage. "And you know this how?"

"If you don't want to be late, I suggest you get out. Or I can just return to Headquarters. Your call."

"Why do you have to take the fun out of everything?"

"Who says I do? I'm having a blast here."

She opened the door and stared outside. Shade covered her path. She should be safe. But what if she had super-sensitive skin like a handful of vampires did? A vampire didn't know until exposed. She took a deep breath and dashed from the van to the front door.

"Hey! You forgot to close the door."

Victoria turned around and smiled. "No, I didn't." Served him right if maybe he was the one with super-sensitive skin.

She arrived at the elevators. She could go down and wait for Ben, but what if he was already there waiting? How would she explain going in the opposite direction? Oh, damn Perry. She pushed the up button.

When the doors opened, the wonderful sea scent greeted her and she smiled. Ben. But when they opened all the way, the twins smiled and said "Hey" in unison when they saw her.

"Hello, boys, Mr. Martin."

"Hello, Ms. Braeden."

Ms. Braeden, not Victoria. Then again, she started it with the Mr. Martin line, so what did she expect?

"Zack and I were wondering which high school you went to," Peter said.

She'd like to tell them the truth, that women of her class were tutored. Too bad the truth wouldn't work here. "I graduated years ago."

"Wow," Zack said. "You're in college?"

"No. I graduated from there, too." She had three degrees to show for it, not that anyone would believe she owned them. They were hers, though.

"You must be some kind of child prodigy then," Zack said.

Ben wore his sunglasses, but seemed interested in her reaction as his head tilted to one side.

"I assure you, I am not. I am old enough to order a drink and not get arrested." And if she could get away with it, she'd manipulate these boys to be quiet. So much for thinking she could have some alone time with Ben, and she couldn't even blame Perry for this mess.

* * * *

Ben smiled at Victoria's frustration. Peter and Zack had about driven him nuts with their incessant questions and found a new target with her. Apparently, she was pretty and did look young, if both boys thought she attended high school.

But she was not a teenager. He'd looked up her record. She was twenty-two. Young, but definitely not jail bait.

"Then how come you don't have your license yet?" Zack asked.

"Because my husband didn't allow it."

Didn't allow it? Something primal inside of Ben awoke at the thought she'd been abused. What kind of person refused to let another learn to drive? Only one who wanted control of that person. Maybe it was a good thing her husband was no longer alive.

"You're married?" the boys said.

"I was married. But he died," Victoria said.

"Was he an old dude?" Zack asked, the nosier brother. "Did he leave you lots of money?"

"What are you implying?"

"Uhh, nothing. You said he died. I just assumed."

"Well, you know what they say about people who assume."

Silence greeted Ben and he would bet his last nickel the twins had confused expressions on their faces. The elevator stopped on their floor and he held the doors open. "Why don't we head on into class?"

The boys footsteps slapped the floor and their mutterings grew fainter, indicating they departed, but Victoria's scent remained by his side.

"Do you need any help?" she asked.

How easy would it be for him to say yes and take her elbow, feel her skin, or maybe her blouse—he had no idea what she wore—but she was a student and he the teacher. He should show some kind of decorum while in public. "Thank you, but I have my cane."

"Oh, you have an electronic cane? No wonder I… Sorry. That was rude of me. I never realized they came electronic."

"Well, they do have their glitches. Works great for obstacles. Not so great for holes. I feel pretty confident there aren't any holes in the building, though."

"And you'd be correct."

Her laughter lightened his mood and he smiled.

"Just so you know," she whispered, "my husband wasn't an old geezer, I didn't marry him for his money, and he didn't forbid me to drive. I said that hoping to shut those two up. Sort of backfired, huh?"

"Good to know." He breathed deep and took a chance. "Are you dating anyone?"

"Why, Mr. Martin. Are you inquiring for your own interest?"

He nodded. "I am. If you don't think I'm too old." Or blind. Cripes. What was he doing?

"Not at all. No, I'm not seeing anyone."

Already in for a penny, might as well go for that pound. "Can you stay after class a bit or do you need—"

She interrupted. "I can stay."

"What about your ride?"

"Not a problem. I can…text him. What about your sister?"

Had she done her own research? He smiled at the thought. "She's working late tonight."

"Guess I better go before the teacher yells at me." Her scent intensified and her breath tickled his cheek. "Can't wait for class to end." That husky voice of hers about did him in and the crotch of his slacks became pleasantly tight.

He couldn't wait, either. Damn. How'd he get so freakin' lucky? After settling behind his desk, he waited the obligatory time before taking roll. He was nothing if not punctual.

"Excuse me, Mr. Martin is it?"

He stood and faced toward the woman's voice. Most people felt comfortable being looked at when spoken to, even if the speaker couldn't see. "Yes. How may I help you?"

"I'm Mrs. Holder. My son, Brandon, is in your class. He said you're blind."

Ben smiled. "That's correct, I am."

"How can you teach this class? I checked. You have to have a valid driver's license. Are you telling me the state of Georgia has issued you a driver's license?"

A boy moaned from the middle of the classroom. Most likely Brandon.

Ben pushed himself to remain pleasant, to keep the conversation civil. He had warned Susannah something like this would happen. "Technically, Mrs. Holden, I'm the assistant. The instructor on record will be testing your son and I can assure you, she meets all the requirements of the state. I am only providing the lessons."

"Well, I just don't see how you can effectively teach these students without sight. Blind people don't drive."

"I have taught this course for many years before I lost my sight. The rules haven't changed and neither have the films. But if you have any other complaints, I can give you the instructor's number. She would be more than happy to discuss this with you at a more appropriate place and time."

"I'm thinking maybe I should call the police."

"Ma!"

Yeah, that was Brandon.

"Maybe we should talk out in the hall." Ben reached for his cane. The police. As if they had the time to be bothered with something so trivial.

"I'm sorry. I don't know what I was saying. You're right. Go ahead and teach your class. I'll be leaving now."

What was that all about? Her tone had flip-flopped and she'd spoken as if she'd been fed the lines.

The door clicked closed, settling the room in silence. Were the students just as stunned as he? Whatever, he had a class to teach and no one was stopping him. For now, anyway.

* * * *

Victoria remained in her chair while the students exited the room. Before they slipped out the door, she sent each a mental command: *Do not tell anyone your teacher is blind.* After that episode with Mrs. Holder, she could kick herself for not doing it yesterday. Too late now, but at least she had gotten Mrs. Holder to leave without wanting to call the police.

Ben looked in her direction. She smiled at him, then stopped. He couldn't see her, so why arouse suspicion? These teeny-boppers would like nothing more than to talk about romantic trysts. Didn't matter whose it was, either. The more inappropriate, the better. And what was more inappropriate than a teacher dating a student?

Not that they were dating. Not yet, anyway. Although, if she had her way… Oh yeah.

The last student's footsteps diminished down the hall. Probably safe from sensitive ears, but better she kept the discussion mundane, at least for now. "If you don't mind me asking, how long have you been blind?"

Ben stood and picked up his electronic cane. Without any effort, he found the desk beside her and sat on the chair. She inhaled his wonderful scent.

"I don't mind you asking anything. I lost my sight almost ten years ago. Car accident. Proof you should always wear your seatbelt. I was lucky I only lost my sight."

"You teach driver's ed and didn't wear your seatbelt? I find that hard to believe."

"Actually, I was in the backseat and took it off for a minute to grab something out of the back of the van. Before I had a chance to put it back on, we'd been hit and I was flying. I don't recommend it." He chuckled. "So how is it you don't have a driver's license? You royalty or something?"

"I wish. Actually, driving never held much interest for me. My husband preferred to drive and I had no issues with that."

"Your parents must have loved you for not raising their insurance rates."

"I'm sure Father would have, if he were alive. He did seem to be all about the money." She leaned toward him and filled her lungs with his tantalizing scent. "What is the name of that cologne you're wearing? It's absolutely wonderful."

"Cologne? I'm not wearing any. I even use unscented soap. I find it interferes."

What? Not a cologne? So how did that explain the similarities to Justin?

Scheisse. Was it possible she found one? Nah. What were the odds? None were found for centuries and then to have three within the last six months? Of course, there were ways she could check.

"But I'll take it as a compliment that you think I smell good."

"Then do." She laughed and mentally ordered him to scratch his nose. To cough. To stand. He did none of those things. Most likely his head injury caused that. She'd just have to watch what she said around him.

"What do you look like?"

"I, uh…" What should she say? Like a seventeen-year-old? Most people thought she looked younger than that.

"Let me be more specific. What color are your eyes?"

She could do specific. "Hazel. How about you? You ever take off your glasses?"

He smiled and removed them, unveiling cloudy green eyes and several small scars. "I've been told they look a little freaky. That's why I keep them on."

"They don't look that way to me, but I could see the students making comments."

He slid them back over his eyes. "Better to keep them guessing, I say. So what color is your hair?"

"Blonde."

"Are you tan or do you sunburn easily?"

She swallowed. "I'm pale. I don't go out into the sun."

"Good. No chance of getting skin cancer then, huh?"

Or turn into ash. "That's true."

"Any freckles?"

"No. But I have a dimple on my right cheek when I smile."

"Kissed by an angel." He paused. Was he thinking about kissing her, too? *Gott*, she hoped so. "Do you mind if I see what you look like?" He raised his hands and wiggled his fingers. "Or is it too soon?"

She shook her head. What an idiot. He couldn't see her. But his touch would rule out her suspicion. "No, not too soon. What do you need me to do?"

"Victoria? There you are. I've been waiting for you downstairs and thought I'd missed you."

Ben's hands were inches from cupping her face and his scent fogged her mind. Who the heck was looking for her? She shook her head and leaned around the only guy who mattered to find… "Graham? What are you doing here?"

He stood in the doorway, his greyish-blue eyes lit up when she spotted him. Besides his yearly requirement, she hadn't seen Graham away from Headquarters since Henrik's death. But then, she'd never left Headquarters, so that could have had something to do with it.

Graham glanced at Ben, who had risen and returned to his desk. "I heard Barnet was making you walk home and thought you could use a ride."

Ben's head jerked up. "You don't have a ride home? At this hour?"

"She does now," Graham said. "What are you, deaf?"

"No, just blind."

Graham scrunched his forehead.

Of all the days to be offered a ride… Victoria couldn't believe her luck. But it was an offer she couldn't refuse. Because if Ben was what she suspected, then there was no erasing his memory and Graham just might be stupid enough to say something inappropriate. Still, she didn't want Ben to get the wrong impression. "Graham, I'll be done in a minute. Can you wait for me in the lobby?"

"Sure." He smiled and headed toward the elevators.

"I take it he's a friend?" Ben asked.

"Of my late husband's, yes. Listen—"

"Were you really walking home alone tonight?"

"No, of course not." That's what her cab fare was for. "But I guess I better get going. Can we do this again tomorrow? Without the interruption?"

Ben smiled. "Consider it a date."

A date. Wonder what an actual one with him would be like? *Hölle*, she just wanted to touch him. Better save that for later. Damn Graham for showing up when he had.

* * * *

The room became much too quiet. Her absence left a void he hadn't expected. Ben fisted his hand. The last time he'd punched out someone he'd been in the eighth grade and Bruce Dorsey had flipped up Teri Armentrout's skirt in front of the basketball team. Ben had earned a week's detention for his actions, but it had been worth it seeing Teri's grateful smile.

And he hadn't felt the need to punch anyone since. Until now.

Who was this Graham and what did he mean to Victoria? And why did Ben have this urge to connect his fist with the guy's face?

He was losing it. Plain and simple. Graham hadn't done anything but offer Victoria a ride. Damn it. All that self-pity came flooding back, something he thought he'd fought off ten years ago. He had come to terms with his blindness, it was his life now, it was who he was. Even Victoria seemed to accept him.

But damn it, he wanted to drive her home. And he never would.

He kicked out, expecting to meet his desk. Instead, the trash can clattered across the floor. Shit. He got down on his knees and reached out.

"Ben?" Susannah hustled into the room. "Are you okay? Did you fall?"

He stopped and lowered his head. "I'm fine. Didn't know the can was there."

"I got it. Sorry I took so long tonight. Hope you found something to keep yourself busy." The sounds indicated she was picking up whatever was inside the trash can. Damn it, he couldn't even do that right.

"What's got you in the dumps? Class giving you a hard time?"

He found the chair and climbed back on it. "Class is fine. Guess I'm just tired."

She settled the can beside the desk and her footsteps shuffled away. "One of your students left her scarf behind. Where do you want it?"

"I'll take it." Susannah placed a thin, gauzy scarf in his hand.

How sad was he for wanting to sniff it and discover if it were Victoria's? He needed to get a grip. He stuffed it in his bag and stood. "I have a student I suspect walks home alone after class. Do you mind if I offer her a ride tomorrow?"

"Her? Who? That child you were ogling yesterday?"

"She's not a child."

"She's not an adult, either."

"Her records indicate she's twenty-two."

"No way. Your program had to have translated it incorrectly. And even if it hadn't, twenty-two is still too young."

"It's only seventeen years. If she doesn't care about the age difference, why should I?"

"You're not seriously considering her, are you?"

He shrugged. "I don't know. I like her, Suze. I think she likes me, too."

"Of course she likes you. You're a great guy. But I hate to tell you this, she probably thinks of you like a father, not dating material. Or she's pumping you for an A. Come on, let's go home."

Victoria didn't treat him like a father figure. He may be blind, but he got the distinct impression her interest extended far beyond any stupid grade. Shoot, everyone in the class knew Susannah was giving the exams.

No, Susannah was wrong. Victoria was interested in him as a man and, hell, he would take advantage of that. It'd been over ten years since his last relationship. He was long overdue.

* * * *

Victoria exited the elevator and Graham greeted her with a kiss on the cheek. "You're kind of early for the meeting, aren't you?"

"I'm not here for the meeting." Graham opened the front door for her. "So, who's the guy?"

"Guy? Oh, you mean Mr. Martin. He's my teacher. I…had a question and stayed after class to ask it."

"Must have been a personal question. You two seemed chummy."

And they would have seemed chummier if Graham had arrived a minute later. Maybe she should be thankful he came when he had. Although, it would have been better if he hadn't arrived at all. "He's a nice man, don't read anything more into it. If you're not here for the meeting, then why?"

"I came to see you."

"Me? Why?" He'd never shown any interest before. Or had he? She'd lost count of his attempts to discredit Henrik while her husband was alive, but that had stemmed from their feud, not because of her. Of course, she never did determine what their feud was about. *Scheisse.*

Graham shrugged. "I know how much Henrik meant to you. When I heard you were seen outside, I figured you were finally moving on."

Moving on? And he'd been waiting? That couldn't be a good sign.

He grabbed her shoulders and looked her up and down. A breeze ruffled his hair, sending dark locks every which way. "You are looking good, Victoria. Widowhood suits you."

She only wanted a ride, not a relationship. Well, not a relationship with him. Graham was nothing more than a former friend of Henrik's. A friendship that had ended badly. "*Gott*, you sound like you still hold a grudge against Henrik. You know he had nothing to do with the Committee. You should be mad at me, not him."

He laughed. "I could never be mad at you. Besides, I know he had great influence with the Committee. Face it. He was more a member than you."

"That's not true. He didn't control me."

"Not directly, I suppose."

"What is that supposed to mean?"

"Victoria." He said her name on a sigh and shook his head as if she'd been some sort of naughty child. "Everyone knows he only had to tell you how to vote, and that's how you voted."

"Everyone?" No, that couldn't be true. Henrik had supported her votes, not coerced them. Or had he? *Scheisse.*

He caressed her cheek. "I'm sorry. I didn't come to upset you. I came to see you. Where would you like to go? Have you fed?"

Feeding was eating as far as she was concerned, but the way he said it with that low voice made it sound almost sexual. If she were to do any sexual activity, she'd rather do it with Ben. But if she rejected Graham's advances she'd be stuck finding a cab, or worse…walking home. No, she could handle Graham. "I did this morning, and while I'd love to reminisce—"

"Sweetheart, I want to do more than reminisce. Don't you know that?"

Unfortunately she did, the bulge in his pants a clear indication. "I'm flattered, but I have homework and I'd like to get to it."

"Why *are* you taking a driver's ed class?"

Telling him the truth was too embarrassing and definitely not his business. "Just thought it was time for me to learn how to drive."

"There are books on-line and you can get a license without the class. So what's going on?"

"Nothing is going on."

"Is the Committee looking into all vampires being legal or something?"

"You know I'm not allowed to discuss Committee business. Every time one of us does, it comes back to bite us."

"That makes it sound like you are."

"You're reading too much into this, Graham. Now, where's your car?"

He pointed at a red Cadillac parked on the street. "I got it from an old man in New York. Ain't it pretty?"

"You stole it?"

"No. He sold it to me. Maybe not for what it's worth…"

"You mean you manipulated it out of him. Now why would you do that?"

He put his hands on hips. "You make it sound like it's never done. Henrik did it a time or two."

"Never."

"Excuse me? Maybe you should look into that plantation home you owned, then tell me he never."

She would look into it. And ask Barnet about it. Manipulation for personal gain was wrong. Henrik had known how she felt about it, too. No way would he have been underhanded like that. Apparently, Graham was still bent on discrediting Henrik.

Graham opened the passenger door and leaned toward her, his sight focused on her lips. She quickly slid onto the seat to avoid any possible kissing. Was a ride to Headquarters really worth this?

After climbing in behind the wheel, he turned toward her. "Are you sure you have to go back so soon? You'll have all day for homework."

And if she had homework, that would be a true statement.

"Maybe another time. I'm still trying to get used to being out."

He took her hand. "Henrik's been gone a long time now. He wouldn't have wanted you to mourn this long, would he?"

She snatched her hand away and opened the door. "I think this was a mistake."

"No, no. I'm sorry. You're right. Please, let me drive you back."

She shut the door and sat quietly while Graham drove. This ride better not be the start of something horrible. If she wasn't careful, Graham could easily become a pain in her *Arsch*.

CHAPTER 4

Victoria threw her purse inside her room and headed for Barnet's office. She'd thought Graham would never let her leave. The man was persistent, she'd give him that. But after what he had told her about Henrik, she needed reassurance it wasn't true.

She turned the corner and nearly ran into Barnet.

"Oh good, you're back," he said, indicating for her to follow. "We're having an impromptu meeting in the conference room. Jack is here and we have Hilde and Abe on the televisions."

"You mean you teleconferenced them in and they're on the monitors?" And he thought she was out of touch.

"Yeah, yeah. Whatever." Barnet sprinted ahead, apparently not willing to speak of anything until he had his audience.

Their conference room was probably no different than any of the ones she'd seen on TV. Except there wasn't a view of the city. Being underground made that feat impossible.

Four monitors lined the wall at the end of the long table. Victoria didn't see the need for so many, but Barnet had faith she would eventually move out and any impromptu meetings could be held electronically. Right now only two of the monitors were lit.

Jack, always the gentleman, rose when she entered the room. Dressed in his standard T-shirt and jeans, he exuded masculinity. There was a time after Henrik's death when she'd given Jack a second look, but he'd always treated her like a little sister. Truth be told, she kind of liked being one, so she never pursued him. "Wow. You look…nice. Did you have a date?"

Barnet glanced at her and raised his eyebrows, as if he'd just now noticed her wardrobe. "You wore that to class?"

"You act like I never dress casually." She wouldn't bother explaining she'd had to purchase the outfit since all she owned were suits and dresses. Thank goodness the Underground had clothing stores.

"You don't," they both said.

She tugged on her blouse before taking a seat across from Jack. "Well, you said I should blend in."

"Victoria, you're fine. Ignore them," Hilde said from the left monitor. The short-haired blonde was the first woman elected to the Committee back in 1898 and someone Victoria had hoped would become a close friend when she became a member in 1932, but that had never occurred. In fact, Hilde rarely came to her defense. That she did now meant a lot to Victoria.

Abe, the newest member of their group—elected in 1940— appeared on the right monitor, wearing a crooked smile. His dark hair hung low, practically obliterating his eyes. How he could see, she could only guess. "Now that Victoria is here, what is this meeting about?"

Barnet sat at the head of the table. "I received a call from Dalton. Seems he's fed from a human he can't control."

"Shit," Jack said. "Another Perfect Mate? That makes the third since December."

The fourth, if Ben turned out the same way. No way would she volunteer that information. Not yet, anyway.

"I sure wish I knew where they were coming from," Barnet said. "The Perfect Mate is a story. How is this happening? And why now?"

Jack rubbed his face. "It's got to be more than that. It must be based on fact."

Barnet shrugged. "Not any fact I know about. I don't even know when it was written. The story had been floating around for centuries when I'd been turned. If it were fact, wouldn't we have evidence of it by now?"

"I'll investigate and see if an author can be found," Jack said. "Someone had to have written it."

"Good idea. Better to get the information from the source."

"Is this vampire going nuts like Katarina did with Justin?" Hilde asked.

Nuts was putting it mildly. When Katarina had brought Justin to Headquarters shortly after Christmas, she had nearly attacked Victoria and Hilde, and all they had done was show an interest in Justin's scent. Of course, at the time no one had any idea Justin was a Perfect Mate—or that Perfect Mates actually existed—and wouldn't know for another two months.

"No," Barnet said. He turned toward Victoria. "The mortal is male."

Victoria's heart lurched. Dalton lived in Detroit, not Atlanta, so why the look? Unless Dalton was in the area. *Scheisse*. She discreetly stuck her hand in her pocket and toyed with the handkerchief. Henrik had given it to her as a gift and since his death it had given her peace whenever she became nervous. But to bring it out now would only draw attention to herself.

Jack chuckled. "So both guys are straight? There's no attraction otherwise?"

Barnet shook his head and looked at Jack. "No attraction. Just one scared vampire who doesn't know what to do. Hell, he practically drained the guy dry."

"Drained him?" She squeezed the handkerchief and nearly gasped. Must remain calm. It was possible Barnet spoke of someone other than Ben.

"Whoa," Jack said. "Do we need to call in Ian?"

"No, we don't need anything cleaned up. Not yet anyway. I've asked John Pennington to go up to Detroit and assess the situation since he lives nearby, but we need to bring the mortal here. Hilde, if you value your marriage, you might want to stay away in case this man affects you. No need to get Rolf upset again."

Victoria let out a discrete sigh. Good. Not Atlanta. Not Ben.

"I understand, but what about the June meeting?" Hilde asked. "It's less than three weeks away."

"Hopefully we'll have him someplace safe by then. Victoria…I'll let you decide if you want to stay or not. If he's a Perfect Mate…" Barnet raised his eyebrows.

She had already found her Perfect Mate. Well, maybe. Even if Ben wasn't one, she was more attracted to him than some unknown male. "He's not a toy. Doesn't he have any rights?"

"He's one against a whole race. There are no rights. If he discovers we exist, we'd have no way to erase his memories. Would you rather we kill him?"

"No, of course not, but we shouldn't offer him up to the highest bidder, either."

"Damn it!" Barnet pounded his fist on the table. "Where are they coming from? Why now? When word gets out—"

"We can't sit on this any longer," Jack said. "Or we'll end up with more situations like this. If vampires are forewarned, they'll know to check before acting."

"Or we'll have a mess on our hands when every unmated vampire goes out looking for their own Perfect Mate. We don't even know everything yet. Two couples in six months don't give us enough data."

"Maybe three could," Abe said. "And we'll have the chance to evaluate from the first meeting. That's if Victoria is willing—"

"Wait a minute." Victoria bolted out of her chair. "Who said I was looking for a mate?"

"You seemed willing when Justin was here," Hilde said.

"So did you!"

"Enough." Barnet extended his arms. "Victoria, sit. No one is forcing anyone to do what they don't want."

Except they were forcing someone by imprisoning him. She slunk to her seat. *Gott*, if they found out about Ben and he turned out to be a Perfect Mate, would their actions be watched as if under a microscope? They weren't zoo animals. "No one's going to want their privacy taken away. No one wants to be observed."

Barnet stood. "No one is observing. Nothing is to be decided tonight. I don't even know this man's condition. It might just be a moot point. Still, I wanted you all aware of the situation. Who would like to go up there and retrieve the fella?"

Barnet might have asked for volunteers, but he looked at Jack because, well, Jack always went. Of course, that was before he'd gotten married.

"Sunshine and I can leave tonight," Jack said.

"Excuse me," Barnet said. "Do you really want your wife near him?"

"I don't feel comfortable leaving her alone. She's still new."

"All the more reason she should stay away from him. Right, Hilde?"

Hilde had the decency to blush. "I didn't know what was happening, she will. Still, would you want to see your wife attracted to another?"

Jack lowered his head. "I trust her."

"Sure you do," Barnet said. "But do you want her to feel guilty for being attracted to another?"

"No, but I can't leave her. She's too new."

Jack's wife, Sunshine—whom everyone else called Sunny—had only been a vampire since January. Most newly turned vampires hadn't been well known in their human life and just relocating would suffice, but Sunny's father was the Governor of Florida, which made her high-profile and likely to be recognized. Something they wished to avoid since she'd been reported missing.

"I'm sure she could manage without you for a few days, but if it'll make you feel better, she can stay here until you return."

"I'll keep her company," Victoria said. "You won't have to worry about her."

Jack nodded. "Thanks, Victoria. Then I'll leave tonight."

"Good, good," Barnet said. "Go rent a van, one with panels. And take some tranquilizers and whatever you need to bind him. Nicely, of course. We don't want to hurt the fella, but we don't need him running away, either."

"No matter what you do, he's going to hate us," Victoria said.

"Better to hate us than be dead," Barnet said.

* * * *

Ben plopped onto the couch. Why couldn't his sister just be happy he'd found someone? Was it because she had no one but him in her life?

"What's the matter?" Susannah asked. "Aren't you feeling well?"

"Why don't you ever go out?"

Her briefcase landed on the table, keys clanked inside the bowl. "Who has time? The business keeps me busy."

"Not that busy. Are you a lesbian? Is that it? I'm okay with it if you are."

She choked back a cough. "What? No. I like men."

"Then why don't you go out?"

"Well, in case you hadn't noticed, men aren't exactly falling at my feet begging to go out with me."

He couldn't see why not. She'd always been pretty. Ten years couldn't have been that harsh on her. "Who said they had to ask?

Maybe you need to make the first move."

"Uhh, no. Besides, like I said, I don't have time. What with the business and taking care of you…"

The words trailed from her lips and imbedded themselves in his heart. "Damn it, Susannah. I don't want to be the reason you don't have a life."

"I have a life."

"Really? Because it doesn't seem like it to me."

"I don't need a man to complete me. You keep me busy enough."

Did she think he was helpless? "You don't have to take care of me."

"I didn't mean it like that."

"Then how did you mean it?" Her silence spoke volumes. "Is that why you don't want me to see Victoria? You don't think I can take care of myself?"

"No, of course not. I just don't think that child knows what she's in for."

He bolted off the couch. "What?"

"I'm sorry. That didn't come out right. Sit down."

"I think it came out fine. You think I'm incapable of taking care of myself."

She grabbed his arm and pulled him down to the couch to sit beside her. "I love you, Ben, but you can be a handful."

"How am I a handful? Because I occasionally run into things? People do that all the time. That's why there are emergency rooms."

"Ben, please don't be this way."

God, if his own sister thought he was helpless, how could he ever hope to win over Victoria? He didn't want her pity or assistance. He wanted a relationship. An equal one. "I can take care of myself and I'll prove it."

"What are you going to do?"

He had no idea. He'd lost his teaching job after the accident due to his lengthy absence. Once he became relatively healthy, he didn't think he could effectively teach math to high schoolers anymore. But now that he'd had a taste of the classroom again, he'd love to have his old job back. Would it be possible? He still tutored at the school so maybe it was worth a shot to ask. Because if he couldn't support himself, it would certainly put a crimp in things.

* * * *

Graham pulled up to the curb and turned off the engine. Victoria might have said Martin was just her teacher, but he'd seen the look of desire on her face. Graham hit the steering wheel with the heel of his hand. Damn, if he'd only arrived sooner, before she stepped foot out of Headquarters, she'd be his right now. Okay, so it would take some work. But eventually, she would look at him the same way and then he would not only have the love of his life, he could have a voice on the Committee. And wouldn't that be perfect?

Unfortunately, if he fiddled with Martin, Victoria might get wind of it. Better he fiddled with the sister instead. What better person to put a wrench into a budding romance?

Speak of the devil. Or should that be angel? Whatever. Susannah Martin stood in front of an open window combing her hair. Perfect. He sent a mental message, *"If anyone is in the room with you, tell them you need some fresh air and will return shortly. Then come outside to the red Cadillac parked across your building."*

Not long after, she stepped outside. She wasn't really all that bad looking for a forty-year-old. And if he was into older women—which was a joke, seeing as how he was older than all mortals—he might even have some fun with her. Heck, he might do it anyway. The windows were tinted and it had been awhile since he'd had any sex. Maybe it would be better to get some relief. And Ms. Martin would sure beat his hand.

Damn. He was getting hard just thinking about it.

He rested his arm along the open window and took control of the woman, sending her around the car and making her climb into the passenger seat. He locked the door, raised the windows, and practically choked on the fumes.

Damn. How much perfume did the woman wear? The scent of lilacs nearly burned his nose. He lowered his window a crack. Didn't help any.

Fine. He would hold his breath, because at this point all he could think about was getting some relief.

He unzipped his pants and pulled out his cock, hard and ready for some fun. "Come give me a blowjob."

Without any hesitation, she bent over and took him in her

mouth. Damn, that was easy. And her mouth was heaven, all wet and suction. He stroked her hair and moaned. Oh yeah. Much better than his hand.

Later he would do something about that perfume.

* * * *

Wearing her bathing suit and a robe, Victoria headed for the pool. She had asked to speak to Barnet privately. Frustrated with the meeting, he declared he needed a swim and that he'd talk at the pool. Since the only other person at Headquarters was Perry and he was busy watching television, she didn't have to meet Barnet in his office to have privacy.

The tile stairs leading down to the pool were smooth against her bare feet and she descended without a sound. When she entered the room containing the Olympic-sized pool, Barnet was already taking freestyle laps. She sat on the side and dipped her legs into the water. Her body temperature matched that of the cool water immediately. She splashed Barnet as he swam past.

"You keep that up and I'll pull you in," he said.

"You'd have to catch me first." She leaned back on her arms. The ripples in the water mesmerized her. If she ever brought Ben to this pool, she'd have to make sure the water was heated. This thing did have a thermostat, didn't it? But if she asked, Barnet would want to know why and she wasn't willing to share Ben yet— Perfect Mate or not. Which made her wonder… "Barnet? Are you hoping you'll find a Perfect Mate?"

He reached the end of the pool and changed to the backstroke. "Well, I won't deny the thought does intrigue me. Doesn't it intrigue you? I thought for sure you'd have jumped all over the chance to meet a prospect."

"Why? Because of the way I acted with Justin? I'd like to think I know better now." Justin had smelled fine, she wouldn't dispute that fact, but had she really been interested in him? She'd like to say no, not that Katarina had ever given her a chance to find out otherwise. Whereas Ben… Sure, her interest had all started with his scent, and maybe his blindness helped a little—okay, a lot—but there was more to him than that. Like his big, strong arms and a sexy voice that could probably convince her to do anything. And his lips, she couldn't forget those. But was his scent causing this attraction or was something more involved?

Barnet swam past her. "Sure wish I knew where they were coming from."

"I'll do some research. See what the four of them have in common."

He stopped and bobbed in the water. "Four?"

Scheisse. She had included Ben. Quick, quick, she had to cover up her blunder. She purposely counted on her fingers and smiled. "I meant three."

Barnet raised an eyebrow. "Is there something you're not telling me?"

"Like what? That I'm bad at math?" And hopefully a better actor?

"Yeah, right." Barnet continued with his back stroke.

That was too close. What was she thinking? Oh yeah. Of Ben. Maybe if there were more Perfect Mates around, she wouldn't feel the need to hide Ben, not that she had definite proof he was a Perfect Mate. Even so, she wasn't willing to share. Would she ever? Then a horrible thought came to her.

"Barnet, why do you suppose Dalton called you about this Perfect Mate?"

"Why wouldn't he call?"

"Because of Derek's actions when he discovered he couldn't control Justin."

Katarina had told Victoria she'd had to incapacitate Derek in order to keep him from killing Justin. And even after she had turned Derek over to the Committee, he still wanted to know why they hadn't killed the freak.

Barnet swam over to her side of the pool. "What are you getting at?"

"Maybe we're not hearing about Perfect Mates because the ones who are discovered are being..." *Gott.* Just thinking about Ben dead wrenched her insides.

"Killed?" When she nodded, he continued. "Why would they do that? Did you want to kill Justin when you met him? I didn't."

"No, but how do you explain Derek?"

"Derek had issues with Katarina wanting her freedom. He was much too protective of her. Still... It is worth looking into."

Barnet was probably correct, but not a theory she was willing to test right now. Not with Ben anyway. "We might want to think about adding some questions to the check-in process. To see if any have been discovered."

By their laws, every vampire must check-in yearly by attending one of the quarterly Committee Meetings and failing to meet this requirement—or break any law for that matter—could be met with a death penalty. Most of the questions were benign, such as what name they were currently living under and where they were currently residing. But each Committee Member also searched each vampire's mind to see if they'd broken any of their laws. A time-consuming process, but an effective one.

"If we do that, then we'll have to let them know why." He rubbed his temples. "This is giving me a headache. I thought I was beyond those. Please tell me this isn't what you wanted to discuss."

She chuckled. She'd forgotten all about her reason for the meeting. "No. I saw Graham. He found me after class tonight."

"Is that how you came home so quickly? I told you no more getting rides."

"I don't see why I can't get a ride if I do it on my own. Isn't that what you had in mind with this class? For me to mingle?"

Barnet laughed. "Touché. So what about Graham?"

"He said something…"

"About what? Perfect Mates?"

"*Hölle*, no. Why did you approach me to join the Committee?"

He rested his arms on the edge, the water glistening on his pale skin. "Henrik suggested I ask you after I told him about adding another female. Why?"

Oh *Gott*. Was Graham right? "Do you think Henrik used me to get a voice on the Committee?"

"If he wanted to be on the Committee, he could have run for the open position. No one would have stopped him."

"But you wanted a female. You made that clear in the meetings."

"No. I wanted balance. I only suggested females would bring that. When we got no takers, we started searching. You were the only one interested."

"Because Henrik encouraged me."

"So what if he did? Say you're right and he used you to get a voice. You've been on the Committee longer since his death than when he was alive."

"And now you want to see me kicked off."

Barnet pinched the bridge of his nose and sighed. "We don't want to kick you off. We need you to be a full participating member. You can't do that staying at Headquarters all the time. What exactly did Graham tell you?"

"That just about everyone knows Henrik was more a Committee Member than I am."

"I have not heard any complaints. Neither before nor after his death. Your inability to leave the Underground is a Committee issue. It is not public knowledge."

"But, Graham—"

"For some strange reason is trying to goad you. Do you care about his opinion?"

"Well, no."

"Then don't worry about it. Anything else?"

There was the issue about her former home, but she would do some checking on her own first. "No."

"Then come race me. I need the distraction." He arched back into the water and swam toward one end.

Being distracted sounded good to her, too. She slipped off her robe and dove into the water.

CHAPTER 5

Susannah stopped the car. "The door is at three o'clock."

Ben yanked the strap of his laptop case over his head to cross his chest and grabbed his cane. "What? You're not going to walk me inside and make sure I find the class?"

"Ben."

"Or make sure I don't fall and hurt myself? Heaven forbid I make another trip to the emergency room."

"Ben, stop it."

Oh no. He was just getting started. "I'm surprised you still want me to teach."

She let out an exasperated breath. "I never said you were helpless."

"No. Just that I couldn't take care of myself."

He reached for the handle, but she grabbed his arm. "I'm sorry. How many times do I have to say it?"

Probably until he believed her. He shrugged free from her grasp. "I gotta go."

"What the hell is she doing?" Susannah asked.

"Who? What?"

"Your little friend. She just hopped out of a van and left the door open. Tell me that isn't the sign of a spoiled teenager."

Ben smiled. Victoria was here, hot diggity-dog. Her mere presence lessened his anger and frustration toward his sister. "I'll see you after class."

In his need to be quick, he managed to trip over an uneven

portion of the sidewalk, collide into a trash bin with his thigh, and elbow a passerby. He shouted an apology over his shoulder as he reached for the door. Where the handle should be, he met with air.

"Are you okay?" Victoria's concerned voice came from directly in front of him.

Had she witnessed his stupidity? Way to be smooth. At least Susannah hadn't followed him in. Wouldn't that be lovely? He entered the foyer and moved to the left, where he'd be out of traffic. "I'm fine. How are you, Victoria?"

"Couldn't be better now that you're here."

That certainly was the case for him. She was like a drug. A nice, soothing drug. "You keep that up, I'm going to think you like me."

She laughed, the sound charming to his ears. "What was your first hint?"

"So is that why you're here early? Hoping to run into me?" Hell, he nearly ran into her. Literally.

"Oops. The secret's out. Do you have to go up now?"

He almost laughed. Seemed they both had the same idea. "Not right away." He ran his fingers over his watch. "We've got twenty whole minutes. What did you have in mind?"

"*Scheisse.* Does everyone have to show up early? Let's go over there." She grabbed his arm and pulled.

"Whoa, wait. Let me take your elbow."

"I'm sorry. Here."

He gripped her softly, so as not to make undue advances, when really everything inside him wanted to charge ahead and kiss her. But she had an agenda and he would hear her out first. Then later, who knew?

Dinging elevators came and went and he counted six steps when she turned left. The slight echo of their footfalls told him it was a hallway. The voices from the entrance grew dimmer.

Five steps. Ten steps. "Where are we going?"

"Someplace private." She stopped after fourteen steps. "Much better." She turned around. "You wanted to know what I look like, so I thought now would be a good time and no one from class will spot us here."

"You make it sound like we're doing something immoral." Although he wouldn't mind being a little immoral if she didn't. He pocketed his cane, freeing up his hands. Hands that ached to touch her more intimately than just tracing the contours of her face.

"No, of course not. But you know how teenagers like to gossip." She placed her hands on his shoulders, pushing him up against a wall. "I'm ready."

And damn, if she didn't make that sound all sexy. If he wasn't careful, he'd give away his desire easy enough. Heck, he wasn't exactly soft. He wouldn't scare her away, though. He ran his hands from her forearms—she wore a silky, long-sleeved blouse—to her shoulders. She was much shorter than he anticipated. Delicate, too. He inched his fingers to her neck and met with the softness of her skin. An electric-like current sprinted up his arms and went straight to his groin. Instant hard-on. His breath caught in his throat and he dropped his arms. Hot damn.

She gasped. "Oh my. Do that again."

"Do what? Did I shock you?"

"*Hölle*, no." She took his hands in hers and that charge returned. His heart skipped several beats. If he was having a heart attack, he hoped it never stopped. She placed his hands on her face. "Oh *Gott*, you feel soooo good. Please forgive me."

Forgive her? For what? For making him feel delirious? While he still held her face, she leaned forward and pressed her lips against his. A spark ignited into a full-fledged fire. Delirious? Hell no, this was Heaven. He pulled her close and plunged his tongue inside her willing mouth. She tasted better than he imagined—a mix of spicy and sweet. Damn, he couldn't get enough of her. Her arms went around his neck and he spun them around, planting her against the wall and rubbing his erection into her. He'd never wanted anyone like this before.

* * * *

Victoria reveled in the heat Ben spread throughout her body. She didn't have to wonder any longer. That one touch confirmed it. He was a Perfect Mate. He was *her* Perfect Mate.

He continued his assault on her mouth, turning her legs into wet noodles. Thank goodness she couldn't control him, or she might have him remove her clothes. They were way too constricting.

Movement down the hall snapped her back to the present. She broke the kiss. "Sure wish I didn't have class."

He laughed, panting. "You could say that again. Although, I still don't know what you look like."

She brought his hands to her cheeks and closed her eyes as his wonderful heat spread. "Look to your heart's content."

He ran his thumbs across her cheeks, eyes, brows, around her ears and ended at her chin and mouth, all while she resisted stripping him bare and taking him on the floor. If he had touched her last night in the classroom, she probably would have.

He leaned his forehead against hers. "You're beautiful."

"I bet you say that to all the people you touch."

He shook his head and gave her another mind-numbing kiss, sending her libido through the atmosphere. "I want to see more of you."

"I think that can be arranged. But maybe we should cool you down."

He rubbed his erection against her and chuckled. "What was *your* first hint?"

"I'm so sorry. I really only brought you here to feel my face."

He backed up and frowned. "You're sorry?"

She grabbed him by the lapels of his blazer and tugged him closer. "Not like that, no. I just didn't mean to make you feel like you need to take a cold shower."

The smile returned. "You always make me feel hot. That kiss just made it feel more…right. I wish we didn't have class, either."

"I'm free after. All night."

"And I'll be counting the minutes until we're free." He pulled out his cellphone. "Why don't you go on up to class while I let my sister know I won't need a ride home."

"Okay. The elevators are at—"

He touched her face. "I know where they are."

"You're smarter than me. I get lost in this building and I can see."

He leaned over and brushed his lips against hers. Damn, he was good. She'd moved so many times and he still found her?

"Try not to torture me too much tonight, okay?" He smiled. "I'm a little out of practice."

"So am I." Over forty years out of practice. Not even Henrik had made her feel unglued with just a kiss. Was it the Perfect Mate thing or Ben? She kind of hoped it was the latter.

* * * *

Susannah had locked up a student-driver vehicle and was heading toward her car when Graham climbed out of his and waved her down. Meeting in secret, or through manipulation only, wasn't in his best interest, nor feasible. He needed a reason to call on her and have her meet him and what better way than to court her.

But in order to court her, he needed her to remember him naturally, which was his plan this evening.

He'd love for her to look at him and see someone else's face— such as Perry's—but like most vampires, he didn't have that ability. Still, he tried, in case Victoria grew suspicious. The worst she'd find searching Susannah's memories was a blurry face.

"Excuse me, ma'am," he said. "I couldn't help but notice you work for the driver's ed school. Can I talk to you about classes? I have this friend…"

While trying his best to project Perry's likeness, as well as sound like the man, Graham made sure not to block his allure. He needed her at his mercy. And maybe more sex. That other night wasn't enough, and to have a willing partner…damn. He was getting hard thinking about the fun they could have.

"Oh, hello." Her face lit up with a smile. "Actually, I'm the owner." She pulled a card out of her purse. "Class information is on the web. Your friend can sign up there."

He took the card from her and stepped in close. His allure must be working since she hadn't bolted. "But then I wouldn't be able to spend some time with a pretty lady."

Susannah sputtered and giggled.

Yeah, his allure was doing the trick all right. "My name is Perry. Are you on your way to meet another student?"

"No, I'm done for the night."

"Wonderful. Why don't you let me buy you a cup of coffee and we can discuss what classes you have?"

"Well…I don't know. It's not like I know you." She stared at him with desire in her eyes and never stepped back. This fish had been hooked.

"I'm asking you to get to know me. You can even drive your own car and pick the place. Please don't make me beg." Or push her feeble brain. He needed her willing to do this—less chance Victoria would suspect anyone manipulating Susannah—and if he turned her on, how could she resist?

She shrugged. "Why not? I don't have to be anywhere."

He smiled. Best news he'd heard all night.

* * * *

Ben ran his fingers over his watch. Only ten minutes left and then Victoria would be all his. He didn't know exactly what they would do but, frankly, he didn't care. He just wanted to be with her.

He'd left Susannah a message saying not to bother picking him up. And he'd told her the real reason why. Let her take that however she wanted.

The music indicated the film had ended.

"Does anyone have any questions?" Silence greeted him. "I hope no one is raising their hand." The students chuckled. "Okay, then. I'll see you tomorrow."

Chairs scooted across the tile floor.

"Will you really? See us, I mean?"

A few students snickered.

Ben wasn't sure if it was Pete or Zack being the funny one. They took turns and their voices were similar. "I'm sure at your age that you understand what a figure of speech is. If not, then perhaps you don't belong in this class."

"Ha ha, he got you, Pete," Zack said. "Good one, Mr. M. See ya tomorrow."

Ben wished everyone a good evening while he stood and unplugged the ceiling projector cord from his laptop. At least Susannah had graduated from VHS tapes. He couldn't imagine trying to maneuver an old VCR without his sight. At least, not without making a spectacle of himself.

"Doesn't it bother you when they make fun of your blindness?" Victoria asked.

The coast must be clear if she was talking to him. "Nah. They're just having fun. I haven't got anything against that."

"Even at your expense?"

"It's only at my expense if I let it. Besides, they aren't malicious." He slid the laptop inside his case, which also contained the scarf. He'd forgotten all about it. "You left this in class yesterday."

She took it from his hands, her fingers lingering, and that strange, wonderful, electric jolt shot up his arm. His heart skipped a few beats. She wrapped the scarf around his neck and pulled him down. Their lips met in one shocking and thrilling kiss. His libido had never gotten such a workout.

"How do you know it's mine?"

He wrapped his arms around her small waist. "Your scent was all over it. Am I mistaken?"

"No. Just wondered. Is your sense of smell that strong?"

"I don't know if it got stronger or if I pay more attention to it. But I love the way you smell, so it wasn't that hard to determine."

She pulled his neck down again. "Wish I was taller."

"I think that can be arranged." He maneuvered her to the desk and easily lifted her, but she didn't seem to have gotten much higher. He laughed. "Or maybe not."

"It's a little better." She grabbed his hips and settled him between her spread thighs. He was already hard for her. "What do you want to do tonight?"

Some kind of macho instinct reared its ugly head, ready to rip off her clothes and discover every inch of her, but they hadn't even had their first real date yet. He needed to be a little less caveman-ish. "How about going out for dessert or coffee? I'm sure there's something open we can walk to."

"Sounds heavenly." She leaned into him for another mind-blowing kiss. "Probably a good idea, too. Who knows what I'll do to you here."

"Victoria?"

She muttered a curse under her breath and Ben straightened. The man's voice sounded oddly familiar.

"Oh there you are. Whoa, did I interrupt something?"

"Perry! What are you doing here?"

Ah, the man from the garage. Ben had a feeling their night just ended. At least Victoria appeared to still dislike the fellow.

Perry snickered. "I was told to pick you up."

"By whom? I thought I was supposed to…make my own arrangements."

"That was before the instructor called. Barnet's not going to be happy if you've been…well, you know."

"I never called." Ben was getting lost in the sea of names. And why were they all male? Didn't she have any female friends?

Discreetly holding his hand out, he maneuvered his way back to the chair.

"You're the instructor? But Barnet said a woman called."

A woman? Ben tripped on the desk leg and stumbled, but found the chair and landed hard. What the hell was his sister doing? Damn, he should have never told her anything.

"Wait a minute," Perry said. "He's blind. How can you have a blind instructor?"

"Perry!"

"Oh man, sorry. That came out rude, still—"

Ben held out his hand. "No worries. Nothing I haven't heard before."

Victoria's feet slapped the floor and the desk moved a smidgen. "For your information, Ben is teaching the class but his sister is administering the tests. And I haven't complained to anyone. So you can go and tell Barnet that. I'll get my own ride back."

Ben's mood lightened. Maybe their night wasn't finished after all.

"There's only one problem with that," Perry said. "Did you forget you promised Jack you'd keep Sunny company?"

"*Scheisse.* That's tonight?"

And just like that Ben's mood tanked. Were they ever going to get a chance to be alone?

* * * *

Victoria's heart sank. At this rate, Ben would be an old man before she ever got a chance to date him.

"I'm sorry," she said. "Jack is a co-worker and he has business out of town. I promised I'd keep his wife company since she doesn't have any friends in the area."

"Hey, it's okay. I understand." He whispered, "And I'm sorry about my sister. I hope you're not in trouble."

Even Ben's whisper was loud enough for Perry's ears—and it was just like the man to not give them any privacy—but she whispered back to keep up the facade. "I'm not. Do you need a ride home? I'm sure I could convince Perry—"

He shook his head. "I'm good. But, thanks."

Kissing him goodbye was out of the question. If Perry hadn't seen anything earlier, she certainly wouldn't give him a show now.

She took Ben's hand and squeezed it. Such strength. Such warmth. She really didn't want to let him go. "See you tomorrow."

The doors to the elevator hadn't even closed when Perry said, "Well, well, well. You and the teacher, huh?" He sang in a high, trill voice, "Victoria and Teach, sittin' in a tree. K-I-S-S—"

She smacked him in the arm, shutting him up. "Stop it." So much for thinking he hadn't seen anything.

Perry snickered in a high-pitch sound that always grated on her. "I'm confused, though. Why did you bother with the new duds if the guy is blind?"

She wasn't about to admit that her new clothes made her feel more feminine or even sexy. Why give him any more ammunition? "Glad you're confused. You can stay that way."

"Does he know how young you look?"

Ben had explored her face and hadn't seemed to notice. Not that she'd noticed much after their touch. "I'm sure his sister has said something. But he thinks I'm twenty-two."

Perry choked. "Twenty-two? Is that what Barnet told them?"

"It's in my records."

The elevator doors opened to the first floor. "You like him, huh?"

No use denying it. Perry could easily tell if she were lying. "Yeah, but his sister doesn't like me. I think she's trying to keep us apart. Probably thinks I'm too young for him."

"Why don't you just 'make' her stay away?" He used air quotes when he said the word "make," probably because a group of ladies stood over in the corner. Not that the group could overhear the two of them. Neither one spoke very loud.

"I don't want to. That's no way to start a—" *Scheisse.* She nearly blurted out the word relationship.

"Start a what?"

"A friendship."

Perry chuckled. "Yeah, right. I think you want more than a friendship. Who knew Vicky had sexual needs?"

"Stop it. And stop calling me Vicky." She pushed on the door and nearly slammed it in his face. Sexual needs, indeed. What business was that of his anyway?

The outdoors greeted her and she would have shied away, but Perry's presence, even with how little she actually tolerated the man, was enough to ease her fears.

He skipped ahead and turned around, walking backwards. "If you weren't such a pain in my ass, I could probably distract her some. She any good looking?"

If she could get Perry to distract Susannah, it might be a blessing. But Perry never did anything free. "She's pretty. But why would you help me?"

"Because I'm such a nice guy. And plus, you'd owe me."

That's what she'd thought. "I don't recall anyone ever saying you were a nice guy. But if I wanted you to keep her busy, what would it cost me?"

Perry laughed, his voice echoing off the buildings. "Oh man, you must really like him if you're willing to use me. This is going to be fun."

His idea of fun was her idea of torture. She should have kept her mouth shut.

He'd parked the van in the loading zone and dashed around the front. He climbed in the driver's side. The sun had set. No need to sit in the back and maybe sitting up front would get her on Perry's good side. She pulled the passenger door open.

"You might want to get in the back," he said.

"What? Why?"

He nodded toward the back. Victoria leaned in. A familiar redhead smiled and waved.

"Hi, Sunny." Victoria sneered at Perry. "You had her wait in the car and didn't tell me?"

"I don't have to tell you everything," he said.

Victoria grimaced as she climbed in the back. "I'm so sorry. If I'd have known you were here, I wouldn't have taken so long. He should have brought you inside."

Crap. What was she saying? She should be thanking Perry for not bringing Sunny inside. How might she react to Ben?

"That's okay. It was kind of fun sending the cop away. I think he wanted to give Perry a ticket."

Perry swung around in his seat. "And that's why I left her in the van. Thank you, by the way."

"My pleasure," Sunny said. "You don't really need to keep me company, though. I told Jack I would be okay on my own."

Victoria had never been alone. She'd moved from her parents' home to Henrik's home. And then when Henrik had died, moved to Headquarters without missing a beat. Sure, she had her own room, but Barnet lived across the hall and was available whenever she needed him. She couldn't imagine living on her own.

"I'm sure you could, but why bother? I'll keep you so busy, you won't have time to miss Jack."

Sunny smiled. "Actually, I was hoping we could go out dancing. I hear there are some clubs near the Underground that are open quite late."

Perry's eyes widened. "Ooh, that sounds like fun. Count me in."

"No one invited you," Victoria said. *Hölle*, she didn't even want to be invited. Dancing? At a bar? With people? Lots of people? *Scheisse.*

"Hey, the more, the merrier," Sunny said.

"Aren't you afraid someone will recognize you?" Not that the three of them couldn't stop something from happening, but Victoria was grasping at excuses.

"She'll be with us," Perry said. "I think the three of us could handle it."

What? Did the guy read her mind or something?

"And I have a disguise." Sunny opened her bag and pulled out a black wig. "It should be enough, right?"

Victoria couldn't deny that. And the odds she'd even be recognized were slim. "What about Jack? Won't he mind you going out dancing?"

"He doesn't own me. Besides, he hates that kind of dancing. Believe me, if I could get him to a club, I would."

Damn it. If she didn't go along, she'd never hear the end of it from Perry.

"Why don't you ask your teacher to come along?" Perry turned toward Sunny. "She's got the hots for him."

Sunny placed her hand on Victoria's arm. "You do? Well then by all means, go get him."

"No, I can't," Victoria stammered. "It's late and he's…mortal and he doesn't know about us." Not to mention irresistible to female vampires. *Scheisse.* So much for wanting to thank Perry for not bringing Sunny upstairs. Victoria would rather murder him.

"Then we won't talk vampires. Go on. Go get him. It'll be fun."

Fun? More like torture. Something Perry loved doing to her. But what kind of excuse could she give and be believed?

"If you're too chicken to ask, I'll do it." Perry jumped out of the vehicle and headed for the building.

Nooo. If she didn't stop him then the whole vampire community could discover what Ben was.

CHAPTER 6

Ben stepped into the elevator. He should have known the night would end with him being alone—again. Was it too much to ask for some intimate time with Victoria? Sure, he should just be patient—they haven't known each other all that long—but whenever he took in her scent, patience flew out the door. One of these days her job or his sister would stop interrupting.

What the hell was Susannah thinking calling Victoria's contact person? All because he had asked to give her a ride home? Guess he'd be having a talk with his sister tonight after all.

The doors opened and Ben readied his cane.

"Hey, Teach. Just the guy I'm looking for." Perry pushed Ben back inside the elevator and the doors closed to Victoria's shouts.

"What's going on?" Ben asked. "What are you doing?"

"Relax, Teach. I'm not here to hurt you, but Victoria is acting a little shy and I need some information from you. You like her, don't you?"

Shit. What kind of trouble had he gotten himself into? "Who are you and what business is it of yours?"

"Oh, sorry. My name is Perry Davenport and I'm an…acquaintance of Victoria's. And while technically it's none of my business, I noticed she's taken a shine to you and I wondered if it was reciprocal. It's okay if it is. Really. Just need to know before I ask you an important question."

Important question? Oh, hell. What did he have to lose? "Yes, I like her."

"Good. Then how would you like to go dancing with her? Tonight?"

More than anything. He just wanted to be with her. "Is this some kind of a joke?"

"No joke. She's afraid to ask, so I'm doing it for her. It won't be only the two of you, though. I'll be there and so will another friend. It'll be all proper and everything. What do you say?"

A night dancing with Victoria? Could that really be possible?

Perry slapped Ben on the shoulder. "I'll take that smile as a yes. Okay, now how do I turn this thing around?" He laughed. "Just kidding!"

The doors opened to a wonderful flowery scent.

"Perry, what did you do? Are you okay, Ben?"

"Relax, Vicky."

The sound of a punch was followed by Victoria saying, "Stop calling me that."

Perry leaned into Ben's ear. "Picky, isn't she?"

The two of them acted like he and Susannah had before the accident. He kind of missed that.

"Can I speak to Ben in private?" Victoria asked.

"Don't talk him out of this. He's already agreed to go."

The front doors swished closed. A few moments later, Victoria placed her hand on his chest. "You don't have to come if you don't want to."

He covered her hand with his own, getting a nice zap all the way to his groin. "Are you kidding? I would love to spend more time with you. But if you're afraid someone will see us—"

"That's not it. Some people think I look younger than I really am. I don't want you to feel—"

He placed his finger over her mouth. "I don't care what other people think. Only what you think."

"I think I got lucky running into you on Monday." She smiled against his finger and he searched for her dimple. Wonderful.

* * * *

Perry slid behind the wheel and smiled at Sunny, who had moved up front. "He's coming."

"Oh, good. I got the impression Victoria doesn't go out much."

He snorted. "She doesn't go out at all. If it weren't for Barnet insisting she take this class, she'd never leave the Underground. Still… I'm not sure if she really likes this guy for himself or if she likes him because he's blind."

Sunny raised her eyebrows. "She has a blind teacher?"

"Yeah, I'm curious about that story, too. Maybe we can get him to spill."

"So why would his blindness be a factor?"

"Because he can't see how young she looks."

"And that bothers her?"

"It must. Why else live like a hermit?"

"Maybe she really misses her husband. Because she didn't get her forever with him."

"Uh…no. I'm not saying she didn't love Henrik, but he's the one who turned her so young. I think maybe that messed with her head a little."

Victoria and Teach emerged from the building. He held onto her elbow wearing a big grin, yet she grimaced as if heading for the guillotine. What was her problem? She clearly liked the guy and the guy was crazy about her. Perry had thought for sure she'd jump at the chance to have some time with him, especially with the sister out of the picture.

"Whoa. I can see what Victoria sees in him. Hubba hubba."

"Aren't you married? To Jack?"

"Yeah, but I'm not dead. I can still look."

Perry supposed Teach wasn't all that bad, for a guy. His sister might even be a looker. Hadn't Victoria said she was pretty? Maybe he'd check her out. Victoria wouldn't have to know, unless she begged again. Then he would make sure he got something from it. No use wasting good bribe material.

Victoria opened the side door and let Teach get in first. "Ben, you've met Perry. Up front with him is our friend, Sunny."

"Nice to meet you, Ben," Sunny said. "Do you like dancing?"

"I did ten years ago. Hopefully, I'm not too old."

"We're only as old as we feel and I feel like a teenager," Perry said. "Now, Teach, I hope you don't have a curfew. I think the ladies want to stay out late. And don't worry about getting home. I'll be your chauffeur."

Victoria snorted.

Teach smiled. "I'm game for anything. Thank you."

Sunny took a deep breath and leaned her head back.

"You okay, Sunny?" Perry asked.

"Oh, I'm fine. What's that wonderful smell?" She turned in her seat. "Must be you, Ben. What's the name of your cologne? I must get Jack some."

Victoria's eyes widened.

Teach laughed. "I don't know whether to feel flattered or strange. Victoria thought I was wearing cologne, too, but I promise, I'm not wearing any fragrance."

Sunny leaned toward Teach and Victoria pushed her away. "Are we going or not?"

What the hell was going on? Sunny looked ready to swoon out of her seat and Victoria was acting all protective of the teacher. Perry hadn't seen that kind of reaction since he'd met Sarah. But Sarah was a Perfect Mate and hadn't yet bonded with Johnny, so when Perry had been drawn to her, Johnny had gone ballistic.

No. Could it be?

He sent Teach a command to kiss Victoria. Teach never moved.

Perry gripped the steering wheel and pulled away from the curb. Son of a bitch!

Johnny had been a hermit since his turning and had stumbled across a Perfect Mate on his first attempt at dating and now Victoria hadn't left Headquarters for over forty years and stumbled across one on her first trip outside? When the hell would he find his own Perfect Mate? Apparently they were coming through the woodwork now. This wasn't fair.

Unless… Was it possibly hereditary? Could Teach's sister also be a Perfect Mate? All the more reason to check her out.

Well, until he had his own, he might as well have fun with Victoria.

✳ ✳ ✳ ✳

Victoria took a seat at the table Perry had claimed after helping Ben find his own seat. Music blared and bombarded her brain. It had been years since she'd had to adjust her hearing. Why did mortals listen to music so loud? How did they even converse over the noise?

At least they were no longer sitting inside that small van. If Jack ever found out Victoria had exposed his dear wife to a Perfect Mate—and if Victoria had any say in the matter, no one would know Ben was one—he would blow his lid. Not toward Sunny. Oh no. He loved her. Whereas, Victoria was a mere friend, a co-worker, a little sister. If he found out, she might as well be crossed off his list. If she survived at all. *Scheisse.*

This whole excursion was such a bad idea. But if she had said anything, Ben would have thought she didn't want to be with him and Perry would want to know why.

"You drink beer, Teach? I'm fetching," Perry said.

Victoria stared at Perry. They were drinking beers?

"Yeah, sure. Sounds great." After giving his order, Ben lifted his hip and reached toward his back pocket.

"Don't bother, Teach. I got this round. Come on, Sunny. Why don't you help me?"

Ben found her hand and squeezed it. "You seem nervous. Is it because of me or this place?"

He had yelled at her to be heard over the music. She would have liked to tell him not to bother, but that would only require an explanation. Instead, she yelled back. "You do not make me nervous. I've never been to a nightclub before. I don't know how to act."

"Well, we could go up and dance. Would that make you feel less nervous, then?" He scooted his chair back, but she took his arm and stopped him from standing.

"I don't mean to be rude, but can you? Dance, that is?"

"It's been a few years, but I think it's like riding a bike, don't you?"

She wouldn't know. She'd never ridden a bike, either. "Can we wait for a slow song, then?"

"I really don't think this place plays slow songs. It'll be fine. As long as we stay close, I shouldn't bump into anyone. Or step on your feet. But just in case, you are wearing combat boots, right?" His grin widened as he placed his palm upward on the table.

She laughed. Henrik had never made her laugh before. But a whole song feeling Ben's warmth? Would she be able to last without ripping off his clothes? Before she had a chance to find out, Perry and Sunny returned with one beer and three waters.

"Let's have a toast," Perry said as he sat beside Ben. "You can do that with beer, right?"

"I don't think the drink matters." Ben reached out and Victoria handed him his drink. "Thank you."

She stared at her own glass. Would he notice she wasn't drinking beer? Or drinking, period? His sense of smell nearly matched that of a vampire's, as did his sense of hearing.

Perry raised his glass and indicated everyone to follow, even so far as lifting Ben's hand. "To opportunities. May they all be *perfect*."

When he emphasized that last word, he winked at Victoria.

The noise dinned. The room spun. Oh *Gott*. He knew. He *knew*. Now what?

The glasses clinked and Ben took a swallow. Victoria lowered her glass without a sip while Perry grinned at her. How soon she'd forgotten. He'd been involved with another Perfect Mate. Something told her he wasn't about to keep the information to himself no matter what she bribed him with.

"I'm ready to dance," Victoria said. "Are you ready to dance?" Maybe they could get one in before their world crumbled around them.

* * * *

Ben collided with another dancer. Maybe dancing wasn't such a great idea after all. The first song hadn't even ended and he'd probably stepped on more feet than the floor.

"Hey, watch it Gramps."

Gramps? How much grey did he have? He touched his temple.

"Don't listen to him," Victoria said. "He's a jerk."

Maybe so, but it didn't stop him from feeling old. Really, really old. This was no place for him, so why was he trying to fit in?

"We don't have to dance," Victoria said. "I'm not even sure I know what I'm doing."

He laughed and leaned toward her. "Guess that makes two of us."

The music changed to something a little more his speed—Phil Collins singing "Two Hearts"—and gave him an idea.

"Come here." He reached out and found her. Pulling her close, he wrapped his arms around her and spoke into her ear. "If you don't mind, I think I'll just hold you during all the songs."

"Sounds good to me." Her arms went around his neck and when their skin touched, he got that pleasant zap she always sent his way. "Now this reminds me of dancing."

God, had he ever enjoyed holding a woman more? So soft and

curvy, she fit against him perfectly. Her scent was more intoxicating this way, too. Should have suggested they dance like this at the beginning, even if the music didn't call for it. If only they were alone. Then again, maybe not. He'd probably rush into something she wasn't ready for and no way would he screw this up.

For the rest of the song they danced without speaking. Her head rested on his chest and for a brief moment he felt whole again. As he if were dancing with his eyes closed. He got lost in the lyrics while he held her close.

"I like this song," she said.

He liked the song. He liked her. She seemed so much wiser than her twenty-two years. Heck, the way she talked at times, she almost sounded older than him. Maybe she had one of those old souls. Whatever, he wanted to keep her. And hopefully she didn't mind the age difference. Or the blindness. Hell, couldn't forget that.

"Sunny and Perry seem to be having a good time," she said.

"And you're not?"

"Oh no, that's not it. I'm enjoying the company very much. It's just dancing never was my thing."

While he enjoyed holding her, the noise level made having any kind of conversation impossible. "Why don't we go outside? Then we won't have to yell at each other."

She tensed in his arms. "Outside?"

"Something wrong with outside?"

"No, no. Of course not." She pulled away and took his hand, putting it on her elbow. "Might want to stick close. It's a bit crowded on the floor."

He got that. As she led him across the floor, he bumped into several people. At least none of them called him gramps.

The muggy air hit him first, but the sheer difference in sound made him relax. "Is there someplace we can sit?"

"Over here." She led him to a bench. "I think this is for a bus."

"Maybe we'll go for a ride, then."

"What?" She gripped his arm.

In his attempt at levity, he'd ended up spooking her. "Hey, relax. I was just kidding. What's the matter?"

"I'm sorry. It's...nothing. I'm being paranoid."

And apparently he was the cause. His chest tightened. "You don't feel safe with me."

She scooted against him—thigh to thigh—and ran her fingers

through his hair. "That's not true. I feel very safe with you. It's just been a long time since I've been… I'm kind of a homebody, okay?"

"You were home schooled?"

She let out a nervous laugh. "Yes, I was, actually. Crowds make me nervous. Not you. Okay?"

"Okay." He could understand her dilemma. There was a time after his accident where he struggled to venture outside. It took his sister's prodding and encouragement for him to move on. Maybe he could be Victoria's encouragement. At least he wasn't the cause of her fear. "So, can I ask you a crazy question? How much grey do I have? And be honest."

"Oh Ben, that's not so crazy." She touched his temple. "Only a little bit here."

"Oh man!"

"It's no big deal. That guy was an idiot. He probably called you that because of the way his dance partner was looking at you."

"Looking at me how?"

"As if she wanted you all to herself."

"Nooo…" She had to be wrong. Who would want an old blind guy?

She took his hand, shooting sparks straight to his groin. "Can't blame her too much. I want you. If it weren't for Perry and Sunny, we could be alone."

God. Alone with Victoria. Would it ever be possible? He didn't know what she saw in him, but he wouldn't take it for granted. Oh no. He kissed her. Tenderly at first. But when she wrapped her arms around his neck, he became more aggressive and she wasn't stopping him. He broke the kiss and focused. Now was not the place to make any moves on her. Anyone could be watching.

He smoothed the hair from her face and placed his forehead against hers. "You make me forget we're in public."

"So do you. I like that feeling."

Well, at least he did something right. She rested her head on his shoulder and he slid his arm around her. She fit perfectly. "So if crowds and dancing aren't your thing, what is?"

"Piano, guitar, flute. I love music, but not whatever it was they were playing in there. Well, except for that last song. Classical is more my style, though."

"You play three instruments? Are you some kind of prodigy?"

Maybe thinking she was an old soul wasn't so far off.

"No. I just have lots of time to practice." She tensed and groaned softly. "*Scheisse*. Doesn't that man have a life?"

Man? What man? Had Perry followed them outside?

"Hello, Victoria. What are you doing out here?"

Graham, not Perry. Ben's shoulders fell. Perry, he could deal with. The man clearly cared for Victoria's well-being, even if she couldn't see it. Graham was a different story. Animosity practically spewed out of him. Did he feel threatened? Victoria didn't seem to be sending him any signals to indicate an attraction, not that Ben could see her face.

"I'm on a date, what does it look like?" She had stood and he could almost picture her with her hands on her hips. Her words were said with venom.

Ben held back a smile. Yeah, she was definitely not flirting with Graham.

"A date? With this mor—"

"Graham! Was there something you needed? Right now?" Her tone had an air of authority to it, as if she were speaking to a subordinate. If Ben went by her voice, he'd never guess she was afraid of crowds or that she was only twenty-two years old. More like decades older.

"What's the matter with you? You can just wipe—"

"Enough. If you have business to discuss, take it up with Barnet. We're through."

"Victoria…I'm sorry. I didn't mean to upset you. Call me later. Please. It has to do with Henrik."

"Fine. Whatever." A few moments passed when she finally returned to the bench. "He's gone."

Man, talk about light on his feet; he never made a sound. And Ben was sure he could hear a fly land now. At least his sense of emotions wasn't lacking. "He's jealous."

"Well, he has no right to be. I've never given him any reason to think we are more than friends."

"And Henrik?"

"My late husband. Graham only dropped his name hoping I'd ignore you and listen. That man is beginning to be a pain in my *Arsch*."

Yep, jealous. "He's not dangerous, is he?" While Ben worked out regularly, being blind had its disadvantages. Like knowing when to duck.

"No. He's more bark than bite. I'll talk to him later and set him straight. Because I only have eyes for one man and that's you." Her lips brushed against his, re-igniting his libido. All thoughts of propriety left his head. He reached out for her, but she pulled away. "Can we go back inside, please?"

"Is it Graham or someone else you don't want to see us?" Because he was fairly certain if his students were hanging around the bar district, they wouldn't want to be spotted.

"I think I prefer the darkness of the bar. And maybe dancing in your arms again."

Everything seemed to scare her. Dancing. Crowds. Outside. Well, he'd do his best to make her forget about anything unpleasant.

* * * *

Victoria rose slowly. She'd love nothing more than to continue kissing Ben, his heat still lingered on her lips, but the four vampires—two men and two women—headed her way had put a stop to that. Taking Ben to a bar in the vicinity of Headquarters with the Committee Meeting only a couple of weeks away was a mistake she wouldn't make again.

He gripped her elbow. "Lead the way."

Gott, she'd love to lead him somewhere safer. Quieter. Guess that's what she got for not having her own place.

The noise hadn't abated any, but the darkness was welcoming. Victoria led the way to their table and arrived at the same time as Sunny and Perry. Why'd he have to find out about Ben? Why? Would he tell the rest of the Committee? Would he be that mean? Maybe if she pleaded with him. He seemed to like Ben. Almost like friends. Friends didn't let friends be locked away like some kind of animal.

She relaxed. Perry might bug the stripes off a zebra, but he was an honorable man. He'd do what was best. And the best thing for Ben was to keep him a secret.

The four vampires she'd spotted outside entered the nightclub and looked in their direction. Perry waved them over. "Come and join the party!"

Nooo! She took it all back. That man wouldn't know what

honorable meant if it bit him in the *Arsch*. If anything, he was an idiot. An idiot pushing her over the edge to insanity.

Ben took a swig of his beer. "Victoria? You're tensing up again. What's the matter?"

"Yeah, Vicky. What's the matter?" Perry smirked at her and she nearly threw her glass of water at the guy.

She stood and pulled Ben up. "Let's go dance."

She managed to get them back on the dance floor, but so were the vampire couples. Had Perry sent them out after her or what?

"I'm beginning to think you don't really want to dance," Ben said.

While it was flattering he could read her so well, it was also unnerving. Was that part of being a Perfect Mate or merely his highly attuned senses? Did it really matter? She could ponder that issue later. First, she had to get them out of there and fast. "I was wrong about coming inside. Can we go sit out in the van instead?"

"Sure. Anything to make you feel better." He took her elbow. "Do you need to use the restroom first?"

"No. I just need some air." And a ticket away from the madness.

She headed in the opposite direction of the vampires and circled the dance floor. She stopped at the restrooms and stared at the exit. Blocked. Damn. Another female vampire stood at the entrance. Was this vampire night or something?

"Did you change your mind about the restroom?"

How could she get Ben safely away before some female became drawn to him? Because once one female discovered him, the others would investigate. News like that wouldn't take long to reach Barnet. Then what? Then what?

"Victoria?"

She couldn't very well ask Ben to accompany her to the ladies room, and even if she did then what? Climb through the window? How would she explain herself? Trapped. She was trapped inside a nightclub with three females. Oh no, make that four. Females who could take Ben away from her. She grabbed her chest. Damn, why was it hurting so much? And why was it so hard to breathe?

CHAPTER 7

"Victoria, speak to me. You're worrying me." Ben reached out and found her hugging herself. He pulled her into his arms. "Baby, what's the matter?"

She grabbed onto him and mumbled, but he couldn't make out her words. He'd take her outside except he had no idea which way it was to the exit. She had walked them around the place in such a zigzag fashion, he'd lost his bearings.

"What's the matter with Victoria?" Perry asked.

Ben relaxed. Thank God. "I don't know. She's not speaking coherently. I think the crowd has gotten to her. She doesn't get out much, does she?"

"No, she doesn't. Hey, Vicky." Perry shook her, which only caused her to squeeze Ben harder. No nasty comeback at using the name she despised. "Well, that's not a good sign. Can you carry her and then follow me outside?"

Ben tugged on her arms to loosen her grip, but she held on tighter. For a little thing she exhibited immense strength. "Victoria, you need to let go so I can pick you up. I'm not going anywhere."

"Pick me up? Why?"

Oh, thank God she was back. "Perry's taking us outside."

"Perry?" She shifted in his arms. "Perry! Don't let them take him. Please. I'll do anything you ask."

Her paranoia was starting to freak him out. Who was here and why would they want to take him?

"Hey, Vic. I'm sorry. No one's taking anyone, okay?" Perry said.

"Let's go back to the van. I'll drive you home."

"Ben first."

"Of course."

Ben relaxed. Okay, so maybe he was safe and she was just having a panic attack. "Should she see a doctor?"

"Nah, she'll be fine once we get out of this place. I'll take you to the van and then come back and get Sunny."

"Sunny?" Victoria squeezed Ben harder. Oh crap, not again. If she didn't let up soon, she'd end up cracking one of his ribs.

"Sunny is not a problem. Okay? Now let go of Teach and take his hand. I think you're hurting him."

Victoria gripped his hand while he took Perry's elbow. After several steps, she squeezed his hand and he nearly yelped. Man, what kind of hand exercises did she practice? She needed to stop.

Heat blew in his face and horns honked in the distance. Her grip relaxed. They continued to walk in silence until the van door opened.

"In you go," Perry said.

Ben climbed in after Victoria.

As soon as the van door shut, she wrapped her arms around his neck. "I am sooo sorry. You must think I'm crazy."

He pulled her into his lap and rubbed her back, reveling in her closeness. "I don't think you're crazy, just had a little panic attack. What happened?"

"Doesn't matter. It's over with."

"Why'd you think someone was going to take me away?"

She buried her head into his neck and mumbled, "Because I'm an idiot."

"You're not an idiot."

"Even after that stunt I pulled?"

"You got spooked. It happens to the best of us. You gonna be okay?"

"Yeah." She relaxed in his arms. "I like you, Ben."

He smiled and took in her scent. "I like you, too."

"Sorry I spoiled your night."

"Hey. I have a wonderful woman in my arms. What do you think you spoiled?"

Both front doors opened then closed. The van shifted with additional weight.

"Everything okay?" Sunny asked.

Victoria tensed for a moment then shifted in his arms. "I'm fine, but I think I frazzled poor Ben, here. Sorry for cutting your evening short."

"Don't worry about it. It wasn't near as much fun as I thought. I miss Jack. I'm glad I'll be staying with you now. I don't think I want to be alone."

"We'll keep each other company, then." Victoria placed her mouth beside Ben's ear. "Because I'm going to miss you, too."

Her words struck his heart. Three days and he was already a goner. Saying goodnight to her would be hard.

"Where to?" Perry asked.

Ben relinquished Victoria to her seat and gave his address. They arrived in too short a time. Not caring who saw them, he leaned over to give her a kiss goodnight when she pushed him back.

"I'll walk you to your door."

He bid good evening to Perry and Sunny and took Victoria's elbow. He'd rather hold her hand, but that would only cause him to trip and fall and no way would he end the night in the bushes.

They stopped at his apartment and he leaned against the door. "Why do I get the feeling our roles are reversed?"

She placed her hands on his chest. "You don't like me walking you to your door?"

"I'm finding it hard to say goodnight, period, so…I'm not minding. Are you going to be okay?"

"How's this for okay?" She took his face and planted her lips against his own. Her soft, sweet tongue explored his mouth while a fiery jolt made a path to his groin. Good thing for the door's support or he would have landed on his ass. "I'll see you tomorrow in class."

"It's a date." He waited two full breaths before attempting to move. Hot damn, that woman knew how to kiss. Floating on a high, he entered the apartment.

"It's about time you got home," Susannah said.

The high plummeted and the tightness in his pants disappeared in record time. Nothing like a reprimand to spoil a good hard-on. Moving out was becoming more appealing.

"I didn't realize I had a curfew. What are you doing up?"

"I'm just… I was worried about you. Don't you have to tutor tomorrow?"

Her tone had flinched. She'd begun to say something else then changed. Was she lying to him or hiding something? But what? It's not like she had a life. Maybe if she did, she'd leave him alone. "I don't have to be at the school until ten." He placed his bag on the entryway table. "Go to bed, Susannah. I'll see you in the morning."

"Ben, wait."

He stopped. "I'm tired. Can it wait until morning?"

The scent of lilacs intensified, but nowhere near as strong as she usually wore it. "I'm sorry for being a mother hen. I only mean well."

"I know, but your mothering is smothering me."

"You didn't seem to have any problem with it until she showed up."

"This has nothing to do with Victoria. And even if it did, why are you so against her?"

"She's putting a wedge between us. I don't like it."

"The only one doing any wedging is you. Which reminds me, why did you call her contact people?"

"You said she needed a ride. I wanted to find out if that was true. Which, by the way, she lied to you. She has a ride. So whatever kind of bullshit she's feeding you—"

"Stop. I never said she asked for a ride. I wanted to give her one. Damn, you're impossible. Goodnight, Susannah."

Punching a wall sounded good right about now, but he couldn't afford another doctor's visit and she'd drag him to one for sure. He settled on slamming his bedroom door instead.

* * * *

Victoria followed Perry into the library. The rows of books—the majority of which she had purchased herself—brought her more comfort than her handkerchief. Or would have if not for Perry. Damn man sure knew how to spoil things.

In a couple of weeks the room would be full of vampires looking for something to pass the time until their Meeting. Until then, it was deserted and private. Thank goodness. She really didn't want to have this conversation in her room. A room across the hall from Barnet's. Of course, if she couldn't pay Perry's price—a price that was sure to be high—it wouldn't really matter who eavesdropped on their conversation. Ben would be outed and she'd be forced to hide him. And wasn't that a wonderful way to start a relationship. *Scheisse.*

She sat in a chair across the table from Perry. "What tipped you off?"

"Your reaction to Sunny."

"You going to tell anyone?"

He leaned back and crossed his arms, wearing a huge smile on his face. "I don't know. What's it worth to you?"

She shot out of her chair, tempted to throw it across the room. "Damn it, Perry. This isn't funny. Do you know what could happen if Barnet finds out?"

"If Barnet finds out what?" the Head asked from the doorway. "That one of the Committee Members was seen freaking out at a nightclub?"

Scheisse. She narrowed her eyes at Perry. "You told him?"

"He didn't have to tell me anything. Not when I get several calls from people who spotted you there. Why didn't you tell me it was this bad?"

Tell him what? If he didn't know about Ben, what did he suspect?

Perry stood. "It was my fault. She didn't want to go. I talked her into it. Thought the crowd would toughen her up. I had no idea her agoraphobia was so severe."

Agoraphobia? She swallowed. Well, it was better than the truth. And *Hölle*, who was to say she didn't have it a little bit. She could almost kiss Perry. Almost.

"Victoria, I'm sorry," Barnet said as sadness and compassion flashed in his eyes. "I wish you had said something. I could have gotten you help."

"I don't need any help. I'm fine. Just keep me out of nightclubs."

"Are you having this same problem in your class? If so, I could cancel—"

"No!" Then she'd never see Ben again. "Class is fine. I mean, I'm fine in class. In fact, it's helping."

"Okay. Perry, make sure you pick her up from class from now on. We don't need to have another incident." He turned to her and placed a hand on her shoulder. "I wish you had confided in me, Victoria. I would have helped you sooner."

She lowered her head. What could she say? She couldn't lie to his face.

His cellphone chimed, saving her from commenting. He still owned an old flip-phone, but then, so did Jack. Guess not every vampire embraced technology. Still, to even get Barnet to carry the darn thing had been her greatest achievement at the time.

He stared at the display and sighed. "Just how many vampires were at that club?"

She or Perry might have answered if Barnet had stuck around for it. Instead, he walked off with his phone to his ear, reassuring whoever was on the other end that Victoria was, indeed, fine.

Perry chuckled as he settled back into his seat. "Man, you really owe me now. I'll have to think of something good."

"I'm surprised you didn't tell him the truth."

"I kind of did. You're not exactly a sociable person. That's the first time you've actually gone out in what, four, five decades? Talk about abnormal. As for telling the whole truth…well, I like Teach and I figure you need some alone time with the guy before anyone needs to know."

"What am I going to do? The closer we get to the Meeting, the more vampires will be hanging around. If we go out…" She shuddered.

"Will you relax? Those vamps aren't here for the meeting. They live around here. We usually meet at that bar…"

"What?" She smacked him in the arm, but could have easily punched him in the jaw. "You knew about Ben and yet you took him to a place he could be exposed?"

"I didn't think you'd go all ape-shit. Have you taken his blood? Is that why?"

"No." She was beginning to have a real appreciation for what Katarina went through after having taken Justin's blood. She couldn't imagine it being any worse, but maybe it could. "What am I going to do? It took all my energy just to keep Graham from saying the wrong thing. How can I stop a mob?"

"Graham? What did that jerk want?"

She smirked at Perry. Funny term coming from him, especially when he was probably the biggest jerk she knew. Although, he had been relatively nice lately. All for a price. "I don't know. I think he expects me to be at his beck and call."

"Tell him to bug off. As for Teach, you have to decide whether or not you want to see him or break it off. And if you continue to see him, you're going to have to tell him what you are or deal with the consequences."

"Consequences?"

"Covering up the occasional goof, avoiding other female vampires. Well, except for Katarina. She's probably immune."

"What do you mean?"

"A bonded mate stops sending out pheromones or whatever it is in their scent. You aren't attracted to Justin's scent any longer, same as I'm not attracted to Sarah's. So why wouldn't it go the other way? Another Perfect Mate's scent shouldn't affect Katarina because she's already bonded to her Perfect Mate."

"That's all fine and dandy, but doesn't help me any. You really going to keep this to yourself? You aren't going to tell anyone?"

"Why don't you want Barnet to know? He's not a threat to you. Hell, he'd probably be happy you found someone."

More like giddy she'd found another Perfect Mate and lock Ben up for sure. "You didn't tell him about Sarah, now did you?"

"Because he was a threat. Competition. Last I heard, Barnet still liked women. Teach won't affect him."

"That may be true, but I can't tell anyone. Not yet. Are you?"

"And lose this power I have over you? No way."

Just the thought of having to trust Perry gave Victoria the shivers. But what other choice did she have?

* * * *

Graham held onto Susannah's hips as she rode him like the stallion he was. The backseat of his car was more than roomy enough for this kind of fuck and the tinted windows were a bonus.

To think he'd only lured her out here for some information. But one kiss led to two and the next thing he knew, she was undressing him.

Her little titties bounced in front of his face and he took one into his mouth. Tongued her nipple. She moaned in pleasure. Maybe she was starved for sex. If so, he may never have to manipulate her again, because having sex that way bordered on being robotic. Like fucking a dummy. He much preferred her enthusiasm. As soon as he'd thought of having sex with her, she'd pulled his shirt off before he could stop her.

Her orgasm rocked him. Damn, he'd never had that happen before either. This little fuck was turning out so much better than he imagined and he came right along with her. He needed this more often for sure.

She collapsed against his chest. "I can't believe I did that. I hardly know you."

"I want to see you again." And that wasn't a lie. "Will you let me?"

"Why are you even interested? I'm more than ten years older than you."

He pulled her hair back. "Age is just a number. You're one hot woman and I want you." He kissed her deeply. If this was going to work, he had to convince her—or actually, Perry had to convince her—otherwise, he'd have to go back to plain manipulation. And after this, no way would he do that. Besides, there was Victoria to contend with. Couldn't have her suspect Susannah was being manipulated. The more real it was, the better.

Susannah moved to slide off him, but he held her in place. "Don't go yet. I'm not through." He sucked on a nipple and made her moan.

"Oh, Perry, what you must think of me."

"I think you're one hot fuck and I thank my lucky stars for running into you the way I did." Now it was time to get to work. He easily took control of her pliable mind and made sure she wouldn't remember the following conversation. "So, tell me about Ben and Victoria."

She pouted. "Ben is mad at me. He won't leave that child alone."

Her dislike of Victoria only made his job easier. "Is there any other reason he might be mad at you?"

"He thinks I think he can't take care of himself."

"Can he take care of himself?"

"He might. But he's always hurting himself. He needs me."

Graham couldn't have Ben mad at Susannah. Not for his plan to work. "This is what you're going to do."

He planted the seeds in her mind while he played with her titties. And they were such nice titties. Would Victoria's be just as nice? He couldn't wait to find out.

CHAPTER 8

Victoria sat at the conference table while Hilde's and Abe's images reflected on the monitors. These impromptu meetings were starting to get on her nerves. Ever since Justin, and then Sarah, had been discovered, Barnet had been on a mission and was dragging the rest of the Committee with him. While she understood why Barnet wanted to keep the whole issue under wraps, all this secrecy took its toll. Once their people discovered the truth, who knew how they might react? Instead of going wild looking for their own Perfect Mate, they might want to replace the whole Committee for lying. And who could blame them?

Then again, how many vampires had hidden their own discoveries?

Barnet took his seat at the head of the table. "I've heard from Jack. Seems our newest Perfect Mate goes by the name of Richard Daugherty."

"Daugherty?" Victoria asked. "Isn't that—"

"It is. You need to see if he's a blood relation to Sarah. If he is, see if Justin works into the equation. This might be the answer we're looking for. At least one of them."

Could it be that simple? A family trait? While Justin and Sarah didn't have any siblings, Ben did. Victoria should have tried controlling Susannah long before now, but if Susannah turned out to be uncontrollable… No, she wouldn't think about that. Dealing with one Perfect Mate on her own was more than enough. She still hadn't figured out what to do with him yet. Well, besides keep him, but it really wasn't only her decision to make.

"So how is he?" Hilde asked.

"Not well. Seems Dalton nearly drained the poor fella dry to shut him up. John has given him a transfusion, but is keeping him sedated. For now."

"Do you think it's possible he might believe he's been given a hallucinogenic drug?" Victoria asked. "Then maybe we won't have to hold him."

"We have to hold him anyway," Barnet said. "At least until everyone is informed about Perfect Mates, and I'm still not convinced that's a good idea. Abe, we need to set up a room for our guest. Make it look like a hospital. Can you swing it?"

"I think I can manage."

"You have until Friday night."

Abe grimaced. "Naturally."

At least that gave her two more days with Ben. Then she would either tell him the truth or break it off. She needed to do one or the other. But telling him would be hard. There would be no going back then.

* * * *

Ben grabbed a mug and poured some coffee. The aroma helped kick start his mental acuity. He'd done nothing but think about Victoria since his argument with Susannah. Sleep hadn't come easily so he'd worked out, hoping that would exhaust him. It had, but not enough to get her out of his mind. Now he'd be lucky to stay awake during his tutoring session.

Susannah padded into the room, no click-clocks of her heels. If he wasn't living with her, he would have never known it was her.

"You forget your perfume?" he asked.

"I got tired of wearing it."

Tired? Since when?

The clattering of blinds sounded. "What a beautiful sky. It's got those big fluffy clouds. Do you think you can get to your tutoring job and home on your own today?"

"I suppose." Would have been nice to get some warning. He'd only taken the bus a couple of times and could have used a refresher. Then there was his lack of sleep. "Why can't you drive?"

"I have errands to run. But if you need me…"

"No. I can do it." And he would, too, if that's what it took to show her he could get by on his own. "What changed your mind? Yesterday you were sure I'd crumble without your help."

The kitchen chair slid across the vinyl flooring. "Yes, I suppose I was. After last night I realized my mistake. I don't want to antagonize you, Ben. I love you. And if letting you go will prove I do, then I'm ready to do that."

Her change in attitude floored him. He sat beside her. "Thank you, Suze. You don't know how much that means to me."

He'd like to think her tune had also changed regarding Victoria, but he wasn't about to spoil the mood. It was enough for now that she trusted him to do things on his own.

* * * *

Victoria stared at the computer monitor and the sea of names in the database all blurred together. Compared to the population of the United States, the number of vampires was miniscule, but thousands of names were still thousands of names. And that included only the North American vampires. *Gott*, what a mess.

"Who knew genealogy could be so draining?" Sunny asked. "Or that there would be so many freakin' Daughertys."

"At least you've got names. Try searching for an unknown vampire."

"That bad, huh? Okay, I'll quit complaining."

Victoria had called Sarah Daugherty and obtained all the family information she could, but there were several sites to fish for data and not all were accurate. Thank goodness for Sunny's help. While she searched for a family link of Perfect Mates, Victoria searched for the author of the Perfect Mate story.

Or had Jack tricked her into it? Since he'd taken the mission, she'd thought it only fair to perform the computer work. Well, there was fair and there was fair. In order to locate the author of the Perfect Mate story, she'd filtered out all but those vampires who had been published in one form or another. But when the list came up short, consisting mostly of vampires who had been turned since Barnet's turning, she scrapped that plan and created a list of all vampires who had been turned before Barnet.

Bad enough some vampires changed their names every twenty to thirty years, adding pen names to the mix made it worse.

Without a team working together, she could spend months at this. And yet with all that work, the vampire might not even be on the list. He could be dust.

This wasn't going to work. Jack would have thrown the computer through the wall long before now.

"Oh my gosh!" Sunny said, her face aglow. "There's a book for sale on the history of Daughertys. Do you think it could be that easy?"

Victoria looked at the link. "You never know. We could stand to use some easy about now." She placed the order and marked it to ship overnight. Small cramps flitted across her stomach and she glanced at the time. Ten-forty-five. Oh good, the mall was open. "I need to go feed. How about you?"

Sunny smiled. "I'm so glad you asked. I've never fed by myself before. Thought for sure I'd screw it up or something."

That must mean Sunny wasn't comfortable with her powers yet. Victoria took advantage. "We'll lure a couple into a room and have some privacy. If you screw up, no one will see and I won't tell. But I'm sure you'll be fine."

"You know, you're a lot nicer than I thought you'd be. All of you are."

"Thank you. I like to think that individually we're all pretty nice. Well, except Jack. I always thought he was the scariest of us all." Victoria laughed. "I like what you've done with him. Made him more...sympathetic. But don't tell him I said that. He might go back to being an *Arsch*."

"Is that why he was sure he'd be executed if he'd been found guilty of turning me? Because that's what he would have done?"

"Unfortunately, yes. As the Committee, we have to be strict. And that means even we can't break the rules. If we weren't strict, if we broke our rules, our people would take it as an invitation to do whatever, and we can't have that. We do have an example to set. If we didn't want to set it, we'd just step down. No one is forcing us to stay."

"Do you like being on the Committee?" Sunny asked.

Did she? If Sunny had asked her that last week, Victoria would have answered with a resounding "yes." The Committee was her family. Without them, she'd be lost. Alone. But now with the prospect of her own Perfect Mate, her world had opened. Her family expanded. At least, she hoped so. Would she want to be on the Committee if she was with Ben forever? Guess only time would tell. "It'll do for now."

"Oh? Does your teacher have anything to do with that?"

"You haven't told anyone—"

"Don't worry. Secret's safe with me. Your personal life is your personal life and friends don't go blabbing."

Victoria placed a hand over her heart. "You consider me a friend?"

Sunny rose and placed an arm across Victoria's shoulders. "Of course, silly. Didn't you just say you weren't going to tell anyone if I messed up feeding? If that's not a friend, I don't know what is. Now, I don't know about you, but I'm kind of hungry. Jack took his time saying goodbye yesterday and I never got a chance to feed after. Not that I'm complaining, mind you."

Less than five minutes later they were strolling through the mall. For a Thursday, the pickings were slim, but two women headed their way. Victoria and Sunny each mentally grabbed one and entered Headquarters as if the four of them were life-long buddies.

Victoria smiled at Sunny. It was nice feeding with someone. She hadn't done that since Henrik.

And if she bonded with Ben, she'd only have to feed from him. Wouldn't that be nice? To never go out in search of food again. Plus, according to Katarina, the sex afterward was phenomenal. Shoot. Just kissing Ben was phenomenal. With Henrik, there hadn't been any sparks. She loved him and what they had together was good, but up until now she never had anyone to compare him with.

"Thank you," Sunny said after they had released the women back into the mall.

Victoria should be thanking Sunny. "What for?"

"For not hovering. I had such a difficult time at the beginning. Jack was always there, just in case. But even after all these months, I think he still has doubts about my ability. Heck, I have doubts about my ability."

"Well, you shouldn't. You did fine."

"Do you mind if we go shopping. I saw this cute store—oh!" She pulled her phone out of her pants pocket. "It's Jack. I'm going to go back inside and—"

"Go on."

Sunny ran toward Headquarters with the phone up to her ear.

Victoria could call Ben. He'd certainly make her day better. But she'd left her phone back in her room. She sprinted inside, nearly bouncing off the walls with anticipation of hearing his voice. She turned the corner to her room and froze. Damn it. Graham stood outside her door.

"About time you got back. Where have you been? I tried calling. Don't you carry your phone with you?"

"What are you doing here?" *Gott*, would she have to suffer with him all day? Bad enough he popped into her life at night.

"I came to talk and if you'd had your phone with you, you'd have known that. Shall we go inside?"

The last place she would ever invite him would be her room. "What's wrong with here?"

He narrowed his eyes at her. "You really want other people to know our business?"

Our business? What kind of game was he playing? "We have no business."

"Why don't you hear me out and then decide?"

"Fine. We'll go out into the mall. Less chance of being overheard." Teach her not to carry her cell. She could have avoided Graham completely and currently be on the phone with Ben. Seemed that call would have to wait.

She found a bench in a relatively quiet area. Most people who walked by paid them no mind, too intent on getting to their destination.

Graham sat much too close—his hip rubbed against hers—and extended his arm along the back of the bench. Scooting away seemed futile. "When are you going to come to your senses and see how good I am for you?"

"Is this what this is all about? Last night you said you wanted to talk about Henrik."

"In a way I am. You need me, Victoria. Admit it."

The man was clearly delusional. "How is it I need you?"

"Well, for one, you wouldn't have to be afraid of going out alone. I saw how scared you were last night."

Oh great. How many more people witnessed that?

He put his hand on her shoulder and squeezed. "I'd be with you. Just like Henrik was. You'd never have to be scared again."

"I'm beginning to think Henrik did me a disservice by being with me all the time. I need to interact with…mortals better." And maybe the outdoors, but no use telling him that. He might use that as another excuse to pursue her.

"Why?"

"If I'm to perform my duty as a Committee Member, I need to be comfortable in all social scenarios. Especially with mortals."

"You were comfortable when Henrik accompanied you. I'll take his place. We've known each other a long time. I would treat you well, Victoria."

"Have you considered maybe I don't want anyone to take his place?" No, she'd already found someone better than Henrik. Someone who fueled her desire. And she could have him forever, too. If he wanted her.

"I don't know. You seem pretty chummy with that teacher. You plan on turning him? Because I can't imagine anyone would want to be blind for eternity."

Blind for eternity? Oh *Gott*. What was she thinking? Ben would never want her that way. Didn't mean she couldn't have a few years with him. Her hopes of having a future with him sank. "No, I have no plans on turning him."

"So it's just a fling, then?"

"Graham…"

"I can show you a good time, Victoria." He grabbed her face and planted his lips against hers. No spark. No flame. At least Henrik had managed to bring about interest. With Graham there was nothing.

She pushed him away. "Stop, please. I'm not interested in you that way."

"How would you know what you're interested in? You've been without a man too long." He grabbed her breast and kissed her some more.

She shoved his hand away and slapped his face. "How dare you touch me without my permission?"

He didn't rub his face because she probably hadn't hurt him, but his brow furrowed in remorse. "I'm sorry. Please forgive me. It's just that I've wanted you for so long. Henrik never treated you the way you deserve."

And she deserved to be groped? *Gott*, if she didn't handle him right, he might do something rash. Not to her, but to Ben. "Graham, I'm flattered, but really, I'm not looking for a new husband."

"Fine. You have your fling then. Get it out of your system. And when you're through, you'll see I'm good for you, Victoria. I'll take care of you. You'll want for nothing."

Nothing except the one man she really wanted: Ben. But would he want to be blind forever? Because that's what she'd be offering him if he consented to being bonded. *Scheisse*. Could she really do that to him?

* * * *

"I don't see why I have to learn this crap," Carson said.

That was the sixth time the fifteen-year-old student had uttered those words. Which was an improvement over last week, when he'd uttered them eight times. Ben ran his hand through his hair. "What, exactly, do you see yourself doing once you're through with school?"

"Well, my friends and I have this band. We figure we'll play in bars and such for practice, then create a video, put it on YouTube, get discovered, and then rake in the money."

Ben nodded. "That's quite a plan."

"It's a perfect plan. So tell me why I need to know algebra for this plan?"

"You'll be making a lot of money?"

"Yep."

"Will you have a manager or an agent?"

"Sure. He'll get us all the great gigs."

"So, he'll be making a percentage of what you make?"

"Uh, yeah, I guess."

"Net or Gross?"

"What?"

"If he takes $75,000 for a show that grossed $500,000 but netted $200,000, how will you know whether or not he's ripped you off?

"That's algebra?"

"That's algebra."

"But wouldn't I have an accountant do all that for me?"

"Sure, but how would you know whether or not the accountant is ripping you off? Overall, you're responsible for paying your taxes."

"Taxes? Ah, man!"

"You think about it and we'll talk more tomorrow."

"Mr. Martin, no offense, but you sure know how to put a downer on the perfect plan." A book slid across the table, followed by the sound of a zipper.

"A plan is only perfect if you're prepared for all scenarios." Like what was Ben doing with a twenty-two-year-old? Why was he dating at all? How could anyone ever want a life with him? Susannah was right. He'd only be a burden.

"I guess," Carson said as he apparently zipped up his backpack. He scooted the chair back. "You need help out?"

"I'm good, thank you." Ben gathered his belongings once the student's footsteps faded away. The day had started out well. Riding the bus had made him feel whole for the first time since the accident. So why the depressing thoughts? Victoria was great and a real boost to his ego. He needed to live life for the moment and enjoy her for however long she wished to stick around. Besides, she might end up having some horrible habit and then he'd have to break it off.

He shook his head. Nah. Not possible. She was perfect.

Damn. Why'd she have to be so perfect? And why'd he have to be so old. And blind. And broke. Yeah, he couldn't forget that part. So much for keeping upbeat.

He pulled out his standard cane and opened it. Most people responded to it better than his electronic one. Maybe if he'd had it on the first day of class, Victoria wouldn't have even talked to him. Remembering the shocked way she'd blurted out "you're blind" brought a smile to his face. Neither his age nor his blindness had stopped her from pursuing him—and she was definitely the one doing the pursuing—so maybe he was making something out of nothing.

Someone rapped on the doorway.

"Ben? Are you finished?" Linda Lewis asked. She'd been the Assistant Principal of the school when he'd taught and her promotion to Principal two years ago came as no surprise to him.

"Yes." He slung his satchel over his head, settling the strap across his chest. "Thanks for setting aside some time to talk."

"Why don't we go to my office?"

He took her elbow and she ushered him down the hallway. A kid's cackling echoed through the corridor and Ben broke out in goose bumps as if he were being marched to impending doom. But that was silly. He was only going to ask for his old job back. The worst she could say was no. So why the nerves?

She guided him to a seat. "You know, it's funny you wanted to see me. I had planned on talking to you after your tutoring session today."

"What about? Am I in trouble?" He wiped his suddenly wet palms on his thighs. It would be just his luck to lose his job.

"In trouble? Heavens, no. I'm hoping you can help me out. I hear you're teaching again. So how would you like your old job back?"

Good thing she'd shown him to a chair or he'd be feeling the floor under his butt about now.

CHAPTER 9

Victoria sat in the darkened classroom while the instructional film played on the screen. In ten minutes class would be excused for the night. In eleven minutes she would be in Ben's arms, kissing him. In twelve minutes, oh, make that thirteen, she would find out why he hadn't come to class early. Or why he hadn't returned her call.

When the agonizing minutes finally passed and he released the class, she took her time putting away her stuff. Her heart sung with joy in anticipation of their night together until his sister walked through the door.

What was she doing here? Hadn't he told her to come later? Disappointment burned in Victoria's chest. Since it seemed she wouldn't get to spend any alone time with Ben, now would be a good time to see if she had any control over his sister.

She'd love to send Susannah away, but if Ben was expecting her, he might find her abrupt departure odd. Besides, how else could Victoria win her over if she never spent any time with her? Instead, Victoria sent a command for Susannah to scratch her nose and lift her right leg. She followed both commands. Victoria slumped in her seat. Damn. So much for thinking it was a family trait.

As the last student departed, leaving Victoria alone with the siblings, Susannah approached Ben. "Are you ready to tell me your news?"

Ben smiled. "Soon." He faced the class. "Victoria? Is your ride waiting for you or are you free to go out for a while?"

His sister frowned at the question, in fact she looked a little ragged with dark circles under her eyes, but Ben beamed in Victoria's direction. Whatever he had going on still included her and her heart lightened.

"I can go out. I'm supposed to call when I'm ready. What's this all about?"

He waved her over. "First, introductions."

Victoria didn't even have to touch him for him to know she'd arrived. He wrapped his arm around her shoulders and kissed her on the temple. Heat spread upon his touch and she did her best not to grab him and kiss him full on the lips. Wouldn't his sister enjoy that display?

"Susannah, this is Victoria Braeden. Victoria, my sister, Susannah."

Victoria offered a genuine smile and her hand. This woman was important to Ben, so she would treat her with respect. Too bad her actions weren't being reciprocated.

Susannah scowled and folded her arms across her chest. "Nice to finally meet you in person. Ben talks about you all the time. I think you've stolen my brother's heart."

Her upbeat tone contradicted her expression, but then Ben couldn't see her. Winning over Susannah would not be an easy task and manipulating her mind was not the path to success.

Victoria lowered her arm. "It's a pleasure to meet you."

"Now are you going to share?" Susannah asked her brother.

"I was offered a full-time teaching position at the high school. Can you believe it? They want me back."

Susannah seemed to be in conflict as to whether she should be concerned or happy and the pause was too much for Victoria. She squeezed Ben around the waist. "Congratulations. That's wonderful news."

Victoria's praise spurred Susannah.

"Oh my God!" She hugged him while nudging Victoria away. "That's great news. When do you start?"

"In the fall. The teacher I'm replacing is retiring this year."

"What kind of class do you teach?" Victoria asked.

"Math. Algebra." He extended his arm toward her and she grasped his hand. After a brief gasp, he pulled her into his arms. He seemed to have the same desirous affliction as she did. "I want to celebrate. Let's go celebrate."

"Oh." Susannah frowned and glared at Victoria. "I'll leave you two, then."

"No. I want to celebrate with both of you. Is there a place close by where we can get dessert? I'm in the mood for pie!"

Ben's enthusiasm rubbed off on Victoria and she laughed. She would have insisted Susannah join them if Ben hadn't beat her to it. It had been a long time since she'd had any family and she'd forgotten how delicate they could be. She refused to come between Ben and his sister and the sooner Susannah realized that, the better.

* * * *

The sound of Victoria's laughter filled Ben with glee. This day had turned out so much better than he could ever have anticipated. First his sister's changed attitude and now a new job.

"Are you sure?" Susannah asked. "I don't want to intrude."

"You're not intruding," Victoria said. "I'd love to get to know you better. Truly."

An awkward silence hung in the air. Victoria was trying and he could kiss her for that—hell, he could just kiss her—but was Susannah giving her a hard time? Probably. He couldn't expect miracles in one day, now could he? "Is there a pie place nearby?"

"No," Susannah said. "But I know where we can go. I'll have to drive there."

"Great. Why don't you pick us up out front?"

He waited while her footsteps retreated, then whispered into Victoria's ear, "Has she left yet?"

He knew the answer, but had used the question as an excuse to feel her cheek against his own.

She chuckled. "Yes."

"Good." He cupped her face and kissed her. In no time at all he slipped his tongue in her mouth and tasted her. God, he'd love to taste other parts of her body, too, and maybe one day soon he would. She wasted no time molding her body to his and grinding against his growing erection. Man, if she kept that up, he was liable to come in his pants. Regretfully, he pulled away and struggled to catch his breath. Hell, his heart wasn't helping any, either, since it decided to go all wild and crazy on him. "I've wanted to do that all day. God, I missed you. You don't mind Susannah coming along, do you?"

She ran her fingers along his cheek. "No. It'll give us a chance to get to know one another. Maybe then she won't hate me."

"She doesn't hate you. She just doesn't know you." He felt around for his bag and found the strap. Susannah probably would have handed him the thing, but Victoria let him do it. As if she knew he was capable. Made him like her even more. He slipped the strap over his head. "I'm sorry I didn't call you back. It's been a crazy day. By the time I finished, I was afraid I might be late to class and I had to pay attention to my stops."

"Stops? Susannah didn't bring you?"

He grabbed her elbow, letting her lead them to the elevator. "Well, she might have if I were home. Crazy day, remember? I rode the bus today."

"Really? Aren't they dirty? And full of people?"

"I didn't notice any dirt and what's wrong with people? Most are very helpful if you give them a chance. Maybe I should get you out more." If Susannah had glimpsed Victoria's panic attack, she would have never agreed to leave him alone with her.

"I think I'd much rather spend a quiet evening with you, without any interruptions."

He smiled. "I like the way you think."

While they rode the elevator down, he fought the urge to kiss her, because after that last one, he might do something foolish and take her against the wall. Now there was a thought that only got him harder. *Way to go, idiot.*

"Are you going to be okay going out? If not, we could do something else." He hated having to ask her, but Susannah didn't need to know about Victoria's insecurities.

"You afraid I'll embarrass you?"

"That's not why—"

She chuckled. "I'm teasing. Sorry. I should be okay, but thank you for worrying."

"You'll let me know immediately if we need to leave, won't you?"

She kissed his cheek. "You're so sweet. Guess that's why I like you so much. I promise I'll do my best, okay?"

That little peck she'd given him sent more blood rushing to his groin. Damn. When had he become such a horny bastard? He needed to get his libido under control or he'd never hear the end of it from his sister.

The elevator doors opened and Victoria led the way. Muggy air hugged him upon exiting the building.

"She's just ahead," Victoria said. "Are you sitting up front?"

He slid his hand across the side of the car and found the rear door handle. "Nope. I'm sitting in back with you. Ladies first."

He couldn't stop smiling. Being with Victoria excited him, made him glad to be alive. Sure, Susannah was tagging along, but how else could she see what a wonderful person Victoria was?

And there was pie in his future. Couldn't forget that.

* * * *

Ben had just stuck his foot inside the vehicle when a loud crash propelled Victoria into the seatback in front of her. What was that? When she turned to see what happened, Ben was gone.

"What the fuck?" Susannah screamed as she rubbed her forehead.

Victoria scrambled to the open door and the sight blasted the air from her lungs. He was sprawled on the sidewalk, lying on his back. His glasses had landed several feet away. She crawled over to him and cupped his face, his heat rushing up her arms. "Ben! Can you hear me?" Then a wonderful, sweet smell invaded her senses. The fabric surrounding the rip on his pant leg was darkening. "Oh *Gott.* You're bleeding."

He grabbed her wrists. "I'm okay." She might have believed him if he wasn't grimacing. "What happened?"

"Some stupid idiot decided to plow into me," Susannah yelled. "God, Ben. Are you all right?"

"I'm fine." He winced as he moved to sit up, but Victoria held him down.

"You're not fine." She turned toward Susannah. "His leg is cut." Her voice broke and she rested her head on his chest. The scent drove her wild with need and her fangs extended. She'd never had such a reaction before. Could it be his blood really was different? It took everything in her not to find out.

"Hey, it's all right," he said as he stroked her hair.

It would only be all right if she got his bleeding under control. But how? She couldn't very well lick him, now could she?

"Here." Susannah held out some gauze. "For his leg."

Keeping her lips clamped together, Victoria nodded and took the offering. Susannah left and examined the car for damage. Perfect timing. Victoria discretely spit into the gauze and pressed it against his leg. It shouldn't heal him completely—and wouldn't that look strange with his pant leg soaked in blood—but at least he wouldn't need stitches and it would keep her from doing something stupid. Like sampling him.

* * * *

So much for a nice evening out. How did he manage to get into so many accidents? This time Susannah couldn't blame him. Could she? Ah, shit.

At least his leg was feeling better. "Can I sit up now? The ground is rather hard."

"Let me help you." Victoria pulled him by his upper arms. "Oh no. You're bleeding from your head, too?"

Ben touched the back of his head and his fingers became sticky. "I guess so." Great. A discount. Two wounds for the price of one trip to the doctor.

"Oh, Ben." She sounded as if she was on the verge of crying.

"Man, you're bleeding everywhere, aren't you?" Susannah said. Yep, he could hear her complaints already. "I can take it from here, Victoria."

"Let me," Victoria said. "Why don't you see if the person who hit us is okay?"

"Like I care what happened to that shit. Ohhh!" Susannah stomped away.

Victoria pulled his head down on her shoulder. Before he could really enjoy her scent, and maybe sneak a kiss in, she applied pressure to the wound. Sharp pain flared and it took everything in him not to jerk off the pavement. Then slowly it faded away, just like it had with his leg.

"What is that stuff?"

She stiffened. "Stuff? You mean the gauze?"

"It's okay if you're numbing me up. Sure feels better. Even my leg doesn't hurt anymore." At least, not like it had earlier. He'd thought for sure the car had taken his leg off.

"You don't think it's my loving touch?" She kissed his cheek sending his libido into overdrive. Nice to know her kisses trumped leg and head wounds, regardless how innocent they were.

"Better not do that again. I might embarrass you in public."

"You couldn't embarrass me any more than I embarrass myself."

Sirens sounded in the distance and grew louder with each second. Just what he needed. Another trip to the emergency room. They should give him a frequent visitor discount. He'd be due some kind of reward by now.

"You don't have to stay with me. You can call Perry to pick you up."

Victoria stroked his cheek. "Don't be ridiculous. I'm not leaving until I know you're okay."

"I feel fine. Really. Almost like I hadn't been injured at all." And if they weren't in public, or in view of his sister, he'd kiss her and show her how fine he felt.

"Why don't we let the professionals decide, okay?"

Doors slammed and footsteps approached. "Okay, miss. We'll take care of your father from here."

Father? Ben could have sworn he heard Susannah snicker.

* * * *

Victoria sat in the noisy waiting room, rubbing her handkerchief, wishing she could mentally silence the two children—a boy and a girl, both under the age of five—who saw fit to scream at nothing. Their mother might even thank her, since she was having difficulty controlling those two. But not only was it wrong, Victoria didn't have the ability. Until those two reached the age of puberty, their minds were unreachable.

Susannah returned with a cup of coffee. She hadn't offered to get Victoria a cup, not that she'd drink it. Still…

"You're awfully fidgety," Susannah said.

"Do you think it's serious?" For the past thirty minutes, Victoria had been afraid to speak. It had taken her that long to retract her fangs.

Susannah rubbed her temple. "Head wounds tend to bleed a lot, so no. He seemed lucid enough."

Victoria nodded. Thank goodness. The way he'd fallen she'd thought for sure he'd been seriously injured. While she could heal small wounds, anything internal was out of her control. Suddenly, losing him to another female vampire seemed silly. She could just plain lose him. "How are you? Did you hit your head?"

"No. I've had this headache all day. Just so you know, this is what he does. I'm not saying the accident was his fault, but he gets hurt a lot and he thinks he's okay, but he's not. Not really."

"Why wouldn't he be okay?"

"Since the accident, he's gotten a bit klutzy."

"You mean, because he's blind."

Susannah shook her head. "No. I mean because he doesn't pay attention. This is his fourth trip here this month."

"But he's not to blame for what happened tonight."

"Whether it's his fault or not is not the issue. Listen, what are you doing with him anyway? What are you hoping to gain? He doesn't have money."

"That's not only an insult to me, it's an insult to your brother. You think someone would only want him for his money?"

"He has nothing else to offer."

"Says you."

Susannah closed her eyes and rubbed her temples again. "That didn't come out right. But you're only seeing a small part of him. You don't see him everyday, trying to do everyday things. Seeing him fail. I help as best as I can."

"Maybe that's the problem. Did you ever think of not helping him? He's not a child."

"Oh, and now you think you know better than I do? Why don't you just go home? We don't need you."

This wasn't going well at all, but Victoria wasn't about to leave Ben. Maybe she and Susannah would never get along, but did it really matter? If she and Ben were meant for each other, they'd live for a long, long time. Susannah would only be a blip on the radar. And if they weren't meant for each other, then Victoria would walk away.

It would be damn hard, though.

"I'm not leaving until I know he's okay."

The little boy screeched and Victoria cringed. She could ignore him, she could. She continued to rub her handkerchief.

"Out of curiosity, is there no hope for Ben's sight?" Because if there was and it was lack of money that kept him from pursuing a cure, he could get his sight back before they bonded. But then he'd see how young she looked. Would that make a difference? He'd certainly cringed after the EMT had mistaken him for her father.

"His optic nerves were damaged and not repairable. He'll always be blind. So if you think someday he'll get better, think again. What you see is what you get."

Maybe so, but what she saw was pretty great.

"You do realize I'm the one responsible for passing you in the class," Susannah said.

Wow, another slap in the face. "And you do realize I could easily take the class on line. I'm over twenty-one."

Susannah huffed. "Over twenty-one, my ass. Why are you taking this class then?"

"That's a strange question coming from the owner. Why don't you like me? I haven't done anything to you."

"You've done plenty."

If plenty included making Ben happy, then maybe Susannah needed time and space to see it differently.

* * * *

Ben sat still while the nurse checked his head. No surprise he'd been the only injured party who needed an ambulance. How'd he get so lucky? "Will I need stitches?"

"Nope. Just a little cut. In fact, it's stopped bleeding. But you've got quite a knot. How're you holding up, Ben? You dizzy? Queasy?"

"No." Of course, he hadn't walked yet. Every time he'd tried, someone put him on a cart or in a wheelchair. Might have had something to do with his blindness, but no one had said. "What about my leg?"

"You know, I would have thought you'd have a gash with the amount of blood on your pants, but that cut is small, too. You got lucky."

"I didn't cause it this time."

She patted his shoulder and placed an icepack in his hand. "I know, sweetie. Just bad luck. Put this on your head to keep the swelling down. Your sister and friend are here."

He applied the ice pack and extended his free hand, wanting Victoria, but getting Susannah instead.

"Time to go home and get you to bed," she said.

"Did you get hurt in the accident?"

"No, I'm fine."

"Victoria?"

"I'm good."

"How's the car?"

"Drivable, but I'm turning it in tomorrow," Susannah said.

"So we can still go out and celebrate." Because he wanted to show Victoria he was younger than he looked. That he could take a few scrapes and survive. That he wasn't her father. Damn that EMT.

"Ben," Susannah scolded. "It's after midnight. And your clothes are all ruined."

Oh. He hadn't even thought of that.

Victoria's scent intensified, indicating she'd stepped closer, and she brushed his hair off his forehead. Her fingertips left a little zing behind. "Susannah's right. You should rest. We'll do something tomorrow, okay?"

He leaned into her. "You promise?"

"I promise." He could almost hear the smile in her voice. "You go home with Susannah. I'll call Perry for a ride."

"No. I'm not leaving you here alone. We'll wait until he gets here."

"You don't have to."

"We insist. Right, Suze?"

"Sure. Not a problem." Susannah fussed over him and he might have objected except she had made an effort to be nice to Victoria, so he didn't want to jinx it. The three of them sat outside on a bench. The temperature was pleasant, but the air a bit on the stale side. Most likely a smoker's refuge.

"I'll go wait in the car," Susannah said. "Call me when you're ready to go."

"Goodnight, Susannah," Victoria said.

Susannah didn't respond, so she must have waved. He searched for Victoria's hand, but she found his first. Even with the pounding in his head, her touch thrilled him. He gave her a gentle squeeze. "Are you okay? You've been awfully quiet."

"I guess I'm still a little shaken."

"You think if I had sight, I could have prevented—"

"Oh no. I didn't even see anything. It happened so fast. One second you were standing and the next…" She touched his cheek. "I thought I lost you."

Her concern affected him deeply. And here he'd thought she wanted to call it quits. Guess that "father" bit disturbed him more than it had her. "Hey, I'm tougher than you think. Can't get rid of me that easy."

He caressed her cheek and leaned in. Found her lips. Soft and yielding. She set his heart racing and he dove in, tasting her. Showing her what he wanted. She sucked on his tongue and he nearly exploded.

His breath came in gasps. "If I got a room for tomorrow night, would you—"

"Yes, oh yes." Her lips had barely touched his when she pulled away. "Ah, damn it. Perry's here."

"He can wait." He held her and devoured her mouth. God, she tasted like heaven. Tomorrow couldn't get there soon enough, but he would finally have her all to himself.

"Hey, Teach! Get a room!" Perry's cackle made Ben laugh because, hey, he *was* getting one.

"Don't tell me you like him," she said as she pressed her forehead against his.

"Okay, I won't."

She chuckled. "I'll see you tomorrow. You get some rest."

Yeah, rest. As if he could sleep now.

* * * *

Graham peered from the rooftop of the building across from the hospital. Susannah's talk with Victoria hadn't gone as he'd hoped since Victoria was currently lip-locked with Martin. Damn it. Had the accident only gotten them closer? Why couldn't it show her how fragile that mortal was? What the hell did she see in that blind guy?

Perry arrived. "Hey, Teach! Get a room!"

A room? No. No room. Damn bastard wasn't helping at all.

It should have been Graham picking her up. And he had suggested as much to Barnet, but the old goat told him it wasn't necessary. Getting close to her the old-fashioned way wasn't working out so great.

So, if Susannah couldn't break those two up, then he'd have to go straight to the source and hope Victoria never noticed. Once Perry had driven off with Victoria, Graham bounded down the stairs and rushed crossed the street. Martin was on the phone and told someone—most likely his sister—that he was ready. Shit, blew that. Should have kept the bastard from calling. Graham would only have to work faster.

He sat on the bench near Martin and took control. *"You will find Victoria to be—"*

"Excuse me, do either of you have a light?" A man in scrubs held an unlit cigarette between his fingers. "My lighter seems to have died on me."

Of all the blasted times to be interrupted. Graham opened his mouth to tell the bugger to beat it, when Ben spoke.

"Sorry, I don't smoke."

What the? Why did he talk?

The nurse or orderly or whatever continued to stare at Graham. Graham shook his head, sending the idiot away.

He mentally suggested Ben scratch his nose. Nothing. Told him to bark. Nothing.

Graham stood and slowly backed away. Damn. What kind of freak was this guy? Did his blindness make him immune? And did Victoria know he couldn't be controlled? Graham smiled. What if she did? Was she keeping Martin a secret? If so, this could be the leverage he'd been desperately seeking. But first, he'd give Susannah another shot.

Well, what do you know? As if on cue, the prodigal sister drove up. Graham ducked inside the hospital.

Thank God he hadn't spoken. Wouldn't that have put a crimp in things?

CHAPTER 10

Victoria logged off the library computer. She had given another go at searching for the Perfect Mate author. If she were to throw in the towel, so to speak, she was going to make darn sure she'd given it her best. Several useless hours later, she'd caved. The name could be staring her in the face, and without any outside help she might as well be fishing in a swimming pool.

After that debacle, she moved her search to the Internet. Graham's accusation about Henrik still irked her. The realtor who helped Victoria sell her home had given her the information on what Henrik had paid for it. Using some algorithms she'd found on line, and based on the current value of the house, she calculated that Henrik had bought their property at market value. Which had been the Henrik she knew. She might not have been in love with the man, but he was a good man—an honorable man—and she should have never questioned his integrity. Graham had only been trying to divert her from his own immorality.

She stood and sauntered over to the bookshelves. Reading seemed to be in order. Anything was better than staring at the computer. Or thinking about Ben and their night—or maybe their weekend—together. She'd never looked forward to a Friday night with such joy before.

Barnet tossed a package on the table. "This came in for you today. Where's Sunny?"

"Probably still on the phone with Jack."

He laughed. "Ahh, newlyweds. It's been a long time since I felt that rush."

She had never felt any kind of rush with Henrik. With Ben though… Would it be different after they made love? Of course it would. How could it not? She just had to make sure not to bite him. *Scheisse.*

"Any luck on finding a link between Sarah and Richard?"

She picked up the package and waved it under Barnet's face. "Not yet, but maybe soon. This is the book on the history of Daughertys."

Barnet's eyebrows shot to his hairline. "There are books like that?"

"Seems so. Genealogy is a big hobby for some. And they love to share their information."

"Great! How about the Perfect Mate author?"

Her shoulders slumped without any effort on her part. Couldn't she have joy for more than a minute? "No, and it's beginning to look like an impossible task. We're going to have to discuss sending out a request."

"Damn it. I had hoped."

"Me, too. There's something else I propose we discuss: Manipulation for personal gain."

"Vampires already know it's frowned upon."

"Yes, but that's not stopping them from doing it. We need to be firmer, set a punishment."

"Victoria, if we go to that extreme, we could all be booted off the Committee, if not looking at another war."

"Are you saying we can't even discuss it?"

"Fine. But not until after this Perfect Mate business is settled. Jack and Abe are due back before sunrise Saturday. Expect a meeting shortly after." He pointed to the book. "Let me know what you find out."

She assured him she would and he left her alone in the library. At least her reading preference had been determined.

She arrived back at her room, opened the package, and settled in her lounge chair. Her sprits rose when she found Sarah's family, but tanked when there wasn't any mention of Ben's or Justin's. Richard might be in there—the name was certainly popular—but without any family history to corroborate, she couldn't pinpoint the man.

Someone knocked on her door. She had told Sunny to come in

anytime, so why the knock?

The one person she never expected to see stood in the hallway. Did the damn man think he lived at Headquarters now? She refrained from slamming the door in his face. "Hello, Graham."

"Good morning, Victoria. Mind if I come in?"

Yes, she did, but before she could tell him, he slithered his way inside.

"You can afford to live anywhere, yet you insist on living here. Why is that?"

She shut the door on a sigh. "What reason would I live anywhere else? I have everything I need here."

"Everything except privacy. Your plantation home wasn't far. Why did you sell it?"

"It got too big living there by myself." Heck, it was too big living there with Henrik.

"I would have—"

"What do you want, Graham?" If she didn't stop him now, he might take it as encouragement to visit more often.

"Besides you?" He held up his hand when she opened her mouth to protest. "Sorry, slipped out. But really, how can you have a relationship with anyone living in this place? You can't very well bring your teacher-friend here, now can you?"

No, she most definitely could not bring Ben here. Especially if Perry were still hanging around. That man didn't know the meaning of the word discreet. "I suppose if I'm ever in a serious relationship, I would move out. But until then…"

He sat in her chair and leaned back. "Fair enough." He opened the plastic bag on the side table and peeked inside before she could stop him. "What are you doing with a slice of pie?"

Damn Graham and his snoopiness. She snatched the bag from his hands. "That is none of your concern."

When she and Sunny had gone to the mall for donors and had passed the bakery, Victoria couldn't resist buying Ben the pie. Hopefully he liked apple. Sunny had said it was the most popular flavor.

"Oh. It's for your teacher, isn't it? Aren't you supposed to just bring an apple to class?"

"Enough, Graham. What do you want?"

"I thought we might hang out together."

"Hang out? I don't hang. Besides, I have work to do."

"Come on, Victoria. You have to give me a chance, here."

"Why? For over forty years I don't see you except at your obligated meeting. If you were so interested, why didn't you show up for every meeting?"

"If I had thought it would have made a difference, I would have. That was my mistake. I truly believed you were still grieving over Henrik. So if you weren't grieving, why haven't you left this place until now?"

"And how do you know I haven't?"

"I've been keeping tabs."

Oh great. She sat on her couch. Maybe if she answered his questions, he'd lose interest and go away. "I was grieving, at first." Maybe not as much as she should have, though. "Then it got easier to stay in than go out." As well as scarier, but she wouldn't admit that. "Resembling a seventeen-year-old doesn't get me very far on the outside world."

"You know, I told him not to turn you so early. I think he was afraid I'd steal you away."

"What are you talking about? I didn't know you then."

"Of course not. I was a vampire. Henrik protected you from us all. But he knew of my interest. I guess he thought marrying you wasn't enough. He was still afraid. Afraid you might leave him."

"For you."

"For anyone."

Henrik had never exhibited any kind of insecurities. He had always appeared confident to her. But had his confidence come from knowing she couldn't go anywhere or do anything looking as young as she did? Or was Graham playing another one of his games by messing with her head?

"So, are you telling me that now you're the insecure one?"

"Of who, your teacher? Not likely. I really can't see him wanting to be a blind vampire, so I doubt you'll convince him to be turned. And when he gets too old, or you get too bored, I'll still be here waiting. Because you see, Victoria, I don't see you as a seventeen-year-old. I see you as a woman. The woman I've always loved."

Loved? He couldn't be serious. If he loved anyone, it was himself. So what was he really up to?

* * * *

Ben slipped his toiletries and a change of clothes inside his laptop bag. The prospect of being with Victoria in every way set his heart racing. He'd never been so nervous before a date. Except this wasn't really a date. More like a rendezvous. Should they have dated more?

He had to stop thinking like that. She had agreed to this. If she thought they were moving too fast, she would have said something. Wouldn't she? Whether she gave the green light or not, it didn't matter. Even if they only spent the time talking, at least it was time alone with her.

Susannah knocked on the door. "Can we talk?"

He placed his laptop bag on his dresser and opened the door. "What about?"

"What are your plans tonight?"

Telling his sister about his personal business wasn't at the top of his conversation list, but since he most likely wouldn't come home until tomorrow, she probably had a right to know. "I have a date with Victoria, so don't bother waiting up. I'll take a cab home."

"You mean you plan on having sex, right?"

"Whatever gave you—"

"If you didn't want me to know you bought condoms, you should make sure the receipt is hidden in the trash can, not lying on the floor beside it."

He sat on the edge of his bed. Shit. Figured he'd miss the trash can. Why couldn't the receipt just state merchandise? And why did she have to treat him as an adolescent? "It's none of your business what I do, you know."

"Ben, you hardly know her."

"Enough to know I want to be with her."

The bed dipped with her weight. "Listen, I didn't want to have to say this, but she said something while we were in the waiting room that maybe you should know."

He shook his head, fearing where the conversation was headed. "You said you were going to give her a chance."

"I was until she asked if your accidents were a common occurrence. She was totally out of her element waiting. She was going to leave until I asked her not to."

"*You* asked her not to?" Now why didn't he believe her?

Victoria had trouble with crowds, but she'd always been kind of protective of him.

"She asked if you were always so helpless. If there was any hope you'd be able to see again."

Now that sounded like something Victoria would wonder about. "And what did you say? Did you agree with her?"

"I didn't want her to get any false hopes. You'll always be blind, Ben."

"And helpless. Don't forget that." It was bad enough Susannah thought that, but why Victoria?

Susannah embraced his shoulder. "Ben… I don't think you're helpless. Just that you need help. She's in over her head and I think she's beginning to realize that and doesn't know how to break it off without feeling guilty. I don't want you to get your hopes up where it concerns her. I love you. I care about you. I don't want to see you get hurt. But you deserve to know the truth."

Had his blindness been the real cause of Victoria's panic attack the other night? But she'd agreed after the accident to meet tonight. Why would she do that if she wanted to break it off? Oh hell, he didn't know what to think anymore. He couldn't believe Susannah would purposely lie. Most likely she'd misunderstood Victoria. That, or his sexual drive led him to believe Victoria was perfect.

Except…she was.

Susannah left Ben alone with his thoughts. He stood and retrieved his bag. Should he unpack? He'd been thinking about Victoria all freakin' day and now he was calling it off? No, he wasn't. He'd wait and see what she had to say first, then decide.

By the time class ended for the night, Ben would have preferred to dig a hole to China with a spoon than have this conversation with Victoria. If he could see, it wouldn't even be an issue. He'd just whisk her off to the nearest hotel, or his apartment—because he certainly wouldn't be living with his sister.

"Coast is clear." Her voice was muffled as if she were speaking from under her desk. The sound of a plastic bag rustled.

"Victoria? Before we go, we need to talk."

"Talk?" Her voice was clearer as if she'd sat up. "Oh. Is it your head? Are you not feeling well? If so—"

"My head is fine. My leg is fine. See? I'm not even limping." Which was a miracle in itself. He'd thought for sure he'd be feeling something by morning, but he'd woken up as if he'd never been hurt.

"I'm so glad. So what do you want to talk about?"

He sat in the chair beside her and took a deep breath. On some level a voice was urging him not to screw this up, but how could he start a relationship with her—and he was certain they were on the verge of doing just that—without them knowing all the facts? "I'm wondering if maybe we're rushing into things."

"What? But last night—"

"Last night I didn't know about the conversation between you and my sister."

She let out a heavy breath. "Ben, I'm trying to be friends with her, but it's hard when she seems to dislike me so much."

"Did you ask her if I would ever get my sight back?"

Silence screamed for a moment and then she quietly said, "I only wondered…"

Oh great. It was true, then. "I'm sorry if I led you to believe otherwise, but I'm forever damaged."

"You're not damaged. Not to me."

"Oh really?" He ripped the glasses off his face. "You don't call this damaged?"

She took his hands, sending a pleasurable zap up his arm. "Ben, where is this coming from? What did your sister tell you?"

"She thinks you're realizing that you're in over your head. And after your panic attack, I'm wondering if you are."

"You said you understood."

"I thought I did. So let me save you the trouble of feeling guilty breaking it off with a blind guy. It's a lot of work. I get it. So don't feel guilty. You're free to go."

"But I don't want to break it off."

"Don't you? You can't even handle a crowd. Susannah said you were even nervous in the waiting room." He said the words meaner than intended, but if that's what got her to see reason, maybe it was for the best.

She muttered, "Well if you've been secluded for forty years, you'd be nervous, too."

Forty years? He couldn't have heard her right. And why would she be secluded at all? "What did you say?"

"Nothing." Her chair scooted across the floor. "If you want us broken up, then consider us broken. Goodbye, Ben." She ran out of the room and a plastic bag rustled in her wake.

What had she forgotten? Waving his hand in the air, he located the item and opened it, finding a plastic fork and a take-out container. When he lifted the lid, the scent of apples and cinnamon filled the air.

She brought him pie? Why would she do that if she didn't care about him? Shit. Oh, what an idiot he was for listening to his sister.

"Victoria!"

* * * *

"Stupid, stupid, stupid." *Hölle.* What made her say forty years? Why'd she have to say anything at all? Victoria ran to the elevators and pushed the button. As usual, it took its ever-loving time to arrive.

Ben emerged from the classroom. "Victoria?"

The elevator dinged as it opened. She hopped on and punched the close door button several times.

He extended his arm as he rushed toward her. "Stop! Please."

The doors closed and she let out her breath. She should have known he was too good to be true, Perfect Mate or not. He was blind. He would always be blind. Why would he want to stay that way forever? Better to break if off now before they got in too deep.

The car stopped twice on the way to the lobby. First to let on the janitor and his wheeled cart, next to let him off. She should have taken the stairs and would have if she knew where they were located. That's what she got for paying more attention to Ben than her surroundings.

Finally arriving on her floor, she approached the glass doors to the outside and stopped. If she called Perry for a ride, she'd never hear the end of it. But if she went outside, alone… *Scheisse.* Why couldn't she do it?

A door slammed behind her. "Victoria?"

She spun around. What? Ben took the stairs? How'd he get down here so quickly? She froze in place. If she ran outside, he might chase her and then get hurt, that's if she could get enough courage to actually go out the doors.

He took two steps and stopped. "I know you're here. I'm sorry. Don't go. Please."

She should leave. She'd already said enough. But she couldn't and not just because of the outdoors. "Why shouldn't I? You clearly don't want me."

He relaxed at the sound of her voice and moved to stand in front of her. "That's not true."

"It's not?"

He shook his head. "Why'd you buy the pie?"

His scent nearly overwhelmed her and she found herself telling him the truth. "You were so disappointed we couldn't go out last night and when I saw it today, I thought of you."

He stepped in closer. "You thought of me?"

She reached out to touch his cheek, but stopped. "I always think of you. And I wasn't looking to break up."

"I know that now. I'm sorry. Can you forgive me?"

If she said yes, he'd most likely want an explanation for her earlier remark. But saying no meant walking away and she couldn't do that. Not if he wanted her. "I think that can be arranged."

"Thank you." He smiled and reached out for her.

Ben wanted her now, but would he later? She stepped into his embrace and he brought his hands up to her face. Reveling in the warmth only a Perfect Mate could create, she closed her eyes. He kissed her lightly on the lips, teasing her for more. "Now, what was that remark about forty years? You meant forty days, right?"

She kissed him back, harder this time, tasting him, sucking on his tongue. If this would be their last kiss, she would make sure it was good. She'd expected the day to tell him everything would eventually come. She just hadn't expected that day to be today. She pulled away slowly and held his face. "No."

"No?" He furrowed his brow as if recalling the question. "But you're twenty-two."

"No."

"No? I don't understand."

"I know." She rested her head on his chest. The thumping of his heart reverberated in her soul. How would she tell him?

"Are you going to explain it?"

"Yes, but we need to go someplace private." Or maybe someplace he couldn't run from her screaming. Was there a padded room nearby?

CHAPTER 11

Ben held onto Victoria's elbow as she led them back to the classroom. He figured it was as private as any other place. Besides, he'd left his cane and everything else behind.

It'd been a miracle he'd tracked her down as it was. Thank God her phobia had kept her indoors because he really didn't want to know what would have happened if she had gone outside. He'd managed to descend the stairs without killing himself—something he would not try again unless Victoria gave him a good reason to repeat that feat—but venturing outside without any aid was altogether something else. If he'd been in his right mind, he might have stopped before stepping outdoors. Might have.

After seeing him to a chair, she shut the door. Several seconds passed and no movement sounded. He stood. "Victoria?"

"I'm still here."

Good. He really wasn't sure he could go through with chasing her again. Oh, he'd chase her, but seriously doubted he'd survive the second time around. He slowly lowered onto his chair.

She sat in the seat beside him. "Guess I'm a little nervous. I've never had to tell anyone this before."

"Tell anyone what?" Her actions were kind of freaking him out. "You're not a spy are you?"

She chuckled. "No, but you might think I'm crazy and I won't blame you if you do. Just hear me out first, okay?"

"You're not making any sense, but sure. No judgment until you're through. Okay?"

She took a deep breath. "Thank you. So basically, what I have to tell you is I'm… I'm… *Scheisse.* Maybe it's better if I show you." She took his hand and he gasped at the pleasurable zap she sent his way. It didn't feel near as great as their kiss back in the foyer, but maybe he could sneak another one in later. She put his fingers on her lips. "Tell me what you feel."

Was she being serious? He'd felt her face before and hadn't discovered any abnormalities. And wouldn't Susannah have told them if there were any? "Lips. And they're very nice lips if I might add."

"Thank you." She kissed his fingers before opening her mouth and repositioning his finger. "And now?"

"Teeth. Straight teeth." He smiled. "Your dentist must love—" Something sharp protruded and pressed against his finger. He pulled back. "What was that?"

"What did it feel like?"

"Like you filed your tooth." And why would she even do such a thing?

"I didn't. Feel again. Please."

"Can't you just tell me—"

"I would if I thought you'd believe me. Please, feel it again."

Her pleading urged him onward. He cupped her face with his right hand and ran his thumb across the top teeth. Alongside her canine, a sharp tooth disappeared, then reappeared. Disappeared. Reappeared. Definitely not a filed tooth.

"Are you making it do that?"

She nodded.

What the hell? He brought his other hand up and explored her mouth. Alongside both canines the sharp protrusion emerged, then retracted. "What are those?"

She took his hands. "Fangs."

"Fangs? Why in the world would you have—"

She touched his cheek, shutting him up. "Ben… I'm not like you."

His heart pounded as he attempted to make light of the strange situation that faced him. "Of course you aren't. I'm a man, you're a woman—"

"I'm immortal. A vampire."

What? Oh God. She *was* crazy. He shook his head. "Not possible. Vampires don't exist."

"I know this is hard to understand. But I'm not crazy and neither are you for believing me. Vampires do exist. We have for centuries."

"Say I was to believe you. How the hell have you stayed hidden all this time?"

"We have the ability to control people and manipulate their minds so they don't remember what they see, if one of us should slip."

"Okay. Then make me do something against my will."

She pulled her hand away and the chair scraped across the floor. "I can't. You're different."

"*I'm* different? I'm not going around saying I'm a vampire." Oh God. Had he said that out loud? This was worse than a horror novel. "Is this your idea of a joke? You said you didn't want to break up with me—"

"I'm not joking and I don't want to break up. I want to be with you, but you deserve to know the truth. But because I can't manipulate you or your memories, what I'm telling you can't leave this room."

"Like anyone would believe me."

She held his hands. "I'm doing this badly, I know. You caught me unprepared and for that, I'm sorry. How can I prove to you what you cannot see?"

Would he even believe her if he could see? He said he wouldn't judge her until she'd finished, and he supposed he owed her that much. But a vampire? Really?

"I know what to do," she said. "Hold onto your chair."

To appease her he did as she asked. "What are you—" His feet left the floor and he teetered. Reaching out, he touched her shoulder. She was holding him up. "How—What—Shit! Put me down before you hurt yourself."

"You don't weigh that much." She placed him back on the floor. "Now do you believe me?"

"I believe you're freakishly strong and have fangs. You going to turn into a bat next?"

She laughed. "I can't do that. I also can't go into the sun or eat food."

"Right, because vampires feed off of…" Holy shit. He grabbed his neck.

She held his wrists, but didn't try to remove his hands from his throat. "Ben, I'm not going to bite you. You aren't food to me. If you were, I'd have had a smorgasbord the other night. Instead, I healed you with my saliva."

"That's what you put on me? You licked me?"

"No. I wouldn't do something like that without your permission. Or in public. I used the gauze."

"Did you want to?"

"I won't lie to you. I was tempted, yes, but I fought the urge."

"Oh God."

"Ben, it's not what you think. Because you're different than other mortals, you're kind of irresistible to female vampires."

"Irresistible how? Are they all wanting to feed from me?" He shuddered.

"No. We're not drawn to your blood. We're drawn to your scent."

"Is that why you liked the way I smell? And Sunny liked… Oh my God. She's one, too? Am I at the top of the smorgasbord?"

"Yes, Sunny's a vampire, and no, it's not like that. We don't want you for a meal, I swear."

He lowered his arms. He supposed if she'd wanted to feed from him, she would have done it by now. So if not for a meal… "Sex? You want me for sex? Is that it?"

"Not exactly, but it is sexual. You feel that, don't you? When we touch?"

"I feel something." Which was a huge understatement. Hadn't lust overcome him after their first kiss? But she wasn't the only vampire he touched, was she? "What about Perry? I'm assuming he's one, too. I touched him and didn't feel anything."

"Yes, he's a vampire, but he's not attracted to males, just like you aren't. Doesn't mean he can control you, because no vampire can. And that makes you a threat to our race. I need to keep you a secret for now because once my people find out about you…"

"I'm dinner?"

She chuckled. "No. More like a prisoner. I don't want them to lock you up."

"A prisoner? Because I can say I know some vampires? I hate to tell you this, but I'd be put in an institution for making those statements." Hell, he might end up there anyway.

"Please know I'm only trying to protect you."

Protect him. Yeah, she had been acting that way. "Is that why you panicked at the club?"

"Partly. Apparently it was ladies night—for vampires."

A snort escaped. He couldn't help it. The whole night was turning into one bizarre-fest. "This is all a scam, right? You're punking me?"

"No. It's real. I won't lie to you, Ben. Ever."

She sounded sincere and he had to trust his instincts. Then again, a few moments ago his instincts had told him to run and he'd stayed. He hoped to God he wouldn't regret that. "Okay, so what other part contributed to your breakdown? Your phobia for the outdoors? Is that real? Can vampires have phobias?"

"Well, this one does. It had several decades to grow, though."

Again with the decades. "How old are you? Your file indicates—"

"I was born in 1628. On my seventeenth birthday, my husband, who I had no idea was a vampire, turned me into one."

"You're almost four hundred years old?" No wonder she'd laughed off his age.

"But I look seventeen. I know I went about it all wrong, but when I ran into you in the garage, I kind of took advantage of your blindness. Not that I wasn't interested in you. I'm very interested. You know that, don't you?"

"Because you were drawn to my scent. Right? You're basically saying you like me because of some chemical reaction."

"No. I mean, yes, it might have helped, but—"

"So what I'm feeling could also be a chemical reaction to you?"

"Isn't all attraction some form of a chemical reaction? You didn't feel a connection with Sunny, did you?"

"Did I even touch her?"

"No." She sighed. "You said you liked me. Has that changed?"

"I don't know what I feel anymore." Except...he *did* like her. Craziness and all. Shit.

"Well, I know I've never felt a connection with anyone since Henrik died."

"But you said you were living in seclusion." For decades, he couldn't forget that. "When did he die?"

"1967."

Shit. That was before he was even born. "Am I the first...mortal you've associated with since then?"

"Well, no, I've been feeding."

Feeding. On people. A shiver went down his spine.

"It's not like that. I don't take enough to hurt anyone."

Good to know, but still strange. Did she just go up to strangers and bite them? He swallowed. Did she get off on that? "Men or women?"

"What? Oh. Women. Okay. I get it. You're right. It's possible what we feel isn't real. Sure feels real, though."

Felt real to him, too, but then what did he know. She claimed to be a vampire and he was beginning to believe her. Lock him up, stat.

* * * *

If Victoria could produce tears, they'd be puddled at her feet. She'd expected Ben's difficulty in believing her story, but how could he doubt their attraction toward one another? Didn't all attractions start chemically in one way or another? What were hormones made of anyway?

Ben rubbed his mouth. "I'm sorry, but I'm having trouble digesting all this information."

"I understand. It's a lot to take in."

He took her hand and her spirits rose. "I have to admit, I do like the way you smell. The way you affect me. You're like a drug…" He frowned and released her. "Are you? A drug?"

"I don't know. Does it matter?"

"Yeah, it matters. I'd like to think I still had some control."

"You have control. We're just sitting here and talking."

"Except every time I touch you all I want to do is rip your clothes off and take you on the floor. How is that having control?"

Oh *Gott*. She wouldn't stop him, either. "Maybe what you're feeling is plain old lust. Did you ever think of that?"

"Right. Lust." He rubbed his face with both hands. "Would you please leave? I can't think clearly with you here."

His words stung, but were understandable. She couldn't think clearly in his presence, either. Still, she'd been looking forward to being alone with him all weekend, now she'd be lucky if he'd even want to date her again. "Okay. Sure. I hope you'll call, but if not, I'll see you Monday." She picked up her purse and stood.

"Before you go, would you answer a stupid question?"

"Sure."

"If you're this nearly four-hundred-year-old vampire like you claim, how come you don't know how to drive? Wouldn't you have learned when the automobile was, I don't know, invented? So why now?"

"My late husband drove me everywhere and it's recently come to my attention that he might have been a little protective of me. After he died, it was hard for me to mingle with mortals, to be taken seriously, looking as young as I do. But in order to keep my job, I was told to start mingling and that I would begin with driver's ed. I swear, it's only a coincidence we met. But it's one I wouldn't take back for anything in the world. You're the first person ever to make me feel alive and I'd like to think you feel the same. But if not, I won't bother you anymore. Goodnight, Ben."

She left him sitting there, looking broken. Her heart was certainly headed that way.

She called Perry for a ride. When he pulled up to the curb, she climbed inside and prepared herself for the barrage of questions he must have.

"Who took your lollipop?"

Victoria shut the door. "He knows. I told him."

"Holy shit. That bad?"

She shrugged. "He thinks he doesn't have free will around me. Like I'm a drug controlling him. I don't know how to prove to him I'm not. *Hölle*, I'm not even sure if I'm not. I'm thinking maybe I do want to meet this Perfect Mate Jack and John are bringing back. If I'm as attracted to him as I am to Ben or was to Justin, or he's attracted to me, then maybe Ben has a point."

"Do you really want to know?"

No, but what other option did she have? She couldn't very well prove she wasn't a drug if she didn't know for sure.

* * * *

With Van Halen blasting in his ears, Ben lay back on the bench and lifted the dumbbells above him. Even the exercises hadn't worn him out enough to collapse in bed. After this set of reps, he would run on the treadmill and hope the noise wouldn't wake Susannah.

Of all the things Victoria could have told him, being a vampire was certainly not on his list. Hell, it wasn't even in the vicinity of any list. How could he not have noticed her fangs? Sure, she seemed to have control over them, but still… Wouldn't they have popped out when he'd bled all over her? But Susannah never said anything. Neither had anyone else. Did she really have that kind of control? Or had she controlled them?

He shook his head. This was all giving him a headache. He should just concentrate on his reps instead. Where was he? "Six. Seven. Eight."

Victoria was certainly nothing like the vampires he'd read about. Of course, those were fictitious monsters and she was… Shit. A for real monster?

Were they really dangerous, though? He'd met three and none of them seemed to show an interest in his blood. Not that he could see if they'd been drooling or not.

A shake of his leg nearly caused him to drop the dumbbells. He bolted upright and yanked the buds from his ears. "Damn it, Susannah—"

"It's not Susannah," Perry said. "I did call you first. You shouldn't play your music so loud."

"How the hell did you get in here?"

Perry took the weights from Ben's grasp. "You'd be surprised what I can do."

It was well past midnight and a vampire was calling? Had something happened to Victoria? That little thought plunged his heart into his stomach. "Is Victoria okay?"

"Yeah, she's fine, physically. Now, mentally…" He chuckled as he placed a towel in Ben's hands. "Sorry, bad habit. Works better when she's in the room."

Ben wiped the sweat off his brow. "Then why are you here?"

"We need to talk."

"Here's not a good place. Susannah—"

"Is asleep. I made sure. You know, your sister is kind of cute."

Ben froze. Perry thought Susannah was…cute? What exactly had he meant by that? "You're not planning on…doing anything with her. Are you?"

"Doing? Oh… No. Now, if she were like you… But unfortunately she's not. Figures." Perry snorted.

"And if she were? Like me?"

"Well… We'd probably be having a different discussion."

"And what discussion are you here for? Or were you looking

for a meal?"

Perry patted his shoulder. "Now, now, Teach. If I was looking for a meal, I'd find someone I could…uh, distract."

"Like my sister?"

"Okay. Yeah, like your sister. But only if she was interested in knowing me. You gonna introduce us?"

Perry and his sister? Could it get any weirder? "Uh…no?"

"Don't think she'll go for a twenty-six-year-old, is that it?"

"You're only twenty-six years old?"

"Well… I was turned at twenty-six. We won't go into how old I actually am. But why are we talking about this? Oh yeah. I'm not here for her, okay? I came here to talk about Victoria and you."

Ben lowered his shoulders. "She's not even going to let me sleep on it, is she?"

"Oh hell, she'd skewer me if she knew I was here. Or at least she'd try. No. I have a little experience with Perfect Mates, so I thought—"

"Excuse me? Perfect Mates?"

"She didn't tell you that's what you are?"

Ben nearly laughed. Vampires must have some strange criteria. "How am I perfect? Because last I saw, being blind doesn't really fit that bill."

"It has nothing to do with you, physically. Well, except for your brain. I guess that would make it physically unless you think that would make it mentally then—"

Ben held his hand out and shut the vampire up. The man knew how to ramble. "Fine. It's my brain. I get it. How does my brain make me perfect?"

"Because you can't be controlled. Which means your feelings are real. And then once you're bonded—"

"Bonded?"

"Oh crap. She said you knew." Perry sighed. "Forget about that part, then."

"No. What do you mean by bonded?"

"It doesn't matter. No bonding can happen without your consent and this really should be a discussion between the two of you."

"Then what are you here for?"

"To tell you that if you feel anything toward Victoria, it's real. Not some drug. Not from someone controlling you."

"But my scent—"

"Is just an attraction. Hell, it should stink for the rest of us, warning us all like that robot yelling, 'Danger, Will Robinson!'"

Ben could almost picture the man waving his arms like the robot on the old television show and nearly laughed. "But I don't smell different to you."

"No, but I don't find you attractive, either. That's not to say you're ugly—"

Ben held his hand out again. "Perry, is there a point to your statement? If my scent does nothing to you, then what's the problem?"

"Your scent might not do anything to me, but I still can't control you. And a mortal who discovers what we are and can't be controlled can get into some serious trouble. But I digress."

Now the man was worried about digressing? "How would I get into trouble?" That sounded worse than being put in prison.

"By blabbing what you know, how else? We can't feasibly discover and control everyone you come in contact with, but we could easily stop you, if you get my drift."

Ben swallowed the lump that had suddenly formed in his throat. "You mean, kill me?"

"We've never been forced to do that, but yeah."

Ben ran his fingers through his hair. Yeah, that was way worse than prison. "Shit."

"So don't blab, okay? Then you'll be cool. Besides, if you truly are Victoria's Perfect Mate, you're not going to want to."

"And how do you know if I am or not?"

"I don't. Not really, But I was attracted to a Perfect Mate who was attracted to another vampire. It's not like I loved her or anything like that, but…well, she didn't like me so much. And if that wasn't a slap in the balls. I mean, what woman doesn't like this?"

The pause lasted longer than was comfortable. "You don't expect an answer, do you?"

Perry laughed and punched Ben lightly in the arm. "You know, I honestly forgot you're blind, Teach. But trust me, I don't have any problem with attracting the ladies and I don't have to use my powers of seduction, either."

Ben nodded. "Good to know." While he was curious as to exactly what kind of seduction powers a vampire possessed—and whether Victoria also possessed this power—that was a conversation for another time. "So what happened with this woman? Did you affect her?"

"If I did, it was minor. But she had someone to compare it to. I only had her, so I couldn't tell how strong or weak the attraction was. But it's just an attraction. Doesn't mean anything other than that. Do you like Victoria? Oh, wait. Stupid question. Of course you do. I saw it on your face that first day."

Sure, he liked her, but a Perfect Mate sounded…permanent. And what did Perry mean by bonding? Shit. He only wanted to date Victoria, not be glued to her. Or did he?

Perry sat on the bench and put his arm around Ben's shoulders. "I know there's a lot to take in. It's not everyday you discover vampires are for real, huh? But Victoria cares about you. A lot. And it has nothing to do with the way you smell or how your touch affects her. I mean, those are great perks, but it's not the reason she likes you. It has to do with you. You have to decide whether or not you can live with a vampire. Because if you can't, the sooner you break it off, the better. Not just for her, but for you, too."

"How so?"

"I'm not sure, but I think the longer you two are together, you might get these urges."

"Urges? What kind of urges?" He already wanted to make love to her. What other urges could there be?

"For her to bite you."

Ben grabbed his neck. "What?"

Perry chuckled. "You heard me, but it's only a speculation on my part. Could be different with you. But if you offer your blood and she takes it, it will lead to bonding, which is a discussion you should have with her. That's if you decide you want to be with her." He rose. "Sleep tight, Teach. I'll let myself out."

Ben cradled his head in his hands.

Vampires? Perfect Mates? Bonding? Hell, he may never sleep again.

CHAPTER 12

Victoria leaned against the hallway wall and rubbed her handkerchief. The Perfect Mate lay in the room across from her, but she wasn't getting any draw toward the door.

If her experiment didn't work, if this unknown man's draw was as strong as Ben's, how could she convince Ben her feelings for him were real? Would she be able to convince herself?

And if she wasn't drawn to Daugherty, would Ben believe her? He might think she'd say anything and he wouldn't be wrong thinking that way.

Abe leaned up beside her and smiled. He really was a cutie, but at six-foot-seven, he towered over her, making her feel younger than her looks. He smoothed the hair away from his eyes. "What are you doing here? I thought you weren't interested in finding a mate."

"I'm not, but I'm willing to confirm whether or not he's a Perfect Mate. I still don't think we have a right to hold him. No one would believe him anyway." But then she wouldn't be able to do what she needed to do and she really wanted some answers. Probably more than Barnet did, and that man was obsessed.

"Victoria, you know it doesn't matter. Besides, he's our best opportunity to find a connection between the three of them and give us some idea of why we haven't discovered that many."

"Oh, I think I know why," Jack said as he approached them. He squeezed Victoria's shoulder. "Thanks for keeping Sunshine company. I sometimes think she still has trouble being a vampire."

"If there's any trouble, it's in your head. But it was my pleasure. I'd forgotten what it was like to actually go out feeding with someone."

"Hey, don't keep me in suspense," Abe said to Jack. "What's your theory?"

Jack leaned his shoulder against the wall on the other side of Victoria. "Seeing what Dalton did to Daugherty, I'm guessing other Perfect Mates have been killed."

"Killed?" Abe said.

The pit of Victoria's stomach churned. Bad enough she'd suspected that, but if Jack did, too, then maybe it was true.

"Think about it. What did Derek want to do with Justin when he discovered Justin couldn't be controlled?"

Abe rubbed his face. "I thought he did that out of jealousy."

"That probably played a big part of it, but he was ready to leave Justin alone until he discovered he couldn't control him. He told me so himself. So it's a good thing we're keeping Daugherty here. We're basically saving his life."

Yeah, but was it a life worth living?

Barnet emerged from the room and stared at the three of them. "What is this?"

"Victoria wants to see him," Abe said.

Barnet raised his eyebrows. "Are you feeling drawn to him?"

"No, not yet. But I didn't notice anything from Justin until after I had met him up close."

"What are you hoping to accomplish?"

A valid question, especially after the way she'd acted. If she couldn't convince them of her deceit, she was doomed. She shrugged. "I guess I'm curious to see if he's really a Perfect Mate. Aren't you all?"

Barnet nodded. "Fine. Why don't we all go in?"

All? While she was fairly certain she wouldn't act like a wild animal, she didn't need an audience if it turned out otherwise. But if she voiced her concern, they'd only grow suspicious.

With her heart rate approaching *allegrissimo*, Victoria walked in and braced herself for the scent of the sea. It's what she experienced with Justin and Ben, so why not Richard Daugherty? But for some reason, she couldn't take but two steps inside the room. *Gott*, she wasn't cheating on Ben, so why the guilty feeling?

A brown-haired woman was sitting in John's lap and she slid off when John stood. He looked at each Committee Member. "Change in plans?"

"No," Barnet said. "Just performing a little experiment. Victoria, Abe, I don't believe you've met Sarah Daugherty yet."

John's fiancée smiled and it reflected in her green eyes. She held out her hand. "I'm so happy to finally meet you. I've enjoyed our talks on the phone."

"Same here," Victoria said, taking Sarah's hand. When touching normal mortals, Victoria might catch an inadvertent thought, but here stood a Perfect Mate, and a bonded one at that. "I'm surprised to see you. I was told you didn't know Richard Daugherty."

"I don't, but I wanted a look around. I wish I did know him. Then maybe he wouldn't have to be a prisoner."

John one-armed Sarah across her shoulders and kissed her temple. "No one's a prisoner."

"Yet," Victoria finished. Everyone turned and stared at her. "Oh come on now. You might want to delude yourselves that we're keeping him for his own good, but that doesn't make it right. The right thing to do is to inform everyone Perfect Mates exist."

"Victoria, please," Barnet said. "This isn't the time."

Maybe not, but at least she wasn't the only one who felt that way.

John smiled at Victoria. "Should I wish you luck?"

She shook her head, but remained by the wall. It would only take about four steps and she'd be beside the bed. But that required taking those four steps.

"What are you waiting for?" Barnet asked.

Indeed, what was she waiting for? Either she was attracted or she wasn't. Knowing wouldn't change her desire for Ben. Would it?

Holding her breath, she shoved her handkerchief back in her pocket and stepped toward the sleeping man. His short-ish hair was as black as the night and his eyelashes would make any woman envious. Dark stubble covered his jaw and upper lip and contrasted sharply with his pale complexion. She pulled the chair alongside the bed and sat. Should she hold his hand or take a whiff? She settled for the latter and inhaled slowly through her nose. A faint scent, similar to Ben's, hit her. A wonderful sea breeze, and it wasn't near as potent as she'd feared.

"Well?" Barnet asked.

She turned and stared at him. "You seem more anxious than I

do. Why is that?"

"You're basically our only confirmation that this man is a Perfect Mate."

"So if I don't feel anything, we'll let him go?"

"No. We still can't control him."

"You mean Dalton can't control him. Has anyone else tried?"

"Victoria," Barnet said, dragging her name out as if she were a naughty child.

She turned back to the man and sighed. Guess there was only one way to confirm or deny what he was. She closed her eyes and took his hand in hers. A pleasing warmth filled her palm and his scent came alive, filling the room. She smiled. *Ben.* Heat shot up her arm and through her chest. She gasped at the suddenness of it and opened her eyes. The sensation was nice, but it wasn't as strong as Ben's. Because this man wasn't Ben. This man couldn't compare to Ben. She dropped his hand.

Barnet placed his hands on her shoulders. "So I'm guessing he is one."

Yeah, Daugherty might be one, but it was Ben she yearned for. Ben she craved. If he was a drug, it had nothing to do with being a Perfect Mate and everything to do with being a man. Her man. But how could she convince him?

She nodded. "I felt the same thing I did with Justin. I'd like to know how I affect him. How soon will he awaken?"

"Not for several hours. I just gave him another dose to keep him out," John said.

Barnet moved in front of her. "Why do you need to know that? I thought you weren't interested in starting a relationship."

"I'm not, but if I'm the one for him…" Except she wasn't. Her heart told her so. But if she was going for proof, might as well go all the way. Victoria looked up at Sarah. "You didn't feel anything with Perry, did you?"

"I did, but not with the intensity I feel with John. But I had a reference. He doesn't. Won't that make a difference?"

Yes it would. Victoria had her reference: Ben. Would that be enough for this man, or would he also need a reference? She looked toward Barnet. "Do you think Hilde would be willing to experiment? Put us both in the room with him and see if he's attracted to either of us?"

Barnet shook his head. "I won't ask her. It wouldn't be fair to her or Rolf."

Victoria lowered her head and pulled out her handkerchief. Barnet was right. It wasn't fair. None of this was fair. But how else would she get the proof Ben needed?

"I'll ask Sunshine," Jack said. "After I explain it all to her first."

No. Not Sunny. She had already smelled Ben. If she smelled Richard, she'd know about Ben and then blurt it out. How could she not? "You don't have to do that, Jack. We'll figure something else out."

"Nonsense. I'm not threatened by this guy. It'll be her decision, but I'm guessing she'll want to help."

"You're braver than I would be," Barnet said.

Scheisse. Victoria could only hope Sunny refused to help or she'd have some explaining to do with Barnet.

CHAPTER 13

Victoria shut down the library computer and headed toward her room. Amazing what information she could obtain with Richard's driver's license and credit card. Armed with useful information, she could now search the Daugherty book for a connection between Richard and Sarah.

Her nerves were shot waiting for the mortal to awaken. Or maybe it was because once Sunny got a whiff of him—and she would since she'd been more than happy to help—she would question why he smelled like Ben. Victoria covered her face. *Gott.* She needed to get Sunny alone and beg her to keep quiet, but Jack was with her, and when the two of them were together… Well, they weren't newlyweds for nothing.

Oh, what was she thinking? Jack could probably read Sunny, especially if she was nervous, and who wasn't nervous keeping a huge secret?

Should she just come clean with Barnet? If she had any kind of inkling that Ben would want to spend eternity with her, she might. Instead, his knowledge could get him locked up as sure as Richard Daugherty was locked up. She couldn't do that to Ben. Not to mention he'd never forgive her if it happened.

Oh, why couldn't it be night? She'd brave the streets and head on over to Ben's. And she could do it, too. Maybe.

As she turned the corner, she nearly ran into Sarah.

"Oh, thank God," Sarah said, her hand on her chest. "I thought I was lost for sure."

Victoria laughed. "It can get confusing in here if it's your first visit. What are you looking for? And where's John?"

"You. And John is still with Richard Daugherty. I was going a little stir crazy and John suggested I help you with your research."

"What? John's not entertaining? I thought you Perfect Mate couples had it perfect."

Sarah blushed. "Kind of hard to be entertaining when you're observing a patient. And that room looks too much like a hospital."

She hugged herself and shuddered.

"Bad memories?" When Sarah nodded, Victoria said, "Well, it just so happens, you can help me."

She took Sarah to her room and then picked up the Daugherty book. "I'm hoping with the information I gathered today I'll find a connection between you and Richard." She opened the marked page. "This is you and your family."

"Oh wow! What do the numbers in front of our names mean?"

"Do you see how your number is the same as your father's, but longer by one, with a number one? It indicates you're his first born. The last number of your father's indicates he was the second born to his father." Victoria thumbed to the index. "Now, let's see if Richard is in here."

After checking all the Richards in the book without success, Victoria searched Richard's father's name. On the third instance she hit pay dirt. "Oh my God! There they are. Richard Daugherty's parents. No wonder I couldn't find them. Their children aren't listed."

"Are we related?"

"Yes. In fact, the first five numbers are the same." Victoria turned to the page indicating the couple. "You descend from the second born and Richard descends from the sixth."

"Hey, I know them!" Sarah tapped the page indicating her shared heritage. "Well, I guess I should say I know the story about them. He'd gotten grief for marrying a witch."

"What? Witches are real?"

"Vampires are real, aren't they?"

"Yes, but I never knew—"

Sarah laughed. "Sorry, couldn't resist. I have no clue if witches are real or not, and she wasn't really a witch. But she did descend from someone who was hung as a witch during the Salem Witch

Trials. Which I guess means I do, too."

"Salem Witch Trials? How interesting."

"Yeah. Her name was Susannah Martin. I think there's a story about her." Sarah's phone went off and she answered it.

Victoria smiled. Susannah Martin? Could it be that easy? Could that be the link to the Perfect Mates? Except Susannah Martin wasn't a real witch. But if Ben also descended from her line… His sister's name couldn't be a coincidence, could it?

Sarah put her phone away. "That was John. Richard is starting to come around. John's already notified Jack and Barnet."

Great, just what she needed. Now she'd never get to warn Sunny beforehand. *Gott*, she was doomed. She put the book down and headed for the door with the enthusiasm of a convicted criminal.

"You act like you don't want to do this," Sarah said as she followed Victoria into the hallway. "Do you still miss your husband?"

Last week Victoria would have said yes. Since meeting Ben… Henrik barely rated a thought. "I guess I'm more afraid I won't have a choice in the matter. If he has a reaction to me…"

"Did you find him attractive?"

"He was okay." And maybe if she hadn't already met Ben, she would have been interested.

"Just okay?" Sarah smirked. "Then he's not for you."

"What do you mean? How can you be sure?"

"I was attracted to John long before I officially met him. Contact only enhanced what I felt. And yes, I did feel something when Perry touched me, but I wasn't attracted to him. You understand?"

"So, it's not like a drug?"

"Well, after John took my blood, yeah, I guess it was. But before that?" Sarah shrugged. "More like chemistry, which, with the right people, is kind of like a drug, isn't it?"

"See, that's what I thought."

"Someone else thought otherwise?"

Victoria yearned to spill the truth to Sarah, but no one could learn about Ben. Not yet anyway. "More like an argument with myself."

Sarah scrunched her eyebrows in confusion. Luckily, they arrived at their destination before Victoria could make it any worse.

The hallway was crowded and there was no getting to Sunny. Even a handhold would help as Victoria could silently beg her not to say anything about Daugherty's scent, but Jack stood between the two of them making it downright difficult to get a touch.

Barnet stood in front of the door. "Before we go in put on these contacts. We don't need him seeing our sparkly eyes."

Since Ben was blind, Victoria had forgotten that bit about Perfect Mates. According to Sarah and Justin, the eyes of vampires glittered to them.

"We?" Victoria took a set of contacts. "Shouldn't only Sunny and I go in? We don't need to spook the man."

"I don't want to spook him, either. Or make him suspicious. What do you have in mind?"

"I thought I'd go in first. If he has a favorable reaction to me, then Sunny could come in, maybe as a nurse. Bring in a pitcher of water or something. We should treat him as if he knows nothing."

"Where the hell are we going to get a nurse's uniform? Or a pitcher?"

"You can probably get away with wearing scrubs. There's gotta be something in the mall."

Barnet rubbed his face.

"Sunshine and I will go look," Jack said.

"Fine," Barnet said. "But don't be long. If the first part works out, I don't want him awake for long."

Jack took Sunny's hand and they rushed away. Victoria let out a relieved breath. If Daugherty didn't find her attractive, then Sunny wouldn't be needed at all and wouldn't that be fine and dandy?

"John stays in the room," Barnet said.

"Of course." As long as Sunny stayed out, Victoria would be fine.

She inserted the contacts. Stupid things were scratchy. How did mortals wear these? After blinking several times to get used to the feeling, she opened the door. Their prisoner didn't move, but her touch earlier brought alive what had lain dormant. Even from the doorway, his scent propelled her forward. Why'd he have to smell so good?

"He's still coming around," John said. "You're drawn to him now, aren't you?"

"Yes." She really wished she wasn't.

"As much as you were drawn to Justin?"

She nodded. "But I wasn't interested in him. Or this man, either."

"If that's the case, then you won't have the added stress of fending off other vampires. Perry never had the desire to fend off me. At least that he admitted to anyway."

As if Perry would admit to anything that made him look bad. "But you…"

"Wanted to strangle every vampire who touched Sarah." John chuckled.

Exactly the way Katarina had acted with Justin and the protectiveness that emerged whenever Victoria was in Ben's presence. She couldn't care less if another vampire showed interest in Richard Daugherty. That gave her hope.

"So then maybe I'm not the—" Before she could finish, Daugherty opened his eyes.

He tugged on the straps securing his arms. "Who are you? Where am I?"

Victoria stood by the bed and was met with the darkest blue eyes she'd ever seen. "Easy, Mr. Daugherty. You're in a hospital. Do you remember what happened?"

"I was attacked. Someone bit my neck. Why am I strapped in?"

"You were hurting yourself in your sleep and you have no wounds to indicate someone bit you." Only because they'd made sure to heal them.

"What do you mean no wounds? That man practically ripped out my neck!" He struggled against the straps. "I demand you free me."

She placed her hand on his arm and his warmth nearly made her gasp. "I'm sorry, Mr. Daugherty. For your own safety, we can't do that."

His eyes widened and he looked down at her hand. "What the fuck did you do to me?"

"Do you have a family member we can contact?"

"What, so you can make them a prisoner, too? No way."

"Mr. Daugherty. We only want to help you." Victoria sighed. He acted as she suspected he would: like someone being held against their will. She nodded to John to administer the sedative. This man was clearly not interested in her, so there wasn't any need for Sunny.

John filled a needle with the drug.

"What are you doing?" Daugherty screamed. "I have rights. You can't hold me against my will!" His words slowly lost their impact as the drug took affect.

Her heart went out to the man. She couldn't see how he'd ever get his life back again. But at least she had her answer. If Ben had any feelings for her, they were real, not manufactured.

Now to get him to believe.

* * * *

Ben dried the last plate and placed it back in the cupboard. Susannah usually washed the dinner dishes, but he'd insisted she let him do it. If he had any fantasies about living on his own, he should make sure he could do it.

The surprising part had been Susannah agreeing with him.

The sad part was wondering if he should even bother. If he couldn't have a life with Victoria—except the thought of not being with her tore him up inside—then why shake things up? Susannah seemed happy to have him around. He certainly didn't mind the company.

"I'm going out," she yelled from the living room. "I don't know when I'll return."

Ben dried his hands on the towel. "Where are you going?"

"None of your business." She kissed him on the cheek. "You gonna be okay?"

He smiled. "You have a date, don't you? Who is this guy? When will I meet him?"

"Stop jumping to conclusions, will you? I'll tell you everything when I'm good and ready, okay?"

He couldn't fault her there. Hadn't he wanted to keep Victoria to himself? Still, if his sister was dating... Shit. She wasn't dating Perry, was she? No, couldn't be. He'd seen her for the first time last night and she hadn't left the house all day. Good, good. She was seeing someone else. Ben couldn't hold the grin back. Hot damn, his sister was dating. "Have fun."

"I'll do my best. What about you? Is Victoria coming over?"

He'd never told her about the other night. In fact, he'd made sure to stay out late enough so it would appear his date went on as planned. If he came to terms with Victoria being a vampire, he certainly didn't want Susannah suspecting anything was wrong.

She'd never like Victoria, then.

"No. She has to work tonight."

"Work, huh? Well, don't get into any trouble. I'll see you in the morning."

The door shut softly, leaving him with the ticking of a clock he'd never seen to keep him company. He'd rather have Victoria keep him company. But could he accept her in his life knowing what she was? And how would he ever be able to decide?

* * * *

Graham lay back on the hotel bed and waited for Susannah. Just one bit of insurance—along with a quick fuck—and then he'd go over to Headquarters. One way or another Victoria would be his. If that meant killing Martin, he'd do it. Accidents happened to the guy all the time anyway. No one would suspect a thing, same as no one suspected Graham had been behind the little fender bender the other night.

He was through with fender benders, though.

A knock sounded. Right on time. He opened the door to a smiling Susannah.

He would miss her. She'd been the surprise through all this. Never would have believed he could get attached to a mere mortal and in only a couple of days, but some things were worth more than a nice fuck.

Like a sweet-looking seventeen-year-old and the back door to the Committee.

CHAPTER 14

Victoria paced the entrance foyer of Headquarters. She'd been waiting all day for sunset—so she could travel to Ben's—and what had she gone and done? Only mention the familial link between Sarah and Richard to Barnet. He had insisted on hearing more, not that there was much more to say. But if she'd asked to leave, Barnet would have grown suspicious.

As soon as he released her, she'd gone to Perry's only to find the man gone. In fact, he hadn't been at Headquarters all day. Figured. The one time she needed the man, he'd found that day to run off doing…whatever.

He wouldn't even answer his damn cell, so she'd texted him a time to meet. If he didn't show in another ten minutes, she'd have to assume he was ignoring those, too. And if he was ignoring those, there would be no visiting Ben tonight. She couldn't very well appear on his doorstep a nervous wreck—a strong possibility if forced to venture out on her own.

"Ah, just the way it should be," Perry said as he entered from the mall. "You waiting on me. I think I like it."

Relief washed over her and joy filled her heart. She would get to see Ben tonight. "Well, don't get used to it." She grabbed Perry's elbow and tugged him in the direction of the garage. "Come on. I need you to drive me…somewhere." Damn. She almost said Ben's name. Who knew what ears were listening in?

"Somewhere? You mean Teach's."

"Shhh! Barnet's office isn't that far away."

He yanked his arm free. "Did he call you?"

"What? Who? Oh… No."

He shook his head. "Aren't you going to give the man a chance to think about it? I'm sure he'll call when he's ready to talk."

Or he'd call to break it off. She wanted to avoid that. "I only want to see him. Make sure he's okay."

"Sure you do. In any case, I'm not your chauffeur no matter what you think. You ever think about taking a cab, or maybe, hmmm, let's see…walk?"

"I don't know the address," she muttered. A weak excuse, even to her own ears. Sure, Ben had mentioned it when Perry drove him home, but that hadn't meant she was listening. Or paying any attention to her surroundings. Of course not. She'd been too busy enjoying Ben.

"Uh huh." Perry crossed his arms and parked his hip against the receptionist desk. "That's never stopped you from finding out before, now has it?"

"No, but I've been busy."

"Sure. Well then, let me save you the work." He pulled out his cellphone. "I'll text you his address. How about that?"

"Why can't you take me?"

"Because maybe I don't want to," he yelled. "Maybe I don't want to witness another perfect mating."

Victoria panicked. "Shush. Do you want everyone to hear?"

"I don't care who hears me."

"What's the matter with you? You didn't seem to mind matchmaking the other night."

"Yeah, well, that was before…"

"Before what? Before you knew what he was or before Sarah's arrival?" Victoria had heard that Perry hadn't even seen John since he'd announced his upcoming marriage to Sarah. "Is that what this is about? Are you saying you felt something for Sarah? Is that it?"

"Didn't you feel something when you met Justin?"

"Who told you that? Katarina? You know her take on the events are a bit biased. I was curious, okay? Yes, he smelled good and I liked it when I touched him. Didn't mean I wanted to make out with him."

"You didn't want to sample him. Just a tiny bit?"

"Truthfully, his scent was intriguing, but he was Katarina's. It never even crossed my mind." And she had no such desires toward

Richard. *Scheisse.* Was it possible Ben was safe from most vampires?

"What about Teach?"

She wanted to more than sample Ben, but wouldn't voice that opinion. Instead, she nodded. "Maybe a little."

He frowned and narrowed his eyes. "I suggest you wait until he calls you; but if you can't, call a cab. I'm busy." With that, he left.

"Wait! Perry!" She dashed out into the mall and ran smack-dab into Graham.

"Hey, sweetness. So glad I ran into you." He chuckled. "You get it? Ran?"

"Funny." Perry was long gone and now she was stuck with Graham? Sure, Graham had a car, but no way would she ask him for a ride to Ben's. She plastered on her Committee smile, hoping a pleasing attitude would get rid of the man. "What brings you here?"

"You. I came to take you out on an actual date. We'll do whatever you want. What do you say?"

"Graham…" How many times would she have to tell him no?

He grabbed her upper arms. "You know that blind guy can't give you what I can, Victoria."

And she could never give Graham what he wanted. "Don't you want someone who's in love with you?"

"You weren't in love with Henrik when you married him, but came to love him. Why not with me?"

"That was different. For one, I was mortal and that's the way things were done back then."

"So…what? You're not even going to give me a chance?"

She wrenched herself free. "I'm sorry, Graham."

"Well, maybe you'll change your tune when I tell you what Henrik was up to prior to his untimely death."

"The only thing he was up to was planning our vacation." After decades of her whining, Henrik had finally given in to going back to Germany. Now she might never see her homeland because there was no way she'd go back by herself.

"It wasn't just a vacation. I know for a fact he was looking to get permission to turn another."

"What? No he wasn't."

"I have proof. A letter he sent to the European Committee Head."

"You have a letter and you're just now telling me? Please, I wasn't born yesterday."

"I was hoping I wouldn't need to use it. If you'll be mine, no one will ever know."

"Why should I care who knows? Henrik is dead."

"Oh, sweet, Victoria. If this gets out, people will suspect Henrik's death wasn't an accident. And who better to kill him than his spurned wife?"

"Are you threatening me?"

"If it gets you to change your mind, yeah."

"I can't believe you'd want me like that."

He grabbed her around the waist. "I'll take you any way I can." He pulled her in and kissed her, ground his erection against her, and slobbered all over her face.

"Stop it." She shoved him away and wiped her mouth. "Tell whoever you want about Henrik. It's not changing a thing."

"Then how about I tell your Committee members about Martin?"

Her heart stilled. He couldn't be suggesting he knew. Could he? "What are you talking about?"

"About how he can't be read or controlled. Seems like a danger to our society if you ask me. I'm sure your buddies will feel the same way."

"He's not a threat to us." Graham, on the other hand, could be a huge threat to Ben.

"He could be if he found out about us."

"But he's not. Why do you think I stopped you from talking the other night?" Somehow she would have to protect Ben. But how?

Graham grabbed her hands and whispered, "No one has to know if you'll only be mine."

Not likely. Her heart was already taken. Guess it was time to come clean with Barnet. "Fine."

He grinned. "You mean it?"

Not in the way he thought. "Come with me."

She only hoped she was doing the right thing. And that Ben wouldn't come to hate her.

* * * *

Graham couldn't believe his good fortune. He should have bribed Victoria before, then he wouldn't have had to go through all the trouble with Susannah. Okay, maybe she wasn't trouble, but thinking of ways to get to Martin without Victoria suspecting anything had been downright exhausting. If he could get away with it, he'd just kill Martin. But then he wouldn't have a reason to be with Susannah and he kind of liked having her around. In fact, he'd left her sleeping in his room in case he hadn't found Victoria.

Once he and Victoria sealed the deal, he'd go back and remove the suggestion he'd implanted in Susannah. He'd never committed murder before, so why start now? Besides, Victoria might renege if anything should happen to Martin. Whatever did she see in that mortal anyway?

He followed her down the hallway. Damn, they were going to do it now. He couldn't wait to strip her bare and bury his cock deep inside her. He'd been dreaming of this day for centuries.

She arrived at a door he didn't recognize and opened it. What was wrong with her room? Maybe this one was soundproof. Was she a screamer? That thought made him even harder.

"What's the matter?" Barnet asked.

Not a room but the old goat's office. She shut the door and Graham turned to Victoria. What was she up to? Getting the Head's permission or some shit like that? Last he saw, two vampires could get it on without the Committee getting involved.

"I have a confession to make," she said.

Confession? What the hell was she doing?

Barnet eyed Graham. "About what?"

"I've found another and Graham knows about him."

Another? Another what?

This news did not bode well with Barnet. He frowned and rose from his seat behind his desk. "So you didn't miscount." When Victoria shook her head, he continued, "Well, that explains a lot. I assume you're interested in this one?"

She nodded.

No. No. No. She was interested in him—Graham. "What are you doing, Victoria?"

"Coming clean. I don't love you, Graham, and I never will. And if I have to expose Ben to save him, I will."

He fisted his hands to keep from throttling her. She would regret this decision. Martin was toast.

* * * *

Victoria paced the confines of Barnet's office. "I can't believe you let him go with only a warning. He's dangerous."

Graham promising to keep his mouth shut was like a bird promising not to fly away. Just wasn't possible. Most likely he was already headed over to Ben's and her sitting in Barnet's office wouldn't protect him from that idiot. But first she might have to protect Ben from Barnet.

"To whom?" Barnet asked. "This Perfect Mate you failed to tell me about? Why would he bother with him?"

"Because he's jealous. I have to go."

Barnet shut his door and blocked her from exiting. "Not right now, you don't. Graham may be jealous, but he's not stupid. Plus he's always been a bit wishy-washy when it came to taking action. Why Henrik ever bothered to turn him, I'll never know."

"What?" How had she known so little about her late husband? Victoria sat in one of the chairs facing Barnet's desk. "I didn't know Henrik turned Graham."

"They were best friends until Henrik turned you. That's when he realized Graham had manipulated him into turning you sooner than he'd planned."

She'd suspected Graham had fed her a story before, but to discover… "Why didn't Henrik ever tell me this?"

Barnet shrugged. "Guilt? He'd sworn me to secrecy, but since he's no longer here and Graham is in the picture, you need to know the truth. Graham had threatened Henrik on numerous occasions, but never went through with any of them. The man is all bark and no bite."

Didn't mean he wouldn't follow through with Ben. Henrik was a formidable foe. Ben was merely mortal. Only she could protect him, but she couldn't very well do that sitting in Headquarters.

Barnet sat in the chair beside her. "Now, why didn't you tell me about this Perfect Mate earlier?"

She wouldn't be able to leave until Barnet got some answers. Well, she'd give him some answers. Only ones he didn't want to hear. "Because I didn't want him caged up like an animal."

"Victoria…" He drew out her name on a sigh. "I'm beginning to understand why we're not hearing about these Perfect Mates. If you care for this man, then what's the problem? Doesn't he care for you?"

The concern in Barnet's voice melted her resolve. He might have a slight obsession with Perfect Mates, but he'd always had her best interests at heart. "He did before I told him what I am. Now I'm not so sure."

"I'm sure he only needs time to consider his options. Is he one of the students in your class? Damn, I can't believe there's one in the Atlanta area."

"He's not a student. He's the teacher."

"Teacher?" Barnet frowned. "That doesn't seem appropriate."

"I'm not a child!"

"I'm sorry. I didn't mean to imply you were. But he doesn't, well, didn't know that at the time, did he?"

"I met him before the class started. He didn't know I was his student and I had no idea he was the teacher. And he did have concerns with my age until he looked up my record. He thought I was twenty-two."

"You're going to have to bring him here. You know that, don't you?"

"Why? So you can cage him up like Daugherty? He's not going to tell anyone."

Barnet stood and rubbed his face. "No one is caging anyone, but you know the rules. He knows about us. That means I talk to him. Tonight. What's your young man's name? Ben, right?"

If she rubbed her handkerchief any rougher, she might end up with a hole in the fabric. Why'd he have to ask the one question she'd rather not answer? "Yes, his name is Ben."

"And his last name?" When she remained mute, Barnet frowned. "Don't tell me his last name is Daugherty."

"It's not."

"Then what is it? Don't make me retrieve that information."

And he would, too, she'd no doubt in that. She put the handkerchief down. "Martin. His name is Ben Martin."

She might as well have said Daugherty. Barnet's eyes widened and his eyebrows shot upward. "What? And you didn't think to tell me that?"

"It's a common name."

"Except when two Perfect Mates descend from one Susannah Martin. I can't believe you kept this from me. You know how important it is to find a connection."

"You mean important to you."

He sat beside her. "Do you honestly feel that way? Can't you see it's important to all vampires? Look at how you're reacting now. This is what I expect will happen if word gets out before we know all the answers. Is that what you want?"

"No, of course not." Didn't mean she wanted to be held as a demonstration, either. Barnet might not plan on it being that way, but how could it not?

"You wait here. I'll go get Perry to drive you over and bring your Mr. Martin here."

Thank goodness Barnet hated using his phone. She wasn't about to tell him Perry wasn't in the building, and she wasn't about to wait for Perry to take his ever-loving time to return. Once Barnet departed, she rushed quietly to the mall.

It was closed for business, but music and voices echoed against the walls. Mortals were drinking and doing whatever at the bars located at the opening of the Underground. She ran down the darkened hall, the lit exit signs guiding her way.

Using the employee entrance, she pushed through the door. People milled about the area and she stayed close to the wall as fear threatened to jettison her heart into space. She could do this. Ben's life depended on it. But where were the taxis?

"Well, well, well. I didn't think you had it in you." Perry stood to her right, leaning against the wall, staring at the throng of mortals.

Scheisse. If he was here, she didn't have much time at all. Unless she got him to help. "I don't, but it's imperative I get to Ben before Graham does. He's jealous and threatened Ben's life. If you won't help me, will you help Ben?"

"That's a low blow, and you know it." He pulled his vibrating cell from his pocket. "What the hell does Barnet want now? Can't I get free from this place?"

Whatever reasons Perry had for not wanting to be around could only count in her favor. "Then don't answer it. Help me—I mean, Ben. Help Ben."

He raised one eyebrow. "What aren't you telling me?"

She hated thinking her only hope hinged on Perry. At least she had hope. She told him everything.

CHAPTER 15

Ben tossed the book on the couch. *'Salem's Lot* lost its appeal, or maybe it just scared the crap out of him. Vampires were real. And one had her sights on him.

Problem was, she didn't seem like a vampire. Not the kind from the horror books he'd read. Not once had she tried to bite his neck—or any other part of his body—so if she had any kind of blood lust, she hid it well.

Several raps came from the door followed by Victoria's panicked plea, "Ben? Ben? Are you there? Please answer the door."

Why would she be so worried? Was she having another panic attack or could something really be wrong? In his rush to the door, he tripped over the coffee table. Damn it! Thank goodness only the carpet met his face. He scrambled up and threw open the door.

She slammed into him. Instead of landing on the floor or crashing into a wall, he stayed upright. She hugged him tightly. "You're okay."

Or maybe her scent had grounded him. One whiff and he decided—he could not live without her. The erotic shock she always gave him was only a perk. How could he not want her all the time? So what if she was a vampire? He was blind and she wanted him.

He smoothed the back of her head. "Of course I'm okay. What's the matter, baby? Did you walk over here and get spooked?"

She pushed him into the room and the door clicked shut. "No,

Perry dropped me off, but Graham knows about you and I thought for sure…" She took a deep breath. "Doesn't matter. You're safe."

He took her hand and relished the jolt she gave his heart. "What does it matter if Graham knows about me? I thought I was only irresistible to female vampires."

"Yeah, but I wasn't ready to announce you to everyone. Not until I understood our relationship. That's if we still have one."

A relationship with a vampire. Sounded strange in his head, but felt right with his soul. As long as the vampire was her. "Perry knows about me. How is Graham different?"

"Perry doesn't want to marry me."

Her words froze his heart momentarily. "Marry? Do you love Graham?" *Please say no.*

"Oh *Gott*, no. I love you." She gasped and tugged to free her hand, but he wasn't giving her up. "*Scheisse.* I didn't mean to blurt it out like that."

"You love me?" He couldn't help but smile. That was way better than a no.

"Yes. And it has nothing to do with you being a Perfect Mate. I—"

"Shut up." He cupped her face and the contact sent a thrill straight to his groin. Instant hard-on. Better than any drug. He kissed the breath out of her until he pricked his tongue on something sharp. Damn. Her fangs. What had Perry said about her taking his blood? He pulled away.

With a ragged breath she sputtered her words. "Oh, Ben. I won't lie to you. I want to bite you, I want to taste you, but I won't. Do you understand? I might not be able to control my fangs, but I can control who I bite and I won't bite you unless you want me to. I won't even beg. You have my promise on that."

Ben caressed her face. He believed every word she'd said. The thought of her biting him didn't seem so scary any longer, but that bonding thing did. Maybe it scared her, too. Right now he didn't care about all that because there was something more important he wanted. "I believe you."

He pressed her against the door and savaged her mouth. But that wasn't enough. He caressed her breast. But that wasn't enough, either. He sought heaven, for he was sure she was it.

"Is Susannah here?" Even her breath was divine on his face.

He shook his head while he nuzzled her neck. "And she's not

expected back anytime soon. We have the place to ourselves."

"Good." She tangled her fingers in his, sending more shockwaves through his system, then ran her hands up his arms and over his biceps. "Ben? Are you okay with me being a vampire?"

The doubt in her voice pained him. She'd done nothing so terribly wrong except share a secret that had kept her safe. Safe from mortals. Well…mortals like him. At least he could ease her mind. He cupped her face and kissed her lightly on the lips. "Why don't we go to my room so I can show you how okay I am?"

"Oh, Ben." She wrapped her arms around him, but when she ground against his erection, he all but passed out from lack of air. "Which room is yours?"

He told her in a voice that might have cracked a wee bit, but how he managed to speak coherently at all became a mystery. If he wasn't so crazed for wanting her, he would have carried her, but with his luck, he'd run her into a wall or drop her. Not exactly a mood enhancer.

When they entered his room, he shut the door and locked it. Didn't need his sister barging in if she happened to call the night short.

"How much do you need me to do?" she asked.

"Do?"

"Do you need me to take charge?"

"Do you like to be in charge? You into BDSM or something?"

She chuckled. "No, although I wouldn't be against experimenting…later, but I mean… You're blind, so I wasn't sure. *Scheisse*. I'm ruining the mood."

"No, you're not." If anything, her talk of experimentation only got him harder. He sat on the edge of the bed and held his hand out. "Come here." When he positioned her in front of him, he grabbed her jean-clad hips and pulled her close so that she straddled his legs. "Sit."

As she settled on his lap, he ran his hands over the silky fabric of her blouse and unbuttoned the top button. "What color is your blouse?"

"It's pink and orange over a white background."

"Flowers?"

"More like flower petals, I guess. Big flower petals."

"Is it see-through?"

"No. I'm not that bold."

No, she seemed more proper than that. He pictured the blouse in his mind. "You look very pretty in it."

"You can see… Oh."

Slowly, he unbuttoned each button, picturing exposing her milky-white skin. As he slipped the garment off her shoulders, something lacey scratched him. He cupped her breasts, finding the source and eliciting a sharp inhale from her. "What color is your bra?"

"Black."

"Mmmm. Sexy. Did you wear it for me?"

She ran her fingers though his hair. "Everything I wear, I wear for you. You might not be able to see it, but you can feel it, right? Plus, it makes me feel, I don't know, sexy, I guess."

God, he wanted her. That she thought about him like that made him smile. He grabbed the back of her neck and ravaged her mouth. "You are sexy. Don't you forget it." Finding the connection in the back, he unhooked the bra, releasing the most perfect set of breasts—perfect because they filled his hands just right. Picturing beautiful rosy tips, he took one in his mouth and sucked, tonguing the nipple and making it grow hard.

Her skin was soft and not at all cold, something he almost expected. Sure, they'd held hands and kissed, but for some reason once he'd heard "vampire," he'd assumed cold. And un-dead. The beating of her heart told him she was far from dead.

Grabbing a handful of his hair, she moaned in pleasure. "That feels good."

"Just good? Then I'm not doing it right." Holding her by her hips, he stood and placed her on the bed. She beat him to the zipper, but he slipped the jeans off her legs. His clothes became history rather quickly and he lay beside her. His heart raced with desire.

While he sucked on her breast, he ran his hand over her flawless skin, along the indentation of her waist and the curve of her hip. As he reached the inside of her thigh, her scent intensified, filling him with a need. Part of her vampire physique or just her? He really didn't care any longer.

She kissed him and gripped his penis, making him harder than ever. "I want this. Please don't make me wait."

He fought the urge to come while removing her hand. "You

keep that up, and it'll be over before we get started. Let me get a condom."

"You don't need one. I can't get or give a disease, nor can I get pregnant. Just get in me already."

He smiled. "Impatient much?"

To tease her some more, he fingered her soft folds and she arched against him. She was wet, but he wanted her wetter. He sucked on her breast again while he flicked her clit.

"Ben Martin, I can overtake you," she said between raspy breaths.

"Yeah, but you won't, will you?"

She shuddered and arched as the orgasm took over her body. A string of German words spilled from her mouth. He covered her and entered her in one thrust. Now there was the heaven he'd sought. Between her tightness and the shockwave that rushed from his groin, he nearly cried out in ecstasy. He pounded into her and she grabbed onto his back. He'd managed to make her come a second time before his own release. And damn, what a release.

He would never let her go.

* * * *

Perry slammed the door leading from the garage. He'd thought he'd gotten away from Headquarters free and clear, but Victoria had to go and blab it all to Barnet. He hoped he'd given her enough time. He couldn't put off Barnet any longer. Now all he had to do was avoid the one person he didn't want to see—Sarah.

Damn Victoria anyway. Why couldn't she be uncontrollable around Justin? If only she'd been tempted to sample him, then maybe Perry wouldn't feel like such a turd for taking Sarah's blood the way he had. He could just blame it on the draw. But after what Victoria had said…he couldn't very well do that. Which meant only one thing…

Sarah might have been his if only he'd met her first. And hadn't pissed her off. Yeah, there was that to contend with, too.

But he hadn't met her first. John had. And she was John's.

Maybe if Susannah was also a Perfect Mate it wouldn't matter so much. But she wasn't a Perfect Mate and it mattered a heck of a lot.

Damn it. When would he find his own Perfect Mate?

As Perry approached Barnet's office, he rounded his shoulders. He had to make this look good unless he wanted his own hide in trouble. Storming through Barnet's office, he yelled, "What the ding dong day is so important?"

Barnet looked up from his paperwork. "What's gotten into you? I expect this kind of attitude from Victoria when it comes to you, but you… Nothing ever riles you."

"Oh, so I'm not entitled to have a bad day? I was feeding and this close to getting some, no thanks to you." He put his thumb and forefinger together to emphasize his point, because that was what everyone expected of him.

"Is that what took you so long to get here? You were after sex?"

"I'm always after sex. It's never bothered you before. So why now?"

Barnet stood. "Victoria's driver's ed teacher is a Perfect Mate."

"Is that so?" Shit. Did he sell it enough?

Fire nearly shot out of Barnet's eyes. "You knew already, didn't you? Damn it! Why didn't you tell me?" No good answer could come out of Perry's mouth, but it seemed as if Barnet wasn't expecting one as he waved his hand in the air. "Doesn't matter. What's done is done. She was supposed to wait here, but does she listen to me? No. I'm going to get her and the two of you will bring Mr. Martin here. Don't leave."

Leave? No way. He might run into the wrong people. But Barnet was sure to return madder than ever when he discovered Victoria had disappeared. Gotta play it cool, though. If Barnet even suspected he'd helped her, his butt would be in a sling.

"Hi, Perry. Wow. You clean up good."

He spun toward the door. Nooo! The one person he had hoped to avoid and there she stood in the doorway. The last time he'd seen Sarah she'd escaped from a serial killer and had been stabbed by a crazy vampire, so she had looked a bit on the ragged and pale side. Now? Her skin radiated a rosy glow. She looked divine. Too bad she no longer smelled of jasmine—of home. Once she'd bonded with Johnny, not only had her draw diminished, so did her scent. She smelled like any other mortal. And if that wasn't another stab in his heart.

Sarah placed one hand on her hip and the other on the outside wall, out of view. "What? No hello? No how are you? Do you hate me that much?"

"I don't know what Johnny's been feeding you, but I don't hate you. I thought it was the other way around." Not that she knew what he'd done, unless Johnny had told her, but why would he do that?

"I don't hate you."

Yeah, no way she knew what he'd done. "Good to know. Now, excuse me, but I have to go." He'd text Barnet to meet him at the van. Problem was, he'd have to pass Sarah to actually head on out to the van, and she wasn't moving.

"Can you spare a minute? We need to talk."

"I don't think that's a good idea."

"Why? Are you still drawn to me?"

Oh, he was drawn to her all right, and probably always would be. Just not in the way she meant. He shook his head. "That went away when you completed the bond."

"I never properly thanked you for saving John. If you hadn't, I don't know if I'd be alive today."

No one knew what would happen to a bonded mate if the bonded vampire perished. That was probably something no one wanted to discover.

"Johnny's my friend. I didn't do anything he wouldn't."

"So why aren't you taking his calls?"

He shrugged. What could he say? That he didn't deserve Johnny's friendship, because that was the truth.

"He told me what you did," she said.

Play it cool, play it cool. "Did?"

"Taking my blood. In Lima."

"Ah, shit. Listen, I'm sorry—"

"I forgive you."

"That's nice, but you see, I don't think I can forgive myself. Just leave me be. You'll be better off."

She shook her head. "Can't do that. I love John and he misses his friend. So why don't you two kiss and make up?"

"You know, I'm not really into that kind of thing."

She moved aside. Was she releasing him to find Johnny? No way would he do that, but if that's what it took for her to let him go, well, she could believe whatever she wanted. Perry headed for the door and Johnny blocked his way. Damn it. Had he been in the hallway this whole time?

"Well I'll be. I didn't think you'd ever get rid of that Hawaiian shirt."

There was no escape for Perry now. He should have never come back to Headquarters until he was assured the two of them had left.

"Yeah, well, Danielle bled all over it when you stabbed her. Kind of ruined it for me."

Johnny chuckled. "Then I guess I owe you a new one."

"Nah. I've gotten used to the new look anyway." He certainly wasn't going to piss off the next Perfect Mate he'd meet by looking grungy. "I hear congratulations are in order. When's the big day?"

"We haven't set a date yet. Kind of hoping you'll be my best man."

Best man? There was no way his friend could be serious. He chuckled. "Good one."

"I'm serious."

Perry swallowed the lump that had suddenly formed in his throat. "Even after what I did?"

"Yeah. Even after. Go figure." Johnny bridged the gap between them. "You're like a brother to me and brothers don't hold grudges. Plus, I know you're sorry. So what do you say, brother? Be my best man?"

Perry never had a brother, even as a mortal. That Johnny thought of him as such was more than he could dare dream. His eyes ached with unshed tears. Damn, was he turning into a sissy? No, he wasn't, but he could be a best man and he'd be the best best man ever. "Does this mean I can throw you a bachelor party?"

Sarah rolled her eyes and Johnny laughed.

Barnet barged inside his office. "Perry! Oh, hi Sarah, John. Sorry for the outburst, but I need Perry. Blasted woman ran off and I'm afraid only you know where she is."

* * * *

Victoria smiled. Ben was beautiful and he was hers.

His face tightened as the orgasm took him over the edge. He barked out her name in a possessive way. Never in her years had she felt so sated. So alive. Somehow she would convince him to become her Perfect Mate. Their connection had to be better than sight. Right? She'd gladly give up her sight for him.

Of course, he'd never said he loved her. Maybe in time. She had plenty of it and wouldn't care how old he became before he agreed to be her mate. As long as he agreed. She didn't want to live without him.

He lightly knocked on her head. "Hello? You okay in there? You've gotten awfully quiet."

"I'm fine. Just recovering from the best sex ever."

"I'm that good, huh?" He grinned and lightly kissed her lips. "And here I thought I needed more practice." He moved to roll off, but she held him tight. Heat spread all over and she wasn't willing to give that up yet. "I don't want to squish you."

"You're not. You feel wonderful." She wanted to announce her love once again, but not until he reciprocated her feelings. Why scare the man away any more than her being a vampire had? Not that he was complaining and she couldn't be more relieved, or happy.

"What do you feel when we touch?" he asked.

"Heat. Glorious heat. Whenever I touch something, my skin temperature matches it, even with mortals, so I don't notice much difference and neither does the mortal. But with you… It's like being out in the sun. I've really missed that."

"So you're never hot or cold? That must save on electricity, huh?"

"Yes, but can also be awkward if I don't dress appropriately for the weather." Not that she'd had that problem until recently.

The front door opened and closed. Keys clanked against glass, a bowl, maybe? Thank goodness Ben saw fit to lock his door before they'd made love.

"Guess we no longer have the place to ourselves." He kissed her long and hard. "Too bad. I could have gone another round."

Another round would have been great, if only they had the time. Right now she had Ben in her arms and didn't want to let him go. "Anticipation will make the next time even better. When did your sister stop wearing that perfume?"

"A few days ago. I don't know what changed her mind. I never cared for it, but she always thought I needed it to recognize her. I suspect she was on a date tonight. Maybe she stopped wearing it for him. I can only hope."

"I could find out for you…if you wanted."

He rolled onto his back. "You mean, like, read her mind? You can do that?" He sat up. "Shit."

Victoria rubbed his back. "I can't read yours and I won't read hers unless you want me to. Forget I said anything."

He turned and cupped her face. "No. I want to know all about you. It's still all kind of unreal, though, you know?"

His words brought her joy. He wanted to know about her. That had to be a good sign. No, a great sign. "Well, you're kind of unreal, too. I should have told you earlier, but you're what we call—"

"A Perfect Mate? Perry told me."

"What? When?"

"He came by the other night. Don't worry, he wasn't trying to sabotage us. I think he truly cares about you and wants you to be happy."

"Perry? You sure we're talking about the same guy?"

Ben quietly laughed. "Yeah, but he didn't tell me everything. Like what bonding is all about. Said that was for a conversation between us."

Music blared from the living room almost as if Susannah was using it to drown out other noises. Those other noises involved metal objects clanking together. "What is she doing?" Victoria said.

"I don't know, but if she keeps it up, the neighbors will complain. I better go find out what's going on. Probably better if she doesn't see you until I tell her you're here. Okay?"

She climbed onto his lap and kissed him. "Okay, but…"

"But what?"

"You also might want to tell her you're going out tonight."

He smiled. "Where are we going?"

She wished it was something that would keep him smiling. "Because I had to tell Barnet about you, I have to take you to Headquarters for…questioning." And hopefully nothing more. "I've heard my phone vibrate a couple of times. I'm sure he'll be on his way once he finds Perry to take him."

He tensed. "Will you be with me?"

"Yes. I won't leave you alone."

He caressed her face and kissed her lightly on the lips. "Then okay. I guess there's a lot I need to know anyway, huh?"

She hugged him. "Thank you for being so understanding."

"I'd do anything for you, Victoria."

Would he really? Guess she would find out soon enough.

* * * *

Ben ran his hands over Victoria's back. He reveled in the silky texture of her skin and the last thing he wanted to do was leave her—snuggling until Perry arrived sounded much better—but the noise intensified. What the hell was Susannah up to anyway? He stood and then remembered he'd thrown his jeans. Somewhere. Across the room. "Crap. Could you hand me my jeans?"

She laughed as her scent wafted past. "Here you go."

After quickly pulling them on, he found her and kissed her again. He would never get enough of her. Not if he had ten lifetimes.

"Go on," she said. "I'm not leaving without you."

When he opened his door, Metallica nearly blasted his eardrums. Since when had Susannah listened to his music? If she wanted to get his attention, she could have just knocked on his door. He found his way to the stereo and turned off the music. The sound of drawers opening and closing lead him to the kitchen, but as he approached, a faint scent of gas lingered in the air. "Susannah? What are you doing?"

"Oh good, you're up. Sit down."

Who could sleep through that racket? "What were you thinking turning up the music like that? You trying to get us kicked out of here?"

"I thought you liked it loud."

Two steps into the kitchen and he stepped on something padded—a potholder. He bent down and found more than one on the floor. Had she emptied the whole drawer? "What's going on?"

"Here they are." Whatever she found, it rattled as if inside a small box.

The scent of gas became stronger and a faint hissing sound came from the stove. "Susannah? Do you have the stove on?"

"Not yet. I can't get it to light. Pilot must be out. You want some tea?"

The rattling must be matches. "Susannah, stop. I don't think you should try and light it."

"Don't be ridiculous. I've done this before. It's not the first time the stove has gone out."

"But it's never stunk this bad." And if the hissing didn't come from the stove, where was it coming from?

"Your nose is way too sensitive. I don't smell anything. I think this headache is messing with all my senses."

There was a knock at the front door. Victoria screamed out his name moments before she slammed into him, sending him into Susannah. Glass shattered just as an explosion ripped through the kitchen.

CHAPTER 16

Pain ripped through Victoria's back as a strong scent of burning material filled the air. How far had they been blown from the apartment? When she attempted to sit up, she couldn't move her extremities. *Scheisse.* The blast must have sent wood into her heart. She wasn't going anywhere on her own.

She had landed hard on Ben, who in turn had landed hard on Susannah. Neither one of them were struggling to get free. That couldn't be good.

"Ben?" She got no response. "Please *Gott*, don't let him be dead." Victoria could hardly speak. Would he even be able to hear her? The blast had affected her hearing so she could only imagine what it did to his. She held her breath and focused. His heart was still beating and his chest rose and fell. Not dead. Thank *Gott*.

After Ben had opened his bedroom door, she'd gotten a whiff of gas. She hadn't thought much of it until Ben questioned Susannah. So Victoria had quickly dressed and took a peek.

If only she had been quicker. No sooner had she peeked, Susannah had struck a match. Victoria propelled Ben and Susannah out the glass door just as the kitchen had exploded.

Victoria's stomach twisted in cramps. She took a breath and Ben's scent triggered her fangs. He wasn't wearing a shirt and, with her face up against his chest, it wouldn't take much to feed from him. But she couldn't do that. She wouldn't do that. Not to Ben. Not that way.

Of course, if she was still in this position by sunrise, she might not have a choice in the matter.

Gott. Is this what Henrik endured during his final hours? She'd never been staked before, so really had no idea she would still be alert and aware of her surroundings. She'd always assumed he'd passed out after the impalement, or had become delirious, but now...

She'd always told him not to go out riding alone. Seems if they hadn't been living on that plantation, someone might have heard his cries for help.

Muted voices carried from the front of the building as people exited. She could only catch bits of phrases from the shocked tenants. If they came back here, would she be able to control them?

"Shit!" Perry's appearance—as well as Barnet's—gave her hope that everything would be okay until Perry pounded on her back with his hands.

Each smack was pure torture. She screamed out. "What are you doing?"

"You're on fire. Or your shirt was. What's left of it. Don't you wear a bra?"

Well, that explained the pain. And the smell. She'd assumed it came from the apartment. If he had arrived any later, she might have burst in flames and taken Ben and Susannah with her. "How'd you know we were out here?"

"Who do you think was knocking at the door before it blew into us?" Perry said.

"We have to get them out of here before we draw a crowd," Barnet said. "Victoria, get up."

"I can't. Wood must have penetrated my heart."

He poked and prodded her back and she gritted her teeth. Was he using a knife? Just because she was paralyzed didn't mean she couldn't feel.

"Damn it. I can't get a hold of it. Hold on, this might hurt."

Might hurt? She already hurt. Barnet hauled her over his shoulder. His poking and prodding were pinpricks compared to the pain that rippled across her back. As he rushed her away from the building, she caught a glimpse of Perry carrying Ben.

More cramps knotted her stomach. "What about Susannah?"

"Paramedics will take care of her." Barnet said.

Yeah, but was she still alive?

Barnet stopped and lowered Victoria to the ground on her side.

They were near some dumpsters, out of sight. Sirens sounded from a distance. "Perry, we need the van."

"Say no more." Perry placed Ben beside her and dashed off.

His face was pale and she ached to touch him, assure herself he was alive, but her arms didn't work. Guess she should be happy she could still talk. If she didn't feed soon, she'd lose that ability, too.

"So that's your Perfect Mate, huh?"

"Yes. Is he okay?"

"He's not bleeding, but he might have a concussion. You appear to have taken the brunt of the blast. What happened?"

"I think their stove malfunctioned. I smelled gas and saw Susannah strike a match. I didn't even have time to stop her. You sure he's okay? I can't hear him."

"When was the last time you fed? You didn't feed from him, did you?"

He would have to mention feeding. The thought of blood caused her stomach to cramp in need, as if her back wasn't hurting enough. She breathed through it. "I haven't taken his blood yet. I fed on Friday morning. But I think the blast affected my hearing."

"Might explain why it's taking you longer than normal to heal. Whatever's lodged in your heart isn't helping matters, either. Relax. His heart is beating strong and there's no apparent injury. John might be able to tell us more. After he fixes you up."

Relief flooded through her. Damn. If she hadn't disobeyed Barnet... "He would have died. If I wasn't here, he would have died. This has to be Graham's fault."

"Now, you don't know that. Sounds like an accident to me."

No. Too perfect for an accident. She would find the truth even if it meant digging it out of Graham's mind.

Perry returned. "Bad news. Van is blocked. Police and firemen are everywhere. I suspect a news crew isn't far behind. It's not everyday an apartment blows up, huh? But never fear, Jack is on his way."

"Did you see Susannah?" she asked.

"Paramedics are with her."

"But is she alive?"

"I don't know. I assume so. They were working on her."

"Barnet, we need to get her. She could be the proof we need to show Graham is involved."

"It's going to have to wait until she's alone."

"But if Graham—"

"Enough." Barnet ran a hand through his hair. "This Perfect Mate is clouding your judgment, causing you to jump to conclusions. Even if Graham is involved—and I'm not saying he is—he can't do anything right now, either. Not without exposing himself, and he wouldn't do that."

Her mind was far from cloudy. She'd never seen things more clearly. Graham was out to kill Ben—possibly going through Susannah—and somehow Victoria would prove it.

* * * *

Ben woke up to one monster of a headache on an unfamiliar bed with unfamiliar scents. He grabbed his head and sat up.

"Easy, Teach," Perry said, his voice sounding all muffled.

Oh God. What was wrong with his hearing? And what was Perry doing here? Shit! The explosion. "Where's Victoria?"

"She's a little busy right now, but don't worry. She's fine."

"Busy?" Too busy to be with him?

"Hello, son," an unknown man said.

Ben jerked. "Who is that? Who else is here?"

Perry answered, "Just the three of us. The voice you don't recognize is Barnet."

"Voice? He's blind?" Barnet asked.

Perry chuckled. "Didn't Vic tell you that?"

"But he's the teacher!"

Ben wasn't about to get sucked into that conversation again. He had tons of questions. "Where's Susannah?"

"Probably at the hospital," Perry said. "We had to leave her for the paramedics since Barnet and I couldn't carry all three of you."

Carry? "Victoria couldn't walk?"

"No, but she's fine. I promise."

"Can I see her?"

A hand landed on Ben's shoulder and the bed dipped with the owner's weight. "That's not a good idea, son," Barnet said.

"Why not? She said she'd be with me when you started questioning me."

"And she's right. She'll be here for that."

"Then why can't I see her?"

Barnet sighed. "She's not in any condition—"

"You just said she's fine."

"She is fine, but she's lost a lot of blood and hasn't fed yet. If you come near her right now, she might…overreact. It'll be better for you to see her after she feeds."

Ben's chest restricted. There was only one way she could have lost blood. "How badly did she get hurt?"

"The blast burned her, among other things. But she'll heal once she feeds. She's not going to die. So don't worry."

She saved his life. He would have perished in the explosion. "If she needs blood, she can have mine."

"Now Teach, do you remember what I told you about bonding?" Perry asked.

"But I can help her."

"So can other donors," Barnet said. "I promise, you'll be able to see her as soon as she's fed. Now, why don't we find you some clothes?"

Ben was still shirtless and shoeless, since all he'd put on were his jeans. At the mention of clothes, goosebumps formed on his skin. "You have the air conditioning on rather high."

"We weren't sure," Barnet said. "I'll adjust it."

"Where am I anyway?"

"Victoria's room," Perry said. "At Headquarters."

A commotion sounded from another room sounding a lot like Victoria yelling. "Where is he?"

Ben stood. "Victoria?"

The door banged against the wall. "Oh, thank *Gott*."

Before he could take another breath, she was hugging him tight.

Barnet yelled, "What the devil do you think you're doing?"

"Yeah, nice view," Perry said.

View? He cautiously touched her shoulders, doing his best to avoid irritating any injury she might have. She was wearing a gown, like from a hospital, and it was open in the back. He closed the gap as Perry snickered.

"Would you two please give us a few minutes?" she asked. "I want to speak to Ben alone."

"Do you think that's wise? You need to feed." Barnet said.

"I will. Later. I feel fine."

"Ahh, Victoria." Footsteps slapped the tile floor, going back and forth, as did Barnet's voice. "Damn it! Ben, don't offer her your blood. Promise me!"

"Why does that matter if I want to?"

She touched his cheek. "He doesn't want us to start the bonding process. Once I take your offered blood, I'll get a little more protective of you until the bond is complete."

"A little?" Barnet said. "Try insanely possessive."

Well, he certainly didn't want to start a feud with this Barnet guy, who seemed important. It wouldn't hurt to know what he'd be getting himself into first. "I promise."

* * * *

Victoria's heart fell a little with Ben's promise. Did that mean he wasn't interested? Probably more likely he wanted to know more. She couldn't blame him there. She loved the way he thought things through. If he agreed to bond, it would be because it was something he truly wanted, not out of some inane desire to repay her for saving his life. Besides, she wouldn't want him that way.

"You will both report to the conference room in ten minutes," Barnet said. "And if you're late, I'll hunt you down. Don't make me regret leaving you alone."

Out of all the Committee Members, Barnet was always the level-headed one. Now with the onslaught of Perfect Mates, he seemed to be losing it. She'd never seen him so angry.

"We'll be there. I promise." After Barnet and Perry departed, she squeezed Ben's hand. "I guess I better get dressed."

Although she had no idea what to wear. Her back was still a burning mess and included a hole John had made to remove the wood. Going through her closet, she found a loose sheath. It should do.

Any kind of movement aggravated her wounds and even slipping the dress over her head became complicated. She gritted her teeth as she eased first one arm, then the other through the sleeve openings. Another cramp rippled across her stomach and she breathed through the pain.

She really should have fed—the only reason John released her was so she could—but the mall was closed and even if John would have been okay with it, Sarah's blood appeared to only be good for him. When another vampire had tried to feed from Sarah, she'd ended up with a mouthful of bitter.

"You're still in pain, aren't you?" Ben asked.

"I've felt better."

"You saved my life. Susannah's too. I know I promised, but if my blood will help you…"

She took his hand. "Ben, as badly as I want to bond with you, I won't start something you don't want to finish. If we bond, you most likely will become immortal."

He frowned. "You mean I'll be a vampire?"

"No. Perfect Mates cannot be turned. You will still be able to go out into the sun. You will still eat regular food. But any new injury you obtain will heal super fast. In fact, we're pretty sure you can't be killed. Not easily, anyway."

"Pretty sure? Not certain?"

"We only know of two so far. Sarah experienced what should have been a fatal injury, but healed from it. That's how we know. We're only guessing she and Justin won't age."

He smiled. "What's so bad about that?"

"Normally, nothing. But…" *Scheisse.* She couldn't say it.

"I'm blind," he finished. "You don't want to be stuck—"

She placed two fingers over his lips. "It's not me I'm thinking about. I would love nothing more than to be with you forever. Blind or not. The decision is yours to make. I'll understand if the thought of living for centuries blind doesn't appeal to you."

He nodded. "So what do I need to do to get you fed?"

"I'll be okay until we get to the hospital. I'll find someone there." She took his hand. "Come on. Let's go get you some clean clothes, then see Barnet and get him to take us to Susannah."

The Committee better approve her plan. Ben's life depended on it.

* * * *

Graham zipped down the hospital hallway and stepped into Susannah's room. He only needed her to do one simple thing. But no. Victoria had to be there and save them all.

Susannah slept soundly. She'd been checked in for observation only, especially since she had no home to return to and no one could reach her brother. Hell, the staff probably thought she was nuts anyway. He'd made sure she sounded that way.

But Martin could arrive at any time, which meant Graham needed to work fast.

He caressed Susannah's cheek. Her demise would have been quick and painless if his original plan had panned out. Now, she might suffer, and all because of Victoria.

If she had only picked him over that blind teacher, none of this would be necessary.

"Goodbye, my sweet." He slipped into Susannah's mind and kissed her for the last time.

CHAPTER 17

Leaning against the van in the parking lot of the hospital waiting for Victoria to return, Ben asked Perry, "How long do you take to feed?"

After Jack had dropped them all off at the apartment to retrieve the van, the firemen on site told them which hospital Susannah had been taken to. Just that bit of information—Susannah was alive—relieved him of his worst thoughts. But once Perry parked, Victoria rushed out and Ben's thoughts turned depressive. How bad off was she?

"Normally, only a few minutes. But she's lost a lot of blood. Between the stake and burns—"

"Stake?" Who the hell staked her? And was it like anything in the vampire book he'd read?

"Okay, poor choice of words. The blast imbedded wood into her heart, which is the same as being staked."

"And that doesn't kill you?" Duh, of course not. Wasn't Victoria walking around?

"Nope. Only makes us paralyzed, which is why Vic couldn't walk. Or roll to put out the fire. Good thing I came along when I did, huh?"

"What? She was on fire?" Suddenly, his legs could no longer hold him up and he slid to the ground.

"Oh shit. She didn't tell you that?"

Ben shook his head. It was one thing to suffer burns but to be actually burning? "Could she have died?"

Perry gripped Ben's shoulder. "It's possible, yes. Fire will kill us. But she's okay, Teach. It'll just take time for her to get back into shape."

Ben rubbed his face. "How long?"

"Once she feeds, a few hours. Then she'll be as good as new. Honest."

Even so, she'd been hurt badly—could have died—and he'd only suffered a headache. Susannah and he owed her their lives. Ben held his hand out for help up and Perry obliged. "That meeting back at Headquarters. Is she an important vampire?"

Perry snorted. "She'd like to think she's important. But she is a member of the Committee. Barnet is the Head."

"You have a committee?" Which was kind of a stupid question. Vampires had a headquarters, it had to house someone.

"Yeah. Crazy, huh?"

"Are you on this committee?"

"Nah. Don't want the bother. Too much work. I'd rather play."

"Play? Like with the ladies?"

"Of course with the ladies. Committee members have a reputation to uphold. Whereas my reputation would probably tarnish the whole Committee, as if I'd ever get voted in to begin with."

Voting? They ran for office? Ben wanted to know more, but figured Victoria could give him more accurate information.

"Ah, back from the Restaurant Alley," Perry said with a fake French accent.

Only a few minutes had passed, so she couldn't have fed long. Ben reached out for her and she walked into his arms. Her scent came to life and he held her tentatively so as not to injure her further. "How is she?" he asked Perry.

"I'm fine," she said into his shirt.

Ben laughed. "I believe I asked Perry."

She turned her head, but not enough to keep him from noticing her facial movements. Did Perry have an obligation to do as she asked?

"Stop it with the eyes," Perry said. "I like Teach, so I am not going to lie to him."

"I don't want you to lie," she said.

"Yeah, right." He tapped Ben on the arm. "She could stand to eat some more, but she's a vampire and still way stronger than you."

"So you can hug me tighter," she said. "I'm not going to break."

Maybe so, but she was small. And her back had been on fire. He couldn't *not* treat her delicately.

"You gonna stand out here all night?" Perry asked. "I thought you were in a hurry."

Victoria released Ben and offered her elbow.

"Think they'll let us see her?" Ben asked. "It's late."

"We don't have to ask," she said. "And they won't call security, so don't worry."

The scent of antiseptic stunk like it had every other time he ended up in the ER. Why couldn't disinfectant smell clean?

The only footsteps that echoed between the walls seemed to come from him. Both vampires were light on their feet. Strange how no one stopped them. Probably some vampire trick. He still had a lot to learn about what exactly Victoria could do and, surprisingly, he was anxious to discover everything.

They stopped and Victoria turned around. "She's asleep, but she's not hooked up with tubes or wires."

The good news relaxed him a bit. He followed Victoria into the room. To his right a chair scraped across the floor. She led him to it.

"Go ahead and wake her. I'll give you a minute alone with her first, but then we'll have to find out what she knows."

He took Victoria's hand and squeezed it. "Thank you." He meant it for everything she'd done.

She pressed her cheek against his. "You're more than welcome."

After a brief kiss to his cheek, she left him alone. He found Susannah's hand and placed his on top. "Susannah?"

Movement came from the bed. "Oh for Pete's sake. Weren't you just here?" Susannah gasped. "Ben? Is that really you?"

She sounded good. She sounded strong. She sounded...confused.

"How are you feeling, Suze?"

"Oh my God." She flung into his arms. "Where did you go? I kept telling them you were there, but they couldn't find you."

"I'm here now, that's all that matters."

"You're right. You're right." She touched his face. "You're okay. Really okay."

"Yes. And you?"

She backed away and the springs on the bed squeaked. "I'm fine. They insisted I spend the night. Something about a concussion. I think they think I've gone a bit bonkers. Have you been to the apartment?"

"Yes, but I couldn't get inside." That hadn't stopped Perry from sneaking in and taking some of Ben's clothes. Too bad it all smelled like smoke. Hopefully the stench would come out in the wash.

"I guess it's ruined, huh? I wish I knew what happened." She gasped. "Perry? Is that you? What are you doing here?"

"You know Perry?"

"Yeah," Perry said. "You know me?"

Susannah's laugh was filled with dread. "Of course I know you. We've been dating. Haven't we?"

What? He turned toward Perry's voice. "When did you start dating my sister?"

* * * *

Victoria glared at Perry. Sure, they'd discussed it originally, but she'd never thought he'd actually go through with it. "Why didn't you tell me you were seeing her?"

"Victoria's here, too?" Susannah asked. "How do you all know each other?"

"I'm not seeing her," Perry said. Victoria raised her eyebrows at him. "I swear. I don't know what she's talking about."

"I'm sorry," Susannah said. "I know you said to keep it a secret, but I assumed because you were here, that you changed your mind. How did you know I was here anyway?"

"Suze, Perry drives Victoria to class. When did you meet him?"

"She didn't," Perry said. "Sweetheart, I think you're confusing me with someone else. Vic, turn on the light, would ya?"

Victoria walked to the switch and muttered, "She didn't get your name confused with someone else."

She flicked the switch. The only person who didn't wince at the sudden brightness was Ben.

Perry stepped toward Susannah. "Now, don't you feel silly? Although, I have to say, I'm kind of heartbroken there are two of me. I always thought I was unique."

Susannah looked him over from feet to face and then leapt from the bed. She planted a kiss on Perry's mouth. And damn it if the man didn't react. He put his arms around her waist.

"Perry!"

"What's going on?" Ben said. "Is he hurting her?"

"No one's getting hurt." Except maybe Perry when she got him alone. Tempted to enter Susannah's mind and stop this nonsense, Victoria settled for being physical instead and wedged an arm between the two kissers, giving the taller one a good elbow to the stomach. "Enough."

Susannah broke away, practically breathless. "I'm sorry if I spilled the beans, but please don't make me say I don't know you. I'm already feeling a little crazy."

Perry licked his lips. His fangs were out.

Scheisse. When he leaned in for some more kissing, Victoria took control. "That's enough, Romeo." She turned toward Susannah and connected with her mentally. *"Go back to bed and go to sleep."*

Susannah walked to the bed and climbed onto the mattress. Her eyes fluttered shut and her breathing slowed.

Ben reached out and found his sister's hand. "Susannah? What's the matter with her?"

"She's fine. I put her into a deep sleep." Victoria smacked Perry in the arm. "For someone who just met her, you sure seemed to be enjoying yourself."

Perry shrugged. "What can I say? She's a good kisser."

"You kissed my sister?"

"Perry, go make yourself useful and get a wheelchair." Barnet was sure to object, but with another vampire involved, Victoria had no choice but to take Susannah back to Headquarters.

"I'm sorry, Teach, but she…started…it." Perry stuttered when he caught the glare Victoria sent his way. Honestly, the man had no brains. He offered up a weak smile. "Yeah, wheelchair. I'll get right on that." He flicked the light off before stepping out the room.

"Victoria, speak to me," Ben said. "What's going on?"

She sat on his lap and caressed his cheek. "I wish I knew. Susannah appears to know Perry. And rather intimately."

Ben groaned. "Shit. He said he wouldn't go after her unless she showed an interest. Guess she's shown an interest."

She placed her forehead against his. "Listen, I know Perry has a reputation when it comes to women, mainly he can't leave them alone, but I don't think he's behind this. Besides, he's a terrible liar and he seemed just as shocked as us when she recognized him. I think he's telling the truth when he says he doesn't know her."

"So, what does that mean? She recognized him. Knew his name."

"It means she's being manipulated."

"Manipulated? Like brain-washed?"

"Yes."

"Who would do that? Graham?"

"I'd love to say yes, but he's never shown that kind of skill before. It takes a strong vampire to make a mortal see them as someone else and I've never seen Graham that strong." Then again, she hadn't seen him in decades. Could he have been practicing? "I do believe he was behind the explosion at your apartment, but I don't have any proof. I think it'll be safer for her if we take her to Headquarters. With your permission I'd like to—"

Susannah moaned. "Ben?"

Startled, Victoria slipped off Ben's lap. What was Susannah doing awake? She should have been out for hours. Something wasn't right. But what?

Ben sat on the edge of the bed and took his sister's hand. "I'm here, Suze."

"I'm thirsty."

"I'll get some water." Victoria snatched the empty jug and stepped into the small lavatory. What was taking Perry so long and why didn't Susannah stay asleep? Could it be because her brother was a Perfect Mate? Did she have similar traits?

Susannah spoke softly, probably thinking she was alone with Ben. "You love her, don't you?"

Victoria kept the water running, in case Ben thought the noise meant he could speak freely. And she wanted him to speak freely. She wanted to know the answer to that question probably more than Susannah did.

"Nah. I hate her guts."

Victoria dropped the jug, spilling water everywhere. "*Scheisse!*"

* * * *

Ben smiled. He figured Victoria could hear even with the water running and he just couldn't resist messing with her. The German expletives—and he recognized some of the curse words—flowed freely after she had dropped what sounded like a full pitcher.

Oh, he loved her all right, but he would tell Victoria before he told Susannah.

Susannah grabbed his arm. "What? Oh, you're joking. When are you going to realize she's not meant for you?"

"Not again." He was tired fighting the same fight with her. "I thought you were going to give her a chance."

"Damn. I think my head's going to explode."

Susannah had never complained of headaches before. Had the explosion caused her discomfort or this other vampire? "Do you need a doctor? Victoria could—"

Something sharp pricked his neck. As he brought his hand up to investigate, numbness set in and he lost control of his extremities. Paralyzed? What the hell? Gravity took over and he fell across Susannah's legs. Had she done this to him? Why? Words failed him as he couldn't even get his mouth to work.

Squeaky wheels announced someone's arrival while Susannah squirmed underneath him. Why hadn't she yelled out? Why couldn't he? Something stung his back. Now what was she doing?

"Couldn't you get a quieter wheelchair?" Victoria asked.

"You'd think," Perry said. "Hey. What's the matter with Teach?"

"Ben? *Scheisse*. Watch out. She's got a knife."

Small arms gripped him around the waist and lifted him off the bed. "Ben? Are you okay?"

Okay? She was joking, right?

"Shit," Perry said. "What the hell? I can't— Ouch!"

Whatever caused Ben's paralysis affected his hearing. Their voices were faint, but discernable, as if they spoke on the other side of a wall.

"Control her!" Victoria said.

"Don't you think I'm trying?" Perry said. "She keeps coming to."

"I'm putting you on the other bed, Ben." Stiff sheets met his face as Victoria settled him on his side. She brushed the hair from his face. "Ben? Can you hear me? Why aren't you talking?" She pulled up his shirt. "She didn't cut you too deep. I'm going to heal you, okay?"

She kissed the part that stung. No, she was licking it. Was he bleeding? Was that it? Well, she could take his blood, he didn't care. Her tongue lingered for a moment and a wonderful flavor filled his mouth. More. He wanted more. She sucked. His groin hardened and his nipples tingled. Man, what a rush.

"What are you doing?" Perry asked.

"Just…heal…ing…" Victoria collapsed on top of Ben.

"Good going, Vicky. Didn't you think whatever she gave him would affect his blood? And why the ding dong day are you taking his blood anyway?"

What happened to Victoria? Why'd she stop sucking? And why wasn't she moving? His eyes became heavy. Maybe if he closed them things would make sense.

* * * *

Victoria snuggled up against Ben in the king-size bed that had miraculously appeared in her room the other day. She'd never thought she would need a bed. It wasn't like she invited men to her room. She would have to thank whoever brought this one over, because she wasn't letting Ben out of her sight ever again.

Well, at least until she proved Graham was responsible for controlling Susannah. Victoria might have had doubts before, but that last stunt erased them. Graham had already told her he had no qualms about using innocents and his dislike of Ben was no secret. Did he not think she would discover his treachery? No vampire was that good. Eventually she and the Committee would get to the truth, she just hoped it came before Graham succeeded in his mission.

When she'd found Ben slumped over his sister, who'd been on her way to stabbing him again, Victoria's heart had nearly stopped. Both she and Perry had tried to stop Susannah mentally, but she kept waking up. Victoria had never witnessed anything like it. With a forcible trait like that, Graham only labeled himself as a dangerous vampire. If she had any say in the matter, his days were numbered.

"You should have left him at the hospital," Barnet said. "They would have been able to treat him there."

She'd already gotten that diatribe from John. That he'd only been an OB/GYN, not an ER doctor.

"I couldn't…leave him."

Even Perry had almost left him behind until she'd threatened to remove a certain body part. Not that she would have gone through with it. He believed her, though, and that was all that mattered. Nice to know she had some control over his actions, even if she was incapacitated. Whatever substance Susannah had injected in Ben, it had affected Victoria for a good hour before she could function properly.

Victoria caressed Ben's face. Why was he still out? He should have come to first. He should be awake now.

Barnet grabbed her arm and dragged her into the living room before shutting the bedroom door. "Sometimes you have to leave the ones you love if it's in their best interest."

She stared at the door to Ben. Yearned to lie beside him. If he woke up and she wasn't there, wouldn't he be confused?

Barnet shook her, bringing her out of her digressions. "What's the matter with you? You're acting like he's given you his blood."

"No. I only healed him. The cut wasn't that deep and he was out of it. He couldn't even talk." But oh, his blood had been exquisite. Got her a little hot, even. It had taken everything in her not to bite him, but she managed a couple of sucks before collapsing as if she'd been staked.

Barnet narrowed his eyes at her. "Are you sure?"

No, she wasn't. Just because Ben wasn't moving didn't mean he wasn't alert. And then there was the feeling she'd imagined of having an erection, something that would only occur if... She covered her face. "*Scheisse*. What have I done?"

"Oh, Victoria," Barnet said on a sigh. "We have two weeks until the Committee Meeting. He can't be here for that. Not unless you're bonded. Do you understand?"

"I thought you didn't want us to bond."

"I've never been against you bonding, but I can't have you partially bonded to a Perfect Mate during the Meeting. Tell me you haven't forgotten what it was like when Justin was here."

Victoria remembered all too well. Katarina nearly skewered anyone who looked at Justin, Victoria included. "Maybe it won't be as bad. I'll know why if I'm acting possessive. I'm also older than Katarina. I have more control." Maybe.

"That's not a theory I want to test. Not during the Committee Meeting."

Not something she wanted to test, either. She still itched to be by Ben's side. Was this how it would be from now on? "I didn't mean for this to happen."

"Doesn't matter what you meant. It only matters that it happened." Barnet paced the small room. "I have to say, I'm a little surprised at your pick. Daugherty looks more like Henrik than Ben does."

"Why does that surprise you? Henrik picked me, I didn't pick him."

"But you loved him. I just assumed…"

"I came to love him, but he never would have been my choice. I was only fifteen. I barely knew him when we got married. And I certainly didn't know he was a vampire. And now I've put Ben into this situation… I can't do that to him."

"You don't know he doesn't want to be bonded."

"If you were blind, would you?" She plopped onto her chair. "Do you think the process wears off if I don't feed from him again?"

Barnet knelt in front of her. "You love him. Do you really think you could stay away even if it did? Besides, from what I've learned, if Ben loves you, he's the one who will talk you into it."

"And then I condemn him to a sightless immortality."

"Only if you give in. And if you decide not to complete the bond, he has to be gone before guests arrive."

So then maybe she shouldn't tell Ben how to complete the bond. Omission wasn't the same as lying, was it? *Scheisse.*

CHAPTER 18

Ben awoke and basked in the scent of wildflowers. If not for the bed beneath him, he'd swear he lay in a meadow, so that only meant one thing: must be in Victoria's room. Certainly wasn't the hospital.

"Ben?" Victoria snuggled beside him. No wonder the scent was strong. "You awake?"

Man, he liked waking up beside her, but what was he doing here? A memory tickled at his mind. Her tongue on his back, followed with some sucking. So sensual. So hot. When it had happened, he couldn't do anything about it. Now? He grew hard and desired her something fierce. He grabbed her upper arms, hauled her on top of him, and kissed her. Her lips were sweet, her mouth even sweeter, and a nice warm buzz shot straight to his groin.

She giggled into his mouth. "I guess you are awake."

"Yes, and you're talking too much." He held her face and continued exploring her mouth with his tongue. Another burst of warmth passed between them.

"Scheisse."

With strength and speed he'd never witnessed before, she straddled his body, grasped his wrists and trapped them against the mattress, alongside her legs. Her bare legs. Naked or wearing a dress? Hot damn. Either one would do.

"We need to talk."

He sat up. Talking was the last thing he wanted to do. Her

enticing breath feathered across his face and gave away the location of her mouth. He took advantage.

"Later." He found those sweet lips again, not that she was actively avoiding him. Maybe he had some power over her after all. Would she let him kiss her forever?

"Ben." She drew out his name, but didn't pull away.

He stopped, just in case. "Is there someone else in the room?"

"No, but—"

"Great, then no talking." He continued kissing her, shutting off her objection. If she'd wanted him to stop, she could easily end it. That she hadn't only got him hotter.

On a sigh, she released him and held his face, kissing him back. God, that tongue of hers. He couldn't get enough. With his hands now free, he grabbed her butt and pushed her into his erection. Her fangs extended. Holy shit. Had he done that? When they scratched his tongue, he nearly bared his neck for her to take his blood. How crazy was that? He wouldn't ask her, though. Not yet anyway. But he wanted more than a kiss. "How's your back?"

"Fine. It's all healed."

"Good." He flipped them over to where she used to lay, garnering a gasp from her. So glad he hadn't miscalculated. Ending up on the floor might have been a killjoy.

He nuzzled her neck and pushed her dress up. Last time he hadn't had a chance to sample her.

The scent of her arousal spurred him lower. He scooted toward the end of the bed and pulled her along so he could kneel on the floor and have total access. God, he wished he could see her right now, all laid out for him. He'd just have to rely on his imagination instead.

Her silky panties were already wet with her desire and he licked them before clamping his mouth over her mound—panties and all. She arched against him as a whimper left her mouth. His dick jerked against his zipper, what little room there was in his pants. If he didn't know any better, he'd swear her mouth was on him.

He slipped the fabric to one side and ran his tongue over her slick folds. She was so wet and he couldn't lap her up fast enough. Every lick made him harder.

"I taste good to you," she said. And it wasn't a question.

"Yes, you do." He sucked on her clit and nearly came in his pants. Whatever the hell was happening, he needed to get in her now or suffer extreme embarrassment.

Quickly, he unzipped and pulled out his dick, half expecting to find a strange mouth on him. Instead he was just wet with pre-cum. No time to remove his pants. No time to remove her panties. Shoving them aside, he thrust his way inside her. Together they gasped.

Some more unfamiliar sensations overwhelmed him. He buried himself deep inside her, her warmth and wetness surrounding his cock, yet it seemed as if something filled him. And every time he moved a certain way, he nearly came out of his skin.

She arched into him and clawed his back. "Do that again."

Yes, she liked it that way. Damn, he liked it that way. He continued pounding into her until she trembled in his arms. Her contractions squeezed him, as some strange sensation contracted within him. What a rush. Light flashed before his dead eyes as he exploded inside her.

She cried out, "Yes, yes," while she thrust her hips upward.

Lightheaded, he collapsed on top of her. Damn. Sex with her was great the first time, but this time was absolutely mind blowing.

* * * *

Victoria closed her eyes. The urge to bite Ben overtook her senses and she turned her head away from his neck. She would not bite him. She would not. If she needed any proof of what she had started, she'd just gotten it. Sharing his experience was one of the side effects of the bond, and she shared all right. Best sex she'd ever had.

He slid out of her, cupped her face, and kissed her hard. "I hope you don't hate me for rushing. I had this insane desire to be in you."

No more insane than her own desire. Would it ever abate? Even now she missed having him in her. "I don't hate you, but you may hate me for what I've done."

"I could never hate you my dear, sweet, Victoria." He planted kisses all over her face.

"You say that now…"

"What did you do?" He stood and pulled up his jeans. "Is it Susannah? Oh shit. Is she—"

"Susannah's fine." Victoria helped Ben onto the bed and

together they scooted to the middle. She snuggled beside him as they lay on the big mattress. "She's here, at Headquarters, and resting comfortably." More like heavily sedated, but he didn't need to know that right now. "This has to do with us. I started the bonding process."

She held her breath. Would he yell at her? She wouldn't blame him if he did.

Instead, he sat up as a smile spread across his face. "All that was from… Damn. But wait. When did you take my—oh." He flopped back to the mattress. "What the hell did Susannah do to me?"

"She injected you with a paralysis drug and then…"

"And then what?"

"She stabbed you."

"She what?" he yelled.

"She didn't know what she was doing and we stopped her from doing any damage. Perry got the worst of it. She nearly sliced his hand off."

"Oh my God. That's why you licked my back."

"You were bleeding. I only wanted to heal you."

He laughed. "So it's my fault. It felt so good I wanted you to take my blood. So is that why the sex was so…intense?"

"Yes. We're sharing each other's experience."

"Holy… And is that why I want you to bite me? Because you want to bite me?"

Her mouth turned dry. "You want me to bite you? Oh *Gott.* I don't know. Maybe."

He rolled to his side to face her. After propping his head in one hand, he took his other and ran it over her stomach, between her breasts, and up her neck before stopping at what she could only assume was his intended target—her cheek. "You make it sound like a chore. Is my blood that bad?"

"No, nothing of the sort."

"So I should have asked you to bite me, huh?" He leaned in close and nudged her temple with his nose before kissing her ear. "I bet it's hot."

Sexy chills ran down her spine. Barnet was right. Ben could easily convince her, especially with talk like that. "I thought if I didn't take any more of your blood, the process would reverse."

"You want to reverse it?"

No. Never. "Don't you?"

"If it means going back to what it was before, no. If you couldn't tell, I'm enjoying this very much. Just out of curiosity, how much time would it take to reverse?"

"I don't know. I don't know if anyone has even tried." Because, really, why would they? Only a stupid idiot like herself would even consider it.

"So it could be never."

"Well, I suppose."

He found her waist and pulled her in closer. "What if I said I didn't want you to reverse it? What would be next? How do we complete the bond?"

"I'm not sure we should."

"Because I'm blind." He rolled away, but not before a trace of sadness snuck through their bond. He might not think his sight mattered now, but what if he was wrong?

* * * *

Why did it always come down to his blindness? Was she really concerned about him, or afraid of being tied to an invalid—and a clumsy one at that?

She placed a hand on his cheek while resting her head on his shoulder. "Ben, can you honestly say being blind for centuries doesn't matter?"

"Are you saying that if there's a cure in, say, two hundred years, I won't be able to benefit from that?" While living that long still seemed unreal, to be with her for centuries would be a dream.

"I don't know. I hadn't thought about it like that."

So there was hope. Would he be able to actually see again? See her? Ben took her hand and intertwined his fingers with hers. "How is it you don't know?"

"Because up until six months ago, we thought the Perfect Mate was just a story. Now we've discovered four and we don't know the connection or why you're showing up now. I don't want to rush into anything until we know more."

"Except I'm not getting any younger while you remain looking, what? Seventeen? I'm sure you won't be able to reverse my age. People are going to think I'm a dirty old man." Hell, they probably already did.

"You know I don't care about that. Your blindness and age

have nothing to do with my love for you."

He nearly laughed. It wasn't all that long ago the thought of bonding scared the crap out of him. Now it was all he desired. Was it possible he had no control over his emotions? That whatever she had started was pushing him to finish?

He hugged her. Reveled in her softness. Her scent. If she was a drug, she was a damn good one. But how was it she could make him immortal but not make him see or appear younger? Guess vampires weren't miracle workers. Somehow he would prove to her she meant more to him than his sight. "If you take my blood now, will it complete the bond?"

"No. It will only stop another female vampire from desiring you."

"But not you."

"No. I would never stop desiring you." She wiggled free and gave him a quick kiss on the mouth. Much too quick, but enough to get a rise out of him. Amazing how soon he could desire her again, but first he needed answers.

"So, if you don't take my blood again, then what? Every female vampire would want me?"

She settled beside him again. "Well… Probably no more than before I took it."

She was holding something back, but what?

"I feel your unease. Why is that?"

"Our emotions transfer when we touch. They're strongest after I've taken your blood, but will fade as time goes on, provided I never feed from you again. Completing the bond stops it from fading."

"That's interesting. Okay, more like mind-boggling, but what I meant is, why are you feeling uneasy?"

"Because…because…" She took a deep breath and blurted, "Because everything inside me wants to complete the bond."

"What's so bad about that?"

"That's not my decision to make and I won't ask you to complete it until I know it's what you truly want. And you won't know that until we understand it more thoroughly."

All valid reasons, although none of them really mattered. He wanted her with him forever, and if forever could last centuries… "So you won't even tell me how to complete it. Will you?"

"No."

At least she was being honest. "How about I tease it out of you by doing this?"

He caressed her breast and tweaked her nipple. His own nipple became hard and his dick jerked. This shared experience was pretty awesome.

"That won't work."

"No? But you like it. I can tell. Then how about this?" He slid his hand under her panties and inserted a finger. She might as well have grabbed him, he nearly came. "Oh damn. That feels amazing."

Her breath hitched. "You do realize that every time you tease me, you're just teasing yourself?"

He laughed as he released her. "Yeah, I'm figuring that out pretty quickly. But wouldn't you want to have that forever?" To know he actually gave her pleasure whenever he touched her was something he did not want to fade.

"Yes, but I'll not have you hate me."

* * * *

Victoria hadn't meant to speak aloud. If Ben ever came to hate her, it would be the end of her world. She would not wish to live on.

He caressed her face. "Oh Victoria. Is that what you really think?"

"It's possible. I've seen it."

"How can I prove that would never happen?"

He couldn't. That was the problem. But what if there was an age limit? What if she had him wait and then he became too old? *Scheisse.* There were too many unknowns.

"Ah, baby, I didn't mean to upset you." He kissed her. Tenderly at first. But his chaste kiss turned into a hungry, must-have-more kiss. He explored her mouth with his tongue and moved his hand down her back until he squeezed her *Arsch.* His sheer possessiveness took her breath away. "We have too many clothes on. I want to feel you, all of you, next to me."

"I think that could be arranged." She slipped the sheath over her head, discarded her panties, and then helped Ben with his clothes. She would never grow tired of seeing his body.

She snuggled against him and he embraced her while kissing the top of her head. This was the life. A life she could have with him if she only knew more. Maybe it was time to really buckle down and search for answers. The news would certainly cheer up Barnet.

She ran her hand along Ben's steely biceps when her stomach cramped. What a way to kill the mood.

"What was that?" he asked.

"Hunger pangs." After recovering from the explosion and then the drug she'd ingested through Ben's blood, she would need to feed a little more often than normal before she was one-hundred percent. The mall was open so finding someone wouldn't be a problem. She kissed him quickly on the mouth. "I won't be gone long."

"Wait." He grabbed her arm as she crawled over him, and a brief flash of fear transferred. "Can you do me a favor?"

She managed an "I'll try," but "anything" nearly slipped out. She couldn't offer anything. Not yet. But his kisses muddled her mind. If he knew the control he had over her… *Scheisse*. She'd give away all her secrets. All he'd have to do was ask.

"Take my blood."

Like that, for instance. She shook her head, yet her fangs extended. "No."

"You said it wouldn't complete anything, so what's the matter?"

"I'm afraid I'll like it too much."

He frowned. "Like, kill me, like-it-too-much?"

"No. Like, I'll want to do it all the time like-it-too-much."

"Then what's the problem? Won't I like it?"

"I'm under the impression you would enjoy it."

He smiled. "Good. Then do it."

He held her on top of him and maneuvered her face into his neck. His vein throbbed and his scent drove her nuts. "I can't."

"But you're hungry."

She was hungry all right. In more ways than one.

He whispered into her ear, "Victoria, the thought of you feeding from another guy makes me want to put my fist through a wall. And I'm not sure how I feel about you feeding from a woman. I want to be yours. Let me prove it to you by offering you my blood. Please."

His words set her heart—and other parts of her body—aflame. She craved to taste him again, and it wasn't like she'd start something new. But taking his blood from an intimate spot—say, his neck—when the bond was screaming for completion, might imply sex. He couldn't possibly be ready for another round and she didn't wish to frustrate him. "Fine. I'll use your arm."

"My arm? That doesn't sound very sexy." He held her tight. "Come on. Use the neck. I know you want to. I can feel it."

Apparently he wanted to be frustrated or he just wanted to frustrate her. "You're evil. You know that?"

"I like to think I'm persistent."

And his persistence would put her straight over the edge. Oh, but what a way to go. After making sure he was lying on the bed comfortably, she straddled his body and placed her hands on his muscular chest. "It might hurt a little at first. I'll be gentle."

He laughed while rubbing her arms. "You make me sound like a virgin. Oh wait, I guess I am."

She inhaled his scent. After kissing him along his jaw, she nuzzled his neck. His pulse pounded against her lips. She pierced his skin.

He gasped.

The sweet, coppery flavor blasted through her system. No other blood had ever tasted so rich. And the amount she drew turned her on so hot she about exploded. So much more intense than the little bit she ingested the previous night. She throbbed in need.

He squeezed her arms and his arousal rose behind her. "God damn! I need to be in you."

No more than she needed him in her. Feeding had never been like this before. He lifted her hips as she helped settle over his erection. He slipped right in. The dual sensations caused her heart to flutter and she stopped sucking. Sex had never been so intense before, either. He was *her* Perfect Mate.

He held her head in place while he fucked her. "Don't stop. God, don't stop."

He didn't have to tell her twice. But once she got her fill, she did just that. If she took any more, he'd feel the loss of blood and she wouldn't harm him in any manner. She licked his neck. Before she could ensure all trace of his blood was gone from her mouth, he managed to kiss her, tongue and all, and didn't seem at all grossed out.

She loved him a little bit more for that.

With a deftness that marveled her, he flipped them over and continued his frenzied pounding, burying himself deep within her.

She met up with him just as fast, urging him on. If she didn't come soon, she would implode. The rubbing and being rubbed, along with filling and being filled, made for one powerful orgasm. Theirs, together. He barked out her name and then collapsed on top of her.

Had he passed out? She nearly had. Before she could shake him, he lifted his head and kissed the top of her head.

"Yeah, you're only feeding from me." With a silly grin, he rolled off her and promptly fell asleep.

She couldn't argue with the man. She wasn't sure she wanted to feed from anyone else.

CHAPTER 19

On his hands and knees and ready to upchuck, Graham rested his head on the floor of the empty room adjacent to Victoria's. He'd give anything not to have heard the sounds that had emanated through the walls. How could she do this to him?

Thank God he had the foresight to enter Headquarters unseen. Jack had departed an hour before sunrise—in a rush to get to his woman, no doubt—and entered the garage from the compound. Graham had managed to slither inside before the door locked shut. Sure, he could have used his card to enter, but then Victoria would have been alerted to his presence, and he had wanted to surprise her. Instead she had surprised him.

He'd raised his fist to knock on her door when Martin spoke to Victoria from the other side. Shocked that the man was still alive, Graham had slipped inside the empty room. Not moments later those two had gone after one another.

Damn Victoria for ruining everything.

She had to have intervened. And now she was doing to that freak what she should be doing to him.

Ever since Graham had laid eyes on Victoria he had wanted her. Unfortunately, she'd already been wed to his maker. Henrik had confided in Graham that he would turn her on her twentieth birthday. He'd thought it would be the perfect age for her. But Graham had wanted her to remain sweet and innocent looking, so he told Henrik he shouldn't wait. That her life was fragile and he was taking a huge risk waiting when he could have her forever right then. But Henrik couldn't bring himself to turn her early. Only when Graham had threatened her life—in disguise, of course—had Henrik panicked and turned the woman.

It should have been enough then for Victoria to despise Henrik, since Graham had learned through her servants that Victoria only married Henrik out of obligation to her father. To find out she was to spend centuries with a man she'd felt nothing for should have had her seeking sexual comfort elsewhere. But no.

If it weren't for the fact Henrik had been on what was now the old defunct German Council, Graham would have done away with him. But the rules were different back then. If Henrik had died, all his possessions—Victoria included—would have been in their control.

So Graham set about to discredit Henrik. If he was no longer on the Council, his possessions were for anyone who laid claim to them. Graham had done a wonderful job. Too good of a job. With his word untrustworthy and his world in shambles, Henrik swooped up Victoria and dashed off. Graham had lost track of them until Victoria became a Committee Member of North America.

Ready to continue with his plan, but unsure how to go about it, Graham had finagled his way back into their lives. While he'd been disheartened to see she'd come to love Henrik, the power within her reach had only made Graham want her more. Henrik had claimed he had no say in what Victoria did on the Committee. But how could he not? She clearly leaned on him; the woman was weaker than a hatchling. Henrik had been an idiot, plain and simple.

Graham had taken advantage of Victoria's position to talk to her alone and often. Each time he'd seen her, he'd plant his seeds of doubt where Henrik was concerned. Victoria thought it all had to do with Committee business, and Graham let her believe it, too. He'd been on the verge of winning, he just knew it, when the bastard up and died on him and sent her into exile.

Graham raised his fist to pound into the floor and stopped halfway, catching himself from making undue noise. What was it about Victoria that drove him wild? Why couldn't he forget her and move on?

He'd been an idiot waiting for her all these years and now she would pay. Just once he'd like something to go his way.

The phone rang from Victoria's room. When she answered it, the caller did all the talking. Even Graham's sensitive hearing couldn't make out the conversation.

"Give us ten minutes?" she asked. "See you then." After a few moments, she called out the freak's name.

"Damn," Martin said. "Did I fall asleep?"

What the hell did she see in that mortal? Graham would never have passed out after sex. Hell, he'd be ready for the next round and show her, too. The woman truly didn't know what she was missing.

She laughed. "Maybe a little. We need to get dressed. We're needed in the conference room."

"What about Susannah? Will I be able to see her first?"

Graham jerked back. Susannah was here? In Headquarters? Hmmm… Maybe his plan would succeed after all.

"After the meeting. I promise. Maybe by then she'll be awake."

"I'll hold you to that."

The bedsprings squeaked. Victoria giggled. What the hell were they doing now? Graham put his ear to the wall.

Kissing noises. *Ick*.

* * * *

Victoria touched her lips before entering the conference room with Ben. They still tingled from his last kiss, which almost led to more love-making. If not for the meeting, they'd probably be at it again. And they hadn't even completed the bond. She could only imagine if they had. How did Justin and Katarina do it? Or Sarah and John?

Barnet sat at the end of the table with John to his left and Sarah to his right. The screens were dark.

"Where is everyone?" And who was staying with their patients? But if she asked that aloud, then Ben would want to know more and she couldn't have him finding out about Richard Daugherty. Not yet anyway.

"Abe is…busy," Barnet said. "Besides, this is just a fact-finding meeting."

"Is he staying with Susannah?" she asked.

"No. Perry is."

"Perry?" Ben said. "After what he did?"

"Perry didn't do anything to your sister," Barnet said.

"You were able to determine that?" Victoria asked.

"Yes. Take a seat. You next to John. Ben next to Sarah." What was wrong with her sitting beside Ben? Before she could ask, Barnet held his hand out. "Don't argue with me, Victoria. I need you both focused and I don't think that will happen with you two touching."

Ben chuckled. "He has a point."

"You make it sound like we don't have any control." She settled Ben in his seat. The need to kiss him came at her hard. *Scheisse.* Why did Barnet have to be right? She settled for a hand squeeze before taking her own seat.

"Take it from me," John said. "You don't."

Barnet introduced everyone for Ben's sake. "I'm hoping this meeting will help us find a connection between Perfect Mates. We believe they might all be related. Ben, do you know of an ancestor in your family by the name of Susannah Martin? Someone your sister was named after, maybe?"

Sarah's eyes widened. "Your sister's name is Susannah Martin? Did your parents—"

"Know what they had done?" Ben laughed. "Oh yes. Dad always joked about being related to one of the witches from the Salem Witch Trials. Thought it made for a good family story. Susannah freaked, though, especially when her friends found out and called her a witch. She finally investigated it further and discovered most of the stories our father told us were untrue, except that we did descend from her. After that, she thought it was kind of cool. But you all realize they weren't really witches, right?"

Barnet laughed. "Oh, we know. But two of the Perfect Mates descend from her line, Sarah being one of them."

"Does that mean Susannah is a Perfect Mate, too?" Ben asked.

"No, which baffles me. You're the first we've discovered with a sibling. I thought for sure she would be one." Barnet frowned, as if he had hoped. He might say he wasn't looking for a Perfect Mate, but it appeared he was lying to himself if he believed it.

But Susannah was definitely not a Perfect Mate. In fact, she'd been easy to control. Maybe too easy. It hadn't taken Victoria but a thought to get Susannah to check on the mortal who had struck them with his car. And if she was that susceptible, then Graham could have easily planted some kind of control bomb inside her.

"Could she be the opposite of Ben?" Victoria muttered.

All eyes turned her way. Oops. Had she spoken aloud?

"Opposite, how?" Barnet asked.

"We can't read or control Ben, yet his sister seems more susceptible to mind control."

"What do you mean, more susceptible?" Ben asked.

"That would explain things," Barnet said.

Ben stood. "Someone better explain it to me, then. What do you mean more susceptible? What have you done with her?"

"Easy, son." Barnet came around the table and placed a hand on Ben's shoulder.

Ben flinched from the contact and jerked away. "Don't 'easy' me. Just tell me what you've done to her."

"We haven't done anything to her, but someone has."

"And that someone is Graham," Victoria said. "I say bring him in. Question him. Read his mind."

"Victoria, we can't do that without just cause. If we start jumping to conclusions, we'll be voted out quicker than it takes a vampire to burn in the sun. And you know Graham will definitely make an issue out of this. We have rules for a reason. We expect our people to follow them, so we must, too."

"Would reading Susannah's mind help?" Ben asked.

"Yes, it would and thank you for offering. But before we go that route, you should know all the facts first. Please sit." When Ben took his seat, Barnet headed back to his own. "First, your sister is physically fine. Well, except for the bruises she received from the blast. You two were very lucky to come out of that unscathed. But we're concerned about her mind."

Ben turned his face toward Victoria. "You said she was sleeping."

Oh crap. Although she hadn't technically lied, it felt it all the same. Why couldn't they stick to the subject of Perfect Mates?

"She is sleeping," Barnet said. "We sedated her, for everyone's safety. Tell me, was she acting strange before the blast?"

"No stranger than…" Ben lowered his head in thought.

Oh, why did Barnet separate them? The need to touch him overwhelmed her. The stupid table was much too wide. She couldn't even reach him with her feet.

"Than what?" Barnet asked.

"Well, she's been antagonizing me ever since I went out with

Victoria."

Victoria nearly slammed her hand on the table. That was the day after Graham had picked her up. But why bother telling Barnet? He'd still want concrete proof. Short of getting a signed confession, Susannah was Victoria's only hope.

"And you don't think it's because you're dating for the first time since your accident?"

"That's just it. I pretty much accused her of that, too. So either she's jealous or someone…" He rubbed his forehead. "Shit."

Barnet sighed. "Still… In my experience, when a mortal can be controlled to perform acts that would cause self injury or injury to a loved one, the vampire would have to be extremely strong to override their instincts, unless the mortal is thinking along those lines to begin with. I don't know any vampire in our district who is that strong."

"You're saying Susannah wants to kill me?"

"No. I'm saying I believe Victoria. That Susannah is the opposite of you. Which made it easier for *someone*," Barnet glared at Victoria as he stressed the word, "to control her in a manner no other vampire can override. This is getting more bizarre by the minute."

"Is she going to be okay?" Ben asked.

"Good question. I wish I had an answer for you."

"Then can I ask a dumb question? How do you not know that much about Perfect Mates? You have a name for them, for Pete's sake."

Victoria figured Ben would get around to asking about the story. She trusted Barnet not to share how to complete the bonding process, but John and Sarah were another matter. Damn. Where was a pen and paper when she needed one?

* * * *

Barnet laughed at the question. If not for the strange circumstances, Ben could see being friends with the guy, even if he did call him "son." Hell, every vampire he'd met he'd liked. Except for Graham. But not because Graham was a vampire.

"You have to realize," Barnet said, "vampires used to be mortal. Turning hasn't stopped us from telling stories. And the story of the Perfect Mate was written centuries ago."

"Centuries? But you're just now finding them. How is that possible?"

"How is that possible, indeed? What's worse, I'm beginning to realize that while I know about the story, not every vampire has heard of it. Or if they have, believe it to be more of a myth. An unrealistic one at that."

Ben couldn't help but laugh. "Vampires are supposed to be unrealistic."

"I understand the irony of that. Trust me. But it was a story no one has ever taken credit for. Like a myth. Which doesn't help at all, if you get my meaning."

Ben did. If met with a mythical creature, what would mortals do? Freak out, naturally. "You think vampires are killing people like me, don't you?"

"I can't say for sure. I hope that's not the case, but it is something we will have to investigate. What I'm actually hoping is that you're all starting to pop up now due to some strange trait passed on through the generations."

"So how does Susannah from the Salem Witch Trials come into play? Is she mentioned in the myth?"

"No. It's a link we recently discovered and are investigating further. It could mean something or it could mean nothing. We're basically grasping at straws here. But if we can determine the origin, we might be able to determine how many there are."

Ben shifted in his chair, his nerves on edge. Barnet was beginning to sound like Hitler. "And this information is needed why?"

"Ben, our numbers are low. It's one of the reasons we've been able to stay hidden for so long and trust me, technology hasn't helped us one bit. It's only made our job harder. Add on top of that a number of mortals who could discover our secret…"

"We're a threat to you." Hadn't Perry and Victoria already told him how dangerous his kind could be to vampires?

"To be blunt, yes."

"And you want to what? Eliminate us?"

"Heavens, no. More like…avoid. If we know who they are and where they live, we could warn our people of the risk."

"If that was the case, why not tell your people they're for real and to be careful? Sounds to me like you'd want to know who they are so you could have your own Perfect Mate. You plan on putting them up for bid or something?"

"Ben!" Victoria said. "We would never."

"Easy, Victoria. He hasn't said anything different than I've thought. Ben, I'm afraid if we don't keep a directory, another vampire could very well do it on his own, for the very purpose you suspect. It's a delicate situation, I agree. And one I don't have a solution for. I only know this has to be kept under wraps for now. If word of the Perfect Mate gets out, I expect pandemonium to ensue. And even asking our people innocent questions about the myth would cause suspicion among the ranks. I can't risk that."

Sarah placed her hand on his arm. "Ben, I felt the same way you do at first. Seems like we're aiding the enemy. But they're not the enemy."

"They feed from us."

Victoria gasped. Shit, he didn't mean it the way it sounded. Although, there wasn't a better way to say it, now was there?

"They feed from those they can control, yes," Sarah said. "And they've been doing it for centuries, without harming our people, none of them the wiser. But vampires can't control people like us. We risk their livelihood. Can you imagine if word got out and people learned vampires were real? What do you think would happen to them? Our people wouldn't stop to think before taking action. Do you think the vampires deserve that? You've been with Victoria. Would you want something like that to happen to her?"

The thought pained his heart. Since meeting Victoria, he'd felt alive and worth something. He shook his head. "God, no."

"Would you want vampires to kill us because we're different?"

"But won't they if they have a list?"

"No," Barnet said. "I don't want a list to make it public. Not initially. But I need a list to understand what we're up against. Are we talking one genetic line, dozens, or hundreds? I think once we have the answer, then we can determine what our people should know and what safeguards should be put in place. If our task ends up being impossible to complete, and there's a good possibility it will be, we'll have to come up with a way to tell our people about Perfect Mates so as not to cause an uproar.

"I want the Committee to protect potential Perfect Mates, Ben. Will we be able to? I don't know. We can only start at the beginning, and the beginning is to know where you're all coming from. We need to know the link."

Barnet made sense, but right now the only link Ben wanted was the one he shared with Victoria when they touched. Let her know how sorry he was for his comment about him being food. And then he'd love to take her back to her room where he could rip her clothes off and make sweet love to her all day. Then maybe, just maybe, she would tell him how to complete the bond. So he could be her Perfect Mate.

Of course, the person sitting beside him already knew that information. He turned toward Sarah. "What's it like? Once the bond is complete?"

"It's like freedom," she said. "Although, you have to understand, when it happened to me, I was under a lot of stress at the time and didn't realize it until later, but I lost the needy edge of thinking I would lose John."

"You weren't going to lose me," John said.

"Rationally, I knew that. But John, I wasn't thinking rationally at the time. Neither were you."

"Only because we didn't know."

"That's true," Barnet said. "I hadn't thought about it like that. Tell me, Ben. How are you feeling since Victoria took your blood?"

"Don't answer him, Ben," Victoria said. "Listen, Barnet. I told you I wouldn't be held under a microscope. It's one of the reasons I didn't tell you about Ben in the first place."

"How do you expect me to understand?"

"Why do you need to? Why do any of us need to?" Her scent hit Ben before he registered any movement. Victoria tugged on his arm. "Come on. Let's go check on Susannah."

"Victoria, wait," Barnet said. "I'm sorry if it seems like I'm poking into your personal business, but as the Committee, we must protect our people. That means understanding the bad as well as the good."

Barnet made sense and Victoria was overreacting. Guess this partial-bond thing would mess with her mind and body until they completed it. Or was she afraid of something else? Ben pulled Victoria back. "Baby, what's the matter? Barnet wasn't asking anything personal."

Tensed, she burrowed her face into his chest and he hugged her close. "Doesn't mean he won't. We're not some creatures on display."

"Listen, I want to help. Barnet is right. Knowledge is key."

"And your experiences are different than John's and mine's," Sarah said.

"The more we know, the better we can inform our people," Barnet said.

Victoria slumped in Ben's arms as if someone had pulled the plug on her. "Okay, I give up." She turned her head in Barnet's direction. "But I'm sitting beside Ben, not across the table."

Barnet chuckled. "Fair enough, Victoria."

Ben kissed the top of her head. Maybe he was being selfish, but if they stayed, the odds increased in his favor that he'd find out how to complete the bond. Because holding her wasn't enough. Being with her wasn't enough. He wanted the freedom Sarah spoke of. To know he was Victoria's and she was his. To feel it in his bones.

* * * *

With his heart still racing, Graham quietly exited Headquarters and merged into the shoppers of the Underground. That had been too close. Victoria could have easily bolted from the room—she had seemed angry enough—and would have surely seen him before he'd made his escape.

When Martin and Victoria had left her room, Graham had been all set to leave before being detected, but his curiosity had gotten the better of him and he followed those two instead. He learned way more than he'd thought possible. Amazing what a little eavesdropping could achieve.

Did they honestly believe Perfect Mates existed? And what was with all the bonding crap? Was that the cock-and-bull story they were planning on spreading at the next Meeting? People who couldn't be controlled were freaks, plain and simple. And freaks should be eliminated. If the Committee couldn't see that, then maybe they needed a new Committee.

Getting rid of the Martins just became a whole bunch easier. If Susannah failed in her command, he'd let the vampire public take care of them. No one wanted freaks in their ranks. Then Victoria would be his after she realized vampires needed to stick together. If Graham required any more proof Victoria needed him, that conversation had confirmed it. The woman seriously didn't have a clue about what was right or wrong.

CHAPTER 20

Victoria held Ben's hand in one hand and her handkerchief in the other. Something was calming her thoughts and she didn't think it was the material.

As the meeting went on and on, everyone had their opinion. Perfect Mates were an anomaly. Perfect Mates were a God-send. Perfect Mates this and Perfect Mates that. She just wanted to take her Perfect Mate and run away. Getting to know the one she loved when their bodies screamed to be bonded was bad enough, she didn't need the Committee looking over her shoulder, too.

The connection with Ben was miraculous. And as long as she continued to take his blood, she wouldn't lose it. Complete the bond and it would become better—all the bonded pairs claimed that fact—but she still couldn't bring herself to tell him what it entailed.

Her apprehension at completing the bond had nothing to do with the act itself. After their last love session, he probably wouldn't care. He'd already gotten a taste with the shared experiences.

The problem? His hope for a cure. If he became immortal, wouldn't his eyes revert to their current form after an operation? Cuts healed on their own. How would his body know the cut was for an improvement?

Truth was, they didn't know anything. And Barnet was right in that regard, they needed to know more. But why did the knowledge have to come at her and Ben's expense?

What was best for Ben? Could he live with being blind for centuries? But to ask him would be to share her theories and she couldn't do it. Not yet, anyway.

Since when had she become so selfish? Maybe since the day she'd met him and discovered he was blind. She'd gone into their relationship for all the wrong reasons. And now she was holding onto him for different wrong reasons.

He was the one for her. No one made her feel at peace like he did. No one brought her such joy like he did. But she was a vampire now and different than when she'd been mortal. Right? He was still mortal. His feelings couldn't be the same as hers. Could they? *Scheisse.*

Ben squeezed her hand, bringing her out of her reverie. "Hey. Are you okay?"

"Feeling her emotions, are you?" Barnet asked. "Victoria, you do look a little lost."

"I'm fine. There's a lot to take in."

"And I appreciate your help. Why don't we take a break and check on Susannah?"

"What's to become of her?" Ben asked.

"Once we determine she's not a threat to you or us, she'll be free to leave," Barnet said. "However, I'm concerned about leaving her alone. Someone has manipulated her—"

"You mean Graham," Victoria interrupted. Seriously, did the man believe it could be anyone else?

Barnet thinned his lips and narrowed his eyes toward her. "As I was saying, someone has manipulated her and they could do it again. Maybe she would be better off here."

"For how long?" Ben asked. "And then you'll erase her memory? How do I explain the passage of time? She has a business to run. You can't expect her to give it up."

"And we won't. I only wanted to put it out there in case you felt the same way. Your apartment is currently uninhabitable. What were you thinking?"

"We have insurance. I thought we might stay in a hotel until repairs are made. I can't watch her 24/7, though."

"You know, Ben," Sarah said, "completing the bond would solve most of your worries. Does the thought of taking Victoria's blood gross you out? Because it's really not that bad and you don't need all…"

No, no, no. *Scheisse!* Victoria shook her head violently.

"…that…much." Sarah's eyes widened as she covered her mouth. "Oh. I'm so sorry, Victoria. I thought he knew."

Ben's eyebrows shot up to his hairline. "I have to take her blood?"

Barnet rose. "John, Sarah, why don't we leave these two alone? Victoria, we'll be in Susannah's room when you're through here."

The door shut with their departure and Victoria placed her head on the table. Now that Ben knew, had her job to convince him to wait become harder? Would he try to bite her now?

"I guess I should have known," he said. "You took my blood, so why wouldn't I take yours. Is that why you didn't tell me? You thought I'd be grossed out?"

How easy would it be to say yes? Because why wouldn't he be grossed out? "To tell you the truth…no. Bizarre, huh?"

"So why not tell me? Didn't you trust me?"

"I can barely trust myself. And the urge is so strong. How can you make a rational decision?"

He pulled her into his lap and cupped her face. "You ever think it's strong because it's right?"

Warmth spread from his contact. He was better than the sun of her memories and she couldn't lie to him. "Yes, it feels right, but you need to consider… It's possible even if there is a cure, you will still remain blind."

"Because I'll heal back that way, right?" He nodded. "I kind of figured that."

"And yet you'd still…" *Scheisse.* She couldn't finish.

"Victoria, as long as I'm with you, my sight doesn't matter. I still see you in my heart. Where you belong. I love you."

He loved her? She wrapped her arms around his neck. "You're just too smart for me, you know that?"

"Nah. You don't give yourself enough credit."

"You hardly know me, though. It's sensible to wait, right? To think about it? I was never given that option."

"Sure, it's sensible. But love isn't sensible, is it? You've brought light into my dark life. I'm ready to take your blood. I'm ready to complete the bond. I can't imagine my life without you in it. Maybe that's new love speaking, or the fact you started a process that's begging to be completed, I don't know. But I'll wait if it makes you feel more comfortable." He hugged her and placed his lips beside her ear. "Just know, I turn forty in March and sure hope you agree before then."

His laughter was infectious and she couldn't help but laugh with him. She hugged him tighter. He might think he was already there, ready for bonding, but how could he know? She'd felt his frustration with every stumble he made. Could he live with that for centuries?

Was she doing right by him by sticking around? Or even taking his blood? Maybe she should stay away, at least until after the Committee Meeting. By then whatever process she had started would have waned. His feelings would be real, without this raging need going on between them. Seeing him in class every night would be torturous, provided Barnet still insisted she go, but it would be worth it. And she could use the week before the Meeting as an excuse to not see Ben.

He pulled back and held her face. "What are you thinking? I'm beginning to recognize some of your feelings, but you've got me stumped right now. Sort of a mix between melancholy and hope."

Scheisse. She wouldn't lie to him, but the truth was out of the question. She squeezed his hand. "See, you need to know me better. Then you wouldn't have to ask."

"Trust me. I'm a guy. I'll always have to ask. I just want you to be happy."

"I am happy. With you." She kissed him on the mouth, which led to their tongues intertwining and their hands groping each other's body parts. She broke away breathless. The next two weeks would definitely be torture. *Hölle*, life without him would be torture. "Come on, let's go find your sister."

"And then later?" He kissed her some more and nibbled on her lips. She relished every second.

But there would be no later. Not until after the Committee Meeting. Somehow she would make sure of it.

* * * *

Ben held onto Victoria's arm as she led them to Susannah's room. Victoria was keeping something from him, his biggest hint coming from the mixture of dread and sadness flowing from her through their link. She probably still thought he'd hate being blind for centuries and he didn't know how to convince her otherwise.

She turned unexpectedly and his shoulder collided with the sharp corner of the wall. His grip on her arm was the only thing that kept him from landing on his butt. Good thing she wasn't some fragile creature; with anyone else he might have left a mark on their arm, if not caused some serious damage.

"Oh Ben, I'm so sorry. Are you okay?" That sense of dread emanated from her again.

"Sure, sure. Nothing I'm not used to. Teach me not to carry my cane. I didn't hurt you, did I?"

"No, of course not. I should have paid more attention."

"You're fine. Nothing practice won't fix." If she wanted more practice. Maybe the problem wasn't she was afraid he'd be blind for centuries, but that she would be stuck with a blind guy for centuries. Sure, she pleaded a good story, but what if she were lying to herself? Could that be where the dread came from?

"Lack of practice is no excuse. I could have hurt you."

"But you didn't." He pulled her into his arms. "Baby, what's the matter?"

She broke free—the act stinging his chest a bit—but took his hand and looped it in her arm. "Nothing. Just thinking too much."

Thinking too much about them or him? Hell, even he had to admit he was thinking too much. Why couldn't he let things be? Except if letting things be meant she left him, well, he couldn't stand for that.

After another turn, this one uneventful, she stopped in the hallway. "Is everything okay, Barnet?"

"Yes. Before you go inside, I wanted to let you know what we've done. How about you? You have everything settled?"

She released Ben's hold on her arm. "We're good. How's Susannah?"

The sting turned into a slash. They were far from good, but why argue with her. She wasn't ready to commit and he had to face that fact. Almost funny when he thought about it. Before he'd lost his sight, committing to one person scared the crap out of him. But he was younger then. A lot had happened since his accident. Besides adjusting to his blindness, he'd grown up.

Whereas, she'd been grown up for centuries. Maybe she just needed to adjust to his blindness. He hoped that's all it was.

"She's coming out of it," Barnet said.

"Have you been able to determine who has been manipulating

her?" Ben asked.

"Afraid not, but that's not a surprise. Whoever is behind this—Victoria, don't go there—has hidden his tracks."

"Didn't you dig?" she asked.

Ben winced at the image of someone actually poking into his sister's head. "Dig? What's that?"

"It's a process we use to go deep into a person's mind," Barnet said. "It's not painful, but since Susannah is more susceptible, I'd like to wait and make sure she's acting rationally before we do any digging."

"Then what did you do to my sister?"

"We planted several suggestions into her mind not to harm you, Ben. But we need to make sure they'll hold, so we placed scissors on the nightstand. Don't worry, they're not real. Just be prepared if she tries and attacks. I have a feeling if she has a trigger, it runs deep."

"Are you saying she'll always want to attack me?"

"No. If this doesn't work, we'll keep at it. We won't leave her alone with you until we're certain she's not at risk of harming you. You have my promise on that."

Now if Barnet could only promise that Victoria wouldn't do something stupid, like try and leave him.

* * * *

After a successful visit, a visit where Susannah not only hadn't tried to kill Ben but had acted sane even, Victoria made arrangements at a hotel for Ben and Susannah. At least Graham couldn't track them down tonight. With Susannah's phone lost in the blast, he had no way to contact her. But that didn't mean he couldn't find her tomorrow or the next day. So what if he'd promised Barnet he'd stay away? Graham's word meant nothing to Victoria.

After leading Ben up the stairs to the garage, she stopped to open the door. "We had to make sure Susannah doesn't see her actual surroundings, so she will still be a little confused. But once you get on the road and Sarah utters the magic word, she should be okay."

He pulled her into his arms. "And what about you? Are you going to be okay? I know something is bothering you. Please tell me what."

Until their bond faded, she wouldn't be able to get anything past him. But she wasn't going to tell him about her experiment. He'd only take it the wrong way. However, there was one reason she could give him and it wouldn't be a lie, either. "I'm worried about Graham."

Ben relaxed. "Is that what's been bugging you? I thought I was safe during the day. That's why Sarah's taking us now, right? So Graham can't follow us?"

So true, so true, but for only one night. "Won't stop him tomorrow after class, though."

"No, but as my mom always said, 'Don't borrow trouble.'"

Victoria chuckled as she led him to the van. "Maybe so, but I like to be prepared for anything. Is your mother still alive?"

"No. She and my dad died in the accident that took my sight." He'd said it so matter-of-factly. Then again it had happened ten years ago.

"Oh, Ben. I'm so sorry."

"Hey, nothing to be sorry about. You didn't know." When she stopped at the van, he pulled her in for another hug. "Will you come over tonight?"

The next two weeks would be pure torture. How could she willingly give up his embraces? His kisses? His blood? His love? But she had to be strong and the only way for her to be strong was to avoid temptation. It was better for both of them. Without his blood in her system, their urges would eventually fade. They had better or her plans were useless.

"I don't know. I'd like to have one worry-free night and if I don't visit you, Graham can't follow me, but I'll call you. And I'll be in class tomorrow for sure." Unfortunately, Barnet had still insisted she finish the stupid course.

"Well then maybe I can convince you to change your mind." Ben kissed her and thoroughly explored her mouth. A sense of urgency passed between them and she nearly didn't let him go. Yeah, phone calls were much safer. Being apart would be much safer.

"Mmmm. I like your convincing. I'll see what I can do." At least it wasn't a flat-out lie. She helped him inside the van.

Susannah already sat inside, under the influence to see a hospital setting until Sarah gave the word. "I was beginning to wonder if you would come up for air."

Ben slipped on his glasses and turned toward his sister. "What are you going to do when I get married?"

"Married?" Victoria and Susannah said at the same time.

Ben laughed and took Victoria's hand. "Yeah, married. Be prepared, Victoria. Because I'm thinking it."

Susannah glared at Victoria. "Well I certainly hope our living arrangements are secure before you go doing any proposing."

So much for Susannah having a change of attitude toward Victoria. But marriage? Oh, she'd love nothing better than to be married to Ben. Hopefully, he still felt that way after their bond faded. If it faded.

And if it didn't? She didn't want to think about that.

Victoria was still waving at the departing van, as if Ben could see, when Barnet came up behind her. "Formal meeting. Now."

She followed Barnet to the conference room. Abe was no longer watching Daugherty and sat at the table while the monitors displayed Hilde on one and Jack and Sunny on the other.

"I thought you said this was formal?" Victoria asked.

"It is. Sunny's included because this was her idea. And I think it's a good one." Barnet took his seat. "First off, John and Sarah will be heading home tonight and I'd like them to take Mr. Daugherty with them. Does anyone object?"

"What?" Victoria asked. "After everything you've said?"

"Which goes to show I am listening to you, Victoria. You're right. We have no right to hold him. But I would like to track him somehow. Can we do that?"

"If he has a cellphone, we could easily track him. But if he loses it…"

"It's only temporary, I hope. Just long enough to see what he says publicly. If he keeps quiet, then I'm okay with leaving him alone. He is, after all, only one person and no female vampire lives in the Detroit area. John will make sure he has traces of a hallucinogenic drug in his system."

"Why the change of heart?"

"We don't need him. We have Ben."

Victoria jerked in her seat. Oh no, he did not just go there. She fought the urge to punch out the Head of the Committee. "We don't have Ben. He's not to be had."

"That's not what I meant. But you know we need to experiment if we're to learn anything. Ben has agreed—"

"What do you mean he's agreed? You can't... I won't... Why are you doing this to us?" Maybe she would reconsider that punch.

"Quit being so dramatic, Victoria. No one's doing anything to you. No one's doing anything in regards to your relationship with Ben. No one's taking him from you. This is strictly a Perfect Mate experiment."

An experiment she really, really wanted no part of. But what choice did she have? Apparently none.

"Do you plan on seeing him tonight?"

She shook her head while pulling out her handkerchief. "No. I thought he should have some away time from all this." A lie, but Barnet didn't need to know. How would he feel if she told him she was holding her own experiment?

"Really? Aren't you afraid Susannah might try something? Or Graham?"

"What are you trying to do to me? You've been telling me all along that Graham isn't a threat. Are you saying I should be concerned?"

"No, but you haven't been acting rationally in regards to Ben. I'm surprised you took the results of our test so well. In fact, I'm surprised you let him go at all."

"You might not believe this, but I do have control."

"Good. Then you won't mind it when Sunny touches Ben."

Had the floor opened up and swallowed her? Ben was hers, not Sunny's. But if Sunny touched him... Frantically rubbing her handkerchief, Victoria looked up at the screen featuring Jack and Sunny. "Why would you want to do that?"

"I don't have this inane desire to touch him, if that's your concern" Sunny said.

"But you might after. Jack, are you okay with that?"

"I'm not afraid of losing Sunshine. If she does lose control, then I'll take her home. No harm will come to Ben."

It wasn't Ben she worried about. Victoria couldn't promise she wouldn't attack Sunny. "So you'll do it without me around."

"Oh no," Barnet said. "We want you there. You say you have control. We want to know how much."

"It didn't go so well with Hilde and Rolf, what makes you think—"

Hilde interrupted. "You're right, Victoria. It didn't. That's only because our relationship is on shaky ground."

This was news to Victoria. "Because of Justin?"

"No. It's just something I didn't want to discuss, but now I guess I should. Rolf thinks I cheated on him. I didn't, but it's what he thinks. When Justin came into play, it only made things worse."

"I'm sorry, Hilde. Do you want me to talk to him?"

"Thanks for the offer, but I doubt it would do any good."

"I love Jack," Sunny said. "And I know he loves me. That's why I think I'm the perfect person to perform this experiment. This isn't something we could do with Mr. Daugherty because we didn't want him to know about us. But Ben already knows."

"And," Barnet continued, "it could help us determine how we should proceed with informing our people about Perfect Mates. If Sunny can control herself around Ben, and we already know you were able to control yourself around Daugherty, then it's feasible to think that with knowledge, vampires won't go off the deep end if they encounter a Perfect Mate. I mean, you didn't when you first met Ben, did you?"

"No, his scent only made me aware of him." Whereas her attraction centered around Ben not being able to see how young she looked. His scent had nothing to do with it. Maybe.

"Right. The problem comes into play when a vampire claims their stake, so to speak. Like you did with Ben the first time Sunny met him."

"Claim my stake? Please. The only reason I got nervous then was because I was trying to keep his existence a secret."

"Okay. Good point. So then you won't mind being there when Sunny touches Ben. Which reminds me, don't take his blood. Let his desire return. Can you do that?"

Well, Barnet just made her job a little easier. Her experiment wouldn't have to be a secret and now she wouldn't have to lie to Ben. "Yes."

"Even being in his class?"

"If you're concerned, I don't have to go."

"If not this class, you will attend another. You're not getting out of it."

She crossed her arms across her chest. "I don't see why. You wanted me out of Headquarters. I'm out. And if things work out between Ben and me…" She stopped when everyone stared at her with googley eyes. What did she say?

"If?" Abe asked. "Don't you love him? Because I can tell he loves you."

"Love has nothing to do with it. I need to be sensible. Look what love has done to Graham. He's acting like a nut."

"Because he is one," Jack said. Sunny elbowed him in the ribs and Victoria nearly laughed at Jack's surprised expression.

"Okay, fine. Bad example. Then look what it did to Henrik. Because of love, he turned me into a forever teenager. How could I turn Ben into a forever blind man?"

Barnet placed his hand on her shoulder. "Henrik did not give you a choice. But you've given Ben a choice. Haven't you? That's sensible."

She shook her head. "As long as we have this raging need to complete the bond, what kind of choice does he really have? No, I'll gladly not take his blood so the bond will fade and he can make a rational decision, because right now no one's rational."

"You think your need for him will fade?" Abe asked.

"Won't it?"

No one could answer her. Guess she would find out soon enough.

CHAPTER 21

Perry parked Susannah's car in the hotel parking lot, grabbed the two suitcases he had packed, and took the hotel stairs to the third floor.

He kind of hoped he'd be taking a trip to Dayton. It would have been nice to travel with Johnny and Sarah now that he'd been forgiven, but he couldn't leave until Victoria had finished her driver's ed course. Even though she could physically walk home (mentally was another matter), thanks to the sun she couldn't walk there. And even if she was finished with the class, he wasn't sure he should leave while Susannah was still under another vampire's influence. Barnet warned him not to interfere, but what did Barnet know? Still, if caught, he might be drained a gallon or two of blood. Or worse—staked for a bit. Either way, it would be worth it to get to the truth.

Someone had done a real number with her mind. The night she'd cut him, he'd been sure he had control. Whatever command she'd been given prior to the incident had held fast and eventually overrode every command he and Victoria had thrown at Susannah. And while it appeared the command had been wiped out or simply expired, she still thought they had a fling. He needed to find out who put his face into that pretty little head of hers.

Perry knocked on the door. "Hey, Teach. Let me in."

Ben opened the door looking more haggard than he should. Or is this what love did to a man? "Is everything okay?"

"Everything's peachy. I was able to gather some more of your stuff at the apartment. I'll put the suitcases by the bathroom. Brought your sister's car over, too. Hope you don't mind."

"Thanks. I'm sure she'll appreciate it." Ben sniffed the air. "After she washes everything. Yuck."

"Yeah, it is kind of rank. Where is your sister?"

"She's in the room across the hall. She wanted one that connected, but I was hoping Victoria…" Ben frowned and shuffled toward the bed.

What the ding dong day was Victoria doing? Was she really giving up a Perfect Mate? "Yeah, well… She probably thinks it's better to stay away, what with the experiment and all."

"But a week? Damn, I wish I'd never mentioned the M word."

"M word? You proposed?"

"Not exactly. But I let her know I was thinking it. I want her to know I'm in this all the way. I don't know how else to prove it to her."

"It's this experiment, I'm sure of it. She's weak around you, and Barnet would have a fit if she spoiled it. A week's not all that long when you have eternity to look forward to."

"But she'll feed from someone else."

"You don't like that, huh?" When Ben shook his head, Perry chuckled. "Well, I hate to break it to you but the majority of you are basically food to us."

Ben smirked. "According to Victoria, the females are more than food to you."

"Well, a guy has needs, you know? Victoria's not like me, though. She doesn't feed all that often. I think she hates feeding alone and she's too stupid to ask for company."

"How do you know so much?"

"I see everything." Perry laughed. "But let me ask you this and I want an honest answer. Can you be happy being blind for centuries?"

"I told her it didn't matter. She doesn't believe me."

"Ah. Maybe she senses something, though. Maybe you aren't being truthful to yourself."

Ben plopped on the bed. "Do I get frustrated I can't see? Sure. But there's nothing I can do about it. What frustrates me more is thinking about a life without Victoria in it. I'd gladly give up any chance of seeing if she were with me."

"And is that you speaking or the bond?"

Ben shrugged. "I don't know. I'd like to think it was me."

"And I'm sure Vic is thinking the same. Maybe this little experiment of Barnet's will also satisfy her. Who knows what goes on in that woman's head?"

"What? Can't you read her mind?"

"Not if I can help it." Perry smiled at Ben's laughter. "So, how's your sister?"

"I guess she's fine. Sarah saw us to our rooms before she left. I haven't had a chance to speak to Susannah alone. She was tired anyway. Come to think of it, so am I."

Someone knocked on the door. Perry peeked through the peep hole. "Speak of the devil." He opened the door to one surprised woman. Then again, she was probably expecting Ben to ask who it was.

"Perry? What are you doing here?"

He still couldn't get over the fact some creep used his face. According to Victoria the creep was Graham, but Perry had never known Graham to be so…smart. And it took smarts to cover your tracks. "I brought your car over and some stuff from your apartment."

"How sweet." She looked around Perry. "Ben? I'm going to grab something to eat. Do you want to come?"

"No, thanks. I'm going to crash."

"I'll go with you," Perry said.

Susannah smiled and it made her look years younger. "Okay. Let me go get my purse. I'll meet you in the hall."

"Sounds good."

She practically bounced out of the room and it pained him seeing her so joyful. Not that she shouldn't be happy having a date with him, but she believed he was someone else and that rankled his skin.

"What are you doing?" Ben asked after Perry shut the door. "I thought you weren't seeing my sister."

"I'm not, but maybe I can find out who was using my face." And make sure Teach was truly safe.

"You're going to dig in her mind, aren't you?"

"You know about that? Well, don't worry. I'll be gentle."

"Gentle?"

"With her mind. She's not a means to an end for me. I promise." No, if he were to hit that, as it were, he'd prefer to have her uncompromised. "You trust me, right?"

"Yeah, I do."

"Good, then I'll see you later." Perry left and found Susannah in the hallway, grinning. She really was cute, in a forty-year-old kind of way. "Hey, Suzie-Q, where are we going?"

She laughed. "You've never called me that before. I like it. Do you mind if I just call in room service?"

"Not at all." He followed her into her room. The privacy would make it easier for him to probe her mind anyway. But once she shut the door, she was all over him. Her lips pressed against his in a scorching hot kiss. He'd give her this, she definitely knew how to kiss. Regardless of her circumstances, if he didn't get control, there would be no going gentle with her. "Don't you want food?"

"Right now I want you." She grabbed his crotch and he became rock hard.

Holy shit. As badly as he'd love to bed her, this was Teach's sister. He wouldn't take advantage, not after promising Teach. Perry cleared his head and mentally ordered her to fall asleep.

She became limp in his arms. He waited a moment. The last time he'd given her that command, she'd only been out a few seconds. When she continued sleeping, he carried her to the bed.

Why couldn't she be a Perfect Mate? He wouldn't mind being with someone like her. She certainly wasn't bad to look at and she seemed fun. And then Teach would be his brother. Wouldn't that be something? Then again, that might make Victoria his sister. He shrugged. He could live with that. Ah, but why bother dreaming? It was never going to happen because Susannah was clearly not a Perfect Mate.

He settled on the bed beside her and cupped her sweet face. Even though it seemed his command wasn't being overridden by the previous command, he shouldn't dawdle. With his luck, she'd wake up and start at him again. She'd weakened his resolve before, the next time he might cave in.

He searched her mind, hoping for a glimpse of the creep responsible, but only found blank spots or worse, his own face staring back at him. Heck, she even remembered him in his old Hawaiian shirt, which he hadn't worn since February. Could it be the work of a strong vampire? Perry was strong—stronger than he'd ever let on—but even he couldn't superimpose someone else's face over his. Most likely her mind was silly putty.

Should he dig deeper? He'd done it to a few vampires, but he'd known what to look for then. What the hell would he look for now? An unknown face? Rummaging around her weak mind might cause more damage than not. The risk was too great. But maybe there was another way.

What he was about to do twisted his stomach. Never in his wildest dreams would he think he'd have to resort to such a stunt and it would certainly destroy any chance at a relationship with her. Well, until he could reverse it, but with his luck it might stick. Didn't silly putty pick up the ink from the comics? Whatever, it was the best for her well-being. Perry went deep into her mind and buried his own command. *"When you look at my face your stomach will churn. You won't want to touch me. If I touch you it will make you sick. Physically sick."*

With her still under, he carried her back to the door and positioned her the way she'd been before. Waking her, he broke the link. "I think maybe we should go out and eat. Isn't there a restaurant in the hotel?"

Susannah blinked several times and then looked up at him. After backing away, she scrunched her face and alternated between rubbing her forehead and gripping her stomach. "You know, I think I've lost my appetite. I'm sorry, but can I take a rain check?"

Perry forced a smile. "Not a problem, Suzie-Q. Not a problem. I'll see you later. You take care of yourself."

He hated causing her discomfort, but it was for the best. Or so he kept telling himself.

* * * *

Parked several rows from Susannah's car in the office building garage, but still within watching distance, Graham strummed his fingers on the steering wheel of the SUV he'd so conveniently borrowed. Okay, stolen. But he planned on returning it when he was finished. He'd rather drive his Cadillac, but Victoria would recognize it for sure and he couldn't risk being seen.

How had Susannah not accomplished his mission? Upon arriving, he'd gone up to the class expecting to find her distraught. Instead he'd heard Martin's voice and high-tailed it out of there.

So now not only was Martin still alive, Graham had no idea where the two of them were living. He'd tried calling her, but only got her voice mail. Most likely she'd lost her phone in the blast. And even if he did get through, how could he explain not knowing where she stayed? Perry most likely drove her and Martin to their new abode.

Wonder how that meeting went over? Had she made advances toward the vampire? Had Perry gone through with them?

Graham scowled. Maybe he should have used someone else's likeness when she first saw him, but at the time he wasn't even sure it would work and Perry had seemed the logical choice. Everyone knew how Perry went about feeding. Even so, he had better not have touched Susannah.

The elevator opened and the Martins exited. About damn time.

"What's going on between you and Victoria?" Susannah asked Ben.

"Nothing is going on."

"Then what was that in class?"

"Drop it, okay? Let's go. I'm tired."

Ooh, was there trouble in romance land? Graham couldn't wait to find out. He took hold of her mind, making sure she wouldn't remember anything. He didn't need her blabbing to anyone, especially Perry, that she'd seen him. For all he knew, the Committee was monitoring her actions.

"Will you excuse me for a moment?" she told Martin. "I have to go talk to another teacher. I won't be long."

"Fine, whatever." He entered the car and slammed the door shut.

Susannah climbed into the passenger seat beside Graham and stared straight ahead. Too bad there wasn't enough time for a little fun, he'd just have to get rid of his boner later. Graham took her hand and connected a link to her mind.

Show me what happened in class.

The events played out as Susannah witnessed them. Victoria sat in the front row of class and asked to be moved to the back. Ben frowned at the request, but Susannah told Victoria that it was fine. She was pleased to see the pained look on her brother's face and the agony in Victoria's, not because she was glad her brother was in pain, but because she assumed they'd had a fight.

Graham didn't know what to make of it. Could the magic of their relationship be wearing off already? Hope sprung inside his chest.

He liked Susannah and really didn't want to see her in trouble. Or dead. Hell, she was the best lay he ever had and if it turned out Victoria couldn't satisfy his carnal needs then why not use Susannah?

Hmmm… Why not, indeed?

He sent the following command: If Victoria and Ben have split, you will not need to kill your brother to save his soul from her. Ben's soul is safe as long as Victoria is out of his life. Repeat your command.

She did as she was told. Who knew he could be so good at this shit? He'd truly never known he had such a gift. All the more reason he should be influencing the Committee and not actually be on it. If anyone suspected his strength, they might want to come after him.

Before releasing her, he found out where they were staying, just in case he needed to visit. Once the class ended on Friday, he'd check back and see how things stood.

He couldn't wait until this whole mess was over and Victoria was his. Then he would have at least one last night with Susannah, if not keep her as a mistress. She deserved the treat and he would make sure it was good.

But not now, no matter how hard his dick got.

CHAPTER 22

By Friday, Ben's mood had tanked. All week he'd suffered in class knowing Victoria was within reach but unable to do anything about it. Each night she came up with one excuse or another to leave with everyone else. Then again, if he was emitting those desirable scents, she was probably going crazy whenever he was near. Certainly would explain her moving to the back of the class or rushing out each night.

But why couldn't she take his calls? He couldn't be affecting her over the phone. She better not be easing into a break-up because, damn it, he didn't want to break up with her. If anything, being apart only confirmed how badly he wanted her in his life. She had to feel the same way, but the uncertainty ate at his gut.

At least he'd see her tonight. The experiment was coming to an end and after class he was supposed to go to Headquarters with Victoria and Perry. He still needed to tell Susannah he'd be out, but her attitude toward Victoria hadn't changed a bit and he didn't want a fight.

"I swear, it feels like my head is going to explode," Susannah said as the car came to a stop.

"Migraine?"

"Yeah. If I didn't know better, I'd say you were transferring your stress over to me."

He could only be so lucky, but it did seem more than coincidental. Especially when she had complained about her head right before each attempt on his life. "Have you seen Perry lately?"

"Of course not. Weren't you standing there when he told me he'd be out of town and unreachable all week?"

"I forgot." Ben relaxed. Sure, that was Perry's plan to keep Susannah from calling the other vampire, but that didn't mean the other vampire hadn't called her. So maybe it was just a migraine. If she hadn't seen Perry then no one messed with her head. Right?

The car moved forward.

"Do you have any plans tonight?" Susannah asked. "I thought we might go out and celebrate finishing your first class. It turned out okay, don't you think? Maybe you'll want to do it again?"

Her voice was full of hope. Continuing to teach the class would certainly help with her finances, especially when he finally moved out. "I had fun, I won't deny that. As for whether it turned out okay, I guess you'll find out from your comment cards. But I'll have to take a rain check on the celebration. I have plans with Victoria tonight."

The car jerked. "Victoria? I thought you two broke up. You haven't been with her all week."

"That's because she had other obligations." Obligations like staying away from him. If only she'd taken his calls, then he wouldn't be feeling so paranoid.

"You ever think that maybe she has a boyfriend more her age?"

"We didn't break up."

"If you say so. But she's acting like someone who's looking to break things off."

No, no, no. She wouldn't have left him hanging like this. She would have told him flat out. It had to be the bond. It just had to be.

The car stopped suddenly causing the seatbelt to catch and cut into Ben's chest.

Susannah's arm came across him, same as his mother's had back when he was little. "Stupid driver. You okay?"

"Yeah, I'm fine." If fine included miserable.

* * * *

"Hey, whaddaya know. We're following Susannah and Teach," Perry said.

Victoria looked between the two front seats and out the window. Her heart lurched at the sight of Ben. And if she had also gotten a whiff, her fangs would probably emerge. It had taken everything in her to prevent that little feat from happening the last couple of nights in class.

"Okay, now I see the drool." Perry peered at her through the rearview mirror. "You're hurting for him, aren't you?"

More like hurting, period. She hadn't fed all week and was paying the price. When Ben had proclaimed she wasn't feeding from anyone but him, he wasn't kidding. She couldn't bring herself to feed from anyone else.

As Perry would succinctly say: she was so screwed.

"Hey, call your boyfriend and find out what's wrong with his sister. She's all over the road."

"Can't you control her?" They were currently in the shade and he'd only have to lower his window for a moment. Victoria pulled her cellphone out.

"Her windows are up."

She displayed Ben's number on the screen. She'd been avoiding his calls. Why? She had no idea. Just seemed better that way—out of touch, out of mind? Yeah, it hadn't worked for her, so most likely it hadn't worked for him, either. So what would she say now? *Scheisse.* She pushed the call button.

"Victoria? Is something wrong?"

He would think that. She mustered an upbeat attitude. "I hope not. Perry and I are behind you. Is your sister okay? Or is something wrong with your car? You're all over the road."

"Hold on." His voice then sounded distant as he held the phone away. "Victoria is behind us. She says you're all over—"

Before he could finish, Susannah slammed on the brakes, squealing her tires. Horns honked from every direction. Perry cursed. Their own tires squealed and the van stopped within inches of ramming into Ben and Susannah.

The van lurched forward as sounds of metal crunching and glass breaking filled the air. Unbuckled, but still holding the phone, Victoria ricocheted off the back of Perry's seat and landed on the floor of the van. While Perry had avoided a collision, the car behind them wasn't so lucky.

"Shit, Susannah," Ben yelled. "Victoria? Are you okay?"

Dust motes of glass remnants glittered in the light that came shining through the broken window in the back. Victoria sat frozen, staring at it as if she could magically repair the damage.

With her blood supply low, it wouldn't take much to burn. She pointed at the threat. "Perry. Perry. Perry."

Perry grabbed Victoria's arm and pulled her into the front. "You're fine." He talked to the phone. "She's fine, but we have a light problem, if you get my drift."

"Do you need a ride?" Ben asked.

Victoria shook her head. "I can't go out there."

Perry cocked his head. "You can't miss your last class. Besides, you'll only be out in it a minute." He spoke to the phone. "Can you take Victoria?"

A minute would probably be all it took. And the windows… "I'll burn in that thing!"

"We have an emergency tarp. You can take that," Perry said.

"I'll come get you," Ben said.

"No!" *Scheisse*. What was she going to do?

Sirens sounded, which did nothing for her racing heart.

Perry climbed over the seats and pulled out the tarp, shaking the broken glass. "I can't leave the accident yet. Go on, we don't need to both be here. I can control this without you."

She took the tarp. "What will you use?"

"Don't worry about me. I'm indestructible. Ah look. There's your boyfriend."

They had stopped in the right lane making Ben's trek to the van possible while the traffic kept Susannah inside her car. He walked toward them as she screamed at him to return.

Using his cane as a guide, he arrived and opened the side door. "I'm so sorry. I don't know what got into Susannah."

"Not her fault. I was too close and apparently the guy behind me was even closer. I think he's okay, but his car definitely isn't. Teach, Victoria might need to do a little manipulation with your sister. You okay with that?"

Only if her manipulation worked after being scorched. And without any fresh blood in her system, how quickly might that happen? Two minutes? One?

Ben nodded. "I understand."

"I can't leave you here," Victoria said. The van had to be safer than Susannah's little car.

"Sure you can. You're more important than I am anyway."

She couldn't believe those words came out of Perry's mouth. When had he ever thought she was more important?

Perry took the tarp and opened it up. "Come on, let's get you wrapped up as best as we can. Sun will be down soon anyway. Heck, the rest of the ride is probably in the shade." He pulled it around her shoulders and over her head. "No zipping to the car. Don't want to draw attention to yourself."

"And walking with a tarp won't do that? It's probably hot out there."

"She's right. It's very humid," Ben said.

"Not enough to worry about." Perry nudged her from behind. "Get out of here before they want to take you to the hospital and then we'll have our work cut out for us."

Scheisse, Scheisse, Scheisse. She was definitely screwed. But she couldn't admit she hadn't fed since Sunday. Which meant she couldn't stick around, either. She'd be absolutely useless if it came to multiple mind manipulation. That would definitely drain her dry.

Ben extended his arm. She held her breath and took it. One whiff of him and she'd be a goner for sure. Not only would her fangs emerge, but she'd probably stop to smell him, if not feed from him on the spot.

"It'll probably be quicker if you lead the way," he said.

"You didn't have to come out here." She took a breath and caught his wonderful scent. Crap. A cramp twisted her stomach and her fangs emerged.

"Stop talking and lead the way."

Not a problem now. If she spoke, she'd lisp or moan and then he'd know something was up. What on Earth was she going to do when she got to class and couldn't control these stupid fangs? Guess she would worry about that once she got to the building. There had to be someone she could feed from, although the thought pained her. She only wanted to feed from Ben.

If she kept her movements to a minimum, she should be able to hold out until after the experiment. Maybe.

Most of the trek to the car was in the shade, but a line of sun hit her exposed hand, burning it. She gritted her teeth to keep from crying out. Thank goodness they arrived at the car before she lost control of her limbs. That little exposure had zapped her energy.

After sending a mental command to Susannah to ignore the tarp and her, Victoria settled in the backseat. To make things easier at the garage, she followed her command with an urge to use the bathroom as soon as they parked. No sooner had Victoria finished, she collapsed on her side. Oh well. She didn't need to sit up anyway.

* * * *

Ben almost spoke to Victoria several times, but caught himself. If she had done something to Susannah, maybe it was best he didn't acknowledge her presence. She was awfully quiet back there, though. Was she even breathing?

The car stopped and Susannah turned off the engine. "I gotta go. I'll see you in the classroom."

She slammed the door shut. Well, that was different. She usually helped him from the vehicle, not that he needed help. Heck, he must have told her hundreds of times he didn't need help, but it had never stopped her before. Victoria definitely had to be involved.

Ben slowly opened his door and fumbled with his cane, just in case Susannah looked back his way. Didn't need her wondering why he wasn't getting out of the car, if she was even caring at all. The elevator dinged, followed by the swooshing of the doors closing. "I think the coast is clear."

"Ben." Victoria's weak voice lanced his heart.

Had the sun affected her after all? How badly was she hurt? He rushed out of the car, tripping over his own feet, and managed to open the back without knocking himself in the head. The tarp crinkled as he lifted it off her. She lay on her side. "Baby? Are you okay?"

"I'm so sorry. So, so, sorry. You should go on to class."

"I'm not going anywhere without you." He found her arm and pulled her upright, then scooted in beside her. She weighed practically nothing. After he closed the door, he placed her head in his lap. He got that tell-tale zap any time he touched her, and she smelled like heaven, but that was it. No emotions transferred. Their connection was gone. "What's the matter? Did you get too much sun? Are you…" God, he couldn't even say the word.

"I'm not dying. Just a little weak." She pushed up against his thighs as if trying to sit up, but fell back onto his lap.

He let out an anxious breath. Okay, maybe she wasn't dying, but she was far from a little weak. "When was the last time you fed?"

"I…uh…*Scheisse.* From you."

"From me?" Shit. Was this all his fault? "Oh baby, no."

"I tried, but I couldn't."

He could just kick himself for his stupidity. "No wonder you've been avoiding me." He pulled her into his lap and placed her head on his shoulder. She never resisted. Either she didn't want to or couldn't. "Come on. Take my blood."

"Nooo. The experiment. It's tonight."

"The hell with the experiment. You're hurting and I can help."

"But I treated you so horribly." She sniffed his neck and even that little movement stirred his groin. Shit. He wanted her to bite him. Hard.

"And I should have never told you to feed only from me."

"That's not why I didn't. It just felt like I was cheating on you. I would never cheat on you. I never stopped wanting you. I never stopped loving you."

He smiled. "Good. I never stopped loving you, either. Now feed."

Several moments passed and she still hadn't bitten him.

"Victoria, I feel bad already. Don't make it any worse, okay? Just bite—"

She clamped down on his neck, cutting off his words. Dear Lord, above. He became instantly hard. Each pull on his neck sent him deeper into paradise. Each pull on his neck strengthened their connection. Her emotions trickled over little by little until her love for him outshone them all. He resisted the urge to grind his erection into her hip. If it weren't for the car and the class and, for her…well…her well-being, he'd take her right then and there.

She broke free and licked him way too soon.

"Did you get enough?" Because he would never get enough of that.

She answered him with a scorching kiss; traces of blood lingered on her tongue and got him hotter. "I love you, Ben Martin. Don't ever doubt that."

"And I love you, too." Life would be sweet now that he had her back. "Can we complete the bond tonight? Or is it done in a special ceremony?"

She backed out of his arms. "What have I done?"

Oh no, she wasn't getting away from him again. "You haven't done anything."

"The bond, it faded for you, had it not? And now…"

"I hate to break it to you, but the only thing that faded was feeling your emotions when we touched. I haven't stopped wanting you to complete the bond. I haven't stopped wanting you, period."

Her fingers were soft against his cheek. "You haven't?"

"No, baby." He kissed her to make his point. Heat spread and sparks flew. He ground the evidence of his desire into her hip. When he slipped his hand under her blouse, she broke the kiss.

"As much as I'm enjoying this, if you don't show up for class, I'm sure Susannah will come back down here. I didn't give her that many commands."

He chuckled. "So it was you." He opened the door. "Can you walk?"

Seemed she could. Amazing what his blood did for her and she hadn't taken all that much.

* * * *

Victoria stared at Barnet across from his desk. Ben fully expected to complete the bond, but she still couldn't bring herself to do it. Not until she knew for sure Ben could handle being blind forever. Barnet was her only hope and, seeing how he wanted to conduct all these experiments, he could put a stop to it. But would he?

"You couldn't wait four hours?" Barnet asked.

"She couldn't wait two minutes," Ben said, squeezing her hand. "She could barely move."

Barnet glared at her. "And there was no one else you could have fed from? No offense to Ben, but wasn't Susannah in the car?"

What was with the third degree? "Yes. But I wasn't thinking clearly at the time."

"Which leads me to wonder how you became so incapacitated to begin with."

"That would be my fault," Ben said. "I told her I didn't like her feeding from anyone else. But I didn't mean for her to go hungry."

Barnet stood. "You haven't been feeding?"

"I've been keeping busy and…" *Hölle.* There was no excuse.

"Damn it, Victoria! Of all the irresponsible… You do remember we have a meeting coming up in eleven days, don't you? I need answers before then."

"I'm sorry."

"I'm sorry is not going to cut it this time. You two will not see each other for five days. That should be enough time to conduct another experiment."

"What? You can't—"

Barnet raised his hand, silencing her. "I can and I will. You are not to leave Headquarters except for your driving lessons, but then I don't expect that to be a problem, do I? Ben, can I assume you will not be involved with teaching her how to drive?"

Ben chuckled. "You could assume correctly."

"This isn't funny," she said.

"It's only five days," Ben said. "I think I can wait five days as long as you promise to take my calls." He turned toward Barnet. "You will let us talk on the phone, right?"

"The phone shouldn't be a problem," Barnet said.

Why were they ganging up on her and why did it matter? Hadn't she wanted to wait to bond with Ben? This was certainly delaying that. But to be treated like a child? She was not a child, damn it. She glared at Barnet. "Why not cancel the class then? Why not put me in a jail?"

"Oh no, you're not getting out of that requirement. Perry will be assigned to you and will not leave your side. That includes feeding and your lessons. You're to get plenty of driving practice in, too. That should keep you busy."

"Maybe I should resign." Not that she wanted to, but damn. Perry twenty-four hours a day for five days? She'd go mad.

"If that's what you want to do, I can't stop you. However, it will not change the fact that you will not be in contact with Ben for five days and Perry will still be assigned to you. The Committee needs answers and you two are the only ones who can give them to us now." Barnet walked to the door. "I'll give you ten minutes together before I send Perry in to take Ben back to his hotel."

"I'm going with him." She'd put Perry to some use, then.

"Yes, you are. And you will practice driving while you're out. Just remember, Perry will not leave your side. Do you understand?"

"I understand I'm being treated like a child and Perry's my babysitter."

"You should have thought about that before going a whole week without feeding." He slammed the door on his way out.

Barnet had every right to be mad at her, but did he have to be such a boss about it? He was worse than her father had ever been. At least there was one good thing about their separation. It gave Ben five more days to think things through. And her, too.

Ben squeezed her hand. "I feel to blame for this. I had no idea…"

"It's not your fault. If not for the accident… Oh well, nothing I can do about that now." She climbed onto his lap. "I'm going to miss you, though."

"I have a feeling Perry will keep you too busy, or maybe too frustrated, to do that. But I'll miss you, too. We'll have to have some of that phone sex I've heard about so I don't explode."

Phone sex, huh? She'd rather have the real thing. She eyed the door. Could they? Was there enough time? Oh, *Hölle*, why not. "Hold that thought."

She climbed off Ben and locked the door. Wouldn't really keep Perry out, but he wouldn't dare break it. Barnet would have a fit. Of course, Barnet would have a fit once he learned she used his office for a tryst. Served him right. She came back to Ben and unbuttoned his slacks. He was already hard for her.

He placed his hands over hers. "What are you doing?"

"Giving you a gift to remember me by." She kissed him and, not only had his warmth spread at the contact, she was met with an electric jolt, too. They both gasped. "*Gott*, I'd forgotten how great that shared experience is."

"Yeah, great. Now stop talking." He grabbed her shoulders, pulled her into his lap, and continued kissing her.

All thought nearly left her head as she was bombarded with sensation. His erection digging into her prompted a reminder and she went back to work on his pants. Good thing she wore a dress. She wasn't sure either one of them could wait.

She freed him and settled over his erection while her mouth never left his. Oh *Gott*, he felt good.

Five days would be murder.

CHAPTER 23

Ben leaned back against the chair and searched for air. That was the quickest quickie he'd ever had and it nearly knocked him out. No time to nap, though.

Victoria climbed off his lap. "*Scheisse.* Where's a tissue when you need it?"

He laughed. "Hey, it wasn't my idea."

But damn, what an idea. Sex in a chair. It was a first for him.

She kissed him. "I didn't hear you complaining."

He had told her five days was nothing, but now… Five days seemed like an eternity. At least he had an eternity to look forward to. An eternity with her. Could life get any better? If so, it might give him a heart attack. Man, he never came so hard.

"Who locked the door?" Perry said as the door knob rattled. "Hey, what's going on in there?"

She sighed. "For once I wish that man would be late."

Ben pulled a handkerchief from his pocket. "Will this do?"

"You carry a handkerchief?"

"Dad always said a gentleman should carry one."

She took it from his hand. "*Gott segnest dich.* Sorry. That means bless you."

"I know. I kind of like the German version."

Perry knocked. "Victoria, open the door."

"Oh, just a minute," she said with a lot of frustration behind it. "You speak German?"

Ben nearly laughed at the change of her voice toward him—all sweet and charming. He adjusted his pants and zipped up. "Not really. Took a couple of years in high school, and we hosted an exchange student from Germany. So I picked up a lot. I'm very rusty, though."

"Well, maybe I can give you some practice. Sometimes I miss the language."

"Hey, we have forever, right?"

She paused for a moment. "Right."

More doubts? Really? He found her arm and pulled her into his lap. "Victoria. I'm in this. Sight or no sight. Do you understand? I'm not losing you."

She rested her forehead against his. "You won't. Okay? I better go let Perry in."

Now, why didn't her tone of reassurance reassure him? Probably because her emotions were all over the place.

She disengaged the lock and a breeze struck Ben's face as the door opened.

"I can't believe you used Barnet's office for a quickie." Perry's tone was laced in shock. Almost as if Victoria had never done anything remotely inappropriate before. Hell, maybe she hadn't.

"I don't know what you're talking about," she said.

"Yeah, right. You two love birds ready to go?"

Silence accompanied their trek to the garage. Several times Ben nearly questioned her comment about not losing her, but with Perry around, no way would she talk freely. Maybe she needed the next five days to come to a decision. But what would he do if she decided not to complete the bond? Well, he'd just have to convince her otherwise.

When they arrived at the van, the sound of keys jangled. "Victoria, you drive. Barnet said you needed the practice."

"I'll drive coming back. Besides, I'm not supposed to drive with a passenger."

Ben fought not to smile. Did she have excuses for everything?

"He's not a passenger. He's the teacher." Perry huffed. "Sometimes I wonder what I did to deserve this kind of punishment."

"You? I'm the one being punished."

"Okay, you two," Ben said. "You're stuck with each other for five days. Might want to make the best of it."

"Teach, there is no best of it. And if you could see the ugly look she's giving me right now, you'd probably run away as fast as you can. She's creepy scary, you know?" Perry's words were followed by a punching sound. "And she hits, too. I'd watch it if I were you."

"As if I'd have any reason to smack Ben," she said. "He, at least, has manners."

She climbed into the back of the van and Ben followed. "Driving's only as scary as you let it," he said.

"I'm not afraid to drive."

"No," Perry said. "She's afraid to go outside by herself."

"I'm not afraid," she said. "I just see no reason for it."

"More like Henrik told you not to and so you don't."

The side door slid shut and Ben took Victoria's hand. "Is that true?"

"I don't know. Maybe."

"How controlling was he?"

"He wasn't controlling. He had his reasons." The front door opened and the van moved with Perry's added weight. "Can we talk about this later? In private?"

He liked how she planned on a later. And private sounded good, too. Five days, though. Yeah, they would be torture.

She climbed into his lap and wrapped her arms around his neck. "What are you doing? You should be buckled in."

"I won't get hurt. Stop worrying." After tossing his glasses who knew where, she nuzzled his neck and nibbled on his ear.

She shouldn't arouse him—it had only been a few minutes since he came—but what do you know, she did. Maybe he was making up for lost time. God knew she was the first since he'd lost his sight. Not unless his hand counted.

The van bounced and Victoria pulled away. "We're here already?"

"It's not like he's across town," Perry said. "So say your goodbyes."

"I'm taking Ben to his room."

"You are not," Perry said.

She kissed Ben on the cheek, her lips lingering and sending out little erotic shockwaves. "Guess we're both coming up with you."

"That's not necessary," he said. Although truth be told, he was having a hard time letting her go. Bond, love, or whatever, it was controlling him.

"Don't be silly. I'm walking you to your door," she said. "He can come with us or not, I don't care."

As they rode the elevator, Ben held her hand and rubbed his middle finger against her palm. She snickered. God, he loved her. She felt that through their connection, didn't she?

He stopped at his door, but didn't pull out his key card. Instead he took her face into his hands and kissed her. Pushed her against the wall and devoured her mouth. If she was having any doubts, he wanted to erase them all. Show her what she meant to him. What they could have together. If he could burn this memory, this kiss, into her brain, into her soul, he would.

Between breaths she muttered, "Perry's right there."

"I don't see anyone," Ben said as he dove into her mouth once again.

"Good one, Teach," Perry said, chuckling.

She tasted all sweet and way too addicting. Ben got her fangs to emerge, which only brought back his hard-on. Guess he'd be calling her soon for that phone sex. He was about to explode in his pants.

"You're killing me," she said.

"Good." He rested his forehead against hers. "I don't want you to forget this. You tend to do crazy things when we're apart."

"I promise I won't do anything crazy. Call me before you retire tonight?"

"Bet on it." He pulled his key card out. "Goodnight, Perry."

She held onto his hand. Hell, he didn't want to let go, either.

"Come on, Vic," Perry said, apparently pulling Victoria away. "Let the man go."

"I love you," she said and then her fingers slipped free.

Man, that bond was tough. Or their attraction. An emptiness settled around his heart and she was probably only a few feet away. Five days. Five long, miserable, lonely days.

Oh hell.

He closed the door and placed his cane on the dresser. He reached for his glasses. Damn it. He'd left them in the van. Or maybe it was a good thing. She'd return with them for sure. He pulled his phone out as rustling sounds came from the bed. He froze. "Who's there?"

"Are you going to marry her?"

Susannah. Not some deranged vampire. He relaxed and placed

the phone on the dresser. Guess the glasses would wait. This is what he got for giving her a key. "Geez, next time warn me, would you? You scared me half to death."

"Answer my question. Are you going to marry her?"

"I haven't asked her." Yet. Hell. Maybe that's what was causing her indecision. What an idiot. He'd certainly remedy that the next time he saw her, like when she returned his glasses. "You might as well get used to seeing her around. She's the one for me."

"No, she's just letting you think that. You have to see she's poison to you."

Poison? Had the vampire manipulated her again? "Have you seen Perry?"

"What does Perry have to do with this?"

Nothing. Everything. If she was being manipulated, he needed to call Victoria. He stepped back toward the dresser, and his phone. "Just answer the question."

"I told you I haven't seen him since Sunday. Why does it matter?"

Great. It was all Susannah, then. "Because I thought maybe someone was poisoning your mind instead. What the hell did Victoria ever do to you?"

"If you could see her you'd know she was wrong for you."

"Since when do you judge a person by their looks?"

"She's evil, Ben."

"I've heard enough. You need to leave."

"And she's poisoned you against me. She's poisoned your soul. I have to fix that."

"You leave her alone. You hear?" Sure, Victoria could take care of herself, but Susannah didn't know that.

"I'll make you better."

"What are you—" a burning sensation formed in his gut and knocked the breath right out of him. When he gripped his stomach, he found it warm and sticky. Blood. "Susannah?"

He collapsed to the floor.

* * * *

Victoria settled behind the steering wheel of the van. Her lips still burned from Ben's kiss. He'd said he was in, sight or no sight, and she was beginning to believe him. She certainly wanted to believe him. Wasn't sure she could live without him.

"Buckle up," Perry said. "Or you'll get pulled over. Don't want that, do you?"

"You're awful bossy, aren't you?"

"Hey, I take advantage when I've got it."

She grabbed the seatbelt and clicked herself in. Five days with this miscreant. However would she survive? She stretched her feet and met with…air. "How am I supposed to drive this? I can't even reach the pedals."

"That's what the seat adjuster is for." He took her hand and placed it on a handle under the seat. "Pull up and scoot forward."

She did as he said and choked when the seatbelt cut into her neck. Perry cackled. Damn man! She unbuckled the belt and moved the seat, then re-buckled. She adjusted the rearview mirror and got a view of cardboard and tape. "You didn't replace the window?"

"You just now noticed that? Damn, you really do have it bad for him. Window's on order."

"How do you expect me to drive if I can't see out the back?"

"The same as any truck driver. Use the side mirrors."

Side mirrors? As if she could see out them. She was about to complain when he pointed to the mirror adjustment. He was showing her the different gears when she spied a familiar set of sunglasses. An excuse to see Ben again. She picked them up and unbuckled. "Ben forgot these."

She had her hand on the door when Perry grabbed her right arm. "Oh no you don't. He can live without them. It's not like he sees."

"That's not why he wears them and you know it. I won't be long."

"Yeah, like you wouldn't be long saying goodbye. I swear, if I wasn't there, the two of you would have done it in the hall."

No, they would have done it on Ben's bed. And then followed up in his shower. *Scheisse.* She really needed to get her hormones in line. "Fine, come with me, then. But he's getting his glasses."

She hopped out of the van and headed for the hotel. Like a puppy, Perry followed. A few steps later, her spine tingled and gut twisted. Did she need to feed again already? She was sure she'd gotten enough from Ben to hold her a day at least.

"Why'd you stop? Did you finally come to your senses?"

She shook it off. "Stomach's acting up. Let's go."

"Well, no wonder. Mine would be too if I hadn't eaten regularly for a week. We'll find a donor after you return those."

She rushed up the stairwell as if something pulled her toward Ben. Probably the bond. Maybe they should complete it as soon as possible. Certainly would get rid of this needy feeling.

She knocked on his door. "Ben, it's me." When it didn't open, she placed her ear against it. Not a sound. "Do you think he's at Susannah's?"

Perry shrugged and knocked on Susannah's door. When she didn't answer, he placed his ear against it. "Not there."

Victoria called Ben's cell. His ringtone sounded through the door and a recognizable scent followed. Her stomach twisted again. "Perry. The smell. The smell."

He swore. "Blood."

The ringtone ended. Her call went into voice mail and her heart stopped. What had Graham done now? "Oh *Gott*, I have to get in there."

"Hold on, I'll go get a keycard."

"You better hurry or don't be surprised to find a hole through the wall. I don't care who sees it, either," she said at his retreating body. He zipped down the stairs. She placed her hands on the door. "Ben? Can you hear me?"

Please let him be okay, she prayed.

She continued to call out for him and by the time Perry returned with the key, she was kneeling on the floor. She snatched the card and opened the door. Ben. Blood. Knife.

She cried out and rushed to his side. Blood pooled around his prone body. Susannah sat beside him holding a bloody knife looking straight ahead at the wall. The woman didn't even blink.

Faint heartbeats came from Ben. Good, she wasn't too late. The front of his shirt was all bloody. She pulled it up to inspect his wound. Instead of healing him, she could only stare at the gash across his stomach. No amount of vampire saliva could heal that. What could she do?

A towel appeared in front of her. Yes, yes. She snatched it and pressed it against Ben's stomach. It soaked through immediately. No, no. "Should we call 9-1-1?"

"Vic, I don't think it's going to matter."

She didn't either. Oh *Gott*, she couldn't lose him like this.

"Victoria? Are you here?" Ben's voice was weak, but he was conscious. And if he was conscious, then maybe, just maybe…

"I'm here, Ben. Do you want to complete the bond now?" Please let him be rational enough to know what she was asking. Sure, he had said numerous times he wanted her blood, but did it matter when it happened? Maybe he had changed his mind.

"I love you, baby. I'm tired."

"I love you, too, but don't go to sleep, Ben. Answer my question. Do you want to complete the bond now?"

"I want to be with you forever."

Good enough for her. Using her fangs, she ripped open her wrist then placed it against his mouth.

"What the hell?" Perry said. "I though they only needed a drop."

She brushed the hair away from Ben's face. "Come on, drink."

He coughed and splattered blood. Hers or his? *Scheisse.*

"If you want to be with me forever, sweetie, you have to drink my blood."

He gave it one suck, then promptly became limp.

"Ben? Ben?" She shook him.

"Ease up, Vic," Perry said. "His heart is still beating. He just passed out."

Ben's shallow breathing eased her fears a little. But his wound was still bleeding. She started licking the cut closed, unsure if anything she did would help him survive. "Do you think he took enough?" she asked between licks. "Do you think it'll work?"

"I don't know. I sure hope so." Perry was holding Susannah, who appeared catatonic.

"What's wrong with her?"

"Looks like she blew a fuse." He fished out his phone and placed a call. "Hey, Barnet. We have a problem and it needs cleaning up."

And there would be an even bigger problem if Ben didn't pull through. Because nothing would stop her from killing the person responsible and she'd hurt anyone who stood in her way.

* * * *

Graham couldn't wait to fuck Susannah and get some much needed relief. Then he'd take a trip to Headquarters and pay his respects to Victoria. Everything he'd seen so far assured him Victoria and Martin were through.

It was about time. But hey, all good things came to those who waited. And he'd waited all right. Way too long.

He drove up to the hotel as Ian walked past carrying a couple of satchels. What the hell was he doing here? Graham lowered the passenger window and called the man over.

Ian smiled and rested his arms on the open window. "Wow. Nice ride. When'd you get it?"

With Ian it was always chit chat first. Graham only wanted information, but he needed to do it without drawing suspicion. He massaged the dashboard. Isn't that what car aficionados did? "A few months ago. Got a great deal, too."

"I bet. So, what are you doing here?"

"Just cruising and saw you." People still cruised, didn't they? Shit. "Thought I'd say hi. So, what's the job?"

"Not sure. Something to do with Victoria and Perry." Ian's face lit up. "Maybe they finally had a knock-down drag-out, huh? Man, I would have liked to have seen that. Anyway, gotta clean the mess before hotel maintenance gets a whiff, you know? See ya."

If it involved Victoria and Perry and this hotel, then it better have meant Martin's death. But if Martin was dead, that meant Susannah had reason to kill him. He slammed his hand against the steering wheel, cracking it in the process. Damn Victoria! Would she ever come to her senses?

CHAPTER 24

Victoria stroked Ben's hand while she rested her head on his chest. As he lay unconscious on her bed, his even-breathing and steady heartbeat lulled her into wishful thinking. It had been several hours since he'd taken her blood and while he hadn't died, he hadn't woken, either.

She had sealed the wound the best she could, reaching as deep as her tongue allowed. It was enough to stop the bleeding so they could transport him and Susannah back to Headquarters. Once back, someone had managed to get their hands on blood and transfuse it to Ben, hoping that would bring him around, but no. Well, not a complete no. The color returned to his face, the warmth that spread when they touched was stronger, and had the little scars around his eyes faded? She thought so, but couldn't really tell. Only problem: would he wake up?

Or would her Perfect Mate be in a coma forever?

A hand landed on her shoulder. "Don't you think you've wasted enough time on this blind freak?"

Graham. She ground her teeth together. Barnet had suspected the man would make an appearance—ever since Ian had seen Graham at the hotel—and had made her promise not to do anything rash. And while Barnet had finally come around to her side, they still needed proof of Graham's illegal activities. Until Susannah snapped out of her catatonic state, they wouldn't get it from her. "Let him hang himself," Barnet had said. But waiting around for that to happen would be the hardest thing Victoria had ever done.

"What are you doing here?" She had to give Graham some credit. He always managed to find her alone. Not that that was too hard. Everyone was more interested in Susannah at the moment.

"We need to talk. Somewhere there are no ears listening in."

She shook her head. "We can talk here. I'm not leaving him."

He grabbed her arm in a painful grip. "Oh, I think you will." He continued telepathically, their touch creating a link, *"Because if you don't, I'll make sure he never wakes up."*

"Are you threatening me?"

"No, it's a promise. I'm in the right here and don't you forget it."

Even if the bond had completed and Ben was immortal, he could probably still be killed, same as she could. And if she wanted to get proof that Graham was behind everything, then she had to go along with him.

"Fine. Let me get someone to watch him."

"I don't think so. Let's go." He dragged her out of the room and into the hallway, heading for the exit to the Underground.

"What are you hoping to accomplish? You think I'm—"

He yanked her hard and brought his face down to hers. His eyes gleamed. "Shut. The fuck. Up."

The man had gone crazy, plain and simple. She went along without struggling. The more he thought she acquiesced, the better her chances at getting a confession.

He pulled her into the darkened and empty mall. Music sounded from a distance. He dragged her away from the noise, tugging her like a wayward child, until they reached the restrooms. He flung open the women's door and threw her inside.

She crashed into the sinks, pain blooming in her hip. Owww. She rubbed the offending spot. Had she cracked the porcelain or her bones? The only source of light came from the emergency exit sign and the room had an eerie red glow. When she straightened up, Graham was brandishing a stake and the light reflected in his eyes made him look insane.

Or maybe it wasn't the light at all and he was already there.

"What are you going to do with that?" she asked.

He slapped the wood against the palm of his free hand. "I'm thinking staking you is the only way to keep you here so you'll listen to reason."

She flashed back to another time, another place, with someone just as menacing. He'd slapped a baton in the same manner as Graham, but wore a mask, so Victoria had never been able to identify him. If not for the passersby, she might have been seriously wounded. It was after that event Henrik had seen fit to turn her. *Hölle.*

"It was you who attempted an attack on me all those years ago, wasn't it? Henrik didn't want me turned so young, but you didn't know how else to convince him otherwise, did you?"

"And yet it did me no good, did it? What is it about me that disgusts you? For centuries I've done nothing but love you, but you don't pay me any mind." Graham paced in front of the exit. "I know you didn't love Henrik when you married him. How did you come to love him after he turned you? Why him and not me?"

"Graham, I didn't know about your feelings then."

"Are you saying if you had, you would have left Henrik for me?"

"I don't know. You're talking ancient history."

"Then how about now? You've only known that freak a couple of weeks and yet you're all over him. He's just a mortal."

A mortal who would do anything for her whereas Graham didn't care at all. "Why do you even want me if I bring you such grief?"

In a flash he was in front of her, caressing her cheek. It took everything in her not to cringe. "I love you, Victoria. Together we could accomplish so much. With your sweet, trusting face and my smarts, we could control the Committee."

"Smarts?" She snorted. "And what makes you think you could control me?" Anger flashed in his eyes and it was all the distraction she needed. She snatched the stake from his hand. "Now listen to me, Graham. We're going back inside and you will confess to everything you've done to Susannah and Ben or this stake will be used on you. And if you're lucky, we won't make an example out of you."

"Example out of me? I haven't done anything to those mortals that another vampire wouldn't have done. What the Committee should have done. Martin is a threat and I can't understand why he hasn't been killed already. You want me to keep my mouth shut then you better dispose of him permanently, and soon. Otherwise the June meeting will be very interesting." He dashed out the door.

Victoria rushed after him, but he was gone.

* * * *

Perry pulled a brush through Susannah's hair. He had never brushed a woman's hair before, but it beat sitting here watching her blink and breathe.

"Are you in there, Suzie-Q?"

No reaction, as usual. She continued to stare out into space, or whatever world she was currently living in.

Guilt wore on him, which wasn't something he was used to. Could he have contributed to the breakdown? Had she been manipulated one too many times? If he dug around in that head of hers, would he just make things worse?

The answer was probably yes to all of the above, so he brushed her hair and told her stories about his life. What little there was to tell, anyway. No woman wanted to hear about the sexual exploits of a man, even if she was in a catatonic state and the man was him.

Wonder how long the Committee would wait until they determined she was permanently damaged? They certainly weren't fit to take care of her.

"She is pretty, isn't she?" Barnet said as he entered the room.

"You hoped she was like Teach, didn't you?" Perry let loose a dispirited chuckle. Hell, he'd hoped the same.

"It would have been nice. I thought for sure if we found one with a sibling…"

"That we'd find a whole nest of them? Or maybe a town with them. Wouldn't that be amazing?"

"Yeah, something like that. Doesn't seem fair to find another male Perfect Mate when the majority of vampires are male."

"I'm sure there are other female mates out there. The men probably won't say." He wouldn't. Hell, he hadn't bothered to tell Barnet about Sarah when he'd found out about her. If by some chance he happened upon another one, he couldn't imagine sharing that information. Why fight the whole race if he didn't have to?

"I've thought the same thing."

"What happens if she doesn't snap out of it?"

"We'll probably have to take her to a hospital."

"Even though she's like this because of us? Do you think

turning her would cure her?"

"Doesn't matter. We can't get her permission, now can we?"

No, but maybe they could get Teach's. And then maybe they could modify their rule. It wasn't fair she should live her life like this if there was a chance she could be better.

Victoria burst into the room. "We've got a problem. I just saw Graham."

Hearing the bastard's name got Perry riled up. When he'd heard that Graham was seen at Teach's hotel, he became a believer that Graham was involved. Not that it took much to convince him. That vampire never did have a lick of sense. No vampire needed to control a partner for sex. That's what their glamour was for. Even then, Perry used it as little as possible. He had his pride. "What did that prick want now?"

"He seems to think it would be for the greater good to kill Ben. Wants to know why we haven't."

Barnet rubbed his face. "So much for thinking the man would keep quiet. We better hope Derek doesn't show up for this meeting. If the two of them get together, it could mean trouble for the Committee as well as for you and Katarina. John, too."

Perry perked up at the mention of Johnny's name. "What? Sarah and Justin aren't telling anyone. Neither would Teach, for that matter." Provided the man ever woke up. He didn't envy Victoria's predicament.

"Doesn't matter what we think. Katarina, John, and Victoria each told a mortal about us, a mortal whose memory cannot be erased. In other words, they all broke the first rule. I need to call a meeting. Come on, Victoria."

"No. I have to get back to Ben. I don't want to leave him alone. Especially now."

"Perry, take Susannah and watch the two of them. Victoria's bed should hold them both." Barnet looked at Victoria. "Was there any change?"

She shook her head. "I'm afraid. What if he stays this way? What if they both stay this way? Graham expects Ben to be killed before the June meeting. I can't... I won't..."

"Easy, now. Let's not jump ahead of ourselves. Go help Perry get Susannah settled and then meet me in the conference room."

After Barnet left, Perry scooped up Susannah. "Lead the way."

Victoria held the door open. "When Sarah was stabbed, she

didn't go into a coma, did she?"

"No, but she was already immortal before the stab and didn't lose as much blood. She did sleep afterward. Maybe that's all he's doing." Hollow words if he'd ever heard them. At least John had been able to wake Sarah when she'd first passed out.

Perry followed her to her room and gently placed Susannah next to Ben.

Victoria sank to the floor and sobbed. "What am I going to do without him?"

Perry squatted beside her. He would have wiped her tears if she could have generated any. "Hey, he's not dead and no one's going to kill him. Don't let Graham get to you."

"You didn't see the look in his eyes. He scares me."

"And if he's gone over the edge, he'll make a mistake. He has more than one enemy here."

"*Danke.* And thank you for watching Ben."

"Hey, it's better than babysitting you." That comment brought a smile to her face and a light punch to his bicep. "You better get going. Don't want to keep the Head waiting."

She stood and took Ben's hand. "I did right by completing the bond, didn't I?"

"I'd have done the same."

She kissed Ben, lingering for several awkward moments. Perry turned away. Love was a messy emotion and one he hoped to never experience. His feelings for Sarah couldn't have been love. He didn't experience that much pain, more like disappointment. Victoria seemed more than disappointed. When he got his own Perfect Mate, there'd be no love involved. Just mind-blowing sex and some wonderful blood, because that would be perfect for him.

Finally, she dashed out of her room, leaving him alone with the siblings. No use sitting in here watching them breathe. Victoria owned a television.

* * * *

Jack and Abe sat at the table with Victoria and Barnet while Hilde's likeness was being transmitted on the screen. Victoria stroked her handkerchief while Barnet caught everyone up on the past events. It wasn't all that long ago she'd thought going to a driver's ed class was the end of the world and the handkerchief did little to soothe her then. Losing Ben *would* be the end of her world. If Graham went through with his plan, she might as well walk into the sun. There wouldn't be much of her left anyway. Ben owned the important part—her heart.

"Is he still desirable to other female vampires?" Hilde asked.

Victoria nearly rubbed a hole in the soft fabric. Who cared if Ben was desirable? She only wanted him awake.

"Good question," Barnet said. "Jack, we'll need Sunny after all it seems."

"What if we let Graham believe Ben is dead?" Jack asked. "That could buy us some time."

The words dead and Ben in the same sentence stopped Victoria's heart momentarily. "And what happens when Graham finds out we lied? We'd never hear the end of it then."

"He'll only find out if Ben is staying here, so we'll put him up somewhere," Barnet said.

"And where would that be? He's not even conscious. He may never wake up."

"Then maybe he should be in a hospital. We could create a false ID for him and put him somewhere where he'll be discovered. And if by some chance he awakens, he'll find a note from us stating what we've done."

"A note? He's blind."

Barnet flattened his lips and rolled his eyes. "It would be in Braille."

"And where would this Braille note be that someone else won't find first?"

"Victoria, stop it! I don't want to argue about the logistics. Those can be decided later."

Victoria's chest tightened. Bad enough to pretend Ben was dead, bad enough he may never wake up, but to be apart from him, too? "You expect me to go along with this?"

"If you're outvoted, you won't have a choice. Besides, it won't be forever. Only until we get this Perfect Mate business settled. Has anyone had any luck?"

"Actually, I was about to call a meeting when you beat me to it," Hilde said. "Rolf stumbled onto something. He was poking around in a chat room and asked about the Perfect Mate story."

"He did what?" Barnet said.

"Oh don't get your panties in a bunch," Hilde said. Victoria nearly snorted at Barnet's comical expression. "Someone else brought it up first. Rolf played the instigator saying the story wasn't true. That's when Alexi Popolov's name came up."

"Alexi," Barnet said, shaking his head. "I should have known."

"Who's he?" Abe asked.

"He's been a pain in the Russian Committee's ass. The man's not satisfied with writing his own stories, he has to tinker with mortals, too."

"Is he the one who's responsible for the outrageous vampire myths?" Victoria asked.

"He's the one," Barnet said. "Doesn't seem like the type who would write a fairy tale, though."

"Well, his name was only batted around," Hilde said. "Everyone on that chat room was speculating."

"I'll contact Dimitri and see—"

"Don't bother. Alexi is missing."

"Missing? Are you sure?"

"I talked to Dimitri myself. Popolov's been unaccounted for for three years now."

Barnet slammed his fist on the table. "Damn it. Now what?"

Victoria really didn't care. Right now there was only one thing she wanted to do and it wasn't sitting in some conference room discussing Perfect Mates.

* * * *

Ben opened his eyes to a semi-lit room. The source of the light came from under the door to the right. Must be dreaming. He could see in his dreams.

He sat up. His sister lay beside him. "Susannah?" He nudged her shoulder, but she didn't react. Maybe he wasn't sleeping. Maybe he was dead. He'd been stabbed, hadn't he? He lifted his shirt. Ran his fingers over his stomach. No wound. Not even a scar. He hopped off the bed, fully expecting to see his body remain on the mattress, but his side of the bed was empty.

The room brightened and his shadow grew on the wall in front of him. Should he head toward the light? But he didn't want to go.

"Well I'll be," Perry, or someone sounding like him, said. "She's not dead, if that's what you're wondering."

Ben swallowed hard. Couldn't bring himself to turn around.

"Am I?"

"What kind of question is that? I'm talking to you, aren't I?"

It sounded like Perry, so what was going on? Ben turned around. A man in silhouette stood in the doorway. "Perry?"

"Teach."

"Then explain how I can see you."

"You can see?" Perry flipped a switch. Soft light filled the room and his eyes widened. Sparkly, green eyes.

Ben blinked several times and probably grinned like a mad-man. He wasn't dead. He was alive. And he had his sight back? In a flash he was wrapped in a bear hug.

Perry slapped his back and spun Ben around. "When she completed the bond, she was only hoping to save your life. Damn. Vic's gonna bust a gut."

"Who are you—" Victoria ended her question in a gasp. "You're awake?"

Perry stopped with Ben's back to the door. Ben turned around. Her eyes glimmered, too, and they mesmerized him. They were the most beautiful eyes he'd ever seen.

"Better than that. He can see!" Perry said.

"What?" She smiled and took two steps toward him when her eyes widened in horror. "Oh!" She fled the room before he'd gotten a chance to see the rest of her.

Not exactly the reaction he expected. "Wait, Victoria." Ben ran after her, but she hadn't gone far. Sitting on a chair, hugging her legs and burying her head, she made herself as small as possible. Which wasn't hard considering she wasn't all that large to begin with. Her beautiful golden locks obscured her face and her sleeveless dress hid everything else. Well, everything except her pale arms. "Why are you hiding?"

"Don't get me wrong. I'm happy you can see. Truly."

"Then let me see you." He brushed her hair aside and pulled at her wrists, but that vampire strength of hers won out. "What's the matter, baby?"

She flew into his arms and hugged him around the neck. A warm electric buzz caused his heart to flip-flop, but he still couldn't see her face. She was afraid of something, but what?

"I completed the bond."

"So Perry said. Are you regretting it?" A mixture of emotions passed between them making it hard to determine exactly what she was feeling.

"No. Never. It's just that…you can see what you're stuck with."

"I don't consider myself stuck with you. If you remember, I'm the one who was pestering you to complete the bond." He yanked on her arms, but she held on tight. "Victoria, baby, let me see you. Please. I would have preferred to see you first, not Perry." He called over his shoulder, "No offense."

"None taken," Perry said as he entered from the other room. "Why don't I leave you two alone? Susannah is resting comfortably."

"Thanks." Ben never would have pegged Perry to be a polo-and-khaki type of guy. The long, blond hair tied in a ponytail fit him, though.

Ben took in the small room, or what he could see with Victoria clinging to his neck. The artwork on the wall—was that a Van Gogh?—the widescreen television, the stack of books on the table. He even stared at his hands.

He could see. He could actually see.

But what Ben really wanted to see was his bonded mate, because he assumed that's what she was now. And man, if that didn't make him feel all caveman-ish, he didn't know what would.

* * * *

Victoria held onto Ben. One look at her and he'd be disgusted. He was a man and she resembled a child.

He grabbed her arms, but she held on tight. "Okay, we're alone now, so what do I have to do to see your face?"

"Close your eyes."

"Close them? Are you kidding? I just got my sight back. I never want to close them again."

"I know, but… Please? For just a moment."

He sighed. "Fine. They're closed. But I'm not letting you go, so if you're hoping to fix your makeup—"

"I don't wear makeup." If only that were her problem. She unwrapped her arms around his neck and took his face into her hands. One last kiss was all she wanted before he decided she wasn't right for him. His lips were warm, and gave her the little buzz she loved. He grabbed her head and plunged his tongue into her mouth as waves of desire flowed through their connection. She closed her eyes. She was his, but did he really want her?

He pulled away and paused. Oh no. She went to cover her face, but he beat her there. Except he was holding her gently, not covering her up. "You're more beautiful than I pictured you."

She shook her head. "I'm too young."

"You're perfect." He proceeded to kiss her and lay her on the floor. Then he stopped. "God, I want you, but I can't do it with Susannah in the other room the way she is."

He might have used Susannah as an excuse, but what if he was just lying to himself? How could he not see her as a child?

Ben stood and pulled her up before walking over to the bedroom. He leaned against the door jamb and stared inside the room. "What happened to her?"

"We don't know. Possible manipulation overload." Victoria wrapped an arm around his waist. "We've never seen anything like it before. Her breathing and heart rate are normal, but she doesn't respond to any stimuli. We assume she's awake since her eyes are open."

"Be honest. You think it's a strong vampire or her mind?"

She lowered her head. "I think Graham's responsible, but he's not strong. I'm so sorry this has happened to her."

He lifted her chin. "Hey, it's not your fault. So…what's the plan for her?"

"Right now? We're waiting and seeing. If she doesn't wake up soon, we'll have to take her back to the hospital. There's not much we can do for her here."

He nodded. "I understand. Man, your eyes are so pretty. Why do they glimmer? I noticed Perry's did, too. Is it me? Or the bond?"

"It's not the bond. It's because you're a Perfect Mate. You would have noticed before if you could see. That's how you can identify a vampire. Look for the sparkly eyes." She touched his temple. The scars were nearly invisible and his eyes showed such life. He'd never really looked at her before and now he was staring. She turned her head.

"I'm sorry I keep staring." He grabbed her around the waist and twirled her around before landing on the couch with her in his lap. "Oh, Victoria. You're the best thing to ever happen to me. I can't get over how lucky I am."

Lucky because she gave him back his sight or lucky because…

Oh, what was she thinking? There was no 'or.'

"Victoria… What's the matter? I can feel your unease."

Before she could come up with an excuse that wasn't a lie, Barnet barged into her room, Perry close behind. Timing couldn't have been better. Let them fawn over Ben's returning sight. Maybe then she wouldn't have to answer Ben's questions.

CHAPTER 25

"So you're basically telling me that Graham, or any vampire for that matter, feels they have the right to kill me? And you'll just let them?" Some immortal he was. Ben shook his head.

Barnet had wanted to take their conversation to the conference room, but Ben refused to leave his sister, so the four of them stayed in Victoria's living room. He and Victoria sat on the couch, Barnet sat in a comfy-looking chair, and Perry leaned against the wall.

"We're not letting anyone kill you," Barnet said. "Or Sarah and Justin, for that matter. But we can't blurt out that Perfect Mates exist. We'll have a mess on our hands."

"Seems like you already have a mess if Graham goes through with his threat of telling everyone you're harboring a freak." Ben clenched his jaw. He'd like to punch Graham just for touching Victoria.

"You're not a freak," she murmured. She kept rubbing her handkerchief and seemed more distant than ever. What was going on in that head of hers? Every time he'd reached for her hand, she'd pulled away. Not in an obvious way, but after the second time he stopped. If he needed a sign she regretted completing the bond, that was it.

"Victoria's right, you're not a freak," Barnet said. "But, like Graham, the majority of vampires won't see it that way. Which is why we need you to pretend you're dead. To buy us some time."

"Dead?"

"It won't work," she muttered. "Graham will think he's been manipulated. And when we tell everyone about Perfect Mates, how do you think it will look then? You always say we need to do things legally. Faking Ben's death might not be illegal, but it's sure blurring the lines."

"Then what do you propose?" Barnet asked.

"Short of declaring my love for Graham?" She shrugged.

"You're not thinking of doing that, are you?" Ben asked.

"I have to think about every scenario. It's what we do. Which reminds me." She turned toward Barnet. "When we finally spread the word, we'll need to implement a new rule. We must protect a vampire who locates a Perfect Mate. I don't want anyone else to have to go through this."

"Good point," Barnet said. "But only if they're bonded or plan to be bonded. We don't need vampires jumping the gun, so to speak. If they tell the wrong Perfect Mate, the vampire should still face the consequences."

"Consequences? What consequences? Are you saying Victoria's in trouble?"

Barnet grimaced. "Technically? Yes. But not just Victoria. John and Katarina, too, and the whole Committee for allowing them to expose our race. Someone like Graham will see our new rule as a protective measure, though. He could still be a problem."

"Meaning, Ben will still be in danger unless I convince Graham otherwise."

Ben fisted his hands at the sound of her words. "I'd rather be declared dead than have you go near him."

"But if it will save you…"

"No." He turned to Barnet. "You're her boss. Tell her she can't."

"He's not my boss."

Barnet laughed. "She's right, but if it'll make you feel better…" He looked at Victoria. "Please don't do anything regarding this issue until you've discussed it with the rest of the Committee, okay?"

She stood with fire in her eyes. Ben bit back a moan. Hearing her voice was one thing but seeing her in action… He'd never been so turned on before.

"Damn it, Barnet! I can't stand by and wait. Graham's only waiting for an opportunity, I know it."

"I don't believe that. I think he'll wait until after the meeting, when he'll hope to have more people on his side. It's what I would do."

She crossed her arms and plopped onto the couch. "Yeah, but he's not you."

Barnet rubbed his face. "I don't know what to do anymore. So let me change the subject. Perry would like to…experiment with your sister."

"What is it with you guys and experiments?"

Barnet smiled. "If you have another suggestion as to how we can learn?"

Ben shook his head. At least these vampires wanted to learn. To understand. And they asked for permission. Better than just reacting, which the majority of humans would do if they ever discovered vampires were for real. "What kind of experiment?"

Perry strolled to the door leading to the bedroom and stared inside. "I'd like to probe her mind and see if I can find a way to snap her out of it."

"Probe? You mean dig, right? Didn't you already do that?"

"Not really. I did a little searching before, nothing deep, though. I was afraid to make it worse. But now? I can't believe she can get much worse, so with your permission, I'd like to give it a try."

Ben scrubbed his face. This was Susannah's mind they were talking about. Would she be a vegetable for the rest of her life?

Victoria touched his arm for a moment then pulled away. "Perry's good. If anyone can find out what's wrong with her, he can. But if you want to think about it…"

He wanted to take her into his arms and never let her go, but it wouldn't help his sister any. Hell, Victoria would probably push him away.

"That's not all," Barnet said. "If she comes out of it, she can't know about…" He pointed to his eyes and then Ben's.

"What? Why not?"

"How would you explain it? And the fact your scars have faded. I have a feeling we're going to have to declare you missing, as if you'd been turned."

Holy shit. He flopped back against the cushions. "You're saying I can never see her again? What about my job?"

"Job?" Barnet asked. "I was under the impression your sister owned the business."

"I got my old job back. I start teaching high school in the fall."

"Oh, Ben," Victoria said. "I forgot all about that."

"Out of the question," Barnet said. "You've changed too much. People will notice."

"So I got my sight back. Miracles happen all the time."

Barnet rose and paced the floor. "Maybe so, but eventually we would have to report you missing. If our theories about Perfect Mates hold true, you will not age. I just figured we'd have more time…"

"Don't I have a say? Or do you plan on imprisoning me?"

"No one will imprison you," she said. "We'll move before I let that happen."

"Victoria…" Barnet said. "You're not making this any easier." He ran his hand through his hair while he continued pacing. "Maybe it's better if we hold off on this conversation. We don't even know if Susannah will wake up."

"Fine." Although it was far from it. Ben stood and turned toward Perry. "When do you want to start?"

Perry grasped Ben's shoulder. "Best if I do it right now. But not here. In her hotel room. That way, if she comes out of it, I won't have to manipulate her mind to forget and if she doesn't, then she'll be discovered soon enough and transported to the hospital."

"I want to come with you."

"I'd appreciate it if you didn't," Barnet said. He held his hand up, silencing any retort Ben, or Victoria, might have made. "Not because I want to hold you as a prisoner, but if you want people believing your sight is due to a miracle, then there should be a reason behind the miracle. Going to sleep blind and waking up with sight is a little too miraculous and would draw suspicion. I'd rather avoid that."

Barnet had a point. One Ben didn't wish to argue. But when—not if—Susannah came out of it, he'd be damned if he would be declared missing or dead. He'd walk down the middle of one of the many Peachtree streets to prove he wasn't. She'd gone through enough, had supported him through his blindness. She didn't need the pain of wondering what the hell happened to him. He would not do that to her.

* * * *

Victoria rubbed her handkerchief. How Ben must hate her.

Barnet and Perry had left to give Ben time to say goodbye to Susannah. And when he headed toward the other room, Victoria couldn't bring herself to accompany him. *Hölle*, he probably didn't want her company anyway. It was all because of her that any of this was even happening.

"You're not going to make me do this by myself, are you?"

"Don't you want some privacy?"

He stepped in front of her and knelt, his scent driving her wild. One touch and she'd be butter. And when he finally broke it off— and why wouldn't he, being forced to live a life he didn't want?— she'd be shattered into millions of pieces. She leaned away from him to clear her head.

He stood, his eyes glistening with unshed tears. "Why do you keep doing that?"

"Doing what?"

He rested his hands on either side of her, against the couch back, trapping her.

She closed her eyes and held still. One touch was all it would take. One touch and she'd crumble at his feet. And where would that leave her when he finally came to realize what his life would be like? When he finally came to hate her.

"That. You keep pulling away. Have you always been like that? Have I misinterpreted everything since I met you?"

"No, *Gott*, no. I love you, Ben. I can't imagine my life without you."

"Then what's the matter? Because I have to say, your actions are scaring the crap out of me."

Her heart raced and she rubbed her handkerchief. Not now. Not now.

He covered her hands and stopped her rubbing. "This. What is this? And why are you so nervous? Talk to me, Victoria. What's wrong?"

His fear slammed into her. She fought the urge to wrap him in a comforting hug, because that would turn into kissing, if not lovemaking, and only prolong the inevitable. Her poor heart couldn't take much more. It was better to be over quickly.

She stared down at the conjunction of their hands. "Everything's happening so fast for you, that when you have a chance to think—really think—about how much your life has changed, how much younger I look than you, that you'll realize, that maybe, you don't like me so much."

She couldn't look at him. Couldn't bear to see his expression when he realized she'd spoken the truth.

"How thick is that vampire head of yours?"

She jerked her head up. "What?"

He stared at her with such love in his eyes. "Aren't we in this together?"

"I'd hope so."

"Do you hate me for ruining your life? Because it sure seems like it's gotten more complicated for you."

"That doesn't matter to me. As long as I have you."

"And you don't think I feel the same way?" He squeezed her hands between his own. "Yes, I have some adjusting to do. And yes, I'll probably argue with Barnet about it. That doesn't mean I hate you. That doesn't mean I don't want you. I don't care what people think when they see us together except to think they'll see a couple in love. Because I love you, Victoria. Always. Nothing's going to change that. Feel our connection. What does it tell you?"

An outpouring of love flowed into her. After everything she'd put him through, he still wanted her. How did she get to be so lucky? She cupped his face in her hands, his stubble scratching her palms. Her heart overflowed and she kissed him. He pulled her into his arms and she went freely. Someday they would get away from everyone and everything. She wanted nothing more than to show him over and over just how much he meant to her.

* * * *

Victoria tasted better than any food. Ben devoured her mouth and inwardly smiled when her fangs emerged. He'd love nothing more than to have her bite him, but unfortunately now wasn't the time. Would there ever be a time for them?

"I'm so sorry I doubted your love and made you doubt mine," she said. "Next time you have permission to kick my *Arsch.*"

He laughed. He loved her language. He loved her. "I might take you up on that." He took her hand. "Come on. Help me say goodbye to Susannah. I'm not sure I can do it without you."

His sister hadn't moved since he'd left the room. Her eyes were still open, blinking every now and then, staring at nothing in particular. For not having seen her in ten years, he couldn't say she changed all that much. A few more wrinkles around the eyes and her mouth, but her hair showed no grey. Had she colored it? She'd never told him.

He sat on the bed beside her. "Do you think she can hear me?"

"Probably somewhere in her subconscious, sure."

"Yeah, if her subconscious even works anymore."

"Don't be like that. You have to have faith."

What the hell? "Did you just read my thoughts?"

Her eyes widened. "I can't read your thoughts." She squeezed his hand and closed her eyes. "I still can't. But…I heard you as if you spoke to me. Say something to me in your mind."

Oh, this could be fun. *Moo like a goat.*

She raised one lovely eyebrow. *Moo like a—* Wait a minute. Goats don't—"

He squeezed her hand and laughed. "I heard you, too. In my head."

Her eyes widened, but her mouth never moved. *"Are you sure?"*

"Yes, I'm sure. Holy crap! How is that even possible?" Sure would beat whispering in a room full of people.

She chuckled. "I knew there was something else those other Perfect Mates weren't telling us. And by us, I mean the Committee. Wonder why they kept it a secret?"

"Maybe they didn't want Barnet doing any experiments. That man doesn't know when to stop."

"He can be rather exuberant. I promise I won't say anything to him. Doesn't mean I won't say something to John or Katarina next time I see them."

He turned back to Susannah. He still had to say goodbye. Who knew when he'd see her next, if at all if Barnet got his way. Too bad he couldn't talk to her mentally. "Hey, Suze. It's me, Ben. I won't be able to see you for a while. Don't you worry about me, though. I'm happy. Really happy. Amazing how sweet life is when you find that perfect person. You have to wake up so you can experience the same. I hope you'll try. I love you, Sis."

Nothing he said made a bit a difference to her. Not a flinch or even a blink. Had she gone and left her body behind? Tears blurred his vision and he buried his face in Victoria's belly. "She's gotta be all right."

"You know we'll do our best." She stroked his hair. "I'm so

sorry this happened."

"Not your fault. You would have never hurt her. I know that."

"But maybe I could have stopped Graham."

He tensed at the mention of the vampire's name. "The only thing that would have stopped that bastard was if you loved him. Promise me you'll stay away from him. He's already taken Susannah, I don't want him taking you, too."

"Ben…"

"Promise me!"

She pulled free from his embrace and sat on his lap. "I promise not to take any unnecessary risks where he's involved, but that's the best I can offer. I can't avoid the man."

"He's dangerous."

"I know."

He would have to trust her not to do anything foolish. However, if he ran into Graham first… Too bad he wasn't as fast as a vampire. Anything he tried would surely fail.

Perry knocked on the doorframe. "Don't mean to intrude, but daylight's coming and I have work to do."

Ben rose from the bed after Victoria slid off his lap. Perry lifted Susannah as if she were breakable.

Ben placed a kiss on her forehead. "Bye, Sis. I love you. Talk to you soon."

He'd like to meet this Graham face-to-face and at least give the vampire a piece of his mind. Maybe one day he'd get his chance.

* * * *

Victoria stood beside Ben as he watched Perry carry his sister from the room. With everything happening so fast, she never got a chance to talk to Ben. "How are you feeling? Your wound. Did it—"

"Heal?" He lifted his shirt and displayed flawless skin. "Seems so. Doesn't even hurt. Was this your handiwork?"

Victoria resisted the urge to run her hands across his skin. He hadn't been awake all that long and he'd been so hurt. Lost so much blood. He couldn't be one-hundred percent now, could he? "I think we both contributed. I did enough to stop the bleeding. The rest you did from being bonded."

"That's pretty…awesome. But to answer your other question, I feel great. Physically. Is that part of being bonded, too?"

"I guess so. You seem very healthy." She pulled his shirt down. The view had been way too tempting.

He grabbed her hand. Sizzling heat shot through her body and flared her desire. "Damn, baby. I love what you do to me. Do we have any other perks?"

Before she could answer, her stomach cramped. One feeding after a week without apparently didn't cut it.

"You're hungry." Ben pulled her to the couch and settled her on his lap.

She ran her fingers along his temple, where he used to have scars. Such a miracle that he was even alive, he couldn't possibly be healthy enough to feed from. "I'm okay. It can wait."

"Wait? For what? I'm right here." He urged her head toward his neck, but she resisted. "Do I have to get you into the mood? Is that it?" He kissed her, ran his tongue along her bottom lip before slipping it inside her mouth for a thorough examination.

Oh, he was getting her in the mood all right and not necessarily for feeding. Was he trying to get her fangs to extend? She focused on keeping them hidden, but found it hard to concentrate when he grew hard against her hip.

"Let's go to the bed, get comfortable and feed you properly."

Get comfortable to feed? She nearly laughed. He wasn't fooling her. She slid off his lap. "Ben… No. It's too soon." Wasn't it?

"Too soon for who?"

"You. I don't want to hurt you."

He leapt to his feet and then scooped her into his arms. "I don't think that's possible. And I feel fine. Better than fine. I've never felt so fine. But if that's your real concern, all the more reason to do this lying on the bed, right?"

"Right." She smiled. It was hard arguing with him when he held her close to his body. And what a body. So hard. So strong. And it had nothing to do with their being bonded, either.

He lowered her to the bed. "First, we need to get rid of these clothes."

"I need to be naked to feed?"

"Hell, yeah. Besides, I want to see you. All of you." He sat on the bed and slid his hands along her thighs and under her dress, leaving a warm, tingly path in his wake. As he pushed the dress up and off her body—with a little help from her—he stared at everything he uncovered. "Your underwear is just as sexy as I pictured it. No, I take that back. Sexier."

He ran his hand over her breast and she arched into the touch. Even through the material of her bra, his heat seared her.

He kissed her while he removed the unwanted garment and when he tweaked her nipple, her fangs extended.

He pulled back. Had she hurt him? The smile on his face told her no. "Ah, there they are. Let me see."

She opened her mouth.

"God, those are hot. Can't wait until they're on my neck." He removed her panties then stood back and stared at her. "Ah, baby. You're so beautiful."

Even his gaze warmed her. "Hey. If I have to be naked, so do you."

"Yes, ma'am," he said with a salute. Clothes and shoes flew every which way. By the time he finished stripping, his desire for her was evident.

He climbed on the bed and on top of her. "I love you, Victoria. Now feed."

"You're awfully bossy. Wouldn't you rather know some of the other perks of being a bonded mate?"

"I'd rather have your teeth on my neck. *And my cock in your pussy.*"

That last bit came telepathically. At his crude language, the lower half of her body clenched in need. "Are you sure you're well enough? It hasn't even been—"

Another cramp, stronger than the last, grabbed her abdomen. She inhaled sharply.

"Enough," he said as he lifted her head against his neck. "Send me to nirvana."

His scent, his desire, and his hand urged her toward his vein. She chuckled. "Impatient much?"

Before he could answer, she bit.

A strong rush of power hit her and she nearly gasped. She'd been warned his blood would be stronger, but she never dreamed how strong.

"God, Victoria. I need to be in you."

No more than she needed him in her. She responded telepathically. "*Then fuck me, Ben.*"

"Oh yeah, talk dirty to me." He thrust inside her and that

double sensation sent a jolt to her heart.

Only two draws gave her the strength and nourishment she needed. After sealing her marks, she then rode the wave to nirvana with Ben.

* * * *

Perry slipped the do not disturb sign into the card slot and shut the door. This was going to be the worst day of his life.

After he and Barnet had left Teach to say goodbye, Barnet had taken him aside and pretty much ordered him not to cure Susannah. Perry had never really disobeyed a direct order from Barnet—maybe a request or two—but following this order didn't feel right. Susannah didn't ask to be a vegetable.

"It's for the greater good," Barnet had said. "We need Ben's cooperation and won't get it if Susannah recovers."

Perry was sick and tired of the greater good. Whose greater good? Certainly not Susannah's or Teach's. Didn't Barnet see what kind of mess he'd create if Teach ever found out his deceit? And how could Perry face his friend—and he truly considered the man to be one—when asked if he'd done everything possible?

Then again, what kind of trouble would he be in if he actually did fix Susannah? Would he be accused of treason? He didn't wish for a stake and bake.

He went back to the bed, where he'd left her. Still no reaction from all the jostling. Maybe he wasn't allowed to fix her now, didn't mean he couldn't discover if she was fixable.

He lay beside her on the bed and took her hand. Taking blood wasn't a requirement for what he had to do, but in her case, it couldn't hurt. Not only would it give him more strength, it might solidify his connection and he was willing to do anything to make this easier. On him and her.

He bit down on her arm. She tasted quite fine, better than most mortals he'd tasted. A trait of being related to a Perfect Mate? Who knew? He took his fill and then healed the mark he left behind. Now onto business.

The last time he'd dug around in someone's head, they were conscious and sitting in a chair. He straddled her body, realizing how bad it looked. Good thing Barnet talked Teach out of coming. He might have gotten the wrong idea.

Perry scratched his head. Hell, he might end up getting aroused anyway. Rummaging around in her memories was sure to cause a reaction. Her kisses certainly had.

He placed his forehead against hers and his fingers on her temples. "Come on, Suzie-Q. Show me where you've been programmed."

He worked his way backward through the memories, but frankly, the command or commands could be hidden anywhere. It was like going through file cabinet after file cabinet of data, looking for that one bit that didn't fit. Didn't matter she had met Graham two weeks ago, the information could be stored anywhere, in any memory. Hopefully Graham wasn't a genius after all and it was only Susannah's easy mind that had made Graham's tactic even possible.

After two hours, Perry was dragging. Draining work, digging. He took another pull from her neck while he continued his search. He wouldn't take much more from her. Couldn't leave her catatonic and anemic.

He came to the time of Ben's accident and her parents' death. The grief caused his own chest to constrict and he almost missed it. There. Not one command, but many, and they all conflicted with her actual feelings. She'd been programmed to believe she was saving her brother and, when she'd seen what she'd done, thought she'd killed him instead. No wonder she'd blown a fuse.

After giving her a tender kiss on her forehead, he slowly withdrew from her mind and caressed her face. "Sorry, Suzie-Q. I'll fix you when I can. I promise."

His head and heart ached. Barnet had better know what he was doing or he might find himself out of a job.

CHAPTER 26

Ben emerged from the shower alone. Not that he'd started out that way. He'd taken quick showers before, but nothing like the whirlwind of Victoria. Who knew a vampire could move so fast? He would have preferred seeing more of that beautiful body of hers, but Barnet had called another meeting and she had to attend.

Man, that guy liked to call meetings. Ben wanted to go with her, to find out if Susannah had come out of her trance, but Victoria assured him it was only Committee business and she'd let him know as soon as she heard anything.

Before she zipped away, she had shown him where she stored his toiletries. As Ben dried off, he searched for a mirror to shave, but the space above the sink displayed a framed print instead. While the beach scene was pleasing to look at, he'd prefer to see his face; it had been too many years. Was it possible she had no reflection, thus the lack of a mirror? He'd have to check it out.

He applied his shaving cream and grabbed his razor. Well, he'd shaved without seeing himself for ten years, what was one more day? After cleaning up, he found his clothes folded neatly inside the dresser. Strange how he could actually see what he wore now. No more feeling tags to ensure the colors matched properly. He was tying his shoes when his stomach growled. Her room lacked a kitchen of any kind. Not even a little refrigerator or a microwave. Surely there was a restaurant nearby, wherever nearby was. Hopefully Headquarters wasn't located in the middle of nothing.

He searched for his phone, but couldn't find it. Was it still at the hotel? He'd make a trip out there later, once Victoria returned. His sunglasses sat on top of the dresser. Take them or leave them? Maybe it would be better if he took them. Just in case. Plus, it might be sunny out. Who knew how his eyes would react.

After leaving a note for Victoria, he exited her room and entered the hallway. A white-tiled floor and sterile-like walls greeted him. He'd seen a homier atmosphere in a doctor's office. An exit sign hung at the end of the left pathway so he headed that way.

He reached what looked like a receptionist area. A sign behind the desk stated Vantage Accounting Management and Personnel Services. "VAMPS? Whose bright idea was that?" he muttered.

"That would be me. You like?"

Perry? If he was here, that meant—Ben spun around. "How's Susannah? Is she—"

Ben didn't need to finish. Perry was shaking his head. "Sorry, Teach. But I'll try again. I promise."

"Is she still in her room?"

"No. I made sure a maid discovered her. And then I waited for the ambulance. I would have followed, but the light was getting to me. The windows in the van kept me from burning, but did nothing for my eyeballs." He blinked several times. "I hope you understand."

"I appreciate everything you've done for her. Are you okay? You seem a little…peaked."

"Don't worry about me. I'm fine. So what are you doing around here? Where's Vic?"

"Meeting."

"Figures. I swear, Barnet lives for those things."

Ben laughed. Nice to know he wasn't the only one who thought that. "So this is a real business?"

"Yeah. Mostly for vampires, though."

"Vampires work for mortals?"

"No, no, no. Our clients are all vampires. Although we've been known to hire a mortal or two for daylight work. But they only think they're working for a temp agency, not vampires. It's one of the many ways the Committee makes money. So, you want me to take you on a tour or would you rather wait for Vic?"

Ben shook his head. "Actually, I came out looking for a place to eat."

"Hungry, huh? Well, good thing I ran into you when I did. I can show you where you can get some grub."

"I don't want to put you out. Besides, it's daylight out there."

"You're not putting me out and we won't be going outside." Perry opened another door that led to a shopping mall.

Ben looked around. "Wait a minute. I recognize this place. Is this the Underground?"

"Very good, Teach. Hiding in plain sight. Not bad, huh?"

"I was in high school the last time I came here." He looked back at the door he came through. Had he seen sparkly eyes back then? He couldn't remember. "Would Victoria have been here?"

Perry rubbed his chin. "They've only been in this location for the past fifteen years. I'm guessing you graduated about twenty years ago, right?"

"Twenty-one." Ben hadn't even bothered going to his twentieth reunion.

"Wouldn't that have been weird if she ran into you back then? Heck, it's still weird you even exist."

"You know, I keep hearing about the Perfect Mate story, but not the story itself. Do you know it?"

"A little. Why don't we get you fed and I'll tell you what I know."

Perry couldn't leave the confines of the Underground, but there was a nice bakery with a place to sit and eat. Ben ordered way more than he needed, but everything looked so good. Seemed he had more willpower when he only relied on his nose.

"Imagine what it must be like if you could see it and not eat it," Perry whispered.

Ben hadn't even considered that. Would Victoria feel the same way? "Do you want to go someplace else?"

"Nah, I was just raggin' on you. You should see your eyes." He bugged his own out and laughed, making Ben follow suit. Guess he had been drooling a little.

Ben retrieved his order, filled his coffee cup and joined Perry at a table. "So it doesn't tempt you?"

"Sure it's tempting. And I could eat it if I wanted. It's just not worth it." Perry eyed the cheese Danish. "Although, in this case… You mind?"

Ben had way more than he really needed. He nudged the plate toward Perry. "As long as it won't kill you, be my guest."

Perry ripped a piece off and popped it in his mouth. His eyes closed in ecstasy. "Ah, damn, that's heavenly. I can see hanging around you will do me no good." He fingered the sunglasses sitting on the table. "What's with these?"

"Wasn't sure if I'd need them outside."

"You going somewhere?"

"Only to eat. Don't have to now."

"Yeah, right." Perry chuckled, but it held a hint of relief. Did he have orders to watch Ben? He wouldn't put it past Barnet.

So much for not feeling like a prisoner.

Well, even prisoners had to eat. Ben bit into the raspberry pastry and washed it down with a sip of coffee. "So tell me the story."

Perry tore off another piece of the cheese Danish. "Once upon a time—"

"Seriously? You're going to start it that way?"

"Hey, it was written a long time ago. How do I know it didn't actually start that way?"

"Fine. Go on." Ben shook his head and took a bite of his pastry. Once upon a time, indeed.

"Anyway, there was this vampire named Gabriel. He liked to travel from city to city and search for the hottest babe—"

"Hottest babe?" Ben laughed. "I don't think they used that phrase once upon a time."

Perry drummed his fingers on the table. "Okay, comeliest woman. Are you going to let me tell this story or not?"

"I'm sorry. I won't interrupt again." Ben smiled. Maybe he should have asked Victoria to tell him the story instead. Heck, maybe he still would, if only to hear her version.

"Okay, where was I? Oh yes, Gabriel searched for the *comeliest woman* to spend the day with. He'd take her someplace dark and secluded and manipulate her mind a bit. Not to coerce the young woman to have sex, Gabriel had his pride, you know, but so the woman wouldn't remember the encounter. He didn't care if the woman was married or not, but a married woman with a husband who left her alone was his ideal candidate."

"This man sounds a little bit like you," Ben said.

"Well, I might have emulated him just a bit. I mean, what's not to like about living like that? Now, as I was saying, one night Gabriel visited a city and met the lovely Mary. She smelled like home, and when he touched her, his body miraculously warmed as if standing in the sun. But none of his mental commands worked on her. Intrigued, and maybe a little stupid, he wooed her the old-fashioned way and fell in love.

"Mary came to love him, too. A love Gabriel knew was real, since he couldn't coerce her. He told her what he was and she accepted him. With her love, he felt true peace and her blood sustained him better than any other human. And it ends, 'So in love they share and forever be together.'"

"That's it? It doesn't say anything about the act of bonding?"

"Pretty much. Vague, huh? Now you see why we thought it was just a story? Or the fact we don't know much about your type?"

"Maybe the writer didn't want anyone to believe it was real."

"If that were the case, why bother writing it at all? Maybe someday we'll find out why."

"So, do you suppose that's what Victoria feels? Peace?" Ben had lost his needy feeling since their bond completed; was Victoria feeling the same? Sarah called it freedom, and in a way he could see it being like that. Freedom from all the anxiety.

A person entered the store and Perry leaned forward. "You'd have to ask her. But it's probably true. I've never seen Johnny so happy and at peace with being a…you know." He discreetly flashed his fangs. "He hated being one before."

"But not you?"

"Oh hell, no. I love it."

"And you've never run into any people like me before now?"

Perry shook his head. "Sarah was the first I found, but Johnny found her first."

"That had to be hard on you."

"I think it was harder on Johnny. He loves Sarah. Sarah was…intriguing to me. Something to explore. Would I have fallen if she'd given me a chance?" Perry shrugged. "Guess we'll never know. Did you get enough to eat, Teach?"

"Yeah, thanks." Ben tossed his garbage into the can and followed Perry out into the mall.

Perry grabbed his stomach. "Damn it. I knew I shouldn't have."

"You okay?"

"Not really. Time to get rid of the Danish. Can you?" Perry pointed to the men's room.

Ben slipped his glasses on and led Perry. Kind of funny when he thought about it. When was the last time he led anyone to anything? Ben tripped and nearly took them both to the ground. "Seems bonding hasn't fixed my klutziness."

"I guess it doesn't create miracles."

As soon as they entered the men's room, Perry dashed to the stall where he proceeded to upchuck in the toilet. For eating that bit of pastry, he seemed to be in a lot of pain. He emerged and stumbled to the sink, splashing water on his face.

"I'm sorry," Ben said. "If I had known, I'd have kept the Danish to myself."

"My fault. One of the drawbacks to being practically immortal. I can eat the food, but not digest it. Nothing I can do about that, though. Well, except maybe not eat." Perry chuckled as he pulled some towels and wiped his face.

Ben pointed toward the mirror. "Hey, I can see you."

"What? You thought we were invisible?"

"Sorry. I just assumed since Victoria doesn't own a mirror."

"Oh, she owns one. I think she keeps it covered up most of the time."

"Why would she do that?" Then Ben got a look at his own reflection. He removed his glasses and stared. "Shit. I look like my dad." He turned his head to the side. "When did I get all this grey?"

"Maybe that's why. She doesn't like what she sees." Perry doubled over. "I need to go feed. I didn't have time after your sister, and with the sun earlier and now with this little disaster…"

"You want to…" Ben stuck out his arm and raised his eyebrows.

"Oh, wow. That's kind of you to offer. No offense, but I don't do guys. Plus, you're bonded now."

"I thought feeding was just feeding. Are you saying it isn't?"

"No, no, nothing of the kind. But if I'm going to get up close and personal with someone, I'd rather it be the fairer sex, you know?" He laughed and winced.

"So what does my bonding have to do with it?"

"From what I've been told, you won't taste all that good."

"What? Does that mean Victoria is forced to feed from someone else?" She hadn't acted like he tasted bad. Wouldn't he have noticed? That Danish was starting to react in Ben's stomach now.

"No, you misunderstood. You're her mate. Once you bonded, you're basically designed for her. Food and otherwise. I'm not sure she could feed from anyone else. I wonder if Johnny or Kat have even tried."

Probably not if Sarah and Justin felt the same way that Ben did whenever he thought of Victoria taking blood from someone else—nauseated. Would she feel the same about him offering his blood? Maybe he wouldn't tell her, then.

* * * *

Graham sat in the shadows of the mall and waited. Perry and that freak had just entered the bathroom. Martin wasn't in as bad a shape as Victoria led him to believe. Besides stumbling around holding onto Perry, he seemed fairly healthy. Damn. Susannah couldn't even do that right.

Once the sun set, maybe he'd go visit her. He never did get the relief he sought. He'd tried with his last donor, but she didn't have the same enthusiasm. She also didn't have the same face and he'd ended up taking her from behind. Might as well have made out with a doll, for all the fun he had.

So what the hell were Perry and Martin doing in the men's room? Making out? Graham smiled. Wouldn't that be something? Then maybe he could win Victoria over.

Oh, who was he kidding? She would never come to her senses. Stupid bitch. Maybe he should just forget about her.

Thing was, he couldn't forget about her. Why else had he been sitting out in the mall waiting for her to make an appearance? Hoping against hope she'd finally find him attractive? Desirable, even?

What if he'd been going about it all wrong? He should force himself on her. Show her what she was missing. Hadn't Susannah thought he was the greatest? Then Victoria would wake up and dump that blind freak. Better yet, she'd help Graham kill the bastard. Vampires didn't need freaks like him knowing about their business.

Which begged the question, why hadn't the Committee done away with Martin? That's what they would have done unless... Damn, had he agreed to be turned after all? That had to be it. Why else would he be here? So what was she waiting for? The Committee Meeting? She was on the damn Committee, she didn't need anything formal, not like everyone else. Most likely Barnet insisted on doing it formally. "Vampire citizens don't get special treatment, so neither should the Committee." Weak bastard, that's what Barnet was. He was in a position of power and refused to use it.

The Committee should be living in opulence. Hell, they all should be. Instead, Barnet and Victoria lived in some boring offices that had been converted into small apartments and the rest of the Committee practically lived in squalor, among the mortals.

When he married Victoria and she became the Committee Head, they would live on a large estate with servants waiting on them. It's what the position deserved and by God, he would get it.

But in order for all that to happen, Martin had to go. Now, more than ever. If he was allowed to turn, Graham might as well hang it up. Killing an uncontrollable mortal was one thing. Killing a vampire, quite another. He didn't need that kind of grief from his people.

For once he'd like something to go his way. Wonder who he could use to do it? Accidents worked better than straight-out killing. Made it hard to prove who was involved, and he needed to keep his anonymity in case he could still win Victoria over. Especially when she grieved. This time he would be by her side.

A couple walked past and the man stuck a cigarette in his mouth. His female companion yanked it out, asking the idiot if he could read. Graham stared at the sign the woman pointed to.

NO SMOKING.

He grinned. Question answered.

∗ ∗ ∗ ∗

Ben grabbed his stomach in sympathy for his friend. Just how long did it take to expel one Danish?

"Next time hit me, will ya?" Perry moaned from the stall.

"Sure thing," Ben said. "Hey, do you know if Susannah is at the same hospital as before? I want to go visit."

Perry gripped the stall door causing his knuckles to turn white. "I heard they were taking her there, but do you really think that's a good idea? How are you going to explain your sight?"

"You said she wasn't awake."

"Not to her. To the nurses."

"I'll find out her room through information and sneak in. Can't be that hard."

"I can't go with you."

"I'm not asking you to."

"No, but…" A guilty look came over Perry's face, confirming what Ben suspected.

"You're babysitting me now. That's it, isn't it?"

"Kind of." He straightened and smiled. "I was hoping—" The fire alarm blared, cutting off Perry's words. He covered his ears. "Shit!"

"Guess someone started a fire. You okay?" Ben pointed to Perry's head.

He lowered his hands. "Yeah. Caught me off guard. My hearing's adjusted now."

Emergency lights flashed and Ben walked to the exit, but Perry grabbed his arm.

"Stop. Check the door."

Wisps of smoke snuck its way under the door. Ben placed his hand on the surface. "It's warm."

"That's better than hot, right?" Perry pulled on the handle and was met with flames. "Shit!" He slammed the door shut, trapping them inside.

Ben froze in place as heat lingered in the bathroom. How had the fire engulfed the area so quickly?

Perry looked up. "Gotta find another way out."

The place had no windows. Just a drop-down ceiling. Perry flipped the ceiling tiles and spurred Ben into helping. The room filling with smoke might have also been a big incentive.

With one pump, Perry jumped into the ceiling and disappeared. Damn impressive. Ben had never been able to jump more than a foot off the ground.

Perry extended his arm. "Grab on."

Ben coughed, his lungs protesting the foul air, and took Perry's hand. A moment later his feet left the floor and he was greeted by an oven. "I don't think it's any better up here."

"No choice." Perry crawled on the supports and Ben followed.

* * * *

Barnet called the meeting to a close and Victoria rose, anxious to get back to Ben. Something didn't feel right and it twisted her stomach. Even the hairs on her neck tingled.

"I need to talk to you," Barnet said. "In private."

"If this has to do with finding a connection between the Perfect Mates, I can get Ben's help in the research. I realize we're running out of time."

"Not necessary. Sunny's been working on it, especially with your preoccupation with Ben, which is who I wanted to talk about. There's something you should—"

A continuous blaring came from the hallway. Victoria covered her ears. "What is that?"

"Fire alarm. Coming from the mall."

She rose. Was this why she felt such unease? "I need to go find Ben."

"You can't call him?" This from the man who never called anyone unless forced.

"We forgot his phone at the hotel." She headed for the door.

"Hold on. Perry will bring him here."

She narrowed her eyes at Barnet. "Why would he be with Perry?"

"It's what I wanted to tell you. I asked him to watch Ben."

"What? Don't you trust him?"

"I don't trust him not to go out into public and have his new-found sight be discovered."

"You had no right."

"I had plenty of right. And you saw him. He'll do what he wants regardless of our situation. We need to treat him the same as a newly-turned vampire and you're going to have to convince him."

She shook her head. "He'll never go for that."

"Even if Susannah doesn't recover?"

She didn't care for his tone, almost as if he knew something. "What did you do? Did you kill her?"

"Now don't be ridiculous. You know me better than that."

She thought she did. Now she wasn't so sure. "You keep saying you want to learn about Perfect Mates, but maybe you should be learning about the vampires bonded to a Perfect Mate. I will do anything to protect him, but I won't go against his wishes."

"Even if he wishes to expose us all?"

"He wouldn't do that. And for you to think he would just goes to show you haven't learned anything from the three bonded couples you've been so-called watching."

Barnet placed his elbows on the table and rested his head in his hands. "You have to admit, your case is different. Ben's different. He might not intend to expose us…."

"That's true, accidents happen. Even with vampires. And just like with a vampire, we deal with each case as it happens. Let's not borrow trouble."

He laughed. "Where did you hear that phrase?"

"A wise man said it to me." And that man better hurry up and get here or she might just tear the place apart looking for him.

CHAPTER 27

Ben bumped into Perry's feet. He'd been so intent on putting distance from the approaching fire that he hadn't noticed Perry had stopped. Heat surrounded them regardless of which direction they went. Was this how a pizza felt?

"Why are we stopping?"

"Outside wall. Hold on." Perry rammed the wall with his shoulder. After the second ram, he broke free. Unfortunately, they forgot to take into account what fresh oxygen would do to a fire.

As if growing fingers, the fire reached out to grab them at an alarming rate, but Perry was quicker. He wrapped his arms around Ben and hurled them through the opening, out into the sunlight. They skidded on concrete for several seconds before coming to a stop. Perry screamed obscenities.

The sun! It hit Perry full on. He covered his face, but not even that helped as every bit of uncovered skin took on the brunt of damage. His hands and arms turned red and blistery and he started to convulse.

Ben grabbed Perry under his arms and dragged him into a shaded alcove. God, would it be enough protection?

Perry was shaking as if in shock. "Gotta call Barnet."

"I don't have my phone."

"Mine. Front pocket."

Ben found it, or at least he thought he had. "This is your phone?"

"Yeah. Smartphone. Button on the bottom. Turns it on."

So this is what they looked like. He'd never actually seen one before. Cool. Ben pushed the button, but nothing happened. "I think your battery died."

"Shit. Knew I'd forgotten something." Perry laughed and then moaned in pain. "Can't stay here. Have to get to Headquarters. Barnet is expecting us. Vic is probably going crazy, too."

Ben hated that Victoria would worry, but at least she was safe. "Yeah, but you're in no shape to go anywhere yet." Ben placed Perry's head in his lap and offered his arm. "Rethinking about taking my blood now?"

Perry chuckled. "I guess bitter is better than nothing." He took Ben's arm. "It'll hurt."

"Hey, you saved my life. What's a little pain?"

Perry pierced the skin and Ben tensed, but the sensation was far from pain. Thankfully, it was far from the pleasure he experienced when he shared with Victoria. Right now it just felt good, like he was helping a friend. He relaxed as Perry's face turned from a black burning mess to a smooth sunburned-red. The speed at which he healed was amazing.

"Holy shit," Perry said. He licked where he bit and miraculously the holes disappeared.

"That bad, huh?"

"No. You got some great blood there, Teach. Got a real kick to it." Perry sat up and watched the blisters on his hand smooth out. "Damn. Never healed that fast before. I really need to get one of you."

"One of me?"

"Yeah. A Perfect Mate."

Ben laughed. "What made you think I'd be bitter?"

"Because that's what Johnny said when someone tried to bite Sarah."

"And she wanted this person to bite her?"

"No." His face lit up. "You think that's it?"

"Hey, you have these strange conditions about offering and all. I just put two and two together. So, how do we get to Headquarters without a repeat performance?"

"We can go through the garage." Perry stood and pulled Ben up. "Do you mind if I borrow those?" He pointed to the sunglasses which had miraculously remained looped on Ben's collar.

Ben handed them over. "Be my guest."

Perry stuck to the shadows, zigging here and zagging there, while Ben walked straight. The sun warmed his face and he couldn't imagine never being in it again. Kind of glad he couldn't be turned. With the bond complete, he got the best of both worlds: immortality and daylight. Not to mention a life with one sexy woman. He couldn't wait to hold her and make sure she was okay.

"Since when did the Underground have a garage?"

"They don't. We do. We connected it to the offices. You need a special key to get in, so no outside riff-raff, if you know what I mean."

Perry swiped a card into a box beside a walk-in door. A similar box stood out from the wall so someone inside a car could open the garage door the same way.

They entered into a cool darkness and their footsteps echoed. Or rather Ben's footsteps echoed. Perry hardly made any noise at all.

"Wow," Perry said. "I don't feel weak one bit. Must be your special blood, huh?"

"You would have gotten weak walking in the shade?"

"A little, but only because the sun is so strong right now. Reflections can be a bugger."

Rows and rows of empty spaces as far as Ben could see. Well, not all the spaces were empty. "Why do you need a garage this big for only two cars?"

Perry returned Ben's sunglasses. "Actually, we only own the van. The other car is your sister's. We weren't sure what to do with it. As for the size, well, it fills up for the Meeting."

"That many vampires own cars?"

"You'd be surprised." Perry strode to an unmarked door. "Come on, let's go ease Vic's mind and get you inside."

The door burst open pushing Perry into Ben. Together, they stumbled to the floor. A man emerged and whipped his arm at Perry before Perry had a chance to rise. Blood sprayed in an arc, but the man—no, make that vampire—dodged the shower. Perry grabbed his throat as he fell to his side.

So much blood. Ben sat frozen to the floor while his heart contemplated leaving his chest.

"I kind of figured you'd get out of the bathroom. Guess if I want a job done right, I'll have to do it myself."

Ben didn't recognize the vampire, but he'd heard that voice

before. Graham. Shit! The dripping knife he held by his side was all the incentive it took to thaw Ben. He scrambled to his feet and dashed for the street. Sunlight was his friend. He'd get help for Perry later. If there was a later. He hadn't made it half-way to the exit when Graham appeared out of nowhere, blocking Ben's escape. Ben skidded to a stop.

Graham furrowed his brows. "Wait a minute. You can see?" He flicked his hands at Ben, who flinched. "Nooo! How can that be?"

Ben swallowed. "You gonna kill me?"

"I should. Freaks like you don't belong in our world. But Victoria has some explaining to do and I'm thinking you'll make good bait because I'm sure she'll do anything to get you back. Not that she will. Get you back, I mean."

Graham stood in front of the exit. He was fast, but Ben might be able to escape with the element of surprise. He charged Graham and knocked the knife free. It clattered on the floor. Ben brought his knee up, but before he could connect, Graham sank his fangs into his shoulder. Damn. Pain radiated from the bite. Ben cried out and shoved when Graham tore away, taking a good chunk of Ben with him. Coughing and spitting, Graham hunched over. Ben took his opportunity. Seemed one quick kick to the groin worked on vampires the same as humans. Graham crumpled in agony. Ben sprinted to the exit. Just as he pushed on the door, pain bloomed on his side and the knife embedded into the door frame with a *thud*. Without looking to see how bad the cut was, he grabbed the wound and ran into the sun.

* * * *

Graham's nuts were on fire. Damn mortal. And what was with that blood? Nastiest stuff he'd ever tasted. He spit out the remaining bitterness.

He straightened gingerly and shuffled over to the knife. He would have gotten the bugger if he could have seen straight. Well, maybe all wasn't lost. Graham had left a rather large gash on Martin's shoulder and the knife had sliced his side. Hopefully he was off somewhere bleeding to death. He certainly couldn't have gone far. But how could Graham chase him in the sun?

The van. Graham yanked the weapon free and stumbled over to Perry, who lay unmoving while blood pooled around his head.

"This is what happens when you're protecting a freak."

Perry stared back at him and blinked. He moved his mouth to speak, but no words came out, and wouldn't for a good long while. If paralysis hadn't set in yet, it would soon. Graham had done a good job of nearly decapitating the man.

"I'm sure you'll recover, and when you do, be prepared to pay for your sins. As should the whole Committee." Graham patted Perry's pockets. No keys. Damn it. He went over to the van and opened the driver's door. Eureka.

* * * *

Ben staggered down the street, holding his side. Blood oozed through his fingers and the wound burned. He looked over his shoulder for the second time. Still no sign of Graham. Maybe he was in the clear. *Thank you, sun!*

Police and fire trucks blocked the entrance to the Underground. If he stepped anywhere near their direction, they would most likely stick him in an ambulance. According to Victoria, he would heal—hadn't he from Susannah's attack?—and he didn't need the hassle with the cops or anyone else for that matter. But was it possible he'd gotten hurt too soon since the last wound? Or maybe too soon since feeding Victoria and Perry? He couldn't remember the last time he'd felt so weary, as if he'd worked out way too hard or stayed up way too long. He had to keep moving, though. Graham could still manage to catch him.

If only he could call Victoria. She'd be able to get him through the police without any problems. All she had to do was use her vampire powers. But his phone was still at the hotel.

Of course! He could get his phone and hide out there. And he'd have plenty of time for a nap.

He searched the street for a cab when the rumble of a garage door sounded behind him. Shit. Graham. No way could he outrun him, not even if he were healthy. A cab idled toward Ben, away from the Underground. He waved his hand in the air and the cab slowed.

The roar of an engine urged him forward. Panting, Ben slid in behind the driver and told him the hotel and street name. "Please hurry."

The driver turned in his seat. "You okay, buddy?"

Ben smiled and turned his bloody side away, which only exposed his bloody shoulder. There was no safe side. "I'm fine. It's paint. But I'm in a hurry. Could you go please?"

The driver raised an eyebrow and shook his head, but at least he drove away. Hmmm… maybe the bond gave Ben some of Victoria's powers. Wouldn't that be a sweet perk?

He looked out the back window. When there was no sign of the van, he leaned back against the cushion and relaxed. Now if he could only stay awake. His eyelids weighed a ton and it took everything in him to keep them open.

He fished out his wallet and pulled out his room key. *Please still work.*

$$* * * *$$

Victoria paced the conference room, her stomach beyond twisted and in actual pain. She'd tried calling Perry, but only ended up in his voice mail. Most likely the man had forgotten to charge his phone—again. And this was the person Barnet trusted with Ben's life? "Where are they? It's been too long."

"It's only been a few minutes."

"And if they were in Headquarters, they'd be here already. You don't suppose they were out in the mall, do you?"

"Anything is possible," Barnet said. "They could also be nowhere near the fire. When did Ben eat last?"

Eat? *Hölle.*

"Did you forget the boy needs food?"

She covered her mouth. "Oh my gosh. And I left him alone."

"So it's a good thing Perry's watching him."

"Don't even go there." She stared at the door. Should she go out into the mall and look for him? But Perry knew to come here. But what if Perry wasn't with Ben? She had no proof. "I'm not waiting here any longer. Call me if they arrive."

She checked her room and discovered the note Ben had left. He had gone out to get something to eat. No mention of Perry, though. *Scheisse.* She rushed out into the mall. Hoses ran down the corridor and firemen applied water to the bathroom area. She'd seen people try to sneak a smoke before, but no one had ever burned up the place.

She checked every place she could get to, manipulating anyone who got in her way. No sign of Ben or Perry. Where could they be? He wouldn't have been in the fire, would he?

She pulled aside one of the firemen. Before he could protest her appearance at the site, she took control of him. No one was discovered in the bathroom, no victims at all. This man assumed someone threw a burning cigarette in the trash. She relaxed. So where was Ben?

Would they have taken the van? Couldn't hurt to look. She dashed back to the reception area and climbed the stairs to the garage. When she opened the door, she stopped cold.

Perry lay lifeless, blood pooled around his head. His neck was slashed open wide. She called Barnet and told him to come to the garage.

She grabbed Perry's hand to connect telepathically. With his wound he wouldn't be able to speak. "Where's Ben?"

"He got away, but Graham took after him in the van. I'm sorry, Vic. He came out of nowhere."

No sorrier than Graham would be when she finally got her hands on him. She stared at the exit and the spatter of blood. "He's bleeding!"

"And he'll heal. Teach is a smart man, but if Graham manages to catch him, he's gonna call you. Use him as bait to lure you. That's what he said, anyway."

"Is that supposed to make me feel better?"

"Just that he's not out to kill Teach. Yet. You have time."

Time to what? Worry?

Barnet arrived. "Shit."

Her phone rang. Could it possibly be? "Ben?"

"Hey, baby. Listen, you have to help Perry. He's—"

"We found him." If possible, she would have cried tears of joy. "Are you okay? Where are you?"

"At my hotel room. How else do you think I got my phone?"

"All right, *Klugscheisser.*"

"Hey, did you just call me a smart ass?"

She would have laughed if Ben hadn't sounded so out of it. "Ben, listen to me. You have to get out of there. You're not safe."

"I can't. I need a nap. The door is secured."

"And Graham can rip through that with no effort. You need to get another room under a different name."

"Baby, there's no way. I just don't have the energy. Probably a side effect from all that healing, huh? I didn't think I'd be able to keep my eyes open getting here. I'll see you at sundown, okay? You might want to bring me a change of clothes."

"No, no. Ben, you need to get another room."

"Love you, baby."

"No, don't hang up." Silence greeted her. *Scheisse.* He'd hung up. She called him back, but ended up in his voice mail. This couldn't be happening. Graham was out there.

"He okay?" Barnet asked as he held Perry's head in place.

"He says he is, but he didn't sound okay. I need to get to him."

"And how exactly do you plan on doing that? We don't have the van."

"But Graham will look for him there. He's vulnerable."

"If Graham knew Ben was at the hotel, he would have gotten him already, right? So it's likely he doesn't even know where Ben went. Weren't you the one saying not to borrow trouble? As soon as the sun sets, we'll all go get Ben. Until then, help me with Perry. Go find a donor and bring him—" He stopped and stared at Perry. "Fine. Bring a female donor up here." He shook his head. "And I thought Jack was picky."

Victoria gritted her teeth. Might as well get busy or she might blow her top. As she headed back toward the mall for Perry's donor, she pulled out her cellphone. Maybe she could get a hit on the van, see it was located miles from here, and relax. When she turned on the app, the signal indicated Graham was still driving in the area. A moment later, she lost the signal. He probably drove into a garage to get out of the sun. Thank goodness. He wasn't anywhere near the hotel, which meant Barnet was right and Graham didn't know where Ben was.

She had time to save him after all.

She found a donor for Perry, although why the sex mattered was beyond her. Feeding a vampire who had nearly lost their head was no easy trick. The enormous loss of blood had paralyzed Perry.

Victoria sliced the donor's arm and positioned it over Perry's mouth while Barnet continued holding Perry's head in place. More than half of the blood either dribbled across his cheek or leaked through his neck. He was able to actually bite the second donor's arm, but even then, a good portion of the blood oozed through the opening in his neck. It took a third donor to finally get Perry's neck knitted together so they could transport him to his room.

"Man, I sure could use some more of Teach's blood." Perry said, settling onto the couch in his room. His voice sounded as if he'd gargled razor blades. He still had plenty of healing to do, but at least he was clean now. It had taken her and Barnet a bit of tender scrubbing to wash off all the blood.

"What are you talking about? What do you mean by more?" Victoria asked as she handed Perry a clean polo shirt.

"He offered." He went on to say how they escaped the fire.

"So you're saying Ben's blood healed you? And it tasted okay?" Barnet asked, getting that experimental look on his face again.

"It tasted better than okay. And it worked quickly. He's like a miracle drug."

"How can that be?" she asked as she sat beside Perry.

"Like I said. He offered. But when Graham bit him—"

"He what?" Oh, she was so going to kill that bastard.

"Relax, will ya," Perry said. "When Graham bit him, he spit it out. Didn't seem to be a pleasant experience for him at all. I'm guessing Perfect Mates have to want to give their blood in order for it to work on a vampire."

"Interesting," Barnet said.

"No, no, not interesting," she said, wagging her finger. "He's not some guinea pig." Or anyone else's blood source and she'd have to make sure Ben understood that, too.

"I didn't say he was."

"You didn't have to. You have that look on your face."

Barnet laughed. "Okay, you got me. At least he's not the only Perfect Mate I can ask. I've got some calls to make. Perry, don't be stupid and go anywhere, okay? Victoria, make sure he stays and rests."

For not being her boss, he sure did sound like one.

"You know he's only doing that to torture me," Perry said with a nudge.

Her smile turned to sobs. Would Graham torture Ben? Would she get to him in time? She still hadn't gotten a hit on the van, but Graham could have moved it and found Ben since the last time she checked.

Perry wrapped an arm around her shoulders. "Hey, he's going to be all right. He got away. Who gets away from a vampire?"

"Graham's going to find him first. I can feel it."

"Are you sensing he's in danger? Like you did last night at the hotel?"

Not only last night, but before the fire alarm had gone off. Did their connection come with a warning system? Or was she just tuned in to him. "I can't tell. I haven't felt right since the alarm went off."

"Why don't you call Graham?"

"Now why would I do that? I certainly don't want to encourage the guy."

"Not for a date, you ninny. He wanted to lure you. Maybe you could lure him back here."

"Lure him, how?"

Perry shrugged. "He doesn't know Teach can heal. Let Graham believe he died. What have you got to lose?"

Not much, that was certain. Could it be as simple as that?

* * * *

Graham parked the van under the hotel awning. All that searching and still no sign of Martin. He'd disappeared, or found his way back to Victoria. Damn, damn, damn!

He needed a release from this frustration. He needed to get fucking laid. And who better to make that happen than Susannah? It was Saturday. What else was the woman going to do? Hotels were made for sex and he would get it on with the best partner he'd ever had.

He left the van behind, not giving a shit what hotel management thought. Hell, most of the time they didn't even pay attention to what went on outside. He could park it there for hours and they'd be none the wiser.

Already hard for her, he took the stairs at a record pace. Maybe they could try something kinky this time. She'd seemed willing enough.

As he approached her door, he looked across the hall. Martin couldn't possibly be in his room, could he? Graham knocked and stood to the side, in case the bastard checked the peephole. When had he gotten his sight back? How? Since when did vampires produce miracles?

No answer. No movement. Graham sighed. Knew he couldn't be that lucky.

Ah, but he could be lucky with Susannah. He knocked on her

door and smiled. Soon he'd be in her. And then he'd be in her again. He would turn this day around for sure.

But she didn't answer her door, either. She certainly wasn't at Headquarters. Could she be asleep? Maybe wake-up sex was in his future. He rushed down to registration and obtained her key.

Little good the key did him. Her room was empty. Cleaning crew hadn't come through yet, as her bed was still unmade. Where was she? Out shopping?

No matter. He'd wait for her. She wouldn't take all day and he could be her present upon her return. He lay on the mattress and took in her scent.

Someone knocked on the room across the hall. "Mr. Martin? Police. Open up."

Police? Graham peered through the peephole. Two cops stood in the hallway.

He opened the door. "Are you looking for Ben?"

The taller of the two turned around. His name tag identified him as Hoffman. "Yes. Are you family?"

"No. I'm a friend of his sister's. Is something wrong?"

"Are you aware of Ms. Martin's condition?"

"Condition? Did something happen?"

The officers looked at one another briefly and shrugged. Hoffman continued, "The maid found her this morning in a catatonic state. She was taken to Grady Hospital."

"What?" Graham didn't have to feign shock. What the hell had the Committee done to her now? "I thought she was out shopping. Oh my. Her brother spent the night with his girlfriend." That word nearly burned his tongue. "I'll be sure to let him know."

He waited until the police took the elevator before shutting the door. His Susannah was catatonic? He ripped the bedding from the mattress and threw it across the room. They would pay for this. Every last member of the Committee.

His cellphone vibrated. *Victoria.* He shoved the phone back in his pocket, unanswered. That bitch would be the first to go, but first he had to find Susannah. He had to fix her.

He walked out into the hallway and stared at Martin's door. If only the bastard was in there now. He'd just finish the job and be happy to do it.

Snoring sounds came from the room.

Graham placed his ear against the door and nearly laughed out loud.

CHAPTER 28

A slap to the face jarred Ben from a pleasant dream. Ah, Victoria. But why did she hit him? And where were his arms? Another slap brought him to consciousness.

"Wake up!"

Oh shit. Graham had found him. Not only that, Ben's arms were tied behind his back and his mouth was taped shut. How had he not noticed all that going on? And how could he get free?

With his heart pounding erratically, he slowly opened his eyes as something tightened around his throat and tugged him upward. *Choking! Choking!* Using his knees, he pushed upward to release the pressure. Another tug sent him sliding off the bed and onto his feet.

"That's better. I'd rather not carry you across the room." Graham held the other end of the sheet that was tied around Ben's neck like a noose. "Not that I couldn't. But I want you awake for this. I find it very interesting you can see, but you're not a vampire. I'd ask you how you were cured, but I really don't want you talking." He lifted Ben's shirt, revealing a faint scar. "I noticed your quick healing, too. What'd you do, carry around some of Victoria's saliva? That's just gross, you know?"

Hey, if that was what the vampire wanted to believe, Ben was okay with that. Hopefully, whatever happened, he'd come out of it alive.

"And what is it with your blood? Must be because you're a freak, huh? Well, we all know what should happen to freaks, don't we?" Graham pulled Ben to the bathroom.

A footstool stood under the dismantled light fixture. Graham took his end of the sheet and looped it around something in the ceiling. He then yanked downward, forcing Ben to stand on the stool. He kicked out, hoping to get a good clobber in, but Graham continued pulling on the sheet causing Ben to stand on his tip toes.

"You gonna try it again?"

With his air supply cut off, Ben's vision became spotty and his neck burned, but he managed to shake his head no. The tension slackened and he stood flat on his feet while catching his breath. Okay, no more attempts. It wasn't as if he could escape from a vampire anyway. At least, not tied up the way he was.

Graham pulled his cellphone out of his pocket and smiled at Ben. "This won't take long, but if you make a sound, I'll pull on the sheet. Understand? " After Ben nodded, Graham pushed a button and placed the phone on the sink.

"Graham?"

Victoria's voice sounded heavenly to Ben. At least she was all right. But she wouldn't be if Graham intended to do what Ben expected. Would his immortality protect him against being hung? Or protect him if his neck broke?

"Well, hello there, Victoria. I seemed to have missed your call. I assume you were calling me about Perry. I do hope the man is okay."

"Perry is fine no thanks to you. It's Ben I was calling about. You had no right."

Graham furrowed his forehead. "No right to what?"

"To kill him. If you think that will make me love you, you've got another think coming."

Ben nearly laughed. She had warned him to get another room, but he just didn't have the energy. If not for Graham, he'd probably still be dead to the world sleeping. Too bad whatever ploy she had cooked up wouldn't work.

Graham stared up at Ben. "I killed Martin?"

"You're the one who bit him. You're the one who cut him. He bled out and it's all your fault. Perry said you wanted to talk, so let's talk. Face-to-face."

"Yeah… I don't think that's going to happen. But let's go back to me killing Ben. I find it hard to believe he's dead when I'm standing here looking at the man blink at me."

"What?"

Ben could hear the panic in her voice and he wished he could reassure her. Not that there was much to reassure her about.

"That's right. But hey, don't worry. He'll be dead when you find him." Graham grinned and tugged on the sheet.

"Graham, you harm him and I'll kill you. Ben is no threat to you. Just let him go."

He scowled at the phone. "Are you fucking kidding me? He's a threat to our entire race! And when our people find out what the Committee has done to hide his kind from us, you'll all be voted out and I'll be voted in. And then I'll hunt you down and we can have that face-to-face before I kill *you*. You've made my life miserable. You made my love for you turn to acid. Good luck getting here before he takes his last breath."

"Nooo! Graham you can't—"

He pushed a button, silencing her frantic pleas.

Ben closed his eyes. Was she acting or for real? Victoria had to believe whatever happened, he would survive. He would survive, wouldn't he?

An evil chuckle sounded from Graham, causing Ben to open his eyes. "Well, that was fun, wasn't it? Much better than I planned. Sorry you didn't get to say goodbye. Actually, I'm not. Now to make sure this holds your weight. Gotta make it look like a suicide in case a mortal finds you first."

The cellphone buzzed on the counter.

"Ah look. She's calling back. Good. She deserves to be tortured." Graham yanked on the sheet.

Please let it be an act. Ben was being tortured enough for both of them. As he rose, he kicked out searching for leverage, anything to help relieve the pressure. All he accomplished was to knock over the stool.

"Ooh, nice touch," Graham said. "Thanks for saving me the trouble."

Ben's lungs burned for oxygen and his neck screamed in pain. As his world darkened, he prayed he'd wake up and see Victoria. This couldn't be the end. It just couldn't. But if it was…

I love you, Victoria.

* * * *

Victoria screamed at the phone. "Pick up!"

Nooo. This couldn't be happening. She must get to Ben. Now. She rushed to the door and slammed into Perry. He had been beside her for most of the conversation and left when Graham mentioned having Ben. Now he returned and with company.

Perry wrapped his arms around her. "Whoa. Where are you going?"

She struggled to free herself. "Let me go. I have to save Ben."

"You're not going anywhere," Barnet said as he closed the door. "You can release her."

Victoria shoved out of Perry's arms. "What? Am I a prisoner now?"

"You are until you come to your senses or the sun sets. Whichever comes first."

"You don't understand. He's killing him as we speak. I can take Susannah's car—"

"And burn before you even make it half-way to the hotel. The windows are not treated. Listen to me. Graham has no idea Ben is immortal, correct?"

"Not that I know of, but—"

"But nothing. You will stay here until it is safe to leave. Ben will survive."

"You don't know that. Vampires can be killed."

"Not that easily and I'm sure Ben is the same. We already know he can survive a stabbing."

"And Graham will most likely notice Ben has healed quickly, too." Victoria shook her head. "He'll do something worse, I just know it." She rushed for the door, but Barnet and Perry blocked her way. She pounded on them. Shoved at them, but they held their ground.

Barnet grabbed her by the shoulders. "Victoria, stop. You're not going anywhere, so just settle down."

Oh, there was no reasoning with the man. She ran to the bedroom, slammed the door and would have locked it if she had owned a lock. How could she stay here and do nothing? Ben needed her more than ever, but there was no getting past those two. At least not through the door.

"Vic, you have to have faith," Perry said through the bedroom door. "You know Teach wouldn't want you to risk killing yourself."

"Leave me alone!" She plopped down on the bed. There had to be someway out of the room, but being below ground meant no windows. However… She stood and stared at the return vent above her dresser. Yes, she could crawl out that way. *Hold on, Ben. I'm coming.*

She turned on the shower and the bathroom fan—not only to camouflage any noise she might make, but also to keep Perry and Barnet from entering the room anytime soon—and climbed on top of the dresser. Luckily, only clips held the grill in place and she removed it without a sound. For once she was glad to be small. But as she hoisted herself to climb through the vent, she rethought her traveling attire. Perry was correct in one thing: Ben wouldn't want her to risk her own life to save his. That meant a change of clothes.

She searched through her closet for something suitable to wear. Long sleeves. Jeans. Oh, and gloves. Those would do. Now for something to cover her head and neck.

Her scarves were all too thin, but a towel might work. She wrapped two around her neck and secured them with a pin. She would wear them if the time came. With money and the phone shoved in her pocket, she was ready. This just might work.

She crawled into the vent—thankful she had room to move—and held her breath in case any dust would cause her to cough or sneeze, thus giving herself away. Too bad the vent extended over her living room. She would have to be extra stealthy.

After what seemed like an eternity and miles of vent, she reached another opening. The room below was empty and she lowered herself. Moments later she entered the garage. Still no sign she'd been found missing. Great.

Victoria ran to Susannah's car. So what if she'd never driven. It couldn't be all that hard. And the windows were treated a bit. Not as strong as the van's, but with the towels she should be okay. The tarp would have been better, but that was still in the van. She climbed inside and reached for the ignition. Empty. Damn Perry! He always left the keys inside. After a fruitless search through the vehicle, she pounded on the steering wheel.

That only left one option before her, and a poor one at that. Only a stupid vampire would venture outside during the day. Seemed she'd have a new label assigned to her. That was if she survived.

She secured the towels around her head and face while staring at the exit door. If she didn't leave now, she might as well walk back to her room. And since that was unthinkable, she prayed for plenty of shade and no people.

She slowly opened the door. No significant light filtered inside; shadows blanketed the whole alley. If only that would be good enough. As she hustled toward the street, she expected to become weaker or at least feel a cramp. But nothing happened. Had the shade really protected her or was it possible Ben's blood was responsible? Whatever, she hurried on her way and stopped when she reached the street. Lots of traffic on this Saturday afternoon and Victoria's heart lurched. She could do this. Ben's life was at stake. After several deep breaths, she was able to block the hoards of people out of her mind, but the sun was another matter. She wouldn't fry immediately, so there was that.

She hailed an approaching taxi. As it slowed, she dashed through the sunlight and jumped inside the vehicle as quickly as possible. Before she could marvel over the fact she hadn't burned one iota, she mentally commanded the driver not to notice her strange attire. She settled in the backseat—ready to move if the sun should reach her—and told him her destination.

Her cellphone buzzed. Guess she'd been discovered missing. "Hi, Barnet."

"Where are you?"

"Where do you think? On my way to Ben."

"Damn it, Victoria. It's not safe out there."

"I'm taking precautions." As well as having some luck on her side. *Gott*, what Barnet would do once he discovered bonded vampires might be able to tolerate sunlight. She might want to broach the subject with the other bonded couples first. Did they even know?

"Call me when you get there."

She assured him she would and disconnected the call. Hopefully her next call would be good news.

The cab pulled in under the awning and, after paying the driver, she departed, leaving the towels behind. She manipulated the front desk into giving her a keycard to Ben's room and trotted to the stairwell. Once out of sight, she zipped up the stairs and down the hall.

Upon opening the door to Ben's room, she noticed the security latch had been ripped off. "Ben?"

She made her way to the disheveled bed and passed the bathroom. He hung from the ceiling, his arms limp by his side.

"Ben!" She untied the sheet that was secured to the closet rod and lowered him slowly to the ground while repeating the same phrase over and over, "Please be alive."

He crumpled to the floor as if boneless. She rushed to him and removed the noose. He wasn't breathing, his heart wasn't beating, and she no longer received that tell-tale warmth whenever she touched him. She performed CPR. No response.

"Wake up, Ben." She breathed into his mouth. Slapped his cheeks. Pounded on his chest. Still nothing. This couldn't be happening. He couldn't be dead. He wasn't supposed to die.

* * * *

Ben stood—no, more like hovered—off to the side while Victoria pounded on the chest of his body that lay on the floor. Funny thing was, he felt the pounding. So how was he not inside his own body?

"Victoria?" He reached out to touch her shoulder, but his fingers disappeared inside her. He flinched and pulled away.

Oh God. She couldn't hear him and she couldn't feel him. Was he even real? Everything around him looked pretty damn real, though. So what the hell was happening?

She carried his body to the bed, sobbing all the while.

"You can't give up," he yelled. "I'm not dead. Oh, please, baby. Keep pounding on my chest. I felt it!"

She sat on the bed and pulled out her phone. Barnet answered, his voice resonated through the speaker.

"He's dead," she said.

"What? Are you sure?"

"Yes, I'm sure. I don't feel him anymore. Even his scent has faded." She covered her face with her free hand.

"I'm so sorry, Victoria. Perry will come once the sun sets. Try to stay put."

"I'm not going anywhere." She disconnected the call and snuggled against Ben's body.

"Hey, I'm right here." If Ben could talk, there had to be a way to get through to her. But his hand went through everything he touched. Hell, he could walk through the bed, not that he was actually walking on anything. How could he get her attention?

"I'm sorry I wasn't there for you. I'm sorry I couldn't protect you better." She inhaled sharply on a sob. "I love you, Ben. I don't know if I can live without you."

Those words sent chills down his spine. "No, no, no. Don't you go talking that way. I'm right here, baby. Maybe my body needs time to heal." That had to be it. "I'll heal. Just give me some time. Don't lose faith."

Of course, his faith crumbled with each second that passed and he remained outside his body.

She sat up and stared at the covered window.

He got up into her face. "That's not the way! Don't you dare."

She pulled her phone out again. Pushed some picture on the screen. A map appeared with a red dot. She enlarged the map. The dot was moving along a line—a street—and then disappeared.

"What are you doing there?" she asked.

He relaxed a bit. At least she wasn't jumping to her death. But who was she talking to and what did that dot represent?

* * * *

Graham took Susannah's hand in his. "What did they do to you?"

He'd never been attached to a mortal as he was with her. And now she was lying there like some sort of vegetable. He climbed into the bed and held her. *Wake up, Susannah. Give me a kiss.*

For an hour he lay there issuing one command after another. She didn't react to any of them. Why wasn't she waking up? What did he have to do to get through to her? He kissed her lips. Nothing. He rubbed his cheek against her cheek. Nothing. He nuzzled her neck. Son of a bitch!

Perry. His scent was all over her neck. That bastard had no right to touch her. Had he made love to her? Fed from her? Were his commands at work here?

Graham fisted his hands. Well, if that's the way Perry wanted to play, Graham could play, too. Susannah was his, damn it. Not Perry's. Not the Committee's.

He confiscated a wheel chair and gently placed Susannah in it. No one stopped him as he rolled her to the elevator. No one stopped him as he arrived in the garage and wheeled her to the van.

No one would stop him from doing whatever was necessary to keep Susannah to himself.

* * * *

Ben paced back and forth while Victoria lay beside his lifeless body. How long would it take for Perry to arrive? He was Ben's only hope in stopping her from doing something stupid—like walking into the sun.

At least that red dot was keeping her alive. For now.

She caressed the face on his body, and like every other time she touched it, Ben felt the associated sensation. How was that possible when she couldn't feel him?

"Graham asked me why I couldn't learn to love him like I learned to love Henrik. I couldn't answer him at the time. But I know why now. It's because I never loved Henrik. Not like a wife should love a husband. I cared for him, sure. He was a good man. But he was all I knew. So when he died, I grieved at the loss because I was lost. Fear crept in. Fear I looked too young. Fear I wouldn't fit in. It became easier to blame my fear on grief." She sat up and stared at his face. "But everything changed when I met you.

"You treated me like a woman, a person, not a possession, and I took advantage of your blindness. I might have gone into our relationship for all the wrong reasons but I fell in love with you for all the right ones. You made me a better person. One who isn't afraid of the world anymore. I just wish…" She hugged his body. "We should have had more time together."

"Oh, baby. We will. Please have faith. I can feel you. That can't be a coincidence. It just can't."

She sat up and brought up the map on her phone. The red dot. It was back and moving. None of the lines on the map made any sense, but it sure spurred Victoria. She rose and pulled the curtain aside.

No, no, not the curtain. He rushed to her—as if it would have done any good—but the sun wasn't a threat. Catching a breath he was surprised to still own, he bent over and placed his hands on his knees. "Don't you dare do that to me again."

"Where are you going now?" For several minutes she kept staring at the map. When the dot stopped she lowered her arm. "That can't be."

"What can't be?" he asked automatically, forgetting she couldn't hear him.

She opened a text to Perry and typed, "There's something I have to do. Please take care of Ben for me."

"What are you doing, Victoria? Where are you going?" The sun was close to setting, but it wasn't safe for her outside, was it? Although, she'd managed to make it to the hotel. Still… He didn't want her to leave.

"Graham will pay for this. You have my word." She kissed Ben's body on the lips.

"No!" That creep was dangerous. Was she looking to get killed? Shit. Was she? There were probably other ways a vampire could die besides walking into the sun. "Please, baby. Don't go."

Victoria touched his face one last time and headed for the door. He rushed after her and blocked her way, but she breezed right through him. *Freaky.* He lost his equilibrium for a moment. By the time it returned, she'd gone out the door.

Should he follow her? She wouldn't hear him anyway. But could he leave his body?

"Oh, fuck it!" He stepped through the door and was instantly pulled back.

Okay, that was different.

* * * *

Victoria stood in the hotel vestibule. Graham had taken everything from her and he deserved to die. Problem was, she wanted to die. In such a short time, Ben had become more dear to her than anyone in her life. They'd never had a chance, though. All because of Graham and his crazy obsessions.

And it seemed he was crazier than she ever imagined.

Without hesitation, she stepped out into the world of people. If she didn't get her butt in gear, Perry would probably stop her and she couldn't have that. Not now.

She turned off her phone and walked toward Graham and her destiny. Once she cleared the city and the sun truly set, she would run. She had a date with death. Whose, she had no idea.

CHAPTER 29

Ben stared out the window. He'd tried leaving the room several times and each time had been pulled back. That had to be a good sign, right? That maybe he wasn't supposed to leave his body because he could get back into it. So why was he still floating outside it?

He had tried sliding into his body, but might as well stand inside a wall for all the good it did.

The door opened. Perry—looking as if he hadn't been nearly decapitated—dropped a suitcase and shook his head as he approached the bed. "Ah, Teach. So sorry."

"Perry, can you hear me?" Ben sighed at the lack of response. It had been worth a shot in any case.

Perry pulled out a folded bag from the suitcase. Was that a body bag? Ben's stomach dropped at the thought. Perry then opened each drawer of the dresser and packed what little had been left behind. When he entered the bathroom, he cleaned up the mess and even replaced the light fixture Graham had dismantled, making everything appear normal, as if no one had intruded and committed murder.

Well, except for the broken security latch. Perry placed that on the sink. Victoria had been correct; it had done nothing to keep Graham out.

Perry returned to the bed and stared at Ben's body. After a few pats on Ben's shoulder, Perry set to work at getting Ben's body into the bag. *Oh shit.* Ben turned away. That zip resonated in the room.

It sounded so…final.

When Perry hoisted the body over his shoulder, Ben's stomach tightened from the pressure. "Please don't cremate me, okay? I don't think I could stand the burn."

Without missing a beat, Perry picked up the suitcase. Then he headed for the door. That elastic string or whatever pulled Ben along. He had no choice but to follow, not that he wouldn't have tried anyway.

Perry peeked out the door and then exited. He strolled to the stairway as if he wasn't carrying a dead body over his shoulder.

Each step down the stairs jarred Ben's midsection. And that elastic grew tauter. Two steps later and everything became dark. What the? He was wrapped up like a cocoon, bent over and moving backward. And what was the issue with his throat? He could barely breathe.

"What's going on?" he wheezed.

The backward movement stopped. He was swung to the side.

"Must be going crazy," Perry said.

The backward movement continued. Shit. Was it possible? Wrapped up. Bent over. Throat on fire. "Stop! Put me down."

Perry stumbled before stopping. "Teach?"

Ben was lowered to the ground and the zipper opened. He whipped off the bag, so glad to be free of that thing. Perry was a welcome sight. "Am I back?"

Perry's eyes widened and he backed up. "Holy shit!"

Ben would take that as a yes. They were on the landing between floors. He pounded his fist on the floor, just to make sure.

"I think I need to sit down." Perry collapsed on the stairs above Ben. "How? What?"

"I don't know. I'm thinking I finally healed enough to breathe." Ben rubbed his throat. "Doesn't feel very healed, though. Guess all I needed was a jolt to the heart." Too bad his lethargy returned. He stifled a yawn. Damn it. Now was not a time for a nap.

Perry pulled Ben in for a hug and patted his back. "Man, wait until Vic hears about this."

"I gotta call her." Ben found the phone in his pocket, but the call rolled to her voice mail. Damn her. "Victoria, I'm alive. Don't do anything stupid!"

His voice sounded like shit. Would she even recognize it?

Perry laughed. "You know you're asking a lot there, don't you?"

"You don't understand. She talked about killing herself."

"Shit."

Ben also sent her a text. "How are we going to find her? I think she's after Graham."

Perry shrugged. "He could be anywhere."

"Could she track him? She had some map on her phone with a red dot."

"What? Was she using a GPS?"

"GPS. Of course. I'd never seen one before."

"Of all the ding dong days. When did they put that on the van?"

"A better question, can you bring up the GPS so we can find Victoria?"

Perry shook his head. "I don't have that app."

"How about Barnet?"

"Oh please. That man is lucky to have a flip phone. Vic is usually the person everyone goes to for that. Wait, maybe someone else can help us." Perry placed a call. "Hey, Abe. When did you put the GPS on the van?"

Ben cleared his throat and glared at Perry.

"Never mind, you can tell me later. Can you track the van for me?"

As Perry explained to Abe what he needed, Ben massaged his throat. He'd never thought pain would be a wonderful sensation. Now if he could only keep his eyes open. All that healing was taking a toll on his system. Well, at least he still had a system. He couldn't wait to find Victoria and hold her again. Provided they found her in time.

"Are you sure?" Perry said. "Yeah, I know how to get there. Thanks." He disconnected the call and stared at Ben. "You okay?"

"I'm beat, but yeah. Hunky-dory. We going now?" Ben grabbed onto the handrail and yanked himself up, but his legs had other plans and he collapsed onto the floor.

"Hunky-dory, huh?" Perry lifted Ben under his arms. "Did you forget you just came back from the dead?"

No, he didn't. But the trip would be worthless if Victoria planned to walk into it.

* * * *

Victoria stood in the long driveway to her former plantation home. Besides the trees having grown considerably and the lawn needing mowing, the place hadn't changed much since the last day she was here. The day of Henrik's memorial service.

He'd been so happy to buy this house for her after she'd been voted to join the Committee—a present of sorts—but it was much too large for her taste. Instead of telling him that and hurting his feelings, she'd thanked him and made do with the vast emptiness.

After his accident, she'd had no trouble selling the estate. It had always been more his home than hers.

She couldn't believe the GPS tracker had led her here, but the van was proof the device hadn't lied. So where were the owners and why was Graham here? He was nowhere to be seen, but the hatch on the van was open and several suitcases filled the back. *Scheisse.* Had he abducted the owners? Was he here to steal? She wouldn't put that past him, although why he'd feel the need to steal from this particular house was beyond her. She hadn't lived here in decades.

Focusing on her hearing, Victoria located two heartbeats in the house: one upstairs, one down. If Graham was here, then he must be upstairs because that heart rate was calm and steady compared to the erratic one downstairs.

All during the trip here, she'd thought about how to approach Graham. Call him out or sneak up on him? Since her fighting skills were pretty much nonexistent, sneaking up on the bastard would prolong her life if she wished to remain living, which she didn't. So she'd decided to call him out. But now with the possibility of an innocent bystander in danger, she had no choice but to go for stealth.

Taking care not to make a sound, she climbed the stairs to the familiar wraparound porch and opened a door she never thought she'd open again.

The stench of gasoline hit her and she held her breath. If Graham was planning on torching the place, she'd make sure he'd go up right along with it. And if that meant burning in flames with him, so be it. But first she had someone to save and the erratic heartbeat came from the living room.

She approached the room and stopped. Was she dreaming? Same furniture. Same wall hangings. Even the same old fireplace set Henrik insisted on buying, as if they would have ever used the fireplace. It was creepy, like walking into her past. Would Henrik come strolling down the stairs next?

Sure, she'd sold the furniture and contents with the house, but that was over forty years ago. Why hadn't the current owner redecorated?

The ceiling creaked above Victoria's head, spurring her to find the victim. And it didn't take long to find her. A woman was lying on the couch. Still as death. Victoria rushed over and found Susannah.

Scheisse. What was she doing here? Was he planning on burning her with the house?

Not on Victoria's watch, he wasn't. She lifted Susannah. Maybe she wasn't really catatonic because her pulse indicated she was reacting to something. Using more stealth than when she entered, Victoria exited the house and zipped to the van. Getting her revenge with Graham could wait. Protecting Susannah became her number one priority.

After Victoria placed Ben's sister on the back seat, she went around back of the van and quietly lowered the hatch. She climbed in the side opening, slid the door shut as silently as she could, and buckled Susannah in place.

Susannah's head tilted to the side, exposing two blue-ish holes on her neck. Only venom would leave that mark behind and cause the irregular heartbeat. That bastard! He'd turned her.

Victoria ran her fingers over the bumps. "I'm so sorry. I'll make him pay for this and for killing Ben. I promise."

But first she needed to get Ben's sister to safety so Graham couldn't do any more damage. Then she'd come back and finish him off for good. She crawled over to the driver's seat and placed her phone in the cup holder. She reached for the ignition. Empty. *Scheisse.* Why weren't the keys where they were supposed to be? Guess she'd have to carry Susannah to safety.

The driver's door flew open.

"You looking for these?" Graham dangled the set of keys in the air then tossed them in the yard, looking smugger than he had a right to be.

She itched to rip his face off so she'd never have to look at him again. Instead, she would kill him. And she'd kill him a thousand times over if possible—he certainly deserved it. Too bad he only had the one life to take.

She lunged out of the van and tackled him to the ground. Big mistake. Not only was he considerably larger, she had no weapon to defeat him with. Well, except her knee. But when she pulled it back, he grabbed her hair and yanked, exposing her neck. She reached for his eyes, his face, anything, but he flipped her around and stood, one arm around her waist and the other around her neck.

Graham chuckled with all the glee of the devil as he rubbed his cheek against hers. "Henrik never did teach you how to fight, did he?"

Maybe not, but she had other tricks. She reached behind and grabbed his balls. "How's this for fighting. Now let me go."

He tensed and she prepared for the release. She'd find a weapon or a stake and put him out of commission.

He bit her neck and sucked.

No! She couldn't let him drain her. As she struggled in his grasp, she squeezed his balls. Hard. Harder. He ripped her neck open and continued sucking while a good portion of her blood flowed down her shirt. Excruciating pain and major stomach cramps incapacitated her. With each ounce of blood she lost, her grip became looser until she could no longer hold him. She made her body limp, hoping he'd stop before it was too late.

He threw her to the ground and wiped his bloody face. "I'd show you what a real man is made of, but I think I deserve better than you."

"You wouldn't know a real man if he bit you in the *Arsch*." Blood gushed from her wound and she applied pressure, not that she had much strength. Could she heal before all her energy left? Or her blood?

"What is it with you and your German? You're not even German!"

No, but Henrik was and Graham knew it. "Just because I wasn't born there, doesn't mean it's not my home. If I disgust you so much, why did you wait for me all these years?"

She really needed to stop speaking, she kept aggravating her wound. More blood seeped through her fingers. Then again, if she didn't keep him talking, he'd drive off with Susannah and leave her here to die.

"Because I was crazy. Crazy to think I was in love with you. But don't worry. It won't take me four decades to get over *your* death." He lifted her by the waistband of her jeans and threw her onto the porch.

She skidded to a stop against the door and struggled to her hands and knees. Must find a weapon.

He zipped up the steps, lifted her again, and tossed her inside the house. Her back met with the bottom step causing something to crack. "*Gott*, please let it be the wood," she muttered.

"What?" Graham placed his face next to hers. "I didn't catch that."

She would have spit in his face, but then he might think she had too much energy. "What are you doing? Throwing me around won't kill me." It sure was hurting, though. And she kept losing blood. If she lost much more, she could go into paralysis and then where would she, or Susannah, be?

"No, it's just fun." He picked her up and threw her into the living room.

She landed near the big fireplace in a puddle of...gasoline. *Scheisse.*

"But you will die. Eventually. I was planning on torching the place anyway. It's not like we'll ever live here now. Better you go up in flames with it."

"*You* bought my house?" The decorations made sense now. And the lack of tenants. "Why?"

"Why else? Are you really that dense? Maybe I'm better off without you, then."

"What about Susannah? You had no right to turn her."

"I had every right. You want to blame someone for her turning, blame yourself. You all broke her, I'm fixing her."

"And if she doesn't come out of it, are you going to kill her, too?"

"If that's what it takes. I won't let her suffer because of your deeds." He zipped toward the back of the house.

Wherever he was headed, now was her chance to get help, something she should have done earlier if she'd had her head on straight. Not that anyone could help her at this point. Her life could probably be measured in minutes now, but so would Graham's if she could find a way to immobilize him.

She reached for her phone, but her pocket was empty. Laughter bubbled up and she fell back on the floor, shaking her head. So much for that plan. Abe would eventually locate the van, but how soon? Hopefully before some mortal discovered Susannah, if

Victoria even succeeded in stopping Graham.

Henrik's fireplace set included one sharp looking poker. If she could grab the poker, she might be able to disable Graham. She crawled to the set while cramps gripped her belly, but managed to get her fingers around the handle. The whole set fell over with a crash. Behind it was the can of gasoline. Empty or full?

Graham stood in the foyer holding a lit match. "Burn in hell, Victoria."

He tossed the match. Flames followed the path of gasoline along the length of the wall. With her last bit of energy, she picked up the poker and the gas can and stumbled to the center of the room, hoping she didn't drag a trail of fuel. He was still standing in the foyer, but his attention was on the dining room, where he was currently setting it on fire. She threw the can at his back.

"What the?" He turned around as she threw the poker. It flew like a javelin. He dodged to the right and the poker embedded in the wall. His laughter caused him to slip in the liquid and stumble backward. The flames leapt to his pant leg. Graham cried out and swatted at the fire, but it caught hold of his sleeve and traveled up his arm. He ran toward the front door, ablaze.

"Now who's going to burn in hell," she yelled after him.

His screams echoed inside the house. She crumpled to the floor, spent.

A vampire might not feel temperature differences, but they could burn. And it wasn't the heat that hurt. It was the damage the heat caused.

Her skin tightened and burned. Her stomach twisted in cramps. But she wouldn't give up. Susannah was still out there and she needed help.

Victoria pushed herself to her knees, grabbed a chair and stood. Pain rippled through her midsection and her hands were stiff from the burning. But she managed to lift the chair and toss it through the window. Then she promptly collapsed.

* * * *

"Wake up, wake up!" Perry shook Ben's shoulder.

Ben opened his eyes. When had he fallen asleep? He'd apparently lost the battle to keep his eyes open shortly after climbing inside the car. He rubbed the crick in his neck. Sleeping in a car wasn't the most comfortable of places. An orange glow lit up the night and Perry was gunning toward it. Ben held onto the dash. "Where are you going?" Then he spotted the van. If the van was here, that meant so was Victoria. "Oh Shit."

Perry skidded the car to a stop and Ben stumbled out. A screaming fireball flew out the front door and headed for the woods.

"Looked like Graham." Perry grabbed the body bag from the back seat. "I gotta go stop him."

"Wait! Where's Victoria?" Ben ran to the house and nearly got hit by a flying chair. "Victoria!"

Flames licked the front window the chair came from and Ben held his arms out across his body to take the brunt of the heat as he peered inside. Victoria struggled to stand. Blood covered her blouse.

"Victoria, over here!" he shouted.

She turned her head toward the window. "Ben? I'm sorry. I didn't mean to die."

Shit. Did she think he was a spirit come to get her? "Baby, you're not dead. I'm not dead. Get out of there!"

"What?"

"I came back when I healed. You have to get out of there. Now!"

Her eyes widened in comprehension. She looked around and then down at her clothes. She undressed in a slow, methodical way. "I've got gasoline on me."

Gasoline? What the hell had Graham done to her? "Then rip your clothes off and jump. I'll put the fire out."

"I have to save my energy." She sat and pulled off her shoes and socks and then squirmed out of her jeans. "Get away from the house."

He ran to the yard. Would she be able to jump if she couldn't even get undressed with any speed? As if diving, she placed her arms above her head and leaped through the window. Flames caught hold of her hair. And her feet. She skidded on the grass and slid several feet past.

Ben pounded out the fire. She moaned, but didn't move. He sat on the ground, pulled her into his lap and placed his arm against her mouth. "Feed."

She caressed his face. "Are you really alive?"

He smiled. "Yeah, baby. Now feed."

"Don't be so bossy." She bit into his arm.

While her feeding healed her body before his eyes, it also awakened a desire in him, giving him one whopper of a boner. He moaned. Thank God Perry wasn't around.

She licked the wound and hugged him tight. "Oh, Ben. You're alive. You're really alive."

"Damn, girl," Perry said. "The fire burn off your clothes?"

Clothes? Shit.

"Hey! Stop looking at my woman." Blocking Perry's view, Ben stood and yanked his shirt off. He helped Victoria up and slipped it over her head.

"Your woman?" Perry asked.

Victoria beamed. "Yes, his woman." She poked her arms through the sleeves and pulled the thankfully over-sized shirt down to cover her nakedness. "Did you find Graham?"

"Yeah. He's pretty much ash. There's no saving him. I hid Susannah's car after I stumbled across the keys to the van. We can come back for it later."

Ben hugged her close. "I can't believe it's finally over. He can't hurt us anymore."

"About Susannah." She looked up at him with wide eyes. "Graham bit her."

His heart lurched and he stared at the inferno in front of them. "She's here?"

"Not in the house. She's in the van."

"That bastard." Perry rushed to the vehicle in a blur.

"What's the matter? If she's in the car, she's okay, right? I already assumed Graham must have fed—"

"Not fed. Bit. He started the turning process."

Turning? As in vampire?

Sirens sounded in the distance.

"Come on. We gotta go," Perry yelled.

"Is she going to be okay?" Ben asked.

"I don't know, Ben. I really don't know. But we'll take good care of her. I promise."

Maybe turning into a vampire would bring her out of her catatonic state. It would certainly mean he wouldn't have to hide from her any longer. But once he got a look at her in the van, he almost doubted the turning would do her any good. She still stared out into space. At least she was alive and that alone gave him hope.

Perry managed to depart the premises without being noticed, and not because of any vampire hocus-pocus. He took the back road instead. Just as Ben gave in to the weariness that settled over him, Perry asked, "So, Vic, when did you put a tracker in the van?"

* * * *

Victoria snuggled next to Ben. It unnerved her how quiet he became during his healing sleep. Almost like he was dead. Which, technically, he had been back at the hotel. She still couldn't wrap her head around the fact he'd been a ghost, and heard and saw everything she'd done. How mad had he gotten when she'd said she didn't want to live without him? She'd have been furious if Ben had said those words.

He woke up and hugged her close to his naked body. Before zonking out, he'd managed to strip, saying he'd always wanted to sleep in the nude but had been afraid he'd flash his sister. "Have you been watching me sleep?"

"Only a little while. I just returned from a meeting."

"You have too many meetings." He nudged his erection between her legs and nuzzled her neck. "You also have too many clothes on."

"Do I now?" She rolled onto her back and smiled.

He straddled her and slid her dress up. "Ooh, no panties. I take back my statement." He kissed her and spoke through their link. *"I love you so much. I want you so much."*

"I'm all yours."

He made love to her slowly and brought her to ecstasy twice before his own release. She marveled at his stamina. His energy. Eight hours of uninterrupted sleep worked wonders on him. What would a good meal do?

Someone knocked on the front door as it opened. "Victoria? Ben? Are you here?"

Damn Barnet. He had better not be calling for another meeting. She just might sock him one then.

"We'll be out in a moment," she said. "Scheisse. I really should get a lock."

"How about our own place instead?"

She liked that idea very much. They quickly got dressed and met

Barnet in the living room.

"Did Victoria tell you about our vote?" Barnet asked.

"He just woke up," she said as she sat on the couch beside Ben.

Sitting in the chair, Barnet raised his eyebrow in a yeah-right kind of look. Her lie became more apparent after Ben smoothed her hair down and kissed her temple.

"So what about the vote?" Ben asked Barnet.

"The Committee decided to inform everyone about Perfect Mates."

She whispered into Ben's ear, "What he's not saying is, he was outvoted."

"Maybe so, but that doesn't mean I'm not on board. We'll make sure to sound upbeat about it and encouraging. We'll also have you, Sarah, and Justin on hand to show you aren't a threat."

"And after the meeting, I'm in charge of sending out a mass text telling everyone to check the website, where we'll post a statement."

"Wait," Ben said, "You have a website?"

"Yes. The server is here. We've got that thing harder to crack than a bank vault."

Barnet growled. "I still don't trust those things. We've never needed them before and had no problems. I still say we're asking for trouble, but I was out voted on that, too."

Ben laughed. "But you all have phones, don't you? Why not text them the information?"

"Are you kidding?" she said. "Phones get lost. Or stolen. The text only says to check the website. Everyone knows what it means."

"Wow."

"So why are you here, Barnet? I could have told him all this."

Barnet lowered his head. "I have a confession to make. When Perry took Susannah back to the hotel, I told him not to cure her."

"What?" Ben stood. "You had no right."

Victoria took his hand and pulled him back to the couch. "I tend to agree with Ben. What were you thinking? It was because of her condition that Graham turned her."

Once Ben settled down, Barnet continued, "You're right, son. I didn't have any right. But I wasn't thinking too clearly, either. Still, my actions caused irreparable harm to your family, and for that I'll be eternally sorry. But I do have some good news. Seems you have a friend in Perry. He didn't care much for my order and although he technically followed it, he did some digging anyway."

"What does that mean?" Ben asked.

"That he found what caused her catatonic state. While she was transitioning, he was able to reach her. I didn't think it was possible, but then I didn't think Perfect Mates were possible either. She's awake. A little confused. Okay, a lot confused, but awake."

"You have to let me see her." Ben stood and tugged on Victoria's hand.

"Hold on. She's still transitioning. I promise, you'll see her soon. Perry is taking good care of her." Barnet rose. "Again, I'm sorry for my actions and I hope you'll be able to forgive me." He offered his hand to Ben.

After a few moments, Ben took it. "You aren't the one who put her into a catatonic state or turned her. There's nothing to forgive."

Barnet smiled. "Thank you. I'll be sure to let you know when you can see her."

Once Barnet left, Ben sat down and Victoria climbed onto his lap. "I'm so glad she'll be okay," she said. "I wonder if she'll like me now."

"How could she not?" He hugged her and kissed her. "It's like a miracle, isn't it? Which makes me wonder…"

"Well, don't keep me hanging. Wonder what?"

"What if I had a miracle operation? One that restored my sight? Then I could continue teaching."

"Ooh, I like that." Then they could go out in public without a problem. She nearly laughed at wanting to go out in public. "Where would this miracle operation occur? It probably shouldn't be in the States, in case schools check for that kind of thing."

"I wasn't thinking States."

"So where were you thinking?"

"Maybe…Germany." He raised an eyebrow and smiled.

Her heart leaped. "What?"

"You heard me," He caressed her cheek, sending warm sizzles to her heart. "So what do you say? Think it would be believable if I had this miracle operation during our honeymoon or should we—"

She grabbed his arm. "Wait. Honeymoon?"

He grinned. "Sure. But only if you want to get married."

"Ben Martin, are you asking me to marry you?"

He laughed. "Yeah, I'm asking."

She held his face and kissed him. *"Then this is me saying yes."*

CHAPTER 30

Ben paced inside the garage, waiting for Victoria. He'd love to go outside and wait—hell, he'd just love to go outside—but he'd promised Barnet he wouldn't venture out of Headquarters until after his "miracle operation." Wouldn't be long now.

The last week and a half had gone by in a blur. Susannah was still adjusting to her new world, but she was thrilled to see Ben and so happy he could see again. Even her animosity toward Victoria had gone, now that she understood Victoria was actually centuries older than either of them and was the reason behind his returning sight.

And then everything had revolved around the meeting. Thank goodness that had gone off without a hitch. Seemed Barnet's worries had been for nothing. So far, anyway. The June meeting was always the smallest of the four and probably the best crowd to break the news to. Only time would tell how the rest of the vampire population would feel after reading the announcement on the website.

Perry emerged from the stairwell. "Hey, Teach."

"What are you doing here?" Ben asked. "I thought you were with Victoria."

"Once the sun set, I saw no reason to stick around."

The garage door opened and the familiar van pulled in.

Victoria slammed the van door. "You *Arsch*. What if I hadn't passed? Then what?"

"But you passed," Ben said "And you drove back all by

yourself."

She stood proudly. "Yes I did. No thanks to him."

Ben nearly laughed. She might have sounded pissed at Perry, but her lips curled at the ends and she stuck her tongue out at him. Had she always been that way or had she changed? Whatever, it was nice to know she didn't hate the man. Might have been awkward since he would be the best man at their wedding.

Ben held his arms wide and Victoria rushed into them.

"Ah look at that. You made old Teach happy."

"Did you have to say old?" Ben asked.

Perry chuckled. "Well…" Then he examined Ben's head. "What'd you do? Use the old Grecian Formula?"

"What are you talking about? I didn't color my hair."

Victoria ran her fingers along his temple. "Your grey's gone. I hadn't noticed."

"It is?" He hadn't paid any attention. Hell, he hadn't even shaved his face in the past week. Victoria hadn't gotten a mirror in the bathroom and she enjoyed shaving him. As far as he was concerned, she could do it all the time. It usually led to sex after.

"You think it's the bond?" Perry asked.

"What are you talking about?" Ben said.

"You're her Perfect Mate. It would make sense that you'd look…younger."

"Younger? How much younger?"

Perry shrugged. "Afraid you'll look seventeen again? Was that a bad look for you?"

"Is it even possible?" Ben asked.

"Would that be so bad?" She spoke mentally and looked up with worry in her eyes.

He caressed her face. *"No, of course not."*

"Who knows," Perry said. "Hey, what do you think about me asking your sister out?"

The change of subject just about gave Ben whiplash. "On a date?"

"Sure on a date. I want to date her."

Victoria laughed. "You want to date someone? And a vampire at that? I thought you didn't believe in dating."

"Okay, I guess I deserved that. So what do you say, Teach?"

"I thought you wanted a Perfect Mate."

"I know what I said, but I like your sister. She's kind of hot."

Victoria smacked Perry in the arm. "That's no way to talk about someone's sister."

"Sorry, man. I mean she *is* hot."

Ben bit his lip to keep from laughing. "You think she'll want to go out with you?"

Perry furrowed his brow. "Who wouldn't want this? So you're okay with it?"

Victoria snorted, but Perry acted as if he hadn't heard her. He continued staring at Ben with pleading eyes.

"I'm beginning to think you're crazy, but yeah, I'm okay with it. Good luck."

"Thanks, Teach."

Victoria buried her face in Ben's chest. "It's over. Germany, here we come." She pointed to Perry. "You. Go."

"You know, ever since you got your license, you've been kind of bossy. Oh wait. What am I saying? You've always been bossy. You sure you want to marry this woman, Teach? I'm sure you could do better."

Ben smiled. No, he couldn't do better. He might be her Perfect Mate, but she was his, too, and he couldn't wait to start their forever together.

Author's Notes

Thank you for reading. If you'd like to be kept updated on the latest news and releases, please sign up for my newsletter at http://eepurl.com/-Auwz. I promise not to bombard your e-mail box.

Want more? Stop by my website at http://stacymckitrick.com/books.php for excerpts and buy links to all my books.

Meet the Author

Stacy McKitrick always had stories in her head; she just never knew what to do with them. Then one day she decided to give writing a try and discovered the passion she'd been looking for all her life. She waived goodbye to accounting and now spends her time writing romance featuring vampires, ghosts, and aliens. All with happy endings, of course. Born in California, she currently resides in Ohio with her husband. They have two grown children. You can learn more about Stacy at her website www.stacymckitrick.com.

www.ingramcontent.com/pod-product-compliance
Lightning Source LLC
Chambersburg PA
CBHW021505110726